Discard

EDEN IN WINTER

EDEN IN WINTER

a novel by

Richard North Patterson

New York • London

Quercus

New York • London

ISBN 978-1-62365-147-3

Library of Congress Control Number: 2013913486

Distributed in the United States and Canada by
Random House Publisher Services
c/o Random House, 1745 Broadway
New York, NY 10019

Manufactured in the United States

10 9 8 7 6 5 4 3 2 1

www.quercus.com

For Dr. Bill Glazer

Wonderful friend, gifted therapist, and superb literary adviser on psychiatry, sailing, and life, with deep gratitude for the pleasure of his company.

Contents

PART ONE

THE INQUEST

August 2011

ONE

For three days, Adam Blaine and his family had entered the Dukes County Courthouse, a modest two-story brick structure with white trim and doors, and passed through a double door to a spiral staircase that rose to the courtroom itself.

Its new carpets were a rich blue, lending it a certain majesty augmented by the high ceilings and four fluted chandeliers. From the raised mahogany bench, framed by the flags of the United States and the Commonwealth of Massachusetts, Judge Aaron Carr presided. At a desk below him the court reporter, a young woman with long blond hair and a grave expression, transcribed the proceedings; still lower were the tables for the prosecutor and the witness's counsel. Black and white photographs of judges, some gazing out from the recesses of the 19th century, gave the room a further aura of gravity. But to Adam, the pallid walls and scarred benches where his family sat watching bespoke a certain world weariness, decades of human missteps and misdeeds, and, on occasion, tragedies—traffic tickets, theft, assault, divorce, domestic violence and, less frequent, a fatal car accident. Murder came to this courtroom every thirty years or so. Now his family was trapped here, suspected of killing one of its own.

On a wall, a schoolroom style clock marked the agonizing passage of time, its second hand twitching from mark to mark. Though four tall windows on each side admitted light, it was dulled by lowering clouds and a steady rain that streaked the glass. Gloom seeping into his soul, Adam could only watch, gripped by the foreboding that his careful plan to conceal the truth would evaporate before his eyes.

His father sat in the witness stand, preparing to deny what Adam alone knew to be true. The stakes for his family were reflected by the media clustered outside, denied entrance to the medical examiner's inquest into the death of Benjamin Blaine, the most famous novelist of his time. A man as arrogant as he was gifted, a great sailor, adventurer, and womanizer, the man everyone believed to be Adam's father. Another lie to be concealed.

The degree to which Adam's mother and brother grasped these perils differed. Sitting to Adam's right, Teddy Blaine was an uneasy mix of worry and gratitude, knowing only that, if this witness were believed, the inquest would clear him of murder. Clarice Blaine understood much more. With a characteristic exercise of will, she projected an aura of patrician calm, as perfectly maintained as her blond, tinted hair, which, even now, helped preserve the beauty of her youth. Beneath which, Adam now understood, lived the fear that had consumed her since the day he was born.

On the stand was Benjamin Blaine's brother, Jack—a man in his late sixties, with stooped shoulders and silvered hair, whose long face was relieved from homeliness by an aura of modesty and kindness. The only person who knew all that Adam knew, and bore for them both the burden of burying it.

With an unwonted look of wariness, Jack faced his interrogator, District Attorney George Hanley, a bulky figure whose white hair and mustache marked him as Jack's contemporary. From the front bench, Sergeant Sean Mallory, the ascetic, sharp-eyed homicide inspector for the Massachusetts State Police, studied Jack fixedly.

So, too, did Jack's lawyer, Avram Gold, a Blaine family friend and, of more import, an eminent law professor and defender of hard cases for more than forty years. Adam could not help but wonder if Gold knew, or sensed, how much hatred festered beneath the surface, and how much more was at risk in the next few moments than Jack Blaine's freedom.

As Gold had explained to Adam, on Martha's Vineyard the medical examiner's inquest was invoked in the rarest of cases—a high-profile death where the circumstances were ambiguous, the media pressure unrelenting, the stakes for public officials high. Its modern genesis was the Chappaquiddick incident—the death of a young woman; the fate of a potential president; a swarm of media; a politically ambitious district attorney. In these circumstances, Gold went on, the authorities had needed an investigative tool to determine whether to impanel a grand jury. But, as Gold had trenchantly added, "No one intended for that tragedy to happen. Whereas a lot of people think someone in your family decided that your father deserved to die."

Though Judge Carr had broad discretion to conduct the hearing, certain rules protected the witnesses and, especially, the person who might be charged. The inquest was closed; the potential subject—in this case, Jack Blaine—could be represented by counsel. The judge could bar all others from attending, though an exception was sometimes made for the next of kin of the deceased—as the judge had for Clarice, Teddy, and Adam, who had already given their testimony. But only Teddy, Adam was painfully aware, had told the truth as he understood it. The other three Blaines had committed, or were about to commit, their own separate acts of perjury or omission.

For Adam Blaine, knowing this, the wait for the judge's final report would be excruciating. The report could precipitate a grand jury, and then a trial, with Jack or Teddy accused of murder. But whatever the result, it would be Adam who had caused it.

Still and silent, he watched the district attorney approach the crux of Jack's testimony. Peering at Jack from the bench, Judge Carr wore a half frown on his bespectacled banker's countenance, the overhead lights illuminating his bald pate. Stepping forward, George Hanley put his hands in his pockets, the forward thrust of his belly lending his questions an air of aggression. To Adam's eye, trained to survive by separating truth from falsehood, Jack leaned back a fraction: the posture of a man about to lie, who is unused to lying in public.

"When you confronted your brother on the promontory," Hanley asked, "what was his appearance?"

Briefly, Jack grimaced. "Worn," he answered. "Almost enfeebled. I didn't know about the brain cancer. But, looking back, death was peering through his face."

Even now, this was hard for Adam to imagine. He had cut off all contact with Benjamin Blaine a decade ago, and had never returned to Martha's Vineyard until Ben's death. But the man he remembered, whose mirror image he was, would forever be imprinted in his heart and mind.

On the day Adam recalled they had been sailing, the joint passion of a great outdoorsman, and the young law student Ben had raised as his son. It was their last sail before the event that divided them forever: at the helm of his sailboat, Ben had grinned with sheer love of the Vineyard waters, looking younger than his fifty-five years, his thick, silver-flecked black hair swept back by a stiff headwind. To Adam, he resembled a pirate: a nose like a prow, bright black eyes that could exude anger, joy, alertness, or desire. He had a fluid grace of movement, a physicality suited to rough seas; in profile there was a hatchet-like quality to his face, an aggression in his posture, as though he were forever thrusting forward, ready to take the next bite out of life. "When Benjamin Blaine walks into a room," *Vanity Fair* had gushed, "he seems to be in Technicolor, and everyone else in black-and-white." As a boy, Adam had wanted nothing more than to be like him.

They had even looked alike, causing others to smile at the stamp of one generation on another—the lithe, rangy frame, the black hair and dark eyes, the strong features that, more than simply handsome, marked them as distinctive men. But much had changed between them that fateful summer; ten years later, Ben's death had only sealed Adam's hatred. In a last, corrosive act, Benjamin Blaine had made Adam the executor of his will, whose provisions were a poisoned arrow aimed at Ben's family. So Adam had stayed to wage war against a dead man, learning more than anyone, save Ben, had ever wanted him to know. More than he had ever wanted to know.

The last piece had come to Adam scant weeks before, at night, brooding over a photo album—a hitherto puzzling bequest from Ben—in the bedroom of the home in which he had grown up.

Stunned, Adam had willed himself to feel nothing.

But dispassion was beyond him. A single fact had transformed the meaning of his life, and his relationship to its central figures— from the first moments of his existence, he had been the catalyst for a web of hatred and deception that had enveloped them all: Benjamin Blaine, Adam's mother; Ben's brother Jack; Adam's older brother Teddy; and Adam himself the unwitting cause. He would not come to terms with this in an hour, or a year. But there was too much at stake not to start.

With deliberate calm, he dressed, walked down the hallway, and knocked on his mother's bedroom door. She answered too quickly to have been sleeping.

Cracking open the door, she stared at him. "What's wrong?"

"Please come downstairs," Adam said. "There's something we need to discuss."

For first time, Clarice looked haggard, almost old. "Can't it wait until morning?"

"No. It can't."

The look of alarm in her eyes was replaced by a fear that seemed years deep. In a weary voice, she said, "Give me time to dress."

He went to the living room, turning on a single lamp before sitting in Ben's chair. For what seemed endless minutes, he waited there, the room quiet, the cool night air coming through an open window. He had never felt more alone.

His mother's footfalls had sounded on the wooden stairs. Then she appeared, dressed in jeans and a sweater, a semblance of her usual calm slipping into place. But her posture when she sat across from him was taut, her hands folded tightly in front of her. The pale light made her face look waxen, accenting the apprehension in her eyes. "What's so urgent?" she inquired.

Adam composed himself. "Tell me about you and Jack. Everything, from the beginning."

She was quiet, her eyelids lowering. He watched her contemplate evasion, the habit of years. Then she said simply, "It started before you were born."

"That much I've worked out. The question is why all of you perpetuated such misery."

His mother searched his face, as though trying to gauge what he knew. "More than I'd understood, Ben was a selfish man. His early success made him hungry for more—more adventure, more accolades and, I suspected even then, more women. For weeks on end, he left me here alone with Teddy."

"And Jack?"

Reluctantly, she nodded. "It happened over time, without us fully realizing how we'd come to feel. But he was everything Ben couldn't be—gentle and reflective, more inclined to listen than talk about himself." Emotion made her voice throatier. "He valued me. With Jack, I was never an accessory."

"Isn't that the life you signed on for?"

Clarice flushed. "I suppose so. But it seems I needed more. Jack provided it."

"By sleeping with his brother's wife," Adam rejoined. "A landmark in their rivalry. Imagine my surprise at discovering where I fit in."

Her eyes froze. "I'm not sure what you mean."

"That since I was young, I always felt that something wasn't right. I'd like to have known when it still mattered who Jack really was to me."

For a telling moment, Clarice looked startled. "Your uncle," she parried. "A man who cared for you."

"Give it up, Mother. The album of photographs Ben left me was his message from the grave, showing that the summer before I was born, my supposed father was in Cambodia. But I look too much like him for that to be coincidence." Pent up emotions propelled Adam from his chair. "Once I grasped that, it explained so much. Jack's kindness toward me, and Ben's ambivalence. Their lifelong breach. The warped psychology of the racing season that last summer, Jack pitting me against his brother." And, Adam thought but did not say, Ben's desire to sleep with Jenny Leigh. "Most important," he finished in a lower voice, "the truth behind Ben's will and, I believe, his murder. That when he presented you with the postnuptial agreement, opening you to disinheritance, you were pregnant with Jack's child. I'm the reason you agreed to it, aren't I?"

Clarice sat straighter, marshaling her reserves of dignity. "Yes," she said evenly. "In legal terms, you were the 'consideration' for everything I signed away."

Hearing this said aloud made Adam flinch inside. "But why consent to all that?"

A plea for understanding surfaced in her eyes. "Is it really that hard to grasp? I did it for Teddy, and for you—"

"For me?" Adam said in astonishment. "Do you actually think making Benjamin Blaine my father was a favor? Then let me assure you that I'd pay any price to go back in time, and stop you from making this devil's pact. For Teddy's sake even more than mine."

Clarice turned white. "Do you think I have no regrets? What you've just discovered has haunted me for years. But I had no choice—"

"Would it have been so terrible to be the wife of a woodworker?"

"Please," his mother said urgently, "consider where I was then. I had no money or skills of my own, and was pregnant with another man's child. The price of being with Jack would have been penury, a bitter divorce, and scandal—with me exposed in public as the slut who slept with two brothers, and you stigmatized as the product of an affair. My choice was wrenching for me, and humiliating to

Jack. But with Ben as your father, both of my sons would have the security you deserved—"

"And you'd go on being Mrs. Benjamin Blaine."

To his surprise, Clarice nodded. "Whatever you may think, I'm not a mystery to myself. My upbringing was a tutorial in dependence—on men, money, and the security of affluence and status. I loved my father dearly. But I understood too late that, to him, a person was whoever he or she appeared to be. And when that was taken from him, Dad withered and died—figuratively at first, then literally." Her tone grew bitter. "I only wish my father had one-tenth of Ben's strength. Ben started with nothing, took what he wanted, and made sure he kept it. I might have been afraid of him, but not once did I fear that he would fail. I'd never be poor, or desperate like my mother became. And, yes, I enjoyed the reflected glory of being his wife, and all the privilege that came with it. That was part of the bargain, too."

"What was in it for Ben?"

His mother seemed to fortify herself, then spoke in a reluctant voice. "Beneath the surface, Benjamin Blaine was a very frightened man. One night early in our marriage, he got terribly drunk. He came to bed and suddenly started rambling about Vietnam, this man in his platoon. He'd been exhausted and afraid, he said—that was why it happened. I realized without him saying so that 'it' involved his fellow soldier. What tortured Ben was that it might be fundamental to his nature." Pausing, Clarice inhaled. "The next day he carried on with false bravado, like he hadn't told me anything. He never mentioned it again. But on a very few occasions, when he was drunk, Ben's tastes in sexual intercourse didn't require me to be a woman. A brutal instance of *in vino veritas.*"

When he rolled me on my stomach, Jenny had confessed to Adam, *I flashed on us in the lighthouse. But it wasn't like that at all. Not what he did or the way he hurt me.*

Sickened, Adam said, "And the others?"

"Weren't enough to banish his fears." Turning from him, his mother continued her painful narrative. "That I was pregnant by Jack made him all the more insecure. But I couldn't bear the thought of aborting Jack's child, and Ben was afraid of anyone knowing he'd been cuckolded by his brother. By exacting the postnuptial agreement as the price for keeping you, he kept Jack and me apart. His ultimate victory."

"Hardly," Adam said. "After that, he tormented all of us for years. I'll never fathom why Jack stayed."

His mother faced him again. "Because he loved me. And you."

"But not enough to claim me," Adam retorted. "I should be relieved that Benjamin Blaine wasn't my father. But now I'm the son of two masochists-for-life—"

"You don't know what it was like for me," his mother protested. "Or for Jack, waiting for whatever moments we could steal, the times he could watch your games—"

"I know what it was like for your sons," Adam shot back. "I always wondered how a father could demean a boy as kind and talented as Teddy. Now I understand—that Ben's only son was gay held up a mirror to his deepest fears." He stood over her, speaking with barely repressed emotion, "I became the 'son' he wanted. I can imagine him trying to believe that my achievements came from him, not from Jack's DNA. But he could never resist competing with me, just as he competed with Jack, my real father." He shook his head in wonder and disgust. "Even now you have no idea how much damage you inflicted, or on whom. But knowing what you did, how could you stand to watch it all unfold?"

Clarice stared at him. In a parched voice she said, "I watched Ben raise you to be the person *he* wanted to be. By accident or design, he made you enough like him to be strong. So strong that you can live with even this."

"In a day or so," Adam responded sharply, "I'll work up the requisite gratitude. But not before we talk about the night Ben died. This time I want the truth."

Clarice met his eyes. "As I told you, Ben locked himself in his study, brooding and drinking. When he came out, he was unsteady, almost stumbling. Alcohol had never done that to him before. But it was his words that cut me to the quick."

She stopped abruptly, shame and humiliation graven on her face. Sitting beside her, Adam said more quietly, "Tell me about it, Mother."

Haltingly, she had.

Ben's face had been ashen, his once-vigorous frame shambling and much too thin—the ravages of the cancer, Clarice now knew, which he had hidden until the autopsy that followed his sudden shocking death. He stared at his wife as though he had never truly seen her. "I'm done with this farce," he told her bluntly. "Whatever time I have left, I'm planning to spend without you."

Facing him in the living room, Clarice had fought for calm. "You can't mean that, Ben. We've had forty years of marriage."

The light in his eyes dulled. "God help me," he replied with bone deep weariness. "God help us all."

Clarice could find no words. In a tone of utter finality, her husband continued, "I'm going to be with Carla. If there's a merciful God, or any God at all, I'll live to see our son."

Clarice felt her bewilderment turn to shock. "Carla Pacelli is pregnant?"

Ben nodded. "Whatever you may think of her, she'll be a fine mother."

The implied insult pierced Clarice's soul. "And I wasn't?"

"You did the best you could, Clarice. When you weren't sleeping with my brother. But please don't claim you stayed with me for our son, or for yours. Your holy grail was money and prestige." His voice was etched with disdain. "You'll have to live on love now. The money goes with me, to support Carla and our son—"

Startled, Clarice stood. "You can't do that," she protested.

"You know very well that I can. That was the price of Adam, remember? For what little good that did any of us." Ben had slumped, as though weighed down by the past, then continued in a tone of indifference and fatigue. "I'm going to admire the sunset. When I return, I'll pack up what I need. You can stick around to watch me, if you like. But I'd prefer you go to Jack's place, your future home. Maybe you can start redecorating."

Turning from her, he left.

Clarice had stared at the Persian rug, unable to face her son. "I never saw him again."

Adam wondered whether to believe her. "How did you react?"

Clarice swallowed. "I was frightened and humiliated. He'd never threatened me like this before, and the other women who preceded this washed-up actress had come and gone. I didn't know then that he was dying. But that Carla Pacelli would bear him a son made it real. To think I could lose everything was devastating."

"But you didn't just sit there, did you? You called Teddy and told him what Ben had said."

"Yes." Clarice admitted. "I've been lying to protect him."

"But you didn't just call Teddy," Adam continued. "First, you called Jack."

Surprised, she glanced at him sideways, then turned away. "He didn't answer," she murmured. "So I left him a message, telling him what Ben had said and done."

"And where he'd gone," Adam said crisply. "Then you lied to the police about both calls. Do you realize what trouble that caused for Teddy?"

Clarice straightened. "What on earth do you mean?"

For the first time Adam was surprised. He gazed into her eyes, and saw nothing but confusion. "What do you suppose Teddy did that night?"

"Nothing." Clarice paused, eyes filling with doubt. "Isn't that what he told the police?"

Adam weighed the possibilities: that she knew nothing of Teddy's actions, or that she had caused Ben's death—or both. "Yes," he answered. "Yet another lie. In truth, he confronted Ben on your behalf and left him still alive, along with a telltale footprint on the

promontory from which Ben 'fell' to his death. Now you've lied him
into a potential murder charge.

"Maybe Teddy thought he was protecting you by concealing
your call and his confrontation with Ben. But here's what I think,
Mother. You couldn't reach Jack, and felt certain that Teddy couldn't
help you. And you were ignorant of one crucial fact—that Ben had
already changed his will in favor of Carla Pacelli." Adam forced a
new harshness into his tone. "In desperation, you went to the promontory. You found him weak and drunk and disoriented, like a man
who'd suffered a stroke. So you pushed him off the cliff, hoping to
preserve the prior will. The one that gave you everything."

"No," his mother cried out. "I never went there, I swear it. As far
as I know, Ben fell."

"True enough. But one of you helped him." Abruptly, Adam
stood. "Call Jack," he finished. "Tell him to meet me where Ben went
off the promontory."

Alone in the darkness, Adam awaited the man he now knew to be
his father. The moon was full, and a fitful breeze came off the water.
For a half hour, he thought about the two rival brothers who, in
their separate ways, had ordained the course of his life.

From behind him, he heard footsteps on the trail. Turning, he
saw the outline of the man for whom, Adam realized, he had been
waiting all his life. Then Jack stepped into the pale light.

"Hello, Jack," Adam said with tenuous calm. "Is there anything in
particular you'd care to say?"

Jack's face was worn, his eyes somber. "That I'm sorry," he said at
last. "I always loved you, Adam. For years my reason for staying was
to watch you grow."

Abruptly, Adam felt his self-control strip away. "As Benjamin
Blaine's son?" he asked with incredulity. "You and my mother
trapped me in a love-hate relationship with a man who resented me
for reasons I couldn't know. Then you pitted me against him in that

last racing season. Do you have a fucking clue what came from that? Or do you give a damn?"

Though shaken, Jack refused to look away. "I never thought you'd leave this place—leave us all behind," he said in a low voice. "I still don't know why you did."

"The reasons are my own, and you've got no right to know them." Adam caught himself, voice still husky with emotion. "There were times, growing up, when I wished you were my father. Now I wish you'd been as strong as the man who pretended I was his son. But for better or worse, I absorbed Ben's will, his nerve, and his talent for survival. Along the way, I learned to trust absolutely no one. A useful trait in a family like ours." Adam paused, then finished with weary fatalism. "On balance, I suppose, I'd rather have you as a father. Yet right now I look at you and Mother, and all I want is to vanish off the face of the earth. But I can't, because the two of you have created a mess I plan to straighten out."

Jack cocked his head. "What do you have in mind?"

"We're starting where you and Ben left off," Adam responded coldly. "Tell me how you killed him, Jack."

Jack hunched a little, hands jammed in his pockets. "So now you're the avenging angel, or perhaps the hanging judge. Whatever you've done in all those foreign countries, and whoever you do it for, you seemed to have developed the soul for that."

"No doubt. But not without help."

Jack seemed to flinch. "Maybe I deserve that. So yes, I'll tell you what happened that night. But before you judge me, listen."

Two

Taut, Adam waited for George Hanley's next question.

With an air of casual interest, the prosecutor asked, "Did you know that your brother had executed a new will, leaving almost everything to Carla Pacelli?"

Jack folded his hands in front of him. "I did not."

That much was true, Adam understood—Jack had believed that a new will was a threat, not an existing fact. Had Jack known the truth, Benjamin Blaine might still be alive. But Hanley raised his eyebrows. "Then for what reason," he inquired, "did you go looking for your brother?"

Jack seemed to steel himself, as though against the distasteful necessity of revealing family intimacies. "Clarice had called me, obviously upset. Ben had been drinking, she said—not an unusual event. Even so, it seemed that he had been unusually abusive."

"Was Mrs. Blaine more specific?"

"She was too distraught to be entirely coherent. But as I understood her, he was flaunting his relationship with Carla

Pacelli—taunting her with it, in fact. I'm very fond of my sister-in-law, always have been. I thought Ben had subjected her to enough."

Sitting beside Adam, his mother bowed her head, a silent portrait of gratitude and shame. "In Mrs. Blaine's account," Hanley asked, "had her husband mentioned that Ms. Pacelli was pregnant with his child?"

Jack shook his head. "No. But Clarice's humiliation—public and private—had gone on long enough. I knew my brother too well to truly believe that I'd persuade him. Still I could damned well try."

Delivering this answer, in Adam's mind Jack evoked James Stewart in a classic movie from the 1940s—a decent man befuddled by circumstance, but resolved to wage an uphill fight for goodness. With willed detachment, Adam replayed Jack's lies in his head, listening for what another man would have taken for sincerity. In this moment, Jack was too good at it for comfort.

Perhaps sensing this, Hanley paused. "Why don't you just tell me, in your own words, what happened that night."

An open-ended question, Adam saw at once—verbal rope for Jack to hang himself. For a superstitious instant, he imagined Jack repeating what he had told him that night. The truth, at last.

Jack had found his brother sitting slumped on the rock, his eyes bloodshot, his gaze unfocused. With terrible effort, Ben sat straighter. "I'm taking a rest," he said tiredly. "I can only assume she called you."

Jack knelt by him, staring into his face. "You can't do this to her," he told Ben. "Not after all these years."

Ben's face darkened, and then he bit off a burst of laughter. "So I should leave everything to Clarice? That way you could move into my house, claim my wife, and take the fruits of all I've done. You may have lived for that, Jack. But by God, I did not." Ben lowered his voice. "I've found someone who loves me, a woman with grace and grit who'll give me a son that's actually mine. They're what my life comes down to, and where my money is going. You and Clarice can do what you please."

Filled with anger, Jack leaned forward, his face inches from Ben's. "This is her home, Ben. You can't take that from her."

Ben smiled a little. "I already have," he answered calmly. "I gave you a home of your own, Jack—our parents' cracker box. Ask Clarice if she wants to live there with you. But I suppose you learned her answer long ago. All these years, she preferred to live with me than in the mediocrity which is your birthright—"

Filled with hatred, Jack grabbed his shirt. "She can file for divorce, and challenge the agreement you forced on her."

Despite the violence of Jack's actions, Ben's face revealed nothing but mild interest. "Not a bad idea," he remarked. "That's what I'd have done in her place, many moons ago." He paused, gathering strength. "Unfortunately for you both, I'm dying. A terrible surprise, I know. Especially because she can't divorce me fast enough. So unless she wins a will contest, which my lawyer and I believe she can't, she'll have nothing but the deathless love you've imagined sharing. She'll be looking for a rich man by Thanksgiving."

Overcome by rage, Jack wrenched him upright, ripping a button off Ben's shirt. In two steps, he held his brother over the edge of the cliff, staring into the face he had always loathed. "I can kill you now," he said in a strangled voice. "I've wanted to for years."

Ben stared at him with contempt. "So did Adam. But even he couldn't, and I don't think you have the guts for it. He got all that from me."

Jack thrust his brother backward, his grip all that kept Ben from falling over the precipice. Ben looked back at him, speaking with his last reserves of will. "You're a loser, Jack. And you're about to lose again."

Jack held Ben's face an inch from his. "Do you think I can't do this, Ben?"

Smiling with disdain, Ben spat into his face.

Jack felt the spittle on his cheek. A surge of insanity seized his body and soul. He stared into his brother's adamantine eyes, then felt his hands let go.

Frozen in time, Ben filled a space above the void. Then he hurtled toward the rocks. For an instant, Jack swore that his feeble cry turned into laughter. Then a distant thud echoed in the dark, marking the death of his brother.

"I was stunned." Jack spoke to Hanley in a monotone that seemed to echo the shock he described. "I stood there on the edge of the cliff, staring down toward the bottom. But it was night, and I couldn't see. Ben had simply disappeared.

"I found the ladder he built down the cliffside and lowered myself to the beach. In the darkness, the eighty feet felt even longer. By the time I reached the bottom, and found him lying near some rocks, I had no doubt he was dead. A terrible accident."

Adam kept watching George Hanley.

Facing Jack, Adam had felt his skin crawl. "You held him over a cliff," he had managed to say, "then let him fall. Murder, plain and simple."

Jack's voice shook. "He'd been spitting in my face ever since he learned to walk. For that one instant, I could do what I'd imagined all my life."

"And save my mother from penury in the bargain. Or so you thought." Adam heard the horror in his voice mingling with despair. "Instead you helped him commit suicide and lock in the new will, putting yourself at risk. No wonder he died laughing."

Jack closed his eyes. Watching him, Adam was overcome by the tragedy of all that he had learned, the incalculable damage to so many lives. "What does my mother know?" he asked.

"Nothing. When I came back to the house, I told her I couldn't find him. By morning, I'd figured out a plan. Incinerate the boots

I'd worn, then stumble across his body on the beach, as though his death were an accident." Jack paused, touching his eyes. "It almost worked."

"Not for Teddy," Adam retorted. "They're about to charge him with killing Ben."

Jack stiffened. "How can *that* be? And how do you know?"

"Doesn't matter. The point is that I also know you're a murderer. But if I turn you in to the police, they may think my mother's an accomplice. On the other hand, there's Teddy to consider. I can't let him take the fall for you."

Jack straightened. "Do you think *I* can? After I tell Clarice what happened, I'm going to the police."

"Don't overdo it, Jack. There's been heartache enough, most of it Ben's doing." Adam paused, finding a calmer tone. "You *are* my father, after all. So I'd prefer that you not pay for getting Teddy off the hook. And given that you're a reasonably accomplished liar, why not make that work for you?"

"What the hell are you saying?"

"You'll have to improve your story, merging it with Teddy's. In my version, Ben never threatened my mother with disinheritance. Because he was drunk and abusive, you decided to confront him in your role as her protector." Adam looked into his father's eyes. "You found him here, and asked him to stop mistreating her. A quarrel ensued. Suddenly he took a swing at you and lost his balance, the victim of alcohol and disequilibrium caused by his brain tumor. When you reached for him, it was too late."

Jack stared at the place where Ben had fallen. At last he said, "Still more lies, after so many. Do you think they'd believe me now?"

"Not really. They'll also think you're protecting Teddy. But I've become familiar with what the police know, and don't know. They have no witnesses to the murder. And Teddy's account will cover all the physical evidence, leaving them with nothing to refute your latest story." Reading Jack's doubt, he added, "Granted, telling it will take some nerve. But once you do, it creates reasonable doubt in Teddy's favor, and he'll do the same for you. George Hanley is nothing if not practical. He'll see the wisdom in letting go of the death of a dying man."

Jack studied him, then shook his head. In a tone of sadness, he asked, "When did you become so cold-blooded, I wonder?"

"The day I left here. All I've done since is refine my talents." Adam paused, struggling with emotions he refused to show. "But that's for another time—if ever. This family has one more thing it needs to settle."

"Tragic," Hanley said, repeating Jack's word as Judge Carr scrutinized the witness. "Yet you didn't report finding him until morning."

For an instant, Jack closed his eyes. "As I said, I was in shock . . ."

"So much so that you didn't tell the police what had happened that night."

"I did not."

"In fact," Hanley said with sudden sharpness, "you told the police that you didn't know how your brother had died."

"True."

"That was a lie, wasn't it."

"Yes."

Hanley gave a curt nod. "On the other hand, there's no physical evidence you were there at all. Unless it's a partial boot print we've been unable to match to anyone. Did you take the boots you wore and get rid of them?"

"Of course not."

Glancing at his mother, Adam saw her jaw line tighten, an almost imperceptible clue to her inner turmoil. Under his breath, Teddy murmured, "Jesus."

"Jack will be all right," Adam assured him. He said this calmly, concealing the tension he felt as the author of a cover-up—which, in protecting Teddy, jeopardized his mother, father, and himself.

"And yet," Hanley bored in, "two weeks after your brother's death, you concealed your supposed eyewitness knowledge of the circumstances."

Jack grimaced. "I was protecting myself," he said—only the second truth, however incomplete, he had spoken in several minutes. "I was afraid that the police might think I'd killed Ben—everyone knew how deeply we disliked each other. Instead, it became apparent that they suspected Teddy. That's when I came forward." He looked down, then fixed Hanley with a look of shamed candor. "I should've told the truth to begin with. Instead, through silence, I put my nephew in danger."

This was another line that Adam himself had crafted. Rehearsal had helped; his father's delivery had improved, though he was not yet as good a liar as Adam had become to survive his secret life abroad.

"You can practice your story on my mother," Adam had told Jack on the way to the house.

As the first light came through the window, he had watched her face as she listened to Jack's carefully crafted falsehoods. In rapid sequence, her expressions betrayed surprise, bewilderment, anger, horror, and, at length, deep anxiety. Unless she and Jack were extraordinarily accomplished actors, Adam concluded to his relief, their unrehearsed interaction suggested that Clarice knew nothing about Ben's death. That Jack had planted another lie at the heart of their relationship was the price of saving him.

Clarice took Jack's hand, shedding the pretense of years. Worriedly, she asked, "Do you really have to tell them?"

"He does," Adam broke in flatly. "What the police have on Teddy could convict him of a murder he didn't commit."

Clarice turned to him. "How can you possibly know all that?"

"Just trust me that I do." He paused, then said, "Like you, Teddy lied to the police about your phone call. That was your idea, wasn't it?"

Slowly, Clarice nodded.

"I assume you were trying to protect him," Adam continued, "and not just yourself and Jack. But I *know* that Teddy was protecting you." Turning to Jack, he finished, "I'm sure that Avi Gold would represent you, and work with Teddy's lawyer. That'll help everyone keep their lines straight."

"So," Hanley interrogated Jack in an acidic tone, "your nephew Teddy also lied to you, concealing that he had confronted his father on the promontory."

"Teddy didn't lie," Jack amended gently. "He simply kept his own encounter with Ben to himself . . ."

"Even when the police identified the boot print he'd left in the mud that night."

Jack gave a helpless shrug. "All of us had a painful relationship with Benjamin Blaine—his wife, his sons, and his brother. Because of Ben's affair with Carla Pacelli, the media descended—especially the tabloids—making the wounds in our family that much more raw. However wrongly, our instinct was for privacy, not truth."

Tense, Adam could only hope that George Hanley never knew how true this statement was, and the role Adam's own paternity played in the Blaines' hidden tragedy. Or for that matter, Sean Mallory, watching Jack with the bleak, pitiless look of a bitter saint.

Hanley crossed his arms, saying coldly, "Even though a man had died."

"Even so," Jack answered softly. "A death is not a murder. But once the police thought it might be, I had to tell the truth. That my nephew Teddy knew nothing about his father's death."

Hanley shook his head in wonder. "Yet there are all these lies— not only Teddy's but yours. And now you tell us that none of you knew that Benjamin Blaine had changed his will to favor Ms. Pacelli. Or even that he was thinking about this change."

"*I* didn't know." Jack's tone was weary but firm. "I'm confident that none of us did. In any event, the business of the will is done with now."

*   *   *

Staring at her son, Clarice had said, "This is just too much for me." Reading his expression, she added softly, "For all of us, I suppose."

"Then brace yourself, Mother. Because there's more." He sat back, speaking in the same clipped tone. "The will contest has become more complex than you know. Thanks to me, you won't get caught trying to pass off the postnup Ben forced you to sign as misplaced self-actualization. On the other hand, I'm now aware of the truth—that you got plenty of 'consideration' for signing it, from continuing to live here to concealing the messy facts surrounding my birth. And I suspect that Carla Pacelli knows that, too."

Clarice looked stricken. "Ben told her?"

"I'm pretty sure he did. So, if you contest his bequest to Carla, I can't lie about that. Right now you've got a decent shot at overturning Ben's will. But between Carla and me, you could wind up with nothing. So here's what you're going do.

"First, your lawyer will offer Carla a settlement of three million dollars, on which you're also paying the estate taxes—"

"No," Clarice protested. "I refuse to treat her as an equal."

"You've got no choice," Adam said coldly. "So feel grateful to get by with that. Carla's got a real chance of walking off with everything: at a minimum, she'll get almost two million for her son. Who, by the way, is Teddy's brother, Jack's nephew, and my cousin. All of us need to see to his well-being. This family has inflicted enough misery on its own."

He paused a moment, allowing Clarice time to absorb this, then looked from his mother to Jack. "The two of you will have more than enough to live here. Though if I were you, I'd sell this place. The karma leaves a lot to be desired."

Clarice seemed to blanch. "How do you know that Carla will agree?"

"Because I'm developing a sense of her. In fact, despite my best efforts, I may have a better grasp of Carla Pacelli than of either one of you. That'll give me food for thought on the flight back to Afghanistan." Briefly, he paused, watching the stunned look in his parents' eyes. "If she consents to this, as I think she will, we're set-tling Ben's estate. Are all of us agreed?"

Clarice looked at Jack, who nodded. Facing Adam, his mother retrieved some of her composure, accenting the sadness in her eyes. "I still look at you, Adam, and see him. The same iron will, the same belief that you can bend the world to your ends."

Despite himself, Adam discovered, comparisons to Benjamin Blaine still pierced him. "Better ends, I hope—especially yours and Jack's. But I'd appreciate it if both of you disappeared for the next few hours. I really do need to be alone."

At ten o'clock that morning, Adam had gone to see Carla Pacelli.

She was waiting for him on the deck, a light breeze rippling her hair. Pregnancy had done nothing to diminish her beauty, that of an Italian-American brunette with dark, intense eyes, tempered by hardship, giving her an aura of sadness and self-knowledge. Smiling a little, she said, "Thanks for calling. It gave me time to dress."

Then I regret that, Adam might have said in another life. But he felt way too tired, and even more confused. At length, he said, "I had to see you."

It came out sounding wrong, not as he intended. Carla regarded him gravely. "You really do look awful."

"And feel worse," he admitted. "How long have you known that I wasn't Ben's son?"

Briefly she looked down, then met his eyes with new directness. "For months now."

Adam shook his head in disbelief. "And yet you had the grace not to tell me. Even though Ben's will had made us enemies."

"It wasn't my place," she answered in a level tone. "And you were never quite my enemy. It was a little more complex between us, I thought."

This was true, Adam realized. "Still, you could have warned me off anytime you wanted to. All you needed was to tell the truth."

"And tamper with your life?" Carla asked with quiet compassion. "It was clear that you loved your family, despite all you'd gone through. I couldn't know how revealing the truth might change that. Once I realized that you knew nothing, it seemed best to keep Ben's secret. At least for as long as I could.

"But there's something else I can say now. Whatever her reasons, the affair between Clarice and his brother caused Ben terrible anguish. That's why I never considered his marriage sacred ground." She paused again. "At least that's my excuse."

"No help for it now," Adam said wearily. "I came here to resolve the future." He paused, searching for the proper words. "There needs to be an end to all this sadness. If I can guarantee you three million dollars, would you take it? That would spare you a will contest, and help both of you quite a lot."

A moment's surprise appeared in Carla's eyes, and then she gazed down at the deck with veiled lids. "More than 'a lot,'" she finally answered. "My lawyer won't like this, I'm sure. But if your mother can accept that, so will I. I don't have the heart for any more of this." She gave him an ironic smile. "As if I'm being so beneficent. I grew up without a dime, made millions as an actress, and blew it all because of my own failings. Now I can give my son the security I lost. That's what Clarice must have thought before you were born."

The comparison—and Carla's honesty—gave Adam pause. "Maybe so," he replied. "But she was also in love with someone else."

"Then accepting this money is easier for me, isn't it?" Carla looked into his eyes. "You persuaded her, I know. But why?"

Adam managed a shrug. "It's simple, really. As I recalculate my genealogy, you're carrying my cousin."

For another moment, Carla gazed at him, then patted her stomach. "Actually, I thought I felt him move this morning. A mother's imagination, probably. But at least I'm not sick anymore."

Adam shoved his hands in his pockets, quiet for a time. "I'm not sure how to say this without sounding stupid. But you're a far better person than I took you for."

Another smile surfaced in her eyes. "I suppose I could return your backhanded compliment. But you're exactly who I took you for, though you did your damnedest to conceal that." Carla paused, then said in a reticent tone, "You're leaving soon, I know. But once you're back, you can come to see us if you'd like."

Adam searched her face, trying to read what he saw there. "Perhaps I will," he told her. "After all, every boy could use a man who cares for him. No matter who."

"Then we'll look forward to it." She hesitated, then added, "Be safe, Adam. Despite everything, Ben worried for you. Now I do, too."

Adam fell silent, unsure of what else he wished to say. Then he felt the weight of what he could never tell her: that his father had killed the father of her child. "I'll be fine," he promised. "Take care, Carla."

Turning from the doubt he saw in her eyes, he left without looking back, still followed by the shadow of Benjamin Blaine.

When Jack's testimony was at last concluded, the four Blaines emerged from the courtroom with Avi Gold, each silent and preoccupied.

Though the inquest was over, nothing was decided; the death of Benjamin Blaine, and the doubts of the authorities, could yet ensnare one or more of them. To Adam's eye, only Teddy showed a modicum of relief. The merciful result, he supposed, of knowing far less than anyone else—not how Ben had died, or who had killed him, or that Adam was his half brother, half cousin. Or how many lies had been told today in this courtroom, all of Adam's invention. Teddy had believed Jack, and Adam envied his innocence.

Shadowed by these thoughts, Adam saw her.

Carla Pacelli paused in the corridor, her level gaze taking in each member of Adam's family—briefly lingering on Clarice, who turned away in scorn and anger. Then her eyes met Adam's. Touching his mother's elbow, he murmured, "Wait for me in the car," and walked over to Carla.

For a moment they faced each other, quiet. "Sorry for this," she said. "I came to see the district attorney, not your family. I thought the hearing would be over."

Adam grasped her dilemma. At the end of his life, she was the one who had cared for a dying man—knowing nothing about the change in his will to favor her—and by her lights, had found the good in him. But she was not family; only Benjamin Blaine's family, who despised him, was allowed inside the courtroom. And so Carla, who suspected that one of the Blaines had killed him, was forced to glean from George Hanley whatever he chose to tell her. Not much, Adam guessed, leaving doubt to gnaw at Carla's mind and heart.

Looking around them, he saw no one; the sheriff's deputies had kept the media outside. "The hearing ran late," he said with an ease he did not feel. "Jack was on the stand for a good while."

"I don't suppose you'll tell me what he said."

"What you've already heard once he went to the police. That Ben's death was an accident."

Her deep brown eyes were flecked with doubt. Burdened with his own deceit, Adam wondered why, of all the deceptions he had crafted, it pained him most to deceive Carla Pacelli. Perhaps because, as he had belatedly discovered, she was the only person involved with Benjamin Blaine who—unlike his mother, uncle, and brother—had always told him the truth.

"Do you believe that?" she asked.

"Consider the circumstances, Carla. There's no evidence that Jack killed him—or, as I understand it, to even place him at the scene. He risked putting his head in the noose in order to save Teddy."

"Which means he's innocent?" For an instant she eyed him closely, the intensity of her gaze fading to a fleeting half smile of skepticism. "I suppose I'll have to wait for the judge's report. For now, you're the person I most want to believe."

Adam had trained his face to show nothing; only another professional, he supposed, might take its studied blankness for what it was. "Whatever the case," she added, "I appreciate all you've done."

He shrugged this away. "How's the baby?"

Carla touched her stomach. "Fine, as far as I know. I have another checkup in two weeks. Ask me then."

"By then I may be back in Afghanistan." Adam hesitated, then heard himself ask, "Can I see you tonight?"

Briefly, she looked surprised, then smiled a little. "Of course." Lightly, she added, "How will you explain this to your mother? Or to anyone, for that matter?"

"I won't. It's like Ben told me, back when I thought he was my father: 'Never complain, never explain.' Truly words to live by."

"Only sometimes," Carla responded. "My life left me with a great deal to explain, if only to the people I choose to care about. But in that spirit, I'll cook dinner for us. I'd rather not have the two of us sitting in a public restaurant, drawing gasps and incredulous stares. There's been too much unwholesome interest in my life, and in my involvement with Ben. I don't want it to bleed into your life any more than it already has."

Adam simply nodded, a tacit acknowledgment of how difficult their relationship was. Whatever it was.

"Seven o'clock, then?" she asked.

"I'll look forward to it," he answered, and went to face whatever waited outside, feeling the conflict within him, guilt at war with kinship.

THREE

Outside, the rain had stopped. For a moment, Adam stood blinking in the light of a changeable August day, feeling like a badger peering from a hole. In this moment of hesitation, he saw the media scrum pursuing his family toward the sidewalk, a swarming organism filled with boom-mikes, cameras, notepads. Then a thin, tight voice said, "Hello again, Adam Blaine."

He knew this voice before he saw her darting at him from the side—Amanda Ferris of the *National Inquirer*, her sharp, birdlike gaze through her glasses filled with venom, her black hair cut short. "Still working?" he inquired pleasantly. "I was worried you'd been fired."

Her mouth twitched in an angry, reflexive smile. Two months before, unknown to the authorities, Adam had deployed her and the tabloid's money to ferret out the evidence against Teddy, then used the information to protect his brother—leaving Ferris without a story, and threatening her with a lawsuit if she printed her suspicions. But now she was back, perhaps on probation, fueled by the desire for retribution by exposing Adam before she lost her job.

"I wasn't fired," she shot back. "However hard you tried."

"How nice for you," Adam said, and began walking. "But I wasn't really trying. If I had, you wouldn't be here."

"But I am. And I think you're still busy covering up a crime. Actually, several crimes. Do you remember the break-in last June, at this same courthouse?"

"Why would I?"

"Because I think it was you who broke into Hanley's office. You read all the files on your father's death, then rearranged all the puzzle pieces to protect your family from a charge of murder."

Over his shoulder, Adam laughed softly. "Print that one, please. I'd like some money to build my own McMansion on the Vineyard. Another monstrosity in Chilmark, only in worse taste. If that's possible."

Ferris shook her head. "I'll wait until I have more—including what happened in the courtroom today. With some reverse engineering of your uncle's story, I'll figure out where you fit in. Maybe even including what you *really* do when you're not attending to your family's very special needs."

He turned to her on the lawn, his face and eyes hard. Instinctively, she shrank back a little. "And then?" he inquired softly.

She stood straighter. "Assuming you don't kill me?"

"For the moment."

Her lips compressed and then she spat out the words. "I'll go to George Hanley and the police, then to Carla Pacelli. I don't know which will make the better story." She paused a moment, then added in a lower voice, "Perhaps Carla will visit you in prison. Far more likely, she'll despise you as much as I do. Your father may be dead, but you'll never outrun his shadow. He was far too big a man."

The words cut to his core. But he did not show this, or any reaction at all. Impassive, he resumed walking to the car, recalling all too clearly the actions that, more than any others, could yet entrap him.

* * *

It had begun on a warm June evening, weeks before.

To assure his solitude, Adam had taken the ladder down to the beach below the promontory, where Ben's broken body had been found. Pulling out his cell phone, he called a former colleague for the second time that week.

"I'm out of answers," Adam said curtly, "How do you get me into the courthouse?"

"Not sure I can," Jason Lew replied laconically. "Even the standard security system you describe is difficult to beat. Cut the power, you trigger the alarm. And you're also dealing with cameras inside, right?"

"Yes. I've got the locations memorized. I also know where the control panel is—a room just off the entrance."

"That's what I need." Lew paused, signaling his reluctance, then said more slowly, "I'd have to pose as a service guy and insert a receiver. That will connect to a switch that shuts the system down from the outside. Pushing the switch is your job."

"My leave's running out," Adam told him. "So I don't have much more time here. How long do you need on your end?"

"Two days to build the receiver, then a day-trip to the Vineyard. Say three nights from now you can go in. Assuming they don't spot me as an imposter, and arrest me on the spot." Lew's chuckle became the phlegmy rumble of a smoker. "Funny work for an old guy. But fifteen thousand in cash would send me to Costa Brava."

Adam felt the encroaching night envelop him. "I'll have it for you by tomorrow."

"Deal." Lew's speech slowed again. "This kind of service doesn't come with warranties. You could hit the switch and find yourself on candid camera, with a shriek alarm for a laugh track. Instead of back in Afghanistan, you'd wind up in jail."

How had he gotten here? Adam wondered again. "If you'd screwed up on the job," he replied, "the guys relying on you could have been killed. They tell me no one was."

"Different times," Lew said. "The technical obstacles are greater now. We'll see if I still have it. Otherwise, you're fucked."

In the next three days, Adam had flown to Washington, met with his superiors, transferred money to Lew through two separate bank accounts, then returned to the Vineyard. On the day following, Lew called him to report. "I got by with it," he said. "I don't think the security guys suspected me. If you're feeling reckless, you can find out if my technical gifts survive."

That evening, at twilight, Adam told his mother he was going fly fishing and drove to Dogfish Bar.

Several men with fly rods were already there, spread like sentries along the surf. Adam stopped to chat, then took his place among the others. For several hours, he tried to clear his mind of tensions, focused on his casting. Only as the rest began drifting away did Adam's thoughts turn from the water.

Shortly after midnight, he found himself alone.

Edgier now, he made himself remain for one more hour. Then he returned to the dirt patch where he had parked his truck, changed into jeans and a dark sweater, and made the forty-minute drive to Edgartown.

He parked on a residential lane two blocks from Main Street. The town was dark and quiet, the last of the drunken college kids cleared from the sidewalks. Sliding out of the truck, he walked near the shade trees lining the road.

Headlights pierced the darkness, coming toward him. Swiftly, he slipped behind the cover of a privacy hedge, kneeling on the lawn of a darkened house. Peering through its branches, he saw that the lights belonged to a patrol car from the Edgartown police. This much he had expected; what he could not know is whether the cop at the wheel would continue on his rounds.

Standing, Adam looked in both directions, then continued past more white frame houses in a circuitous route toward Main Street. Then he veered again, quietly but quickly crossing a yard before concealing himself behind a tree next to the courthouse.

Its parking lot was empty, the rear entrance lit by a single spotlight. Putting on his father's old ski mask and gloves, he took Lew's device from his pocket. It was no larger than a car fob, with a simple switch that would disarm the security system. Unless the device was defective—in which case, arrest was the least of Adam's worries.

He paused, envisioning the challenge ahead. A sheriff's deputy would monitor the surveillance screen in the room near the main entrance, watching images sent by cameras in the hallway and just above the rear door. Assuming that the shriek alarm did not go off when he opened the door, any one of the cameras could reveal his presence inside the courthouse, bringing a troop of cops and deputies. His choice was to back out, or trust in Lew's skill.

For a moment, recalling the young man he had been, who once imagined himself a lawyer, Adam was paralyzed by disbelief. But in the ten years since then he had learned to ignore boundaries, and to mold events to his purposes. Stepping from behind the tree, he felt the coldness come over him, his heartbeat lowering, his breathing becoming deep and even. His footsteps as he crossed the parking lot were silent.

Nerveless, he pushed the button.

The first test would be the door.

Adam inhaled. The door had unlocked; so far, Lew's bypass had worked.

Slowly, Adam edged inside. Dim light illuminated the hallway. A camera aimed down at him from the ceiling, meant to reveal his presence at once. But if the device functioned properly, the monitor would show the empty space that existed a moment before Adam filled it. No one inside seemed to stir.

With painful slowness, Adam crept down the hallway toward the stairs to the second floor. As he reached them, he glanced into the security room and saw the broad back of a sheriff's deputy gazing at a TV monitor, watching the door through which Adam had entered. The intruder was safely inside.

Catlike, he started up the stairs. He willed himself not to look back at the deputy who, simply by turning, would catch him. Reaching the top, he turned a corner, out of sight once more.

The second floor was quiet and still. If he got in and out without being seen, Lew had promised, no one would ever know he had been there. But Adam had more complex plans. Reaching the door of George Hanley's office, also wired to the system, he turned the knob.

Once again, Lew's device had disarmed the lock. Slipping inside, Adam softly closed the door.

Through the window, Main Street appeared dark and silent. Using his penlight, Adam scanned the surface of Hanley's desk.

Nothing of interest. Kneeling, he slid open the top drawer of a battered metal cabinet, then another, reading the captions of manila folders. Only in the bottom drawer did he find the file labeled "Benjamin Blaine."

Taking it out, he sat in Hanley's chair.

The sensation was strange. But for the next few minutes, Adam guessed, he was safe. The danger would come when he tried to leave.

Methodically, he spread the contents of the file in front of him. Hanley's handwritten notes, suggesting areas of inquiry. The crime scene report. Typed notes of the initial interviews with his mother, brother, and uncle—as well as Carla Pacelli, Jenny Leigh, Nathan Wright—the last man who admitted to seeing Ben before his death—and Adam himself. And, near the bottom of the file, the pathologist's report.

For the next half hour, he systematically photographed each page, blocking out all thought of detection. He had no time to read. But once he escaped, and studied them, he would know almost as much as George Hanley and Sean Mallory—and, unlike them, would know that, too. Especially advantaged would be Teddy's lawyer in Boston, who would receive them in the mail from an anonymous benefactor, and who, himself innocent of the theft, would have no ethical duty to return them.

Finishing, Adam reassembled the file and placed it in a different drawer. This last was for Bobby Towle, his policeman friend who, needing money to pay for his wife's rehabilitation from drug addiction, had been vulnerable to Ferris once Adam had betrayed him. Now Hanley would know that someone had rifled his office, but not who it was, creating a universe of suspects who might have sold information to the *Inquirer*. A gift of conscience from an old friend.

Opening the door, Adam left it ajar.

At the top of the stairs, he stopped abruptly. The deputy was padding down the hallway, perhaps sensing that something was wrong. If he glanced up, Adam was caught.

Utterly still, Adam watched him. The man disappeared, the only sound the quiet echo of his footsteps.

Adam stayed where he was.

Moments crawled by while the deputy inspected the first floor. At last, Adam heard more footsteps, and prayed that the deputy would not come upstairs. Back toward Adam, the man plodded to his station and sat before a monitor Adam knew to be disabled.

With agonizing care, Adam walked down the stairs. With each step, the distance between him and the deputy lessened. As Adam reached the bottom of the steps, it narrowed to ten feet.

Head propped on his arm, the deputy gazed at the frozen screen.

Turning down the hallway, Adam passed beneath more cameras, still unseen. A few last steps, swifter now, took him to the entrance.

Slowly opening the door, Adam reentered the night.

As he stepped onto the asphalt, headlights sliced the darkness. In an instant, Adam grasped that the patrol car was arriving. As its lights caught Adam, the driver hit the brakes.

Whirling, Adam sprinted down Main Street, footsteps pounding cement. In one corner of his mind, he gauged the time it would take the patrolman to swing back into the alley toward the street, picking him up again.

Suddenly, he swerved, cutting back through the lawn of the Whaling Church and then a stand of trees bordering a neighbor's backyard. Behind him, he heard brakes squealing, a door opening, the footsteps of the cop scurrying from his car.

Adam had little more time to run; in minutes, more police would converge, on foot or in patrol cars. Nor could he drive away. His last hope was to hide.

Bent at the waist, he crossed another yard, heading for his truck.

It was parked in a line of cars along the crowded lane. As head-lights entered the lane, Adam reached his truck, sliding to his stomach at the rear. Clawing asphalt, he pulled himself beneath it, invisible to anyone who did not think to look.

He heard the patrol car pass, then his pursuer, still on foot, reaching the lane near Adam's truck. Listening to the man's labored breathing, Adam imagined him looking about, mystified by the absence of sound, the sudden disappearance of his quarry.

Move on, Adam implored him.

Another car passed without stopping, and then the man's foot-steps sounded again, fading as he moved away.

Adam removed his mask and gloves. Damp face pressed against the asphalt, he glanced at his watch.

Three-twenty. Two hours until dawn. Head resting on curled arms, Adam waited.

First light came as a silver space between the tires of his truck. Sliding out, Adam looked around him, and saw nothing but the still of early morning.

He climbed into his truck, started the motor, and drove out of town at a slow but steady pace. Glancing in the mirror, he saw that no one followed. As had been his plan, he headed back toward Dog-fish Bar.

The beach was empty, the only sign of human existence the foot prints left by fishermen. Satisfied, he changed back into his fishing gear, and drove to a restaurant overlooking the Gay Head cliffs. He ordered breakfast amidst the tourists and tradesmen, a nocturnal angler as determined as Ben Blaine had been, refueling after hours of solitary fishing. He made a point of joking with the waitress.

On the way home, he tossed the garbage bag filled with his clothes in a pile of refuse at the Chilmark dump, and dropped Lew's device in its incinerator. Parking at his mother's, he saw Clarice drinking coffee on the porch. "You look terrible," she observed.

Adam fingered his dark stubble. "The price of watching the sun come up. All that's left when you catch no fish."

"Get some sleep," his mother suggested with a smile. "You're not twenty anymore."

Climbing the stairs, Adam closed himself in a room that still held the artifacts of his youth. For a moment, he had contemplated Jenny Leigh's photograph, a painful remnant of the time before his break with Ben. Then he downloaded the images he had taken into his computer, reviewing the documents he would provide to Teddy's lawyer.

The process took two hours, more disturbing by the minute as the mosaic of evidence began forming in his mind. The witness statements conformed to what he knew: the Blaines, Jenny, and Carla Pacelli all denied knowing about the will, and his mother and Teddy's central assertion—which, in his brother's case, Adam had no longer believed—was that neither had seen his father once he left the house. Far more lethal were the crime scene and pathology reports. He was not surprised that someone besides Benjamin Blaine—no doubt Teddy—had left distinctive boot prints at the promontory. But there had been drag marks in the mud as well, mud on the heels of the dead man's boots, suggesting that someone had dragged him, perhaps struggling, through the wet earth near the point from which he fell. Worse yet, there were circumferential bruises on Ben's wrists, heightened by his regime of chemotherapy, appearing to confirm that a murderer had grasped him by both arms. It was plain that the police and prosecutor believed, as Adam did now, that someone had thrown Benjamin Blaine off the promontory.

Adam felt a coldness on his skin. His next task was to print these pages, mail them to Teddy's lawyer, then erase the images from his camera and computer before getting rid of both. But he paused to absorb what he and the authorities now further believed in common—that Teddy had killed their father. The job Benjamin Blaine had left him was not just to undo a will, but to save his own brother.

And so he had, Adam believed now. But that Benjamin Blaine was not his father was far from the only surprise awaiting him after the break-in. Another was that Teddy was innocent of murder; Jack—his real father—guilty. But this did not change the risk to Adam himself. Now he, too, was guilty of a crime—obstruction of justice in order to save one member of his family, then another. All that was left him was the hope that, despite the suspicions of George Hanley and Sean Mallory—and now Amanda Ferris—no one could ever prove that. Another secret Adam carried alone.

Ignoring the reporters' shouted questions, he opened the door of the SUV and slid into the passenger seat, beside his father.

PART TWO

The Devil's Pact

August–September 2011

ONE

At the end of a long, silent ride, the Blaines arrived at a rambling white frame house once owned by Clarice's parents, placed on a spacious meadow in Chilmark with a view of the Vineyard Sound through a cut in the trees overlooking the water. In his youth, this bluff had been Adam's favorite place to watch the sunset with Benjamin Blaine. But now the site was marred by all that had come since, the most haunting of which was what had happened there the night Ben died.

Touching Teddy's shoulder to signal that he wanted a word, Adam walked with him across the rain-dampened grass to the guest house where his brother lived and painted. At the door, Teddy turned to face him, worry showing through his quizzical smile. "I know that look by now, Adam—the indecipherable expression that conceals a cool brain at work. So the problem is?"

"A tabloid reporter named Amanda Ferris. The *National Inquirer*'s gift to journalism, and now to us. She's after me, which means she's after you."

At once his brother's tepid smile vanished. "I don't even know her. But it seems that you do. Would you mind telling me how?"

Once again, Adam found himself regretting all he could not say, even to the brother he was determined to protect. "I prefer reminding you what to avoid—talking to anyone at all about our father or this inquest. If you hear anything about her, tell me. We need this locked down tight until the judge issues his report, and George Hanley decides what to do."

Doubt clouded Teddy's eyes. "You think they believed Jack's testimony?"

"Not really. Their problem is that they can't disprove it."

Teddy looked at him more closely. "Do you believe it?"

"I know *you* didn't kill him." Adam paused, steeling himself to follow this simple truth with yet another lie. "And why would Jack volunteer this story if it weren't true? Easier to say he was home in bed."

Slowly, his brother nodded. "I owe Uncle Jack a lot."

"You do." Briefly, Adam smiled. "But then what is family for? Even this one."

Pausing outside, Adam took fresh stock of the house he had salvaged for his mother despite Ben's malice. It had been built in the 1850s: in the 1940s, a then-wealthy couple from Boston, Clarice's parents, bought it as their summer home. Long before Adam and Teddy had played hide-and-seek in the woods and swum off the rocky beach below, Clarice had spent the best summers of her childhood in this house. As with many homes of this vintage, the porch that looked out at woods and ocean had been more generous than the rooms, a reminder that what was most compelling about the Vineyard lay outdoors. Adam could still remember the summer evenings when his mother and Benjamin Blaine would sit on the porch at night in moments of marital peace, talking or listening to the crickets.

But, like their lives as a whole, the space inside bore the mark of a dead man. Ben had knocked down walls to suit himself, and now the living room was large and open, filled with the comfortable furniture he liked and mementos of his travels—Asian vases, African masks, scrolls in Arabic and Hebrew. Amidst this sat the other remnants of Ben's life—his wife and brother, Adam's father. Sitting across from them, Adam could only wonder how it felt for Jack to be there.

It was to Jack's credit, Adam supposed, that his sensitive eyes—though resolutely fixed on Adam—betrayed his shame at the concealment of his guilt, as well as the deeper truth that Adam's mother also did not know: that Adam had protected him. But Clarice's innocence allowed her to regard her younger son with a look of hurt and anger. Coolly, Adam said, "Go ahead, Mom. I hate to see you feeling repressed."

"You know what it is. How can you humiliate me in public by being friendly with that woman?"

"Actually," Adam corrected, "it's worse than that. We're having dinner tonight."

His mother bridled. "Dinner with your father's whore."

Adam felt the familiar whipsaw of hurt and anger. "He wasn't my father, and Carla's not a whore. If it weren't for her willingness to settle the estate, there's a good chance you'd be out in the street, with nothing I could do for you. So you might save a bit of the gratitude you lavish on me for her."

At this, Jack turned to Clarice, silently imploring her to stop. But Clarice did not see him. "Forgive me," she told Adam stiffly, "but giving her three million dollars feels like gratitude enough. Beyond that, I expect more loyalty from a son."

Though stung, Adam answered softly. "And I might've expected more candor from a mother. So let's be candid now. For years you put up with my quasi-father's affairs. You hate Carla because she's the woman Benjamin Blaine took seriously. For you, the real tragedy is that he died too late for you to maintain the illusion of your marriage."

At this, Adam saw his mother summon the willed self-control that had governed her life reassert itself. "To be wholly fair," she responded in a more even tone, "the core of my difficulties preceded Carla Pacelli's arrival here by roughly thirty-four years. The postnuptial agreement through which I gave up my rights in my husband's assets—including the house he had bought from my father. The reason you were born in comfort instead of scandal." She paused, concluding softly, "Or born at all. Everything else came from that."

"Meaning?" Adam could not help but ask.

Though Jack placed a hand on her wrist, Clarice kept looking at their son, speaking with quiet vehemence. "If I'd terminated the pregnancy, Adam, my husband never would've known. Instead, on returning after four months away, Ben knew to a certainty that the child I was bearing wasn't his. But I insisted on having you. Not for any religious reasons, but because you're my son, and Jack's son, and I wanted you to live more fiercely than you can ever understand. As a purely practical matter, you were the last thing I needed in my life. But this wasn't a practical decision, unlike so many that I've made. I loved you before you were born, and I love you now.

"So, please, spare me the moral outrage about how Jack and I misled you. I could have ended your life before it began, and saved you all this disappointment. Little did I imagine that you'd end up blackmailing me, more or less, to help his mistress and the unborn child he favored over you and Teddy."

It was a mercy, Adam supposed, that the last decade of his life had, so often, required that he feel nothing. "Then you made the wrong choice, didn't you? It seems that I've been the agent of your problems before I was ever born, right to this moment. No doubt it's rich with irony how poorly I've repaid you." Seeing Jack wince, he paused to choose his next words with care. "I appreciate what you did, Mother—or at least tried to do. But my whole life was distorted by Ben's ambivalence about me, and the rivalry between my supposed father and my real one. I can't inflict our family pathology on another unborn child.

"Like you, Carla is choosing to have a child who is a result of an affair. Her son may be nothing to you, but he's Teddy's brother and my cousin. So I'm going to make a place for him in my life. That requires me to have a relationship with his mother. As much as you want me to hate her, I can't—and don't. If you resent me for that, try to remember that this boy will outlive us all. And outrun us, if he's lucky."

For an instant, Clarice looked wounded, and then her face closed. "Surely you don't expect me to forget who this woman is. Let alone to accept her."

Before Adam could answer, Jack turned to her. "None of us can forget any of this, Clarice. Be we're asking Adam to accept quite a lot. So he's entitled to some forbearance on our part, including on the subject of Carla Pacelli. There's enough for the three of us to sort out as it is."

Watching his mother absorb this, Adam felt a deep ambivalence. Only Jack and he knew why his father was free to sit here. But Adam also remembered all the kindness Jack had lavished on the boy who had thought himself lucky to have such a caring uncle. Deeply, pointlessly, Adam wished never to have learned all that he had, and to love Jack still.

"Thanks," he told Jack with a casual air he did not feel. "It's not like I'm marrying her, after all." He sat back, looking from his father to his mother. "Anyhow, we've got the present to worry about. As I've already told Teddy, there is a *National Inquirer* reporter lurking about, a particularly feral specimen named Amanda Ferris.

"Ferris will stir up all the problems she can, including with Carla Pacelli. You don't want that, believe me. So there may come a time when you're grateful that I'm in touch with Carla. After all, I'm the only member of this family who she's certain didn't shove the father of her child off a cliff. If only because I was in Afghanistan."

Quite deliberately, Adam looked at his mother, not Jack. But he did not truly see either one; he was suddenly, unspeakably soul weary, and the spacious room felt claustrophobic. Without saying more, he got up and went to see Carla Pacelli.

Two

Carla Pacelli was living near the Blaines, in a guesthouse behind the summer home of the novelist Whitney Dane. That Whitney and Ben, her contemporary and fellow writer, had routinely avoided each other had always been a puzzlement to Adam, all the more so because of his understanding that, in their childhood and youth, his mother and Whitney had been the closest of friends. But this estrangement, whatever its cause, had made it possible for Whitney to continue giving Carla a refuge from all that had beset her—alcohol and drug abuse, the collapse of her career—while she tried to build the foundation for a new and different life.

At seven o'clock, it would still be light for another hour, and Carla had set the table on the deck outside, affording them a sweeping view of a Vineyard Sound that glistened with the falling sun. Wearing a loose, flowing dress, Carla was placing napkins when Adam arrived. Glancing up at the sound of his footsteps, she gave him a wry smile, as though to acknowledge the incongruity of the occasion. "What excuse did you give them at home?" she asked. "A poetry reading?"

"I said we were going to Lamaze class."

To his surprise, Carla laughed lightly, the first time he had ever heard this. The effect was charming, lending a human touch to a woman whose appearance was so stunning that, even now, Adam experienced the involuntary jolt of attraction he had felt when seeing her on the screen. But there was something else, he realized: even with the weight of all he was concealing from Carla Pacelli, after the strain of dealing with his family he was simply glad to see her. "Men will do anything to appear useful," she replied. "How are things among the Blaines?"

"Trying," Adam paused, then decided on the novelty—at least for this day—of speaking an unvarnished truth. "He left a lot of wreckage, Carla, ending with the will. All the more so because it set you and my mother at each other's throats. All in all, it's been a long day, and I'm very, very hungry."

Carla pulled out a wooden chair, inviting him to sit. "Then I hope you like chicken cacciatore," she replied. "One of my few specialties. My mother's family was Irish; my father's Italian. So there was only one direction my cooking could take."

Adam realized that he had rarely heard Carla mention her parents, and then only in passing. "You know all about my family," he said, then recalled at once how untrue that was. "What was yours like?"

Her smile faded. "Another time, perhaps. While I'm up, what would you like to drink that contains no alcohol at all?"

In the event, the chicken was succulent, its sauce tangy but not too rich. When Adam said as much, Carla answered, "You can thank my grandmother, who taught it to my mother. Mom was desperate to please my father in any way she could. You're the incidental beneficiary."

There was more behind this comment, Adam was quite certain, just as he knew that, at least for tonight, he should not probe this. Instead, he asked, "Are you staying here until the baby's born?

It's nice right now, but Martha's Vineyard in the winter is like the world's longest Bergman film."

The sun had fallen into the ocean, its red disk bathing the water in a last painterly orange-gray glow as night began enveloping them. Lighting a candle, Carla observed, "I'm not looking for excitement—I've had too much already. This is a better place for me to stay sober."

Adam could still remember the photographs of Carla that were splashed across cable news, taken after a one-car crash caused by her cross-addiction to alcohol and cocaine. Though he had not imagined knowing her then, her eyes were filled with shame, drawing from him a sympathetic wonder that a woman with so much could fall so far, so fast. In a tone that he hoped was encouraging, Adam replied, "You look like you're doing fine."

Carla gave a fractional shrug. "It helps to be away from there. When I was running on the hamster wheel, I thought substance abuse was my friend—alcohol helped me relax, and coke jacked me up to learn my lines and keep the weight off. So I started doing more coke so I could drink more, which accentuated all of my less than desirable traits: impatience, fear of failure, and a tendency to wall off feelings." She looked at Adam more intently. "I'm a born loner, it seems. Maybe you know what that's like."

"Let's say I'm familiar with the species."

"Anyhow, alcoholism was another part of my birthright—my dad had it, and my grandfather before him. It was always waiting in ambush, until the right combination of pressure and stuff I'd never resolved brought it out of hiding. God knows what would've happened if I hadn't cracked up that Porsche."

For a moment, Adam watched the candle, flickering in a fitful breeze that caused its light to shimmer on the table. "How did you pull out of it?"

"By accident, at first. As a matter of self-preservation, I had to show how contrite I was. So I figured a respite drinking vegetable juice at Betty Ford might retrieve my career." Carla's tone became sardonic. "Naturally, I showed up drunk in the backseat of a limousine. I vaguely remember a sense of disbelief as I entered a driveway lined with palm trees, ending up in a reception area that was so serene I thought I was in one of those movies where you imagine the afterlife. My keepers took one look, gave me something to keep me from crashing, and led me to a room with a single bed. God knows how long I slept, and how little I wanted to wake up."

"What happened when you did?"

Carla rolled her eyes, a surprisingly droll expression. "Do you really want to hear all this? You don't seem like the type who goes to AA meetings for fun."

"You have no idea of the things I consider fun. If I weren't interested, I wouldn't ask."

She fell quiet, considering him with renewed gravity. In that moment he wondered if he reminded her of Ben, perhaps of the evenings before he died when she must have explained her life. Then Carla collected herself to answer. "Actually, I felt horrified. I'd gone to sleep in the afterlife, and awakened in a summer camp for junkies. Not only was I jumpy and strung out, but my new counselor was explaining the routine: daily sessions for fitness, spiritual care, diet and nutrition, counseling, and—worst of all—group therapy. If I'd had the strength, I'd have run screaming into the night."

"But you didn't."

"How could I?" Carla responded wryly. "Before, I had a crew of employees who depended on my career. Now I had all these lovely people dedicated to my recovery—a doctor, nurse, psychologist, spiritual counselor, dietitian, fitness trainer, chemical dependency technician, and, God help us, an alumni services representative for when I got out, just like at UCLA. And they had a schedule for me that ran from six in the morning to ten at night, with wonderful new friends to meet in what was essentially a women's dorm.

"I wanted to crawl under my bed. But what made it even harder was group therapy." Her tone softened. "I wasn't a very trusting person then. I'm not sure I really am now. But I'm better."

"Group therapy," Adam remarked, "is not something I can imagine doing."

"Neither could I. But it turned out to be what I needed. I learned my problems weren't special—they were just mine. The more these women were honest around me, the more honest I became. Ironically enough, there's something addictive about candor when you need it to save your life." Carla took a sip of her coffee. "It's hard to delve into your deepest secrets, especially in a business where predators publicize your every slip. But the day I found myself weeping without being able to stop, I realized how much pain I'd been in, and for how long. And I knew that nothing about my life—the money, the celebrity, all the people who needed me enough to suspend the rules—could protect me from what I'd been carrying around."

To Adam, the memory lent a raw note to her smoky voice. "Hence, Martha's Vineyard."

Carla nodded. "The cliché in recovery is 'change your playground and your playmates.' But I also realized that escaping wasn't enough—that wherever you go, you take your demons with you. My first ninety days on the island, I went to ninety AA meetings. The other part, which I still can't quite believe, is that I've renewed diplomatic relations with Catholicism. If one seeks help from a 'higher power,' as AA says you should, better the version you already know."

Adam smiled. "God and I have never been formerly introduced. But it seems like it's worked for you. I saw that mug shot, and you're not the same person."

"She wasn't the girl I wanted to be," Carla answered ruefully. "Not when I was young, and certainly not now. But celebrity makes it that much harder. Another reason that I came here."

Adam found himself thinking of Amanda Ferris and then, with piercing quickness, of the scandal Carla had evoked by becoming involved with Benjamin Blaine. Imagining them together, he felt a sudden resentment, then stifled it. "I guess becoming a mother changes things, too."

In this moment, she looked vulnerable. "Everything," she said softly. "For a bunch of reasons I thought I could never have children. You can't imagine how fiercely I want this child, and to be the mother he deserves. A psychologist might say that I want to give him the parenting I didn't have." She met his eyes. "For better or worse, family really is the gift that keeps on giving. All we can do is try to understand it, and do better for whoever follows us."

Once more, Adam felt an unspoken kinship. But his own family had trapped him in a web of secrets he was forced to hide from her. "In my family," he responded, "whoever follows us comes down to your son. As matters stand, he's the last of the Blaines."

Carla regarded him curiously. "Did you ever want kids?"

"I thought so, once. But my job gets in the way."

"I'm sure," she retorted with a trace of irony. "It can't be easy persuading Afghan farmers to grow other crops than opium poppies. As a former addict, I can say first hand that you're performing a service."

"Thank you," Adam said solemnly. "Not everyone appreciates my self-sacrifice."

"Oh, I do," she rejoined. "Too bad Ben didn't believe a word of it."

"I find that odd, Carla—seeing how we hadn't spoken in ten years. He must've been reading the entrails of goats."

His dismissive tone did not seem to faze her. "Actually, Ben was reading maps and talking to your mother. Believe it or not, the trajectory of your career worried him—Pakistan, Iraq, and then Afghanistan. Everywhere jihadists seemed to be. He even made *me* wonder about you a little."

Adam chose to laugh. "You really *don't* trust anyone, do you?"

"I've already admitted to that," she replied in an unimpressed tone. "As for Ben, he thought you were CIA."

"Then he was wrong." More easily, he added, "Anyhow, you played a spy on television. So you know that if I tell you the truth, they'll have to kill us both."

Carla hesitated. "Does it matter that I worry for you, too?"

"Only that you're wasting your time. I have a foolish job, not a lethal one. I may be leaving in two weeks, but I'll be coming back."

"And then they'll send you someplace else?"

"Somewhere nicer, I hope. But my company is under contract to USAID, and they don't give foreign aid to farmers in Tuscany or

Bordeaux. Which explains the pattern of travel Ben seemed to find so sinister." He paused, searching for a change of subject. "Anyhow, I'll let you know how to reach me. Just so I can hear if you're getting along okay."

She looked into his eyes again. "I'll stay in touch," she answered. "But we'll be fine. If we need help, there are people in AA I can call."

"Then you're having the baby on the island?"

Carla nodded. "Whitney has told me I can stay, and I like my doctor here. So yes, unless there are complications."

For a moment, Adam sensed she wanted to say more about her pregnancy. But there was no easy way to probe this, and their conversation about his job was one he did not care to revisit. Glancing at his watch, he said, "This has been nice, Carla. I didn't realize how late it is. You must be tired."

"And no doubt they're waiting up for you at home. But I hope this won't be the last time I see you." She paused, as though hearing herself. "In the next two weeks, I mean."

"I know what you meant," Adam assured her. "Do you know another Italian dish?"

"Several." Briefly, Carla touched his hand. "You can bring wine, Adam—for yourself. As long as you take it with you, I won't mind."

THREE

That night, Adam Blaine awoke from the recurring nightmare of his own murder.

The bedroom of his youth was pitch black, the thin silver light on his window cast by a crescent moon. He could feel the sweat on his forehead. In this dream, like the other, at the moment of his death he became Benjamin Blaine.

Turning on the light, he looked at the framed photographs that had remained there since he had left the island a decade before. A picture of the man he had thought his father; another of Jenny Leigh, the young woman he had loved until his break with Ben. Opening the drawer of his nightstand, he slid them inside, and closed it.

Enough, he thought. He could not kill these dreams alone, nor did he wish to take them back to Afghanistan. In the morning, he would call Charlie Glazer.

* * *

At 10 a.m., as agreed, Adam found Dr. Charlie Glazer sitting on the porch of his home overlooking Menemsha Harbor.

A family friend from Adam's youth, Glazer was an eminent psychiatrist who for years had taught at Harvard. On Adam's return to the Vineyard, faced with the complexities of Ben's death, he had turned to Charlie for advice on how to navigate the labyrinth of his family—a group Charlie himself had given considerable thought over forty summers spent there. A bright-eyed man in his late sixties with white hair and mustache, Charlie did not affect the walled-off gravity often associated with his profession, instead combining a sweet-natured good humor with the tough-mindedness of the skilled psychoanalyst beneath. Adam had always liked him; now, Charlie was the only person he could trust with a semblance of the truth.

"So," Charlie said without preface. "It sounds like you need to talk a little more. No surprise—even viewed from the outside, your family is an inexhaustible subject."

Adam sat in the canvas chair across from him. "This isn't just about them," he responded, and felt the tug of his own reluctance. "It's about what's going on with me."

For a moment, Charlie appraised him in silence. Dryly, he said, "That sounds dangerously close to actual psychotherapy."

"I guess it does."

"Then as a friend, and a professional, I should refer you to someone else. I know far too much about your family to be a neutral therapist, and I formed too many opinions about its members too long ago. One of which is that untangling all of that requires a serious commitment to a rigorous analytic process."

Adam felt a sliver of despair. "No time, Charlie. I'm going back to Afghanistan in two weeks. Explaining my family to a stranger would take a year." He hesitated, then finished, "Whatever happens to me over there, I need more peace of mind than I've got."

Charlie frowned. "A tall order in two weeks' time. Especially—and I hope you'll forgive me—for someone as locked up tight as I perceive you to be."

"I know that. But I'm not hacking it alone."

Charlie's probing gaze softened. "You really are alone, aren't you."

For a moment, the words struck in Adam's throat. "I can't tell anyone the truth. You're the only person on this island I can trust, and who it's safe to trust. In fact, the only person in my life. By profession, and I guess for deeper reasons, I'm not a very trusting person. And there are other lives at stake than mine."

Charlie cupped his chin in the palm of his hand, staring fixedly at the water. Finally, he said, "The circumstances are hardly ideal. But I'll help you to the extent I can. What I need from you is an absolute commitment to honesty. You can't hide the ball from me— or yourself."

Adam grimaced. "I understand. The one thing I ask is that we meet here, or maybe on your sailboat. In the last ten years, whenever I'm in an office I feel cooped up."

"Fair enough. Three meetings then, at least two hours at a whack. No bullshit. Are you prepared for that?"

"Yes."

Charlie nodded briskly. "All right then. I'll get us some coffee, and we can start. You take yours black, right?"

Handing Adam a steaming cup of coffee, Charlie sat back across from him. "What brought you back to the island?" he asked. "The last time I saw you, maybe a month ago, you were leaving for Afghanistan."

"I was. The medical examiner's inquest got in the way."

"And I suppose you felt responsible to look out for your mother, brother, and uncle. Or, or should I say, your father."

The conversation was barely started, Adam reflected, and there was already something he could not say, even to Charlie—that, whatever the justice in it, Adam was covering up his father's murder of Adam's father figure. "There's a lot to worry about," he answered. "Especially Teddy, whom I know to be innocent of murder. There's also Carla, and what happens to her and the boy. Nothing good can come from further conflict between her and my mother, whether it concerns the estate or the circumstances of Ben's death."

Charlie gave him a shrewd look. "I'll let that answer pass, Adam—at least in part. As to Carla and your family, I certainly credit your concern—and the reasons for it. But you and I both know that your feelings about Carla, however complicated, transcend merely looking out after everyone's interests. Though I can't imagine you're anywhere close to sorting them out."

"True enough," Adam acknowledged. "But then it hardly matters, does it? I'm going back to Afghanistan. That's what brought me here this morning—my work."

"Which you admitted to me is dangerous, and nothing like the story you tell your family—and everyone else. But it would help if I knew a little more." Reading Adam's expression, Charlie added, "Unless you plan to kill someone before you leave here, anything you tell me is confidential. Including about what you're really doing in the world."

Adam smiled without humor. "I may kill someone pretty soon, Charlie. But I don't yet know whom. And unless it's a certain tabloid reporter, no one on this island." He drew a breath, fighting the habits of a decade. "I'm a CIA officer. Ben and Carla guessed as much, and I imagine you have, too."

Charlie nodded. "That much, yes. But tell me more about what you do."

Adam sat back, marshaling the answer he forced himself to give. "I'm on the paramilitary side of the agency—the special activities division. I'm fluent in Arabic, Pashto, and Dari, the principal languages of Afghanistan and Pakistan. I'm also schooled in running agents, avoiding surveillance, and using pretty much any weapon you can imagine. Part of that training involves the quarter of a second rule—the time within which human beings can respond to danger. I'm conditioned to kill someone just a little quicker."

Charlie showed no discernable reaction. "How does that work in Afghanistan?"

"Mostly self-protection. My assignment is to operate against the Taliban and al-Qaeda by recruiting agents, getting information, and targeting their leaders for assassination. If I get caught at it, my best hope is to die quickly."

"Sounds challenging enough," Charlie observed phlegmatically.

"Yup. One of the hardest parts is sorting out the people I recruit—who's a double agent, or when might they become one. My life depends on getting it right." He paused a moment. "Even harder, at least for me, is that I'm responsible for their lives. So far, I haven't lost one. I never want to."

Suddenly it struck Adam that he had deployed Jack like a double agent, placing him at risk to save Teddy. Another thing he could not say. "And so," Charlie was observing in measured tones, "your survival, and that of others, depends on a very complicated series of calculations and deceptions."

The statement gave Adam a leaden feeling. "I've arranged my life into boxes," he acknowledged. "Each box contains certain people, situations, experiences, and emotions, carefully arranged so that no box touches any other box, placing me or others in danger. I've even got boxes for Martha's Vineyard: for Carla; for each member of my family; for the DA; for this tarantula of a tabloid reporter. For what I believe are good reasons, I'm deceiving every one of them in different ways—letting them believe things that aren't true, and withholding things that are. All because I'm trying to protect my brother, mother, father, and Carla from each other, as well as to protect myself. But Afghanistan is worse—betrayal comes in many guises, any one of which can kill you."

Charlie frowned. "A hard life to lead, Adam. It seems you've lost the habit of feeling safe, or even the ability to know who you're safe with."

"Also true," Adam replied with a trace of irony. "Though I seem to be suited for the work. When I went into special ops, they put me through a battery of psychological tests. To everyone's great pleasure, I came out as able to tolerate a high degree of risk and stress without cracking up, and being unusually unconcerned with my own safety."

Charlie considered him over the rim of his coffee cup. "In psychological terms, what do you suppose that means?"

"I don't know. I just know that's who I became once I left this island." He paused, disconcerted by the admission he was about to make. "In the last three years, I'd thought I proved to myself I can live with pretty much anything. But since Ben died, and I came back here, I've been having these nightmares. That's why I called you."

Charlie smiled a little. "I think there are many reasons why you called me, all of which are closing in on you. But tell me about these nightmares."

For a time, Adam gazed out a Menemsha Pond on a perfect August day, the sky clear blue, a steady breeze propelling trim sailing crafts across spacious waters bounded by woods and meadows. It seemed so alien from the life he led that the scene, once so evocative of his youth on the water, now struck him as surreal. The coffee felt sour in his empty stomach. "Both dreams take place in Afghanistan," he said at length. "In one, I'm next to a cliff, surrounded by Taliban fighters who are about to execute me. My only escape is to jump off the edge. But when I do that, I realize I'm falling toward the beach behind our house where Ben died on the rocks."

"And the other?"

"I'm driving my truck when I hit an IED concealed in a dirt road near the Pakistani border. Suddenly I'm outside myself, looking at my own dead body by the side of the road. I know that my life is over, cut short in a way that lacks any meaning. But my head is that of Benjamin Blaine the last time I ever saw him."

Charlie looked at him keenly. "So in both of them, at the moment of your death you become the man you believed to be your father. What does that raise for you?"

Adam shrugged. "You're the shrink, Charlie. You tell me."

Charlie shook his head in demurral. "I don't know enough to do that. So anything I'd say is a guess. Obviously, Ben Blaine is central to both dreams. For reasons we've yet to fully explore, your break with him was traumatic. I could posit that you couldn't overcome that trauma simply by leaving. If so, I suppose the dream could imply a visceral need to kill him—not only literally, but in your heart and mind.

"But there are other ways to look at this. The dream could symbolize your deep entwinement with your supposed father, and your fear that you've become like him. Or even that something about his death makes you feel guilty." Charlie gave him a searching look. "As I said, I don't think you've told me everything you know, which leaves me more than a little in the dark. But all in its own time."

By training and habit, Adam avoided the implicit question. "So it's all about Benjamin Blaine. Like everything else."

"Not necessarily. Another way of analyzing a dream is to imagine that everyone appearing in it is some element of yourself. So part of you in the first dream may identify with the Taliban who are about to kill you." Charlie hesitated. "There's an aspect of our last conversation, a month or so ago, that I recall quite vividly."

Adam put down his coffee cup, responding in clipped tones. "You mean that just before returning here I'd shot a double agent for the Taliban who was about to kill me, drove fifty miles at night with his corpse in the passenger seat, then dumped his body by the road where I thought no one would know him. It's funny, Charlie, what sticks in your mind."

Charlie laughed softly, his eyes still fixed on Adam. "What stuck in my mind is that an hour or so later you learned that Ben was dead. One can be forgiven for thinking that one experience might relate to the other. Was that the first time you'd killed a man?"

"The third," Adam responded evenly. "The first was shooting a Russian arms dealer in his suite at the nicest hotel in Eilat, Israel, the Queen of Sheba Hilton, terminating his business of selling sophisticated explosives to al-Qaeda in Iraq. The second was cutting the throat of a key al-Qaeda operative in Croatia, who'd been enjoying a small bed-and-breakfast on the shore. For that one, I pretended to be an international tax attorney. No one can say my superiors lack a sense of humor."

Charlie cocked his head. "What did you feel about killing these two men?"

"Not much. They'd been responsible for too many deaths already, and would've facilitated many more. When it's trading one vicious life for many innocent ones, it's not that hard to do the moral math."

"And the last guy?"

"Was a reflex—I'd killed him before I'd even had time to think."

"So this time, the life you were saving was your own."

"Yes."

"As I calculate it, that was about six weeks ago. Then, in swift succession, you learned your father was dead; came home to a place you'd left for unknown but painful reasons; found out that Ben had disinherited your mother and brother, exposing them to financial ruin; learned that the police suspected a member of your family of murdering the father you despised; proceeded to steal or illicitly acquire evidence that enabled you to arrange for Jack to exonerate Teddy; discovered that your mother had lied to you about critical facts of your life, including that your uncle was actually your father; and forced her to agree to a settlement with Ben's pregnant lover." Charlie's tone became rueful. "A rich and full two weeks, Adam, which still leaves you on the hook for obstruction of justice should the police and DA ever figure out what you've been up to." He paused, then inquired gently, "Does that about cover it, or are things even worse for you? Which I somehow suspect they are."

"Let's say it's close enough."

Charlie shook his head, a gesture of sympathy. "And you wonder why you're feeling a bit troubled. The average person would get his very own wing in Bellevue."

"Sounds nice," Adam replied. "But I have a prior engagement in a war zone."

"So let's look at what you're taking back with you. Have you had nightmares like this before?"

"No."

"Then let me suggest that your life—not just the CIA, but its entirety—is catching up with you. True, your tenure at the agency has enabled, even required that you avoid confronting your own emotions. You've developed all sorts of defenses exacerbated by stress—compartmentalizing, vigilance, extreme caution in relationships, emotional distance, and serious levels of distrust. But you haven't stopped being human." Charlie leaned forward, looking at Adam intently. "What those nightmares call up for me is that part of you that is connected to your deeper feelings, many of which precede your work with the agency. Including your fear of death—or, as troubling, your expectation of dying."

Adam found himself without words. Watching his face, Charlie prodded. "You expect to die young, don't you?"

Adam stared at the deck, unsure of how to answer. "It's crossed my mind."

"Do you think that's all about your job? Or is there something more to it?"

"I don't know."

"But you do know when those feelings started. You didn't have them when you were young, did you?"

Painfully, Adam tried to remember the boy he had been. "That's like recalling another life, Charlie. But I don't remember having those feelings then. At least not consciously."

"Yet at some point you started feeling disconnected from relationships—a loss of joy, of wanting to be fully in the world."

Adam shrugged. "Sounds like a pretty good job description."

"So you say. But you sought out that job. I wonder if, at some earlier point, you began feeling expendable. Or were made to feel that way."

Adam found that he could say nothing. Looking at him closely, Charlie asked, "If you look at it honestly, Adam, how do you cope with the risk of dying?"

For a moment, Adam closed his eyes. "I'd say I've become 'familiar with the night.' If I die, I can accept that. I've come to believe that I won't have long relationships, or children of my own. I try to imagine it, and I can't anymore."

Charlie bit his lip. "Actually, I'm not sure you *do* accept that—at least not quite. Beyond that, I'd say you just described a fairly typical response for someone with your profile."

"Which is?"

"Damaged," Charlie said bluntly. "In your case, an attractive, smart, and inherently empathic man, with unusual abilities and the capacity to work your will on the world around you. But someone whose experience of family involved increasing levels of uncertainty, ambiguity, and dishonesty. Your 'father' lied to you, competed with you, and, I think, betrayed you in some terrible way. Your mother deceived you, and didn't protect either of her sons when Benjamin Blaine demeaned Teddy for being gay and treated you as a rival. Even your supposed Uncle Jack, who was kind and consistent in that role, didn't come to your defense. And he, too, was keeping a terrible secret from you. Then something even worse caused you to break off with Ben, leave this island, and change the entire course of your life. Take all that together, and the message I think you got is that your feelings don't matter—that on some subliminal level, *you* don't matter.

"Often such people become hedonists, losing themselves in drugs or sex. Instead, you put yourself in a dangerous situation with a high risk of death. One might suppose that the CIA allowed you to try outrunning your own demons, while pursuing self-annihilation in a way that preserves your self-image as a capable, autonomous person . . ."

"Actually," Adam cut in sharply, "I'd say my career choice was a pretty natural response to watching madmen from al-Qaeda blow up two high-rises and kill three thousand people. Call me sentimental."

Charlie watched his face. "I understand that part, Adam. But when you're back in Afghanistan, ask yourself whether you want to survive, and if you can imagine a life you can embrace on the other side." He paused for emphasis, then finished slowly and succinctly. "I'd like to think that's the truest meaning of your dream. That you're afraid of dying, because the deepest part of you still hopes for something better."

FOUR

Roiled by memories, for the first time in ten years Adam drove to Quitsa Pond.

Benjamin Blaine's classic wooden sailboat, a beautifully maintained Herreshoff built in the 1920s, was still moored where it had been when he first set foot on it. Though less painful, the image was as vivid as the last day Adam had seen this boat, in the race where he had beaten Ben for the sailing cup they both coveted.

"Well into this century," Ben had explained to the seven-year-old Adam, "the Herreshoff brothers designed eight consecutive defenders of the America's Cup. They built boats like this for the richest, most sophisticated families of their times—the Vanderbilts, the Whitneys." His voice lowered, to impress on Adam the import of his next words. "To own one is a privilege, but to race one—as you someday will—is a joy. I mean for you to learn the primal joy of winning."

Too late, Adam had discovered what it meant to surpass this man, on this boat, on these waters. Or where and how their competition would end.

Sitting at the end of the catwalk, he gazed out at the Herreshoff, then heard the soft footfalls on wood. Instinctively, he was on his feet before he saw the young woman walking toward him.

There was something familiar about her, though he could not place where he had met someone so striking and distinctive—a tall, lean body, fuller where it should be; curly black hair that ended in a widow's peak; olive skin; large brown eyes that suggested a touch of amusement and, he somehow sensed, a volatility of mood; chiseled but strong features that, taken together, lent her an offbeat and distinctly exotic appeal. The smile she gave him contained a hint of challenge and adventure, though Adam could not imagine what he had done to earn this. Then she said, "Hello, Adam Blaine."

"Hello."

His tone of puzzlement caused her to appear even more amused. "You don't remember me, do you?"

"I should, obviously. I just don't know for what."

The woman laughed. "Nothing a man should be embarrassed to forget. The last time you saw me you were twenty-three and I was seventeen, and a little gawky. Since then, I'd like to think I've 'blossomed,' as they say in those terrible romance novels." She extended a cool, dry hand for him to shake, a gesture clearly meant to be ironic. "So let me reintroduce myself. I'm Rachel Ravinsky."

"Whitney Dane's daughter?"

"The very one. You might remember me better if our mothers had been on speaking terms."

This was another of Clarice's many mysteries, and, as with the others, she had been notably elusive. Remembering what everyone still believed, Adam said, "It was usually my father who offended someone—he had so many weapons in his arsenal."

Rachel's smile became a grin. "One in particular, I always heard. I suppose everyone says you look just like him."

"Yup. But that's where the resemblance ends. So are you living here?"

"Not now, but I will be for a while. I'm a writer—like my mom, but not like her at all. I'm here for a day or two, moving some stuff from New York. Come the fall, I'm hunkering down at my parents' house to start on my first novel."

"Then you write fiction?"

She put her hands on her hips, gazing at him in mock offense. "You haven't read my short stories in the *New Yorker*?"

Adam smiled. "Sorry. I've been in Afghanistan. My peer group is more into *National Geographic* and *Guns and Ammo*. I don't suppose you've written for them."

"Not yet." She cocked her head. "Aren't you the slightest bit curious about what I'm doing on this dock?"

"A little. But I somehow sensed you'd get around to telling me."

Once more, Rachel looked amused. "I introduced myself to Mom's arresting new tenant, who seems to have added further intrigue to your family's all too intriguing story. Among other things, I took the opportunity to ask her about you."

There was something mercurial about her, Adam sensed, a certain pleasure in stirring things up. "That must've been interesting," he remarked. "You don't recognize the normal conversational boundaries, do you?"

"That was our mothers, Adam. I take the modern view that conversation involves an actual exchange of information. To my complete surprise, Carla volunteered that you were on the island. Given the familial strains, I couldn't very well call your mom. But talking with Carla reminded me of you and this place, how you always sailed from here." Her voice took on the quiet of reminiscence. "I didn't really expect to find you. But I always thought this one of the most beautiful spots on the island, and now it brings back my summers here when I was young. Another life, another girl." She gave Adam a curious look. "Back to the present," she inquired, "how *do* you feel about Ms. Pacelli?"

Adam felt an edge he tried to keep out of his voice. Casually, he said, "I feel fine about her. Why wouldn't I?"

Rachel shot him a skeptical look. "Oh, I don't know. Maybe because she was your father's lover, pregnant with his child, and an enormous embarrassment to your mother—as well as an expensive one. I can't imagine you have no feelings about that."

"I have a number of feelings," Adam answered coolly. "Among them that I choose not to judge people by one sliver of their lives—short of theft, rape, child abuse, or the murder of someone who doesn't deserve it. I don't much like malice or unkindness, either. So I'll leave maligning Carla to people who don't know her. It's good sport for the summer crowd in Chilmark, too many of whom require distraction from their lousy marriages and empty lives."

Rachel looked defensive and a bit startled, betraying a vulnerability beneath her surface poise. "I seem to have touched a nerve. If so, I'm sorry." She hesitated, adding quietly, "You've become a hard man, Adam Blaine."

"So I understand. Also an honest one, given the choice. So what *are* you doing here, exactly?"

Rachel looked down, then up at him again. "Let's start over, all right? Would you mind sitting down for a minute?"

Adam hesitated. "Seems like there's room."

They sat beside each other on the dock, legs dangling over the water, looking at the hilly, tree-lined meadows beyond. "I was curious," she confessed. "When I was a teenager, I had a serious crush on you. Then suddenly you just vanished, and nobody knew why. It seemed so strange to me, and I couldn't get you off my mind."

Another person who wondered, Adam thought, another answer to avoid. "I certainly hope you found some surrogates."

Rachel smiled a little, still tentative. "A few."

"I can imagine," Adam responded more easily. "I'll bet there were whole weeks in the last decade when I never crossed your mind."

"Days, anyhow. But I'm cursed with a literary imagination. Sometimes I found myself making up stories about you—what happened that summer, where you were. Now you're back, and I can ask."

Adam shrugged. "Why spoil a good story? I'm sure whatever you dreamed up is far better than reality."

Rachel looked at him askance. "You really won't tell me, will you?"

"Nope. If only because there's really nothing to tell."

"I guess I'll have to wait, then. For all the thought I've given you, we really never knew each other. Though we may have more common history than you're aware."

Adam gave her a puzzled glance. "How so?"

Rachel's returning gaze was serious. "Your mother never told you, I'm sure. But in her middle years, mine has become less buttoned up. After your father died, she explained why childhood friends became so distant."

"So enlighten me."

Rachel faced the water. "When they were twenty-two, your father and my mother had a summer romance. I gather it was pretty serious for both of them—though Mom won't quite say why, the end sounds quite shattering. Including for your father, though I find that sort of difficult to imagine."

Surprised, Adam asked, "Because he was a compulsive womanizer, you mean?"

Rachel nodded. "That, and the idea of the two of them together. I love my mom, of course—when I was a teenager, she had the patience of a saint or a stone, and needed it. She's kind, even-tempered, and so reliable that it's incredibly annoying. But she's a classic WASP. There's nothing surprising about her, and she's certainly not a sex goddess like Carla."

This was so like the remark of a much younger woman that Adam found himself laughing. "I wonder how your father struggled by."

"Oh, *he* thinks my mother hung the moon."

"So do a lot of people," Adam replied. "At least as I recall. It's heartening, if somewhat astonishing, to attribute such good taste to my father at twenty-two. Or at any age, with rare exceptions. But then you're Whitney's daughter, and there's something solipsistic about how children view their parents." Adam paused a moment, then added, "Just because you can't imagine the man you knew looking at your mother like he did Carla Pacelli doesn't mean it didn't happen. It just means that she was fortunate to escape."

Rachel looked somber now. "You didn't like him much, did you?"

"No. Not much."

Contrary to Adam's assessment of her, she decided to let this go. "Anyhow," she assured him, "the summer romance I imagined for us might have ended better."

Adam smiled at this. "My loss, I'm sure. My only excuse is that I had a girlfriend."

"I remember—Jenny Leigh. Whatever happened with that?"

Adam felt his face go blank. "We were too young, that's all."

For a moment, Rachel seemed to study his expression. "So is there anyone now?"

"No. The company I work for is an agricultural consulting firm that moves me around a lot. So I'm not an ideal candidate for long-term relationships."

A glint of mischief surfaced in her eyes. "What about short-term? Fortunately, I'm here until tomorrow."

Adam shook his head. "I have plans, regrettably, and I'm going back to Afghanistan in two weeks. So one day's a little *too* short."

"Coward," Rachel said in mock dismay. "Are you planning on coming back?"

"I hope to. Maybe in four months."

"If you do, I'll still be here." Ruefully, she added, "No way I'll finish with my novel in four months. Or anything like that."

Once more, Adam could feel her uncertainty. "Whatever time it takes," he assured her, "my father always said that the key was showing up."

"My mother says that, too. I just hope I've inherited her character and perseverance." Abruptly standing, Rachel touched his shoulder. "It's been nice to see you, Adam. If you do get back here, please come find me."

Without waiting for an answer, she was off, taking the catwalk toward the grassy bank with graceful, determined strides.

Pensive, Adam watched her go, then turned back to his contemplation of the pond and the sailboat. Inevitably, his mind turned back to what he could never talk about—to Rachel, or anyone else. The last fateful race when he took the Herreshoff Cup from Benjamin Blaine, striking a blow to the older man's voracious ego. The catalyst for a chain of events that nearly destroyed a young woman, and led to Adam's absence from Martha's Vineyard until the moment he had come to wish for deep in his soul—the death of the man who had betrayed him.

FIVE

In search of distraction, Adam and Teddy repeated a ritual of their boyhood, paddling a two man kayak across the Tisbury Great Pond.

They spoke little, preferring to enjoy the breezy early morning, still temperate as the sun began its ascent, the pleasant strain of their smooth but vigorous strokes propelling them through choppy waters toward the stretch of sand that separated the pond from the Atlantic Ocean. Arriving, they beached the kayak and walked barefoot toward the pounding ocean surf. Teddy preceded Adam, standing where the dying waves lapped his calves and ankles, wind rippling his curly brown hair. For a moment, he reminded Adam of the gangly teenage older brother he had always loved and defended to Benjamin Blaine. But now the first strands of silver had appeared in Teddy's hair—overnight, it seemed—and his sensitive face, evocative of Jack's, seemed careworn. Adam guessed that he was still not sleeping well.

Quiet, Adam stood beside his brother, leaving Teddy to his thoughts. Then he asked, "Still worried, Ted?"

Narrow eyed, Teddy gazed at the horizon as the water became a brighter blue. "Wouldn't you be?" he asked, then added pointedly, "And *aren't* you?"

"Sure. I still think you and Jack are okay, and that they'll decide to let the death of a dying man alone. But we won't breathe easy until the judge and Hanley announce their decision."

Ted frowned, regarding Adam with curiosity and concern. "This isn't just about Jack and me, is it? Or, for that matter, Mom."

"It's certainly not about *me*," Adam rejoined with a casualness he did not feel. "Unless wishing someone dead from ten thousand miles away is a capital offense."

"Stop bullshitting me, Adam. I don't know what you did, but I'm damn sure you were looking out for me in ways George Hanley wouldn't appreciate. Every piece of advice you gave me suggested that you knew what George and the police were doing and thinking." Teddy dug his feet in the sand, looking stubborn and discomfited. "Have you ever met with my lawyer?"

At once, Adam felt on edge, though the answer he framed was truthful. "Richard Mendelson? I only met Richard at the hearing, when you were being questioned."

Though Teddy nodded, the concern in his expression was unchanged. "That's what Richard told Hanley yesterday, when George called to ask the same question. But Hanley made a date to meet with him in Boston. He also wants to interview Richard's secretary." He paused for emphasis. "Richard doesn't think it's about me—what could my lawyer tell him, after all? He believes that, for whatever reason, Hanley is sniffing around you."

Adam shrugged. "Let him, Ted. There's nothing for George to find. I'm leaving here as innocent as I came."

To shut off the conversation, Adam began walking along the water's edge, as though intent on savoring the day. Teddy fell in beside him. "Why don't we go out to dinner tonight?" he proposed in a lighter tone. "Like normal people. It's been a while since we showed our faces in public, except to answer questions, and some fresh fish at L'Etoile might go well with a crisp white wine."

"Sounds good. But it'll have to be tomorrow—I've got dinner plans tonight."

Teddy looked at him askance. "Carla? Again? I understand you're serving as a bridge here, protecting the family's interests. But isn't this becoming a tad incongruous?"

Smiling, Adam put a hand on Teddy's shoulder. "Why would you say that, Ted?"

Walking from his mother's house to the guesthouse where Carla was staying, Adam could not help reflecting on the psychic distance he would cover in ten minutes. From Benjamin Blaine's wife to his ex-lover; past the promontory from which Ben had "fallen" in his family's account, the scene of a homicide; to the spacious grounds where Rachel Ravinsky's mother and his own, had spent countless hours as girls and young women before something—quite possibly Ben—had come between them. But his mind kept returning to all he had done to protect Teddy. Most worrisome, that he had mailed stolen documents to Teddy's lawyer, leaving himself vulnerable to George Hanley's suspicions and Amanda Ferris's malice and resentment.

He had been as careful as his training demanded. After printing out the documents he had photographed in Henley's office, he had put his cell phone and computer in a bag filled with rocks, driven a powerboat far offshore, and dropped them to the bottom of the Vineyard Sound. Farther out, he had done this with his hard drive. Before putting the documents in a mailbox, he had made sure that neither they nor the envelope bore his prints. He did not think he had made any mistakes; he knew that he could not afford one.

Reaching Carla's guest house, he paused for a moment, to dispel his thoughts. Being in her presence required a clear head.

As Carla cooked dinner, Adam sat watching her at the kitchen counter, sipping a glass of the Pinot Noir he had brought from Benjamin

Blaine's cellar. He could not help but wonder, uncomfortably, how many times the dead man had sat where Adam did now—watching this beautiful woman, knowing that, as night fell, he would have her. The swell of her stomach was more visible now.

"How are you feeling?" he asked.

"Fine," she said over her shoulder. "I'm pretty careful about what I do and don't do. I want to give this baby every chance."

"Because you thought you'd never have one?"

She was still for a moment, as though captured by some memory or reflection. Adam found himself looking at her long neck and back, no less elegant for the ripening of her body. Quite deliberately, he thought, she did not turn to face him. "My son is a gift," she said softly. "I tell myself he's why everything happened—crashing and burning; coming here; meeting Ben, yet never imagining that whatever came of that would include a child. So there's nothing I can regret without regretting him."

Adam was struck by the emotion in her voice. "Did you always want children?" he asked.

Without responding, she served dinner—fresh linguine with clams, cooked in garlic and olive oil; a salad of tomatoes, romaine hearts, radishes, and a savory dressing she had made herself. "To understand what this means to me," she said at length, "you have to know more about my childhood than you'd care to hear. But the idea of kids kept coming up for me in different ways. My home life was difficult. So, as an antidote, I fantasized about being a good mother, protecting my kids from the harshness of life, and some of the things I'd seen.

"When I started acting, I'd observe other families, and try to imagine what they were thinking and feeling." Sitting across from Adam, she looked at him with a clear, candid gaze. "One afternoon, toward the end of it, I was being driven home from the set in a limousine with tinted windows. I'd quit early; I was too drunk on vodka and edgy on coke to bring the last scene off. We got stuck in traffic. I was staring out the darkened window, at nothing, when I noticed an SUV stalled next to me—a mom, dad, and a small boy and girl, laughing, heedless of time. All at once, I was filled with confusion and self-pity. I wanted to *be* that mother, and in this fleeting, pointless moment of envy, I imagined that her husband was the kind of dad I'd longed for but never had. Then I realized that I could never be anyone in that picture, and turned away." She shook her head dismissively. "Maudlin, I know."

"Human," Adam demurred. "Any thoughtful person from a difficult family understands one of its cruelest aspects—the distance between the archetype people long for and the reality they face. So maybe you start hoping that you can somehow press the reset button and replicate what you wished for, rather than what you lived."

Carla nodded, and then her expression clouded. "True enough. Perhaps that's made me superstitious."

She had a more specific worry about her pregnancy, Adam sensed. But at the core, Carla Pacelli was a deeply private person, and, he intuited, a lonely one. "After I leave," he ventured, "would you mind if Teddy checked in on you now and then?"

Carla gave him a look of surprise. "I doubt he'd be that interested. And I'm not sure I'd be comfortable with someone suspected of killing my baby's father. Not to mention his own."

The bald statement made Adam feel foolish, an emotion at war with his fierce love of Teddy, his knowledge that his brother was innocent, his own father guilty. "Teddy didn't kill anyone," he said flatly. "He's a good soul—the best of us, really. The only reason anyone suspected Teddy is that Ben was a primitive homophobe."

He watched Carla consider responding, then decide to let it go. Instead, she asked, "Does Teddy know Ben wasn't your father?"

"No. Better that he not know that his father's favorite son wasn't his son at all, and that Ben knew it. Not that you should care, but it would also complicate Ted's view of our mother." Not to mention, Adam did not say, that the truth would take Teddy one painful step closer to comprehending the reasons for Ben's death.

Carla considered him. "You carry a lot of secrets, don't you? That must make life difficult."

This was uncomfortably close to home. "Thanks to Ben," he replied, "I share this particular secret with you. I'd appreciate it if you never enlightened Teddy."

"I didn't enlighten *you*, did I? You're not the only one who's good at keeping secrets." Her gaze became curious and probing. "Are you ever going to tell me why you broke off with Ben?"

Adam met her gaze. "I can't," he said simply.

"Because it's too painful?"

Adam chose not to answer this. "Among other things, because it involves someone else who's still alive. I know you're curious, but we need to let this go."

Carla studied him another moment, then said simply, "I'm sure you have your reasons, Adam."

In the uncomfortable silence that followed, Adam searched for a change of subject, then asked, "Are you still hoping to become a therapist?"

She nodded. "After the baby comes, I plan on going to graduate school. The life I lived before was all centered around me. What I learned in recovery was that I can help other people, just as they helped me." She glanced at his wine glass. "By the way, you're helping me complete a successful experiment. When I first met Ben, the smell of alcohol tempted me. But sitting here with you, it seems like drinking has lost its appeal. Good to know, given most of the people I'll meet won't be in a twelve step program."

"I'm sure you'll be fine," Adam assured her.

"I intend to be," she answered firmly. "For myself, and for this baby."

Adam felt a moment of disquiet, the fear of what might happen to Carla if her pregnancy went awry. "Don't worry, Carla. I'm sure the kid will find other defects to complain about. Just be glad he'll never be a teenage girl."

She laughed. "I remember how I was, believe me. But I'd take one of those, too, if given half the chance. I was an only child, and it didn't improve my character a bit. Having a younger sibling might've helped."

Adam smiled. "If you ever speak to Teddy, ask him. Then you can decide what to wish for."

After dinner, he helped her wash dishes, looking out the kitchen window at the ocean glistening with moonlight. He remembered passing by this guest house at night, perhaps a month before, and seeing Carla washing dishes by herself, her face framed in the same window. Then, he had imagined her as an enemy, yet he had sensed the vulnerability of a woman alone with her losses and regrets. He had not known that she was pregnant, nor grasped her determination to stand on her own.

They went on like this, Carla handing him dishes, silverware or glasses before he dried and put them in a dish rack—a form of communication, no less companionable for their relative quiet. He was suddenly aware of how close they were, of all he saw in her now. She caught him glancing at her, and turned to face him.

Impulsively, he took the dish from her hand, putting it aside, looking into her deep brown eyes. Gazing back, she seemed neither welcoming nor fearful, as though somehow she had expected this.

Gently, he put his hand on the nape of her neck, drawing her face to his.

Her mouth was full and soft and warm. Their lips stayed where they were, gently pressing, and then his parted slightly, as did hers, the tips of their tongues touching, then more. He held her tight against him, their kiss deep and lingering until, at last, she drew back and, seeming to shudder, laid her head on his shoulder. He could feel the swell of her stomach against him, reminding him of her womanliness, yet all that kept them apart. But still he had wanted this.

"Sweet," he murmured.

"Yes," she answered softly, a trace of sadness in her voice as she raised her head to look at him. "What do you want from me, Adam?"

"I hadn't thought beyond this moment," he answered honestly. "I wasn't expecting this."

"You shouldn't have, for good reasons." His eyes were filled with confusion. "There's so much to this, isn't there?"

Adam felt the pulse in his throat. "Yes."

"Then just hold me for a minute. Before you go."

For a time he did this, silent, then murmured, "I won't stop thinking about you, though."

"Nor I you."

She took his hand, walking him to the door. Opening it, he turned back again. He could not seem to stop looking at her.

"Before you leave," she asked, "will you at least come to say goodbye?"

"Of course."

Bereft of words, he touched her face with curled fingers and walked into the darkness. The night felt warm, yet solitary, save for the shadow of Benjamin Blaine. Adam could still feel her behind him, in the shelter of the house where she and Ben had conceived their son.

SIX

Two mornings later, Adam sat with Charlie Glazer on his sailboat in Menemsha Harbor. The boat was the Herreshoff Charlie had raced against Ben and Adam that fateful summer. The venue had been the therapist's choice; Adam wondered whether this was meant to evoke feelings he preferred to repress.

For a time, Adam watched battered fishing boats labor through the mouth of the harbor. Charlie cupped a mug of coffee in his hands, wearing an alert but pleasant expression. "I've been reflecting on our last session," he began, "and what you want to accomplish here. Ordinarily, I don't challenge my patients—especially at first. But I already know a lot about your life, and we don't have that much time.

"It's obvious that over the years you've built up some very strong defenses. So I'm going to push you pretty hard—because I may need to, and because I think you can take it. Are you okay with that?"

Adam met his gaze. "Sure."

"Okay. I've thought some more about the CIA. Both about the nightmares of your own death, and the choice you made to choose a path so dangerous and so consuming. Maybe we should talk about who you were before that, and what triggered your decision to leave here."

Adam felt himself tense. "About the nightmares, sometimes a cigar is only a cigar. People wanting to kill you raises the possibility they'll succeed. On that level, the dreams are simple enough."

"Sure. But you didn't have them until Benjamin Blaine fell off a cliff, forcing you to confront your family's past." Charlie leaned forward. "That you came to me suggests you're grappling with some profound psychological and existential questions you may have entered the agency to avoid. I think they may have started with your parents. Perhaps Clarice most of all."

The last statement took Adam by surprise. "If you say so."

"I don't 'say' anything. But let me ask you this—when you were a kid, did you believe your mother loved you?"

"Come off it, Charlie. Why don't you just ask if I owned a sled named Rosebud? I don't think I'm suffering from maternal distaste for breastfeeding, if that's what you're after. She was my mom, and I took it for granted that I mattered to her."

"Then let's move past early childhood. Was there a time when your feelings about Clarice became more complicated?"

Adam took a swallow of black coffee. "Maybe in adolescence, when kids begin to differentiate. Some of that had to do with Ben. He was tough on me, worse on Ted, and she let him do it. Then I started hearing rumors about other women." Adam paused, sifting uncomfortable memories. "As a teenager, I started feeling protective of her. But I also began to wonder if she was willing to sacrifice her sons and her own pride to preserve her social status. And part of her simply felt unreachable. I remember describing her as 'the most pleasant person I've never really known.'"

Charlie gave him a keen look. "To whom?"

Adam hesitated. "Jenny Leigh."

"Was Jenny the person you confided in?"

"Yes. But she had problems of her own. So I tried not to lean on her too much."

"In other words," Charlie prodded, "you decided to be strong. Like you imagined that Ben was."

Adam gave him a skeptical smile. "That implies I had a choice."

"I meant something more instinctive. By accident or example, your parents forced you to be capable and self-reliant. So you became the son who could make things turn out the way you wanted. The son in Ben's own image."

"Think so?"

"I do," Charlie said bluntly. "Not every man would break into a courthouse and steal police evidence to protect his mother, uncle, and brother. So why did you do that?"

Once again, Adam felt the weight of what he could not say. "I had the skills to do it," he answered. "Without me, Teddy might've been convicted for something he didn't do. In the bargain, I protected my mother from suspicion and insured that she kept the house and enough to live on. No one knows better than I how important that is to her."

"But do you resent that on some level? Once again, Clarice has reversed the role of parent and child, and now you've risked everything to save her and the rest of the family. How do you think that's affected you?"

"You tell me, Charlie."

Charlie shook his head. "I'm not a mind reader. But I've seen men with dependent, somewhat elusive mothers replicate that model into other relationships with women. How would you describe Jenny?"

Silent, Adam gazed out at the choppy wake of a grimy fishing boat. "She was fragile."

"Like your mother?"

"No. Not like my mother at all."

Adam saw Charlie consider pursuing this, and then decide not to. "Since you left the island, how would you describe your relationship to women?"

"My job is pretty consuming, and my relationships reflect that." Adam's tone flattened out. "I'm not like Ben, if that's what you mean. It's more like serial monogamy, with a high turnover."

"Don't people in your business get married?"

"Some do. But it's hard for me to imagine."

Charlie raised his eyebrows. "And yet you imagine yourself dead. Is it a fair guess that you don't let women get too close?"

Adam shrugged. "If you're suggesting I have 'issues with intimacy,' I suppose you could make that argument."

"What do you get from these relationships?"

Adam paused, and then forced himself to be honest. "I like the pursuit, as Ben did. But then I find myself pulling back."

Charlie cocked his head. "When you have sex, how do you feel?"

Adam looked down. "Detached," he responded tonelessly. "I'm sure that makes me technically proficient. That's the virtue of not getting caught up in the moment. I never stop being aware of myself, and what I'm doing."

"Sounds lonely," Charlie observed. "For both of you. It also suggests an anomaly. You can have protective feelings toward a woman—as with your mother and, perhaps, Carla Pacelli—but you can't let them in. Ever wonder if your cover story as a spy isn't a cover for something deeper?"

"Meaning?"

"Your career requires you to conceal who you are. That doesn't lend itself to enduring relationships, and any slipup carries the distinct possibility you'll be killed." Charlie paused for emphasis. "To survive, you're always changing identities and cover stories, keeping people at a distance. And you can abandon a woman before she abandons you."

Adam mustered a derisive smile. "Is that really what you think?"

Charlie stared at him, letting their silence build. At length, he said, "I wonder if you realize how defensive you sound. And look."

Adam felt his own stillness. More quietly, he said, "Do I?"

"What do you think?" When Adam said nothing, Charlie added evenly, "I'm not a Taliban interrogator, Adam, or trying to be some sort of demeaning authority figure. I'm on your side, and you and I are in this one together. Can you try to remember that?"

"All right."

"Then bear with me. What I just said about abandonment has a certain logic. Even as a boy, you must have been longing for someone you could trust. But you don't trust a soul, do you?" Charlie looked at him intently. "Tell me why you called Jenny 'fragile.'"

Adam crossed his arms. "What I knew about her then? Or learned later on?"

"Let's start with when you were together."

Adam tried to remember how he had felt. "She was very poetic and sensitive, I thought. But she had mood swings, was afraid of alcohol, and had to take medication. Her drunk of a father had bailed out on her, and her mother was weak and erratic. Even then, I sensed she was afraid of falling through a trap door."

"What did you think would become of her?"

Adam felt his chest constrict. "That I'd love her, and take care of her. That someday we'd have a family. A better one than mine."

Charlie gave him a grave look. "So you thought you could rescue her? That she'd be devoted to you, and you to her?"

"Something like that. I was young."

"When you left the island, you were twenty-three. I think something terrible happened that summer. Not just with Ben, but with Jenny."

Mute, Adam nodded.

Late that summer, Adam had driven to New York.

His second year of law school would start in two weeks. In the spring Adam had found a new apartment in Greenwich Village with two friends from his class; now he moved his stuff—PC, television, CD player, winter coats and jackets—looking forward to another year in the city on the way to his chosen career. His mission completed, he met up with Teddy and took in Village life.

Teddy was living with a guy, and seemed to be pretty good—Adam had missed him, and was glad they could spend time beyond Ben's shadow. But after a couple of days, he found himself looking forward to Jenny's first visit to New York, and then thinking about her pretty much all the time. On impulse, he decided to return to the Vineyard, intent on spending his last free days with her. His life in the law would resume soon enough.

He drove back in five unbroken hours, high on images of the time ahead. He loved the Vineyard and, he decided, loved Jenny Leigh. Whatever she struggled with, they would be okay.

Driving fast, he caught the noontime ferry from Woods Hole to Vineyard Haven, then sped down State Road toward his parents' place. His mother was gone, visiting a cousin. But if his father were not writing, he would share with him some stories of the Village, renewing a bond frayed by the racing season and Ben's hatred of defeat. Then he would go find Jenny.

The house was empty, including his father's study. But Ben's truck and car were there. Perhaps he was on the promontory, or walking the beach below. Eagerly, Adam went to look for him.

His path took him past the guesthouse. Through its open window, he heard a male voice. Though he could not make out the words, they carried a rough sexual urgency that stopped Adam in his tracks.

For a moment, he stayed there, torn between anger and revulsion. The man could only be his father, once again slaking his relentless desire for other women. But this time was a terrible violation—a betrayal of his mother committed within sight of the house she had loved since childhood, the home they now shared as husband and wife. Inexorably, Adam found himself drawn to the window, his footsteps silent on the grass.

There was a bottle of Montrachet on the bedside table, Ben's signature. Adam turned his gaze to the bed and saw his father's naked back, the woman beneath him lying on her stomach, moaning as he thrust into her with brutal force. Then Adam took in her long blond-brown hair and long slender legs and felt himself begin to tremble.

An animal cry erupted from his throat. Wrenching open the door, he saw blood on the sheets. His father turned his head, eyes widening at the sight of him. As Adam grabbed his hips and wrested him from inside her, Jenny Leigh cried out in anguish.

With a strength born of adrenalin and primal hatred, Adam threw his father on the stone floor, the back of Ben's skull hitting with a dull thud. Gripping the wine bottle by the neck, Adam mounted his father's torso, knees pinning the older man's shoulders as Ben's eyes rolled, unfocused by shock and blinding pain. Then Adam clutched his throat with his left hand and shattered the wine bottle on stone. Holding its broken shards over Ben's eyes, Adam saw the wine dribbling across his face like rivulets of blood.

Shuddering with each convulsive breath, Adam lowered the jagged glass closer to Ben's face. His stunned eyes widened, the look of a trapped animal. Adam could smell the alcohol on his breath.

He raised his weapon in a savage jerk, prepared to blind this man for whom no punishment was enough.

"*No*," Jenny cried out.

His hand froze. Beneath him, Ben began writhing in a frenzied effort to escape.

Adam dropped the bottle, glass shattering on the floor. Then he took his father's head by the hair and smashed it savagely against the stone. The groan that escaped Ben's lips made Adam slam his head again, the other hand pressing his Adam's apple back into his throat.

"Please," his father managed to gasp.

Adam forced his own breathing to slow. In a near-whisper, he spat, "I could kill you now. Instead I'll spend my life regretting that I didn't. And you'll spend yours remembering that I know exactly what you are."

Legs unsteady, Adam stood. He stared at his naked father, then faced his girlfriend as she knelt on the bed, tears running down her face, hands covering her breasts as if he were a stranger.

Turning his back on both of them, Adam walked blindly from the guesthouse. By the time he heard its door closing behind him, he knew that he would never speak to his father as long as they both lived, or disclose his reasons to anyone. Only the three of them would know.

Without leaving a note for his mother, Adam left the island the way he had come—Vineyard Haven, the ferry, the long drive back to New York. But he did not go to law school; never again would he take money from Benjamin Blaine. Adam Blaine, no longer his son, would find another life.

Until Adam finished, Charlie watched him fixedly, his face expressionless. For a moment, he regarded the polished floor of his boat. Then he said, "No wonder you wished Ben dead. But damaged or not, Jenny betrayed you, too."

Adam expelled a breath. "I understand her much better now. When I first came back, I saw her several times. She'd always wanted to be a writer, and idolized the man she thought was my father. What no one knew was that her own father had molested her, making her the perfect victim." His voice softened. "After I found them, Jenny tried to kill herself. Perhaps that's why Ben left her a million dollars, one of the few good things he ever did. So she's entered the creative writing program at the University of Iowa, something she always wanted. I hope it helps her. I know now that I can't."

Charlie nodded. "Nor could she help you. So you went undercover, both literally and emotionally. Does that sound right to you?"

Adam looked away. "I guess it does. I'm with a woman, and suddenly I feel myself split off."

"A form of self-protection, perhaps, which metastasized when you found your 'father' sodomizing the young woman you loved. But is there even more going on than that?"

"Such as?"

"One possibility is that you feel repressed anger against all three parents: Jack, who never claimed you; Ben, who betrayed you; and Clarice, who deceived you and failed as a mother. Then throw in Jenny." Charlie gave him a look of compassion. "I *do* think you're still grieving over all you've lost. Which, for me, raises why you're drawn to Carla Pacelli."

"I wouldn't think that's a hard one. I don't require a seeing eye dog, Charlie."

"That," Charlie said pointedly, "is hardly an adequate response. Your mother is damaged. So was Jenny. Carla is a recovering alcoholic and drug addict who's pregnant by a man you loathed. And her choice of Benjamin Blaine begs the question of whether the attraction you both feel is equally unhealthy."

"I get *that* much," Adam retorted. "But every instinct I have tells me that Carla is better than that."

"Quite possibly she is. But you know all too well what your mother, Jenny, and Carla have in common—Ben Blaine." Charlie's voice softened. "When you make love to another woman, do you flash on Ben with Jenny Leigh?"

"Of course not," Adam snapped. "This isn't like PTSD."

"But when you look at Carla, do you imagine her with Benjamin Blaine?"

"I can't help that. And there's always the pregnancy to remind me."

Charlie steepled his fingers. After a time, he said, "Do you still want to get back at Ben, Adam? By doing to Carla what he did with Jenny?"

All at once, Adam felt sick. "If that's what I'm feeling, God help me. And Carla."

"I'm not saying that it is," Charlie responded gently. "But you need to figure it out, don't you. For Carla's sake, and for yours."

SEVEN

Two days before Adam was to leave, a violent hurricane swept past the mid-Atlantic states headed toward Martha's Vineyard.

Getting up at first light, Adam found Jack fitting the boards Ben had designed into the windows of the house, a precaution to prevent the projected hundred mile an hour winds from shattering the glass. Silent, Adam picked up a board and placed it in the window he recalled Ben expanding to brighten his writing den. Farther down the deck, Jack spoke without turning from his task. "Are you ready to go back?"

Adam forced a hinge into place, locking in the board. "It's not like I have a choice."

Jack glanced at him, the worry surfacing in his eyes. "Then I hope you'll watch out for yourself. It sounds like things over there are getting worse."

Glancing around to make sure his mother or Teddy were not within earshot, Adam faced his father. "I'm more concerned about keeping things buttoned up here. George Hanley is still taking an unwholesome interest in our family—including a highly imaginative sense of my activities for the last few weeks. If you hear anything about him or our friend from the *Inquirer*, go straight to Avi Gold."

Jack put down his hammer. Quietly, he said, "Do you have any idea how miserable this feels?"

"That depends on what 'this' is."

"The distance between us. Watching you try to take care of us despite everything you've learned, feeling your anger and resentment." Jack paused, lowering his voice. "Sharing this secret, knowing the burden you carry for what I did."

In the confusion of his feelings, Adam could find no words. At length, he answered, "As John F. Kennedy once said, 'Life is unfair.' Anyhow, killing him was the least of it. In your place, I might have done it myself."

The cool response made Jack wince. "You really do despise us, don't you?"

Adam faced him. "I can't sort out everything I feel, so don't expect me to. All I know is that this family makes me tired, and unspeakably sad. Maybe I'm tired, period. But that's nothing you can fix."

Turning, Adam picked up another board and walked to the next window.

Finishing his work, he entered the house, and saw his mother in the kitchen, taking stock of what they could eat once the power blew out and plunged the island into darkness. He passed her without speaking, went to his bedroom, and called Carla Pacelli.

Without preface, he asked, "What do you know about preparing for hurricanes?"

Carla laughed. "Nothing—I never made that movie. So what should I do?"

"Wait for me. I'll be over in an hour to give you a short course."

The grocery store was jammed with Islanders buying food and candles and flashlights and extra batteries. Adam did the same, adding bottled water and first aid provisions. Even in their hurry, other shoppers stopped to glance at him—he was, after all, a Blaine, the look-alike son of a famous father who had died in murky circumstances.

When he emerged, the gusts of wind had stiffened noticeably, rattling the trees at the edge of the parking lot and lending the air an eerie crispness that was the harbinger of destruction. Glancing at his watch, Adam saw that it was four o'clock. In one hour, a curfew would bar all traffic from the roads. If he went to Carla's, he would be with her until the storm passed.

Amanda Ferris was standing by his truck.

Stifling his surprise, Adam said, "Still here? Were you I, I'd have taken this storm as a sign from God."

She gave him a rancid smile. "*I* would've thought you'd be hearing my footsteps. George Hanley has become a friend. Once this blows over, your problems will only get worse."

Adam opened the rear door and began loading groceries inside. "Someone's will," he said over his shoulder. "Monomaniacs always end up flying too close to the sun."

She touched his sleeve. "Tell me what you did, and I'll let your family off the hook. Or you can bring them down with you."

Adam knew better than to believe this—she had already set the wheels in motion, spurring Hanley's call to Teddy's lawyer. He turned to face her. "There's no story here. So you'll have to take your chances."

The vulpine smile returned. "You're forgetting Carla Pacelli. There will *always* be a story *there*, and someday she'll want to help me. There are only so many people you can lie to, and only so many lies even a man like you can tell."

Without more, she turned and walked away.

When Adam arrived at Carla's place, he struggled to push the car door open against a heavy gust of wind. The skies were darkening; the forecasters were still uncertain about whether the hurricane would veer, sparing Martha's Vineyard the worse, or visit the level of destruction that toppled telephone poles and power lines, beached ruined boats, and turned homes into junkyards of wood and water-logged furnishings. It was fortunate that the guest house was in a clearing; there were no trees which, torn from their roots, were large enough to come crashing through the roof. But soon the massive power outages would start, taking with them the running water supplied by wells and pumps. This was no place for a preg-nant woman alone.

Head down, Adam lugged the bags full of supplies and groceries toward the house.

Carla had left the door unlocked. When he came in, she rose from the couch with noticeable care, coming over to take a bag from his hand. "You're good to do this," she said. "I can guess at how to cope, but this isn't what I'm used to."

Adam smiled. "No, it isn't. In Hollywood, the toilets might still work."

"And these won't."

"Nope. You don't have city water here. Let me show you what to do."

He hurried to the bathroom, filling the tub and sink with water. "Do this everywhere you can. In a while, it'll be the only water you'll have to boil eggs or flush the toilet. There are ways in which you really wouldn't enjoy living with yourself."

Carla gave him a droll look. "I can imagine."

As she filled the kitchen sink, Adam laid out bottled water and cans of soup and vegetables. "With luck, the propane won't go. You'll have gas to heat those with."

A burst of wind rattled the windows. Apprehensive, Carla asked, "How long could this go on?"

"Unless this thing veers, the power outages will last for days. I brought a transistor radio so we can follow the reports."

As he said this, the kitchen light flickered and went out. The low-ering skies cast the pall of evening through the windows.

Walking carefully, Carla placed candles on the table and lit them. Adam watched her for a moment. "Are you feeling okay?"

Carla hesitated. "I felt some cramping this morning. I know that can happen, but it scared me a little."

She was paler than before, Adam realized. "Then sit down. I'm staying here until this is done. I'll take care of whatever you need."

With palpable relief, Carla sat on the living room couch, resting her head as she closed her eyes. Amidst the antique furnishings Whitney Dane had used to decorate, in the flickering candle light Carla resembled a woman in a daguerreotype from the 19th century. For an odd moment, Adam thought of Rachel Ravinsky, who would soon be living in the main house, and felt relieved she was not here. Then he turned on the transistor radio, hearing the crackling voices of forecasters speculating about the hurricane's path. "Would you like a cup of soup?" he asked. "It looks like you can stand to eat."

Appreciative, Carla nodded "I'm usually not this much of a wimp."

"You're not a wimp, Carla—you're performing a storage function. So take it easy. Believe it or not, I can weather this without your help."

He turned on the gas stove, pouring the minestrone in a pot and stirring with a wooden spoon. Neither of them, he realized, wanted to broach the last time they had seen each other—the kiss, and the confusion that had followed, bringing the evening to a close. Then he noticed Carla watching him with a look of contemplation he could not quite read. He filled two mugs with soup and sat on the couch, handing one to her. "How are you feeling now?" he inquired.

"Grateful."

She bit her lip, as though struggling with an emotion he did not comprehend. Setting down his mug, he looked at her inquiringly. "It's not just the cramps," she confessed. "I've got good reason to be afraid of losing this baby, and never having another."

Adam nodded. "I'd guessed that. What's the problem, exactly?"

Distractedly, Carla smoothed her dress. "Heredity, to start. Before I was born, my mother had a string of miscarriages—much to the displeasure of my father who considered her defective. He never did get the son he wanted." Briefly, she glanced up at Adam.

"Mom got pretty desperate. To prevent any more miscarriages, she started taking a drug called DES . . ."

"Didn't they start banning that?"

"Only after I was born. To be blunt, DES babies grow up with abnormally shaped uteruses. That further decreased my chances of getting pregnant, and increased the likelihood of miscarriage if I did." Carla resumed picking at her dress. "Not that I counted on that for birth control. But when I started taking the pill, I developed blood clots. So I had to use an IUD.

"Bad to worse, it turned out. The IUD led to pelvic inflammatory disease, which makes it still harder to get pregnant, and can lead to an ectopic pregnancy. I always found it ironic that someone who men purported to find so sexy felt like an extinct volcano. Imagine my surprise that—at least this once—I wasn't." She gave him a fleeting embarrassed smile. "So now you know more about my plumbing than you ever wanted to. But you can also understand how precious this baby is to me. However awkward the circumstances, he may be my only chance to become a mother."

Instinctively, Adam felt for her. "What does the doctor say?"

"To rest, and be careful. That's why I've been tiptoeing around today." Briefly, she touched the back of Adam's wrist. "You can't know how worried I was before you called."

"My family can do without me," he said carelessly, "and me without them. So why don't you finish that and go get some rest. If we're about to get blown away, I'll let you know."

Carla looked relieved. Sipping the last of her soup, she slowly stood and rested her hand on Adam's shoulder. "Go," he said in mock sternness.

In the doorway of her bedroom, she turned to glance at him, then closed the door behind her. Outside the wind howled and whistled with new ferocity.

Adam lay on the couch, listening to weather forecasts cutting through the static. Near midnight, it became clear that the hurricane would veer toward the mainland, sparing Martha's Vineyard. As the wind buffeting the windows became more fitful, he allowed himself to sleep.

Deep in the night, Adam awakened with a start, reaching for the gun he did not have. Disoriented, he stared into the darkened room, then felt his pulse racing and the sweat dampening on his forehead. Breathing in, he tried to relax, even as he cursed his dreams. But when the bedroom door opened, he started.

In the candlelight, Carla crossed the room to kneel beside him. "What was it?"

"Nothing," Adam said tersely. "Go back to sleep."

Carla did not move. "You called out, Adam—not to me. You were somewhere else."

"I wouldn't know."

Carla grasped his wrist. "I think you do." She hesitated, then said bluntly, "Ben had nightmares—bad ones. When he awakened, he knew exactly where he'd been. Back in Vietnam, reliving horrors that had stayed with him for forty years. All he would tell me is 'there are some things men aren't made to outrun.'" She placed the back of curled fingers against Adam's forehead. "So be fair to yourself, please. Whatever they've taught you, you're not a stone."

Adam released a breath. "No, I'm not. But these are new."

"Can you tell me about them?"

Adam hesitated, caught between the iron rules he lived by and his desire, this once, not to feel alone. At last he said, "I'm either about to kill someone, or about to be killed. Christ knows why I'm having them now."

"Maybe because you're going back. This job you have—it's more dangerous than the one you described, isn't it?"

For a time, Adam was mute, the words caught in his throat. "Much more."

Carla nodded. "Can you quit?"

"No. If I quit now, other people who rely on me might get killed." His voice hardened. "The Benjamin Blaine I knew was a heartless, selfish bastard. No way he wanted to go to Vietnam. But he didn't run away to Canada, or weasel out of the draft.

"In almost every way, I pray to God I'm nothing like him. But I signed on for this one, whatever the risks, and now I have to see it through. These nightmares are the price of self-respect."

To his surprise, he could feel her irritation even before she said, "Too bad that I've quit acting. That line would come in handy in a war movie." Catching herself, she said swiftly, "Sorry. But it actually matters to me what happens to you, all right?"

Adam tried to smile. "Then I'll remember to avoid any clench-jawed heroics. At least when I'm sleeping on your couch."

Carla retrieved a candle, placing it so that she could see his face. After a time, she asked, "Once this job is over, will your 'company' send you somewhere else? Or will you actually make a choice?"

Adam had no answer. At length, he said, "Ten years in, I'm not sure what else I'd do."

"Maybe live a normal life," Carla responded with renewed gentleness. "That's what I'm trying to do, and some days it feels okay."

"You were always a good actress," Adam responded, "because you inhabited your roles. I may not be quite as gifted. Anyhow, go back to bed. I'm fine now, and your current role requires resting for two."

When Carla emerged again, the kitchen clock was working again, and Adam was gazing out the window at a crystalline morning cleansed by the storm. "How are you feeling?" he asked.

"Better."

"Then we got off light."

He saw Carla begin to say something, then think better of it. "Need to shower?" she asked. "If you're feeling grungy, you can always borrow my Lady Remington."

Adam smiled. "Unless you have fresh clothes for me, I probably should get going." Then he realized that she might have men's clothes there because of Ben.

She seemed to read his expression. "Anyhow, thanks for coming. And for staying."

"Sure." He hesitated. "If you run into a problem, are there people who can take you to the doctor?"

Carla nodded. "Friends from AA, if I need them."

"What about when the baby's born? Is anyone going to be there with you?"

Carla looked amused. "You mean like *there*, there? Back in the dark ages, I've heard, women had babies alone."

Adam shrugged. "My mother did, I'm told. I guess Ben didn't want to be there. Understandable, I suppose. But not ideal." He paused again. "Maybe I'll be back by then. I can't imagine why mere childbirth would faze me."

Giving him an incredulous look, Carla shook her head emphatically. "I won't be at my most attractive, so don't even dream of it. Besides, you've missed out on all the birthing classes they've cooked up to make fathers feel useful. Given everything that will be going on, I don't feel the need to keep you entertained."

"I get that. But maybe you could draft a girlfriend. Given 'everything,' as you put it, I don't like to think about you being alone."

Her expression became more serious. "Thank you for that. But in a lot of ways, except for the months with Ben, I've always been alone. I'm not feeling sorry for myself, just saying I'll be fine."

For a moment, Adam searched for what he wanted to tell her, then stood to leave. "Call me if you need anything, Carla. I'll come by before I go."

She hesitated, then came to him, giving him a swift, surprising kiss. "I'll take that as a promise," she said softly. "Both of us will."

EIGHT

The morning before he was to leave, Adam put on shorts and tennis shoes and began running along South Road, headed for Menemsha.

It was part of his routine, honing his endurance for whatever might happen in the field. He ran hard, as if he were being pursued; though the early morning sun was cool, he could feel the sweat clinging to his T-shirt. In the ten years of his exile from Martha's Vineyard, Spartan exercise had become like breathing to him, feeding his energy while allowing him to escape into a Zen-like trance. It was a metaphor, he supposed, for how he had chosen to live.

But today his emotions did not dissipate into the ether—Carla was too much with him. The questions Charlie Glazer had raised stung him, all the more so because he feared they might be true. It was his habit to avoid the darkest recesses of his inner landscape; his survivor's instinct told him that no good would come of it. But at least for today, his last meeting with Charlie, he would confront them. If his life ended in Afghanistan, there really was nothing to lose.

Charlie Glazer was sitting on the porch with his usual mug of coffee, gazing out at the expanse of Menemsha Harbor. When Adam loped onto the porch, he placed his hands on the railing, catching his breath and taking in Charlie's view.

"On mornings like this," Charlie remarked, "I feel like the luckiest man on earth. When I think about it, maybe I am. Start with the odds against being born, beginning with the cavemen through every man and woman who had to meet for any one of us to exist. Throw in the fact that my immigrant parents had no money or education, but that I was born into the American century and educated at Yale. Then take this morning, as fresh as Creation, with me sitting in this place. I can't escape the feeling that my life is a gift. Nor do I want to."

Though Charlie's tone was musing, Adam sensed that he intended this observation as a message—that Adam could still seize the life that had been given him, and remake it for himself. Though Adam no longer believed this, some part of him—however sentimental or deluded—must want to. Or why was he here?

He sat across from Charlie, ocean breezes cooling his face as the therapist passed him a cup of coffee. Crisply, Adam said, "Seems like we were talking about Carla."

A trace of humor surfaced in Charlie's eyes. "You remember."

"Hard to forget you asking if I wanted to fuck her to get back at a dead man. Is that what you really think?"

Unfazed, Charlie answered, "I was simply raising one possibility. Given all the other women you could be spending time with, it's pretty hard to avoid the implications. What do you think?"

"That I was with her during the hurricane, and it didn't feel like that."

Charlie watched his face. "What were you doing there?"

"What do you suppose? She'd never been through one of these. My mother has Jack and Teddy, but Carla is pregnant and alone."

"And you're also attracted to her, it's clear. Can you tell me how that feels?"

Adam struggled to label emotions he could not quite grasp. "When I first met her, I thought she was the most beautiful woman I'd ever seen. Because of Ben, it made me that much angrier or, perhaps, envious. More than that, she was my enemy—an extremely smart and acquisitive woman who had set out to steal my mother's inheritance. But even then, I realized there was something sexual in our hostility toward each other—or, at least, mine toward her. And, no, I'm not suggesting that was healthy."

"Or inexplicable," Charlie offered mildly. "I remember when I was young, seeing Jackie Kennedy at Logan Airport. As striking as she was in pictures, there was a vitality about her you could only feel in life. The next time I reacted to a woman like that was forty years later—when I saw Carla Pacelli, leaving an AA meeting in Vineyard Haven." Charlie sipped his coffee. "So taking that as a given, what did you perceive about her over time?"

"A number of things. There was this watchful intelligence that seemed to permeate each expression." Adam paused, summoning images from their early encounters. "I'm used to observing people closely. I began to feel that Carla was somehow like me—that beneath the celebrity persona, gracious and superficially approachable, she had a guarded, elusive quality, the ability to control and channel her emotions.

"At first, I thought it was because she was clever, and an actress. Now I think she's extremely self-protective, and that her reasons for that go far deeper than having to cope with being face-famous. There's something wounded about her, I think, which is where the substance abuse comes from. Even her sense of humor—which seems pretty good when she allows it to show—is shot through with irony."

Charlie regarded him with a trace of surprise. "That's a fair amount to grasp about a woman you haven't known that long."

Pensive, Adam nodded. "This may not say anything good about either of us. But sometimes I have this sense that I've met my own species. Right down to the sense that she's afraid to reveal herself for fear that something bad will happen."

"Except that she's not working undercover," Charlie observed. "At the core, who do you think Carla Pacelli really is?"

Adam considered this. "A survivor, with deep feelings she's afraid to reveal—except about this child she seems to want so desperately. The one emotion she'll admit to is how afraid she is of a miscarriage. For good reason, it turns out."

Charlie sat back, cradling the mug in his hands. "In other words, the focus of her life is bringing Benjamin Blaine's child into the world. What does that say to you?"

"It's complicated." Adam could hear his own reluctance. "As I've admitted, I don't like thinking about them together."

"What about this baby she's carrying?"

"That's easier. I feel sympathy for him."

"Hard to avoid," Charlie observed pointedly. "Like you, he's the product of an affair. As you were, his existence was a serious inconvenience to Clarice, threatening her security and public image. And, again, like you, he won't have a father. Your real father didn't claim you; this boy's dad—your fake father—is dead. Which might make him seem, at least symbolically, more like you than any prospective baby on earth."

Adam gazed at the deck. "I suppose that's possible."

Silent, Charlie seemed to withdraw, as if sorting out his thoughts. "If that's true," he said at length, "this baby could represent a second chance to repair the past. You may hope Carla gets the chance to be a better mother than Clarice. You may even want to be a better father figure than Ben or Jack. But Carla's pregnancy is also a constant reminder of her sexual relationship with a man who violated your girlfriend, propelling you into a wholly different life.

"True, she seems to have coped with Ben more successfully than any woman I'm aware of. But she'll forever be the last woman your quasi-father slept with. So everything about Carla and this child brings you back to your own past, in a way one might well describe as incestuous. If not downright Oedipal."

Reading Adam's expression, Charlie held up a hand. "I know you resent me for saying all this. I'm not entirely comfortable with it myself. But you're perilously close to the belly of the beast, psychologically speaking, dredging up every aspect of a family history that—through no fault of yours—is best described as twisted." Charlie's tone became gentle. "Ben brought you back here by dying, made you his executor in a final act of sadism, and stuck you with resolving his posthumous cruelties to your mother, brother, real father and—not least—you. Whatever laws you broke, the fact that you've brought any moral order to this mess is impressive beyond words. But if on any level you're imagining being with Carla, you risk perpetually playing out your tortured relationship with the father of her child. Unless you can confront the complications head on, that could be devastating for all three of you."

To Adam, each word felt like a blow. "That's a pretty dire picture, Charlie—especially for a man who may have no chance to live it. Right now, all I want is for Carla and this boy to be okay. No matter what happens to me."

"I believe that's true. But there's more to this, it's clear. I assume there's a physical component to all this altruism."

"For both of us," Adam acknowledged. "But it's fair to call that situationally limited, so don't let your imagination get out of hand. That hasn't been our focus."

"So what has?"

"We've talked a fair amount—including about her recovery. She's opened up a little, which is why I have a better sense of her."

Charlie gave him a querying look. "But you're less able to reciprocate. Does that trouble you at all?"

Adam felt a fresh wave of resentment, though he was not sure at whom. "There are a *few* things I can't tell her," he said tartly. "Some of them involve Ben's death."

Charlie looked at him intently. "I won't ask what you're holding back. But all the walls you've built, plus the need to lie about your job, must make it hard to be authentic. I wonder if she senses that."

Restless, Adam stood, walking to the railing. Without looking at Charlie, he said, "Maybe she does. But something happened to me. On the night of the hurricane, I told her more than I should have."

Charlie's voice was quiet. "What were the circumstances?"

"I was sleeping on a couch, waiting out the storm. I had the nightmare again, the one where I'm dead with Ben's head on my body. I must've cried out—Carla heard me, and came from her bedroom to find out what had happened." Adam paused, remembering the moment. "When she saw me, she seemed to understand. Ben had nightmares, too, she said—about Vietnam. All he'd told her, Carla said, was that there were some things men weren't made to endure. Then she asked me what I really did, as if she already knew."

"What did you reveal to her?"

"Not much. But I admitted my job was dangerous, and different than what I'd described." Saying this, Adam experienced the same queasy mix of relief and vulnerability. "Ben had already guessed aloud that I was CIA. Now she's sure I am."

"What was her reaction?"

"That she hoped I wouldn't go back there. When I insisted that I had to, she became angry. Then she said it was because she cares about what happens to me."

Charlie cocked his head. "How did that make you feel?"

"For that moment, good. Then I was ashamed of breaking the rules." Pausing, Adam watched a sailboat breasting the choppy waters of the Vineyard Sound. "If anyone confronts us—and no matter how harmless their suspicions may seem—we're trained to 'lie, deny, and make counter accusations.' If necessary, you deploy deflective humor, or infuse your lies with a grain of truth to make them more credible. You're supposed to be like an onion—peel off the layers, and there's nothing left. But I'm not sure that works with Carla. At least for one instant, I didn't want it to."

"What *are* the rules about when you can tell a woman the truth?"

"The relationship has to be very serious—engagement, if not the brink of marriage. I was way off the reservation."

"Literally, yes. But emotionally speaking, wasn't that your way—if not exactly a proposal of marriage—of telling Carla that you want her in your life?" Charlie's voice softened again. "Perhaps the only chance, in your mind, given the foreboding in your nightmares."

Adam turned to him, resistant. "It was a bad moment, and Carla happened to be there. Don't make too much of it."

"And don't make too little of it," Charlie rejoined. "Frankly, it's the most hopeful thing I've heard from you since we started. Setting aside the obvious problems with this particular relationship, in this so-called 'bad' moment you wanted to be closer to another human being. Whatever the reason, Carla seems to call on that in you—you broke the rules for *her*, not someone else. Which raises the question of how those feelings will affect you in Afghanistan."

Leaving the railing, Adam sat across from him. "I'm not sure what you mean."

"Then let me try an analogy," Charlie proposed. "By your account, Carla has worked hard to find out who she really is. The more she succeeds, the less skilled she may be at imagining she's someone else. Perhaps that's another reason she decided to give up acting." He paused, as though to underscore his point. "What you may be saying to Carla, whether she understands it or not, is that you hope for something you haven't let yourself imagine since Jenny. Even if Carla's not right for you, that could be a very good sign.

"But it may complicate your life in Afghanistan. All the weapons you deploy against everyone else—disconnection, avoidance, deception, and fatalism about death—have kept you alive. By embracing the possibility of a different future, you may lose the detachment you've relied on to survive." Charlie seemed to inhale. "So here's the challenge you're taking with you—to hope for a better life, and still live to find it."

Adam could say nothing. But when he stood to leave, to his surprise Charlie clasped his shoulders, looking into his face. "Good luck, Adam," the therapist said. "Like Carla, what happens to you matters to me. I want you back here sitting on this porch. After all, we've still got work to do."

NINE

Refreshed by the 6:45 AA meeting in Vineyard Haven, Carla emerged into the slanting sunlight of a crisp, cool morning, the first harbinger of fall. At this hour, the streets were still empty, and no one would notice her. A good time to take stock of herself with others who understood.

This morning, her sponsor—a formerly popular singer—had celebrated five years of sobriety. Carla felt pleased for her, and buoyed by the example she set. Standing by her car, she paused a moment, reflective, then drove to the Catholic Church in Oak Bluffs.

Carla had left the church years before, and she still did not know if anyone heard her prayers. But a central tenet at Betty Ford was to seek help outside herself, and the rituals of Catholicism were familiar to her. Our Lady Star of the Sea, the most modest church on the island, was set amidst gingerbread houses on a tree-lined street, away from the bustle of a resort town where tourists thronged. The white wooden structure was plain in design, with a clapboard steeple topped by a simple cross. Its lack of pretense pleased Carla, and its parishioners—many of whom were immigrants whose first language was Brazilian Portuguese—had more pressing concerns than the travails of a fading celebrity. So Carla had begun attending the 8:00 a.m. mass on Sundays, slipping into the back just before services began.

Today, a Monday, Carla considered her choices. The grassy park across from the church offered benches beneath the shelter of venerable oaks, and often Carla would sit there to pray and reflect. But this morning she decided to enter the church itself.

The interior was hushed. Its stained glass windows cast a serene dappling of light and shadow on the pews, and the carved image of Jesus behind the altar portrayed a man in prayer instead of a tormented martyr. No one else was there. Sitting near the front, Carla began renewing her connection with the rituals of her youth.

As a child, such a place had been her refuge from the fear she had felt in her parents' home. Now, when the enemy might be herself, she sought a sense of peace and order, and Christ's divinity meant less to her than his compassion. Eyes closed, she recited the Hail Mary, the Our Father, and the Act of Contrition, seeking the strength to achieve the life she now envisioned. Then she prayed for the safety of her unborn child and, at last, for Adam Blaine.

When Carla returned, Adam was sitting on the porch of the guest-house. Seemingly surprised, she told him lightly, "Funny you should be here. I was thinking about you a while ago."

Adam stood, hands jammed in his pockets. "In what context?"

"The other night. I still owe you money for soup, candles, and a flashlight."

"Then let that be on your conscience, Carla. I'm just here to say goodbye."

Carla nodded, looking down. After a moment, she said, "Actually, I was wishing we had more time, just to talk. It feels like we've been interrupted."

The same feeling of regret made Adam wordless for a moment. Wondering if they would ever see each other again, he felt the loss of something precious. "I know," he acknowledged. "But there's no help for that right now."

She looked up at him again. "Can you at least write letters? Back in the Victorian age, I'm told, men and women used to do that."

Adam smiled. "The postal service on the Afghan–Pakistani frontier leaves something to be desired. But I can send e-mails. They just can't be about my day at the office."

A shadow of worry crossed Carla's face. "I was hoping you could tell me more about yourself. Anything, really—memories of being young, your greatest sports heroics. Maybe even what you think and feel."

If only it were that easy, Adam thought. "As long as you reciprocate," he answered. "I already know about my own life, for better or worse. But I'd like to hear more about how you got from there to here."

"Fair enough," Carla answered, and smiled a little. "Anyhow, my new incarnation seems to require that. Something about a 'fearless moral inventory.'"

"One more thing, then. Please keep me posted on how you and the baby are doing. Otherwise, I'll wonder."

Her eyes grew serious again. "I'll be fine. But if you want me to, I will."

Though Adam did not wish to go, he could think of nothing more to say. Instead, he reached out to cradle the side of her face, his own face moving closer. With a questioning look, he asked, "I get to do this, yes?"

Her expression was grave and, he thought, a little sad. "Yes," she answered softly. "Later on, maybe we can figure out what it means."

Adam felt a thickening in his throat. Then he kissed her, gently, lingeringly, feeling her body move into his, the warm reciprocity of her lips. It was he, finally, who leaned back to look at her. "Take care of yourself, Carla. For both of you."

He touched her face again and then, turning, walked away. He did not look back. Saying goodbye to Carla Pacelli hurt too much for that.

Before Teddy drove him to the airport, Adam went to see his mother.

Fleetingly, he kissed her on the cheek. Feeling the thinness of her shoulders, he had the first premonition of Clarice Blaine, always trim and beautiful, as an old woman. Tears welled in her eyes.

"Ten years," she said in an uncharacteristically thick voice, "and I hardly saw you. Now you're going again, carrying such resentment. And I don't know what to do."

"Just give it time, mom. I'll be back soon enough."

Her throat worked. "Will you, though? I'm sorry, but I can't keep myself from worrying."

Adam tried to smile this away. "I'll be okay. I always am."

Clarice shook her head in demurral. For an instant, he imagined her saying, as she had many times before, how much he was like Benjamin Blaine. Instead, she asked, "Have you been to see Jack?"

"No. Please say goodbye for me, all right?"

Her lips parted in an expression of sudden anguish. "Will you ever forgive him? Or us?"

Once more, Adam felt the weight of all that he concealed from her. "This isn't about forgiveness, Mom. I just have to unlearn some things, and accept others. I'm sure that next year will be different."

Assuming, Adam thought, that next year ever came.

When Adam climbed into the passenger seat of Ben's old pickup truck, his brother asked, "How was it?"

"More or less as usual. Like two people looking at each other through glass."

Pulling away from the house, Teddy glanced at him. "Sometimes it feels like all of us are looking at you through glass."

Yet again, Adam wished that he could tell his brother all he knew. "I may have my emotional limitations, Ted. But I'm always home to you."

"I know that," Teddy answered. "But where is your home?"

Silent, Adam gazed at the road ahead, winding past pristine ponds and old houses sheltered by trees. "I have a favor to ask," he said at length, "and you're the only one I can ask."

Teddy gave him a quick, curious glance. "What is it?"

"Look in on Carla now and then, and make sure she has your phone number. She has no one, really, and I think she may be worried about the baby."

Teddy looked bemused "What's this about, exactly?"

"Carla's a decent person, that's all. If she hadn't agreed, I never could've reclaimed the estate for you and mom. If you're not feeling grateful enough, just do it for me."

"For you, then," Teddy allowed with a smile. "You're a mysterious person, bro—in many ways. Am I permitted to guess that your feelings about Ms. Pacelli—however astounding this may be—involve more than humanitarian concern?"

"Guess away," Adam responded easily. "And when you figure it out, please let me know. I grasp so little about myself."

Turning into the airport, Teddy stopped in front of the shingled one-story building, speaking with palpable reluctance. "There's one last thing I need to tell you. Richard Mendelson met with George Hanley yesterday. As Richard suspected, George didn't ask anything about me, at least not directly. What he did ask put Richard on edge—whether he'd received any investigative files concerning our father's death."

At some cost, Adam gave his brother a look of perplexed curiosity. "What did Richard say?"

"He refused to answer. Unfortunately, George also interviewed Richard's secretary. She told him what she felt compelled to, I guess. That Richard had received what looked to be police files— anonymously, in the mail, and much to his apparent surprise. So George demanded the files themselves."

Adam mustered a shrug of indifference. "Awkward. But not a problem for Richard—if he didn't solicit them, he didn't break any laws. Neither did you."

"True enough," Teddy retorted pointedly. "But whoever sent them broke all sorts of laws. Aside from Jack—or me—that's the guy George is after."

Adam shrugged. "Good luck to him, then. But do me another favor. If anything happens with this or the medical examiner's inquest, e-mail me in Afghanistan. I always hate being the last to know."

Swiftly, Adam embraced his brother, and was off.

PART THREE

THE GAUNTLET

Afghanistan–Martha's Vineyard
September–November 2011

ONE

Leaving his concrete redoubt, Adam wondered how his life in Afghanistan would appear to Carla Pacelli.

His quarters were protected by a high wall and ringed with Afghan security guards the occupants hoped would never betray them. The others were American workers to whom he lied about his true mission—targeting Taliban leaders, any one of whom might have tribal or filial relationships with their guards. An existence as lonely as it was surreal.

Now he drove through the countryside with his translator, Hamid. Around them, jagged mountains capped with snow were the backdrop for villages that were tan and dirty. Swerving to avoid rocks with shards so sharp they could slice open their tires, their Jeep kicked up dust as fine as talcum powder. Hamid was his closest associate, and the nearest he had to a friend. To preserve his cover as a contract employee for the Central Poppy Eradication Force, Adam communicated with his case officer in Kabul as little as possible. As for the decision makers who directed his fate, he had never met them.

All this Adam accepted. The hardest part, he would tell Carla if he could, was running Afghan agents when the Taliban sought to capture and kill them both. He still did not know what had tipped off Messud, the Afghan he had killed barely a month before—he could never be certain about who the Afghans he dealt with truly were, or where their deepest allegiances lay. But what haunted Adam most was his duty to protect the agents who—whether motivated by greed or dislike for the enemy—remained loyal to him. One slipup, and a man he knew and perhaps even liked could end up tortured and killed, followed by his family, no matter if he betrayed Adam in an effort to save them. It had always been the most draining part of his job, and Afghanistan was more treacherous than anywhere he had worked. That Adam still cared was, he supposed, the clearest sign that concealed within him was a decent human being.

This mission made him edgier than normal. Adam had to assume that the Taliban was tracking his every movement, especially after Messud had disappeared. Quite likely there were Taliban stationed behind rocks in the hilly terrain along the route; the men he was meeting at its end could well be double agents. His usual practice was to pick agents up on the fly, meeting in a car instead of at a specific location that could be watched. But today, his agent had specified a medical center that would soon be occupied by Americans. Its only virtue was that Adam had never been seen there—it was not safe to meet an agent in the same place twice.

Nor did he trust the man he was to meet. The Pakistani's history was shot through with duplicity—today he could be working for the Taliban, or have become a target of their suspicion. Adam preferred agents whose motives for helping him were as obscure to others as the coin in which he paid them. Briefly, he imagined telling Carla of the village elder he had given a lifetime supply of Viagra in exchange for identifying a key Taliban leader, whom the CIA had then obliterated with a drone. But the elder had lived happily on, his ego and potency replenished.

Driving beside him, Hamid scanned the countryside, his worries running parallel to Adam's. The Afghan was in his late twenties, six feet, yet so broad and muscular that he appeared stocky, his hair cropped under his knit cap, his blunt face sporting a mustache. He had served as a guard at a military base near Kabul while being vetted by the agency, then joined the Afghan security services, which had placed him at the airport to spot suspicious people in transit. So keen was his eye that the CIA had recruited him. Now he was indispensable to Adam—talking to locals; making up whatever cover story was needed; helping assess the character of agents who, if his judgment was faulty, might end their lives. He was that rare person in Adam's life—someone he trusted.

Hamid did not like the man they were meeting, his reservations expressed by a deeper than usual silence. The colonel commanded the Northwest Frontier Scouts, the element of the Pakistani army charged with patrolling the border and monitoring those who crossed it. His more lucrative sidelight was selling weapons in both Pakistan and Afghanistan to whoever paid him most, while slipping the information he gained to Adam. He could as easily, Hamid and Adam knew, sell them to the Taliban.

Adam had encountered the colonel while moving through the tribal areas near the border, meeting with local leaders on both sides. Along the way, he spotted a Pakistani guard post on the border. Stopping, he got out of his Jeep and began chatting with three Pakistani soldiers. After a while, he saw the dust of an army truck coming down from a fort that commanded a sweeping view of the border. Then the truck arrived, unloading a Pakistani colonel bent on finding out who Adam was.

In his aviator sunglasses and neatly pressed uniform, the fortyish man projected a certain arrogance, accented by strong features and a hooked nose that gave him an air of command. Though his manner with Adam was polite enough, his seemingly casual questions probed at who Adam was. He registered no reaction when Adam described his supposed work with the poppy eradication program. "You're an idealist," the colonel had remarked in a tone that mingled amusement and a hint of disbelief. "The least I can do for such a noble fellow is invite you to tea."

Adam and the colonel had driven to the fort and sat in the shade of a makeshift canvas awning. As they exchanged further pleasantries, Adam sensed the Pakistani trying to place him in a personal ecology not bounded by his ostensible job. Either the colonel was trying to trip him up, Adam concluded, or he had some relationship in mind that he could shape to his personal advantage. Adam resolved to do the same.

At the end of an hour, they parted, each pledging fervently to nurture their new friendship with future visits. Returning to his quarters, Adam called his case officer on a secure phone and asked him to run a check on the colonel.

The response had suggested a man whose deceit was even greater than Adam had surmised. Within the CIA, Colonel Ayub Rehman was suspected of doubling as an arms dealer, selling weapons to the Taliban that were stolen from the Pakistani army by corrupt soldiers under his command. Adam could not help but appreciate the irony—his new friend was getting rich on the Taliban's' chief source of financing, opium money, derived from a crop Adam was pretending to eradicate. After some reflection, he came up with a scheme that, with apparent reluctance, his case officer took to their superiors. To Adam's surprise, his man in Kabul came back with permission to proceed.

More visits to the colonel had followed, each man politely but pointedly probing the other. At length, Adam allowed that his real job was somewhat more complicated than persuading farmers not to grow opium—he was working undercover for the DEA, trying to disrupt the flow of opium money to the Taliban. For this, he went on, he needed to identify Taliban leaders. "We're on the same side," he had solemnly told the Pakistani. "After all, your mission on the border is to keep the Taliban from expanding its influence in your country. For such an act of friendship, I would pay you in return."

For a long time, the Pakistani simply watched him. Adam imagined him trying to calculate the advantages of feeding him to the Taliban—one reason, among many, for portraying himself as a minion of the DEA, whose death might be less of a priority.

Finally, the colonel said, "You are asking me to work for two governments."

"What I'm asking you," Adam replied equably, "represents further proof of my good will. For whatever reason, my government believes that you are selling weapons to the Taliban, stolen from the army. Should anything happen to me, this information will be relayed to your superiors, with unpleasant consequences you've no doubt already considered. But should you choose to help me, I can promise that the American government will keep this information to itself. Your life can go on as before, only with another source of income."

The Pakistani studied Adam further, his eyes glinting with resentment and a certain sour humor. At length, he said, "I will give this new partnership a try. I only hope that, whoever you are, your skill matches your nerve."

With this, Adam acquired another agent, at considerable risk to himself. Now, driving with Hamid to meet the colonel, Adam reflected that, on Martha's Vineyard, he had effectively run his father as his agent, jeopardizing Jack and himself at risk to protect his brother Teddy. He still did not know whether George Hanley or Amanda Ferris might unravel his machinations. In which case, his own country would be no sanctuary from danger.

Dismissing the thought, Adam returned to the dangers of the present. "See anything?" he asked Hamid. The translator merely shrugged. Anyone they might spot was likely harmless; their enemies were skilled at staying invisible.

At the bottom of a hill, they drove through a wadi and back up a slope toward a walled compound, the would-be clinic. In due time, a doctor would be located, supplies brought in, and word put out that the Americans offered medical assistance to Afghans. Until then, the colonel had suggested that this was a good place to meet—easy to secure, with a commanding view of the area and the road traversing it. On this basis, at least, Adam could not fault his reasoning.

Hamid drove them through the narrow gate of the compound and spun the Jeep around, parking it just to the right of the gate.

Then they began scouring the rooms inside to ensure no one was there. Opening each door, Adam felt the tension in his shoulders.

No enemies awaited them. Meeting Adam back in the courtyard, Hamid raised his eyebrows and shrugged. They walked to the entryway, and saw a group of shepherds moving their flock in the distance. Otherwise, the harsh terrain showed nothing.

Edgy, the two men watched and waited, chatting absently about Hamid's family. After a time, they saw an SUV kicking up dust in the wadi. Silent, Adam watched it close the distance to the compound.

Abruptly, the SUV stopped by a mud hut near the road. When the driver got out, Adam recognized one of his agents. As planned, two men unknown to the driver emerged from the hut and got into the SUV—the Pakistani colonel and, apparently, the Afghan he had insisted on bringing. Adam had proposed this tradecraft to prevent the Pakistani's vehicle from being associated with the clinic. He could only wonder if the Afghan's information—if real—would justify the risk.

At last, the SUV dropped its passengers inside the compound, and left. Then Hamid closed the heavy door and the four men were alone.

Adam greeted Colonel Rehman with elaborate warmth, then faced the Afghan—Mahmud Hakeem, or so the colonel said. He was a man in his midforties, Adam judged, with liquid brown eyes and a seamed walnut face, more wary than friendly. The face of a survivor in a hard place.

Often with such men, Adam spoke in English, using Hamid as a translator to conceal his language skills. But pretense was useless here—the colonel knew better. In Pashto, Adam said, "It is an honor that you have traveled this far to meet with us. We appreciate your willingness to help."

Hakeem simply nodded—whatever life he had led seemed to have cured him of the need for persiflage. Accepting this invitation to directness, Adam said, "We need some information from you."

Phlegmatically, Hakeem responded to Adam's questions—where he was born; where he lived; how old he was; what he had done in the years before. His answer to the last pricked Adam's nerve ends—as a young man, Hakeem had worked for the Afghan army intelligence, which meant that he reported to the Russians. This made him no friend to Americans or, contradictorily, to many Afghan leaders of the Taliban, who had worked with the CIA to drive the Russians from their country. Adam's one certainty was that he was not meeting with an innocent. But then he already knew that—the man was keeping company with Colonel Rehman.

As the dialog continued, the Pakistani watched Adam keenly. Since the Russians left, Hakeem told him, he had settled down with a family of five boys and two girls, all of whom lived with him across the border with Pakistan. He owned a large truck; his business was delivering food and supplies throughout the border areas. But, with so many mouths to feed, he could always use extra money. Adam surmised that he was already smuggling weapons for the colonel.

At the end of Hakeem's account Adam nodded politely, arranging his features in an expression of doubt. "How would you feel about working with America after working with the Russians?"

Hakeem shrugged. "The past is the past."

"Your home village," Adam said abruptly, "is in an area known to harbor al-Qaeda and Taliban. Have you seen them there?"

The Afghan seemed to measure his words. "Al-Qaeda, yes— Arabs from outside Pakistan and Afghanistan. But they don't stay in the village."

"Where do they sleep at night?"

Again, the Afghan weighed his answer. "I only know the general area."

"Are there Taliban in that area?"

Hakeem hesitated. "Yes."

Adam went to his Jeep, taking out a notepad and pen. "Draw me a map of your town, and the area where al-Qaeda and the Taliban hide."

Hakeem took the pad and pen and, frowning, began to draw. As he did, Adam felt the colonel watching him, no doubt confirmed in his suspicion that Adam was hunting the Taliban for the CIA. For his part, Adam felt sure that Hakeem was the Pakistani's cut out: the colonel meant to use him as a go-between—limiting his contacts with Adam and therefore his own risk—while taking more money from the Americans. It was Adam's job to manipulate them both, ever alert to the chance that he was being manipulated.

"Who is helping al-Qaeda in your village?" Adam asked.

The Afghan did not look up. "A man named Salim."

Adam took the proffered map, primitive but clear enough. "Can you write out directions to where al-Qaeda and the Taliban are?"

Hakeem smiled faintly. "With all your satellites and electronics, can't you do this already? Why rely on my humble drawings?"

Adam's own smile did not reach his eyes. "I appreciate humor. But we are very serious about this."

At once, the man's expression changed. "And I am serious about making money. For that, I will help you find the men you seek to kill. But the rewards must equal the risk."

Curtly, Adam nodded. "If your information is good, they will."

In a crabbed hand, the man wrote out directions, describing the terrain between his village and the place where, in his telling, al-Qaeda and the Taliban had taken refuge. Handing back the notepad, the Afghan glanced at Colonel Rehman.

"There is something else," the colonel told Adam tersely.

Silent, Adam turned back to the Afghan. In a softer tone, Hakeem inquired, "Is there an American soldier missing?"

Adam felt himself tense. Two years before an American private, Bowe Bergdahl, had become the only American POW of the Afghan war. To impress on Adam the importance of finding this single American soldier, his case officer had shown him the videos provided by the Taliban. In the first, Bergdahl looked young and frightened; the later videos traced his emotional deterioration. When the Taliban had demanded one million dollars and the release of Taliban prisoners in exchange for Bergdahl's life, the Pentagon had determined to free him by other means. Now the POW's fate might be in Adam's hands—unless, of course, this was an elaborate ploy.

"We have a soldier missing," Adam replied evenly. "You know that. What else do you know?"

Again, the Afghan glanced at Colonel Rehman. "I was bringing supplies to a village in Pakistan near the border, closer to where I believe al-Qaeda and the Taliban have taken refuge. While I was there, I overheard two men guarding a building, one asking the other if they were moving the American. From how they acted, the man they spoke of was inside. That's all I know."

"When was this?"

"Perhaps a week ago."

Adam handed back the pad and pen. "As best you can, draw a map of the village, showing the building where the guards were."

With a pained expression, the man did so. Studying the drawing, Adam was careful to reveal nothing.

"We will be in touch with you," he told Hakeem, "through the colonel. If this information bears fruit, you will certainly be rewarded. But we may need more from you."

The meeting was over. Facing the Pakistani, Adam said simply, "Thank you, Ayub."

The Pakistani gave him a faint, sardonic smile. "What else would I do? We are friends, are we not?"

With this, the two men got in Adam's Jeep, lying on the floor so that they could not be spotted. Under cover of darkness, Adam and Hamid left the compound and dropped them behind a massive boulder where another car would meet them.

Leaving, Adam asked Hamid, "What do you think?"

The translator shrugged his heavy shoulders, gripping the wheel as he looked for rocks captured in their headlights. "No point in guessing. You'll have to test him, and even then you can't be sure."

Adam felt an apprehension he could not name. "Agreed. But certainty may not matter here. Not this time."

When they reached the compound, Adam went to his room and called his case officer in Kabul.

Two

"Tell me about *your* childhood," Adam had asked her in an e-mail. "I know too much about mine, but nothing about yours."

Sitting with her laptop as early sunlight brightened her windows, Carla wondered how to answer this, even as she pondered the weight and meaning of her sometimes painful memories. At length she resolved simply to begin.

"My father was Italian—obviously—a policeman in San Francisco. Mom was Irish, and worked as a secretary for the parish. Neither was terribly well educated; both were conservative Catholics, especially my mother, for whom the rituals of the church were sacred. We lived in the Sunset District, a last stronghold of the city's middle class, among people whose stucco houses, and beliefs, were much like ours. So it was a given that I, the only child they were able to have, would go to parochial school from beginning to end. Before living, they assumed, a life much like theirs."

Fingers resting on the keyboard, Carla wondered if this seemed too condescending—patronizing her parents from the lofty perch of her precious self-awareness, having failed so completely to manage her own life. There was something arrested in hanging onto the wounds of childhood; after all, her parents had once been children too, scarred by their own parents' flaws and weaknesses. But Adam had asked and so, after typing in this qualifier, she continued with her narrative.

"My father was abusive—physically and verbally. When he drank too much, which was often, he hit my mother for no reason. It was as if Irish whiskey had flipped a switch in his brain that made him erupt in violence. Sometimes he hit me." Involuntarily, Carla paused, and realized that she had closed her eyes. "I knew that other girls saw their fathers as a source of comfort and security. But early on, I felt like Mom and I were living with an enemy who could turn on us at any moment. We were only safe when he was gone. I learned to dread the turning of the doorknob when he came home, never knowing what might follow. I started pulling the covers over my head, as though he might not be able to find me."

Another memory struck Carla—the night that her father, whiskey on his breath, had gently kissed her forehead. In the wave of gratitude that followed, she had begun to fall asleep, then heard her mother crying out in pain. Now turning to the window, she reminded herself that she was thirty-three years old, pregnant with her own child, gazing out at a green meadow on a bright and peaceful Vineyard morning. "Night after night," she continued typing, "I saw the stoicism with which she accepted this as her fate. And so, like my mother, I learned to keep my father's secret."

She had also learned, Carla now understood, to block out the most searing pictures. But nothing could erase the damage to her own self-image. "As children will," she told Adam, "I wondered if this was my punishment for being a bad person—as though God knew that I fantasized that another bad person, some criminal, would shoot my father dead in the streets. But every night he kept coming through our door.

"The night I begged him not to hit my mother, he whipped my bare legs with a belt. She stood between us, begging him to stop. Instead of staying with her, like a coward I ran to my room, crying from pain and fear. Then my mother came to me, one eye swollen from the beating she'd taken for me, and put ointment on my legs. 'It's the drink,' she whispered. 'Tomorrow he'll feel sorry.'

"Falling asleep, I tried to forget the despair I heard in her voice. But the next day, I put on my school uniform, and realized that the other girls could see my bruises. And I was afraid they'd know what happened in our home at night."

Carla was not ready to explain to him how these hardships had bonded her to Benjamin Blaine, whose own abusive father had scarred and shaped him. Instead, she wrote, "This e-mail is beginning to sound like a Dickens novel, only way more self-pitying. So instead of all this bathos, I'll try to explain how this seven-year-old girl came to look at the world."

Even so, Carla reflected, why should Adam care about the hurt of a lonely child? But he had asked, and despite his self-possession, Adam struck her as a deeply wounded man. Though it made her wary, she cared for him, and she had valued his honesty on the night of the hurricane, a brief window into all he kept locked inside him. The only way to reach him was to be honest in return.

"To my childish mind," she continued, "the way Mom and I covered up for my father merged with our religious faith. In my imaginings, 'God the Father' was a stern and bearded patriarch whose rules we could never question, enforced by our Father in Rome through the presence of our parish priest. Though Father Riley seemed benign enough, all this male authority was a one-way street. My mother never once imagined confiding in him about the darker secrets of our home."

Sitting back, Carla touched the swelling of her belly, resolving yet again that her own child would come before any man. Then she felt her thoughts drift to an ironic memory. "My first confession was telling," she typed as its images fell into place. "It was the day before my First Communion, and confession was an absolute pre-requisite. I left my mother and walked into the confessional—this hushed, sepia place—filled with dread at my own void, desperately scouring my imagination for some sin to confess, one worthy of this moment. If only I could have seen into my future, I'd have tied up Father Riley for quite some time. But my mind was so blank that I felt myself trembling.

"In retrospect, my solution was both desperate and revealing. My real sin, I remember mumbling through the screen, was making my father so angry he was forced to hit me. As soon as the words escaped my lips, my eyes filled with tears, and I couldn't speak anymore. I must have hoped that in the guise of confessing my own sins—my father's, really—I could get Father Riley to help my mom and me. But all he said was that I should obey my father. So I recited the act of contrition for my sins, just as my mother taught me.

"I left feeling empty and bereft, knowing that no one would protect us.

"By then, I'd learned to lose myself in motion—some activity that took me out of my own thoughts. So I got on my bike and began peddling like the furies were after me, and I had to outrun them or die.

"As I rounded the corner, the neighborhood Irish crone, Mrs. O'Gara, was watering her roses. She made it her business to know everything, and to pass judgment on the propriety of everyone around her. When I nearly hit her, she began screeching like a banshee that no girl should ride her bicycle before her First Communion. I felt my heart sink—it didn't occur to me that there was no such prohibition, and that this bitter old woman had no business visiting her misery on a child. The next day I went through the First Communion—supposedly this sacred moment—filled with dread, certain I was not in a state of grace, and that my bicycle had become a ticket straight to hell." Rereading these words, Carla smiled a little. "I know it sounds funny now, and it is. But my interior world at seven was a pretty scary place."

Fingers resting on the keyboard, she imagined the much more frightening reality in which Adam now lived—and, she feared, might die. She bowed her head, a moment close to prayer, and then wondered where to go next before typing, "'Gee, Carla,' I imagine you saying, 'this is absolutely fascinating. Please tell me how you became an actress.' So I will.

"Within the confines of our home, Mom couldn't save either of us. But my father was handsome to look at, and I early on sensed that he enjoyed the attentions of women. So I learned to deflect him with humor and charm, trying to please him while becoming my mother's protector." It was odd, Carla thought—this seemed so obvious now, but only at Betty Ford had she fully comprehended it. "As a defense against reality I escaped into an imaginary world, casting myself as someone else. I began to play act for my father in scenarios that I'd invented—like the absentminded hairdresser who gave Mrs. O'Gara a Mohawk, in which I triumphed in both roles. Pretty soon, Dad was insisting that I do this for the neighbors.

"Without knowing, he created a monster, desperate to appease him. My performance as the baker whose wedding cake collapsed was my absolute apotheosis, a masterpiece of overacting that moved Mrs. LoBionco to tell my dad, 'with that talent, Carla should be an actress—God knows she's pretty enough.' The word 'actress' sounded so magical that pretty soon I was in every play at school, always in the lead. Acting was better than riding my bicycle—a transcendence so complete that I forgot myself and everything that troubled me." Briefly, Carla experienced a residue of guilt and sadness. "My other reward was that Dad stopped hitting me. Unlike Mom, I'd became special in the eyes of others and, therefore, to him.

"The irony is that my mother saw this. She implored my father to enroll me in acting lessons at ACT—the theater company in San Francisco where Annette Bening got her start. I became addicted in the true meaning of that word—only acting gave me the approval I craved and, on stage, it was immediate. My mother was giving me an escape she could never have.

"She began sitting up with me at night, listening to my ambitions and my dreams. When my drama teacher said I should consider acting as a career, I knew that everything in my life had destined me for this. And when my mother heard the news, tears of joy ran down her face, and she told me she had prayed for this."

Remembering her mother's arms around her, Carla felt herself swallow. "The church," she went on, "remained the center of her life. Every night, to please her, I recited the Hail Mary, the Our Father, and an Act of Contrition. I never let on that they were white noise to me now, like the rules that came with them—that birth control violated God's will, or that sex outside marriage was a mortal sin. My high school, the Convent of the Sacred Heart, had begun accepting non-Catholics, girls who believed in nothing at all. I was moving outside my parent's world."

She was making an act of confession, Carla reflected, addressed to Adam Blaine. "For the first time I was special—an actress, and pretty, a girl other girls envied and admired. And I'd begun hearing rumors about my father and other women. One night, cruising with friends in another neighborhood, I saw my father coming from a bar with his arm draped around a much younger woman—wearing too much makeup, but nice looking enough, with a body that made the obvious even more so. The kids I was hanging out with didn't recognize him. But I was devastated and then furious—this was the ultimate insult to my mother, still more punishment for all that she'd endured, and a complete denial of all the rules they'd pressed on me. The next night I slept with my first boy, a guy I barely knew and cared about even less.

"That Sunday morning I took a certain savage pleasure in my confession. I'd been taught that if you sincerely repent your sins, God would forgive them, and if you went outside and got hit by a bus, you'd immediately go to heaven. So I confessed my sins with a vengeance—drinking, smoking pot, the guy I'd just slept with. When dried up old Father Riley admonished me from behind the screen to avoid boys—the 'near occasion of sin,' he called them— then gave me a penance of six Our Fathers and ten Hail Marys, I could barely keep from laughing. All this incense and mirrors had ever gotten my mother was another beating from her adulterous husband, my father.

"To me, she was more than my father's victim. She was the victim of her church and all the rules enforced by men—no divorce; mute acceptance; redemption in an afterlife I no longer believed existed. But still I'd go with her to church—to refuse would have shattered her, and she'd already endured too much. So I was relieved when a new young priest, Father Vasquez, took Father Riley's place. He seemed friendly, and more approachable, not pickled in the stifling Catholicism I'd grown up with. Through him, I decided to give the church a final chance.

"The opening I chose was confession. Instead of the usual sins, I began telling Father Vasquez about my childhood, what went on within our four walls—my father's brutality, my mother's silent suffering. As I spoke, I imagined his silence as compassion, and the words began escaping in a rush—my mother needed help, someone to protect her. 'Please, Father,' I implored, 'tell me how to help her. Please, help us.'

"Behind the screen he was still quiet. Then he said, 'You must come here to seek forgiveness for your own sins, not your parents'. I will pray for your mother and father, as you should. But it is not your place to confess your father's sins.'

"Suddenly I imagined my father confessing to brutalizing my mother, and this priest sending him back home to beat her up again with six Our Fathers on his lips. 'All right,' I answered. 'You want to hear *my* sins. My father is a policeman—you know him well. Every night I pray that someone will kill him and set my mother free. When I'm not praying for that, I wish it with all my heart. Because there's no other hope for my mother—trapped in this marriage and this church, by men who care nothing for her.' Shaking with rage, I placed my lips close to the screen, and whispered, 'Fuck you, Father Vasquez. What's the penance for that?'

"I left before he could tell me."

It was a moment before Carla realized that the tightening in her stomach was not a delayed reaction to the past.

Rushing to the bathroom, she stripped off her clothing, and saw the spotting of blood—the first sign of miscarriage, she knew from her own mother. Filled with apprehension, she dressed again, and went back to the computer.

"I'm sure this is more than enough," she typed for Adam Blaine. "Please keep safe, and know that I think of you often."

She hit the send button, then walked gingerly to her car, driving to her doctor's office without calling ahead.

THREE

Alone in his quarters, Adam stared out at the starkly beautiful mountain ranges, waiting for the call from his case officer.

He had been blunt about his own misgivings. "This Afghan could be a plant," he had told Brett Hollis, "and his POW tip completely bogus. They may be thinking we'll respond like Pavlov's dogs, salivating at the chance to retrieve one of our own—the kind of showy operation that got bin Laden. That would confirm me as CIA. Way more important, they could lure us into Pakistan and expose our assault teams operating against al-Qaeda and the Taliban inside the border. All on the word of an agent we don't know and have never tested."

"All true," Hollis said tersely. "But I need to report this now. If the information is solid, they may be moving Bergdahl soon."

"That's another thing that bothers me," Adam replied. "Maybe everything he says is true—or, at least, he believes that it is. But why hide our guy in a populated village instead of in some cave? This story is perfectly designed to make us rush into a trap, get a bunch of guys killed or captured because we just couldn't stand to wait. Instead of one POW, they could have a whole fucking platoon."

"I'll pass on your reservations," his superior responded glumly. "But this one's not our call."

So Adam waited.

Restless, he read Carla's e-mail for the second time that morning. He was thinking about her too much. For the last decade, he had lived without a past or future, functioning in the moment. Now, against all of his instincts, he had begun to imagine a life beyond Afghanistan. Another reason, perhaps, why he was so wary of the Afghan's story—he wanted to leave here alive, and sensed some new danger at hand. In the curious logic of his job, the fear of death could make him more hesitant and edgy, dulling the reflexes he needed to survive. He should never have risked himself with her.

And yet, in her own way, Carla was also taking chances. Her e-mail made light of this, mocking its supposed self-absorption. But she was giving him a part of herself, so that he might understand her better, and perhaps respond in kind. It was no accident, he suspected, that she had chosen to reveal truths about her family—as Carla surely knew, what haunted Adam resided there, unresolved.

Still, she had written, and he should answer.

Sitting at the computer, he began by describing things he could talk about—the terrain, the people, the semifortress in which he lived. "In a way," he told her, "the walls around us symbolize the pointlessness of our mission. We don't want Afghanistan to be the base for another 9/11. But we won't leave a positive imprint here, any more than foreigners did before us. This isn't a country at all, as we understand that—it's a bunch of tribes. Outside of Kabul, Karzai is a joke—he's the mayor of a city, not the president of anything. Each tribe runs their self-allotted territory, and mountain ranges divide them from each other. So the locals depend on Mullahs and religious leaders, a lot of whom hate the government for taxing them, or for helping us cut down opium production and kill their friends with drones. When we go, we'll leave nothing behind but corpses. Including our own."

This was what he would tell anyone in a moment of honesty, Adam knew. But all it would mean to Carla was that his death, should it happen, would be as meaningless as the rest—a pointless sacrifice to his own personal code. He owed her better, if he could find the words, and Charlie Glazer would say that he owed this to himself.

Like Carla, he had memories of a father—first poisoned by betrayal, then by the searing discovery that Benjamin Blaine was not his father at all. For years, Adam had sealed them in a psychic box he never opened. Now he allowed himself to recall Ben teaching him how to sail the Herreshoff on Menemsha Pond—how patient he was, how different than on land. As if recalling someone else, Adam felt a distant, odd affection for the boy he had been, so trusting of his father, so innocent of all that lay ahead. He could not reach back and protect himself—he had learned to be a fatalist, dealing only with whatever he had to face. But he wished better for Carla's son.

That was the festering core of things—the man who had been the foundation of Adam's life, then changed it irrevocably, had been Carla's lover and the father of this boy. Yet there were good memories, as painful as they were to resurrect, and perhaps it would help her to know this much. After gazing at the screen, lost in time, he wrote, "I know you wonder what happened between Ben and me. That's for another day, if ever, and certainly not for an e-mail. But the way in which your father planted the seeds of acting, without meaning to, reminded me of the things Ben did as a father that were for the better.

"One memory stands out. Baseball was the spectator sport he most loved, and he grew up worshipping Ted Williams, the left fielder for the Red Sox who he insisted was the greatest hitter who ever lived. He told me everything about Williams—how he sacrificed five years of baseball to be a fighter pilot in two wars; how he played to his own exacting standards, and not for the adoration of the fans; above all, the molten, uncompromising integrity with which he drove himself to get the most out of his talent.

"This statistic may not mean anything to you, but seventy years ago Williams became the last man to hit .400—an average of four hits in every ten at bat. That's a stunning athletic feat. I still recall Ben telling me 'to accomplish that by swinging a wooden bat at fastballs coming at ninety miles an hour from sixty feet away, or curveballs that dip just when you're swinging, is incalculably difficult. But on the last day of the season, that's exactly where Williams stood.'

"His manager offered to take him out of the lineup for the final two games, a doubleheader, so that Williams could preserve this record. At this point in the story, Ben would begin speaking in a gruff Ted Williams voice. 'If I don't earn this record on the field,' he'd say, 'it isn't worth a damn, and neither am I.' Then Ben would smile, and deliver the punch line, 'That day Ted Williams got five hits and raised his batting average to .406. No man has done it since.'

"It was a message about integrity and risk, the idea that a man should have of himself. It was how Ben strove to live, and drove me to live."

Adam paused, caught in images he once had cherished. Then he decided to give them to her.

"My own training started early," he went on. "When I was six, Ben began taking me to a baseball diamond in West Tisbury. At first, the bat felt almost too heavy to lift. But Ben pitched slowly, underhand, until I learned to time the contact of bat with ball. Every session got harder; each time, I got better, a little more confident. Finally, he deemed me fit for the ultimate challenge—facing his alter ego, Ace Blaine, the fearsome pitcher for the hated New York Yankees, the Red Sox's bitter rival, the pinstriped scourge of Boston's hope of winning a pennant after forty years of heartache.

"In these imaginary—but to a seven-year-old, very real— contests, it was always the last game of the season, and the Red Sox and Yankees were playing for the pennant Boston fans had craved for decades. Their hopes were all on me. I was the Red Sox's entire lineup, all nine batters, faced with batting against the fearsome Ace, whose swagger and towering ego were a parody of Ben's own. The game was always played at Fenway Park, in front of a rabid crowd; it was always the last of the ninth inning, with the Sox one run down, and the gloating Ace smelling another humiliation for the entire city. And the Sox—meaning me—had to get three hits to load the bases, then drive in two runs to win.

"The fans were going crazy, the broadcaster—also Ben—building tension with each pitch. As for me, I was carrying the burdens of an entire team, and my heart was in my throat."

He could feel it still, Adam realized—heart beating, muscles taut, nerves jangling with apprehension and yet this strange adrenalized exhilaration, the nascent belief that he lived to face down challenges. In high school and college, his apparent nervelessness had awed his teammates. Now it kept him alive.

"Remarkably, I later realized, at times both the broadcaster and the ferocious Ace lost track of the count, allowing four strikes before I hit the ball. For a great athlete, Ace was also an erratic fielder, who sometimes made inexplicable errors when I slapped a pitch right back at him. Every so often, with two outs, Ace would blow a third strike right by me—teaching me that I couldn't always win, would sometimes have to bear up under defeat until the next time. But more often than not, I triumphed, and I learned to thrive on challenge and adversity. And I could see through the veneer of Ace's disappointment and frustration how much that pleased the man I loved more than anyone in the world.

"Later on, I understood that he was training me to be nerveless under pressure, the one who never folded. I still carry that, his gift to me."

Gazing at these words on the screen, Adam felt a tightness in his throat. Before his breach with Ben, he had always cherished this memory; later, he had refused remember it at all. Now it hurt.

Sitting back, he steepled his fingers. Ben, who was not his father, had nearly destroyed Adam's life. His true father, Jack, had killed him. Now Adam concealed this from the world. From Carla.

Still, for her sake, he forced himself to go on.

"There were other people in my family, of course. I knew my mother loved me, and she had a sense of fun then, the desire to do new things. She was at her best when Ben wasn't around, and she could have life the way she wanted it. And Jack—my uncle, then— was a calming presence, much gentler than his brother. As for my own brother, I loved him—Teddy was always good to me, no matter what a nuisance I was, and I admired his talent even then. When it became apparent that he was gay, I was the one who confronted Ben on Ted's behalf.

"But that was later. It was Ben who taught me to love the out- doors, and gave me a model of success—determined, unsparing of himself, unwilling to accept anything less than the best. He showed me how to compete—when I was older, he gave no quarter, and expected none." Here Adam paused, caught by a brief, wrenching image of Jenny Leigh. "I've never forgotten what he told me about how to face the world. 'Don't make excuses for what you've already done, and don't complain if people dislike you for it. Don't whine, fell sorry for yourself, or hide from your mistakes. The past is dead; all you can change is the future. So learn, and move on.'"

Easier to say, Adam thought, when you are the protagonist— although, in the end, it seemed that Ben himself had not quite outrun the damage he had done to Jenny. But Ben had also passed on his test for friendship, developed when, as a young man with no money and no prospects, he had observed the underside of the Chilmark social scene, which he had scathingly labeled, "high school for the rich and vapid."

"'If you want a friend,' he admonished me, 'don't choose the insecure, the envious, or the needy. They're the ones who will sell you out. Those you can trust are confident and secure, men and women who like their lives, and don't have to meet their needs at your expense. So no gossips, back stabbers, or celebrity fuckers. No one who has to tell you who they know, what they own, how impor- tant they are, or whose self-concept depends on the acceptance of others. The only people who can truly care about you are those who are sufficient unto themselves.'"

Here, Adam paused again. In his own experience, this last was largely true. But he wondered now whether Ben was also saying that he, himself, was too flawed to be trusted—or, perhaps, that his own resentments of Adam for existing were too great. Growing up, Adam had seen many of Ben's flaws: too much drinking; Ben's derisiveness and harshness; the whispers about women he never bothered to deny; his growing compulsion to compete with Adam—his own son, or so Adam had thought. But he had never expected Ben's last brutal violation of his trust, because Adam had not known that he was at the heart of his family's bitter secrets. Knowing this was no help now, except to explain what could not be helped. The past, as Ben had told him, was dead

Except that it lived on in the woman he was reaching out for, if only through a letter.

The cell phone on his desk rang, the one he used for secure calls.

"They agree with you," Hollis said without preface. "So far your Afghan's background checks out—what he told you about himself is true, at least as far as it goes. But they want you to test him, ask for more information. Who's in charge of the village, a detailed description of the house he claims our boy is being held in—walls; windows; whether the doors swing in or out. Tell him you want pictures, if possible."

Adam tensed—the information they wanted was necessary to an assault plan. "All that's fine," he answered. "But if this is a trap, they'll be more than glad to give it to us."

"We know that. At the next meeting, you'll give him a surveillance device disguised as a rock, which contains a box that picks up telephone calls or voices and relays them to NSA in the States. You'll have it by this afternoon. Make sure this guy knows the equipment is valuable, then ask him to plant it near where he says they're keeping Bergdahl. If he sells it, then we know he's slippery or a double. If he plants it, then we'll see whether there are any voices we can match to known al-Qaeda people. We may even pick up clues as to whether they're actually hiding someone."

Adam gazed out the window in the direction of Pakistan, the no man's land where any assault force would have to go. "But if he's working for al-Qaeda or the Taliban, and not just a scammer, he might do that just to set us up." He hesitated, thinking as he spoke. "Of course, that would expose the colonel to a lot of danger. If *he's* selling us to the Taliban, he'd have to think his own neck was on the chopping block. So either this Afghan is legitimate, or he's doubling the colonel *and* us."

Hollis laughed softly. "Yeah, that's where we wound up. So get your new friend going, quickly. When he's done, we'll figure out what to do."

Adam hung up, his own misgivings a knot in the pit of his stomach. He wondered how much of this was due to Carla Pacelli, and whether his effectiveness was already compromised. Wanting to live could kill.

Typing a last cursory paragraph, he hit the send button.

Four

Head bent over her unfinished dinner, Carla lapsed into a half-conscious reverie, her thoughts like shadows in the candlelight.

Even in the dregs of her addiction, she had never felt this solitary. She had known in an instant that her spotting might precede a miscarriage—her mother's accounts of the five heartbreaking losses preceding her own birth, a prelude to telling the teenaged Carla what a miracle she was, had darkened every day of her pregnancy. But the rushed visit to her doctor had confirmed her fears.

A trim, pleasant man in his forties, Dr. Dan Stein had an easy way of talking meant to mute his patients' anxieties. But there was no changing his admonition. "You're at risk of a miscarriage," he told her after closing the office door. "But there are things you can do to help—no sex, no strenuous activity, as little moving around as you can manage. If possible, I suggest you go someplace where all you do is loll in bed."

Sitting across from him, Carla thought of her mother, and then her father. "Not possible. And a long plane flight would be risky, wouldn't it?"

The doctor nodded. "Your job is to take this baby as close to term as you can. We're pretty good at dealing with premature births—especially if we can get you to Boston before delivery. In the meanwhile, do you have someone who can do your shopping and drive you to appointments?"

Once again, Carla realized how isolated she was. She had come to Martha's Vineyard to heal herself, not to seek the company of others; with the baby's father dead, and Adam gone, the only people she saw with any frequency were fellow alcoholics at AA meetings. "I can find someone," she said at length.

The doctor considered her a moment. "There's something else," he ventured. "I want to give you an ultrasound and send the results to a specialist."

Carla sat straighter. "Is there some problem with the baby?"

He's not a baby yet, she imagined Stein thinking. "I'm certainly not saying that, Carla. This is a precaution."

"So what is it that worries you?"

The doctor tilted his head slightly—in his body language, Carla had discerned, a signal of unease. "Nothing, yet. Your spotting could simply reflect the difficulties your mother had, back when fetal care wasn't nearly this advanced. But it could also suggest a potential anomaly. For your sake, I'd like to rule that out."

Mute, Carla nodded. Unable to look at him now, she gazed at the tile floor.

"Just take care of yourself," Stein said gently, then felt compelled to add, "If you feel the baby isn't moving, please call me right away."

Carla had made it to the car before she felt tears in her eyes. We'll make it, she had promised her son. No matter what's wrong, I'll take care of you.

Two mornings later, Adam and Hamid headed into the harsh terrain of Afghanistan's southeastern borderlands—parched, tan, and dusty—on a rock-strewn road Adam had chosen over a better one.

With every jolt, Hamid grunted his disapproval. "You're getting soft," Adam told him. "What would your forefathers say?"

Hamid shot him a sour look. "My forefathers," he rejoined, "cut the heads off British soldiers and used them to play polo. Consider yourself fortunate."

Adam grinned at this. "I'm already an organ donor," he said. "But you can take the rest." Lapsing into silence, he acknowledged the bitter truth beneath his companion's jibe: someday soon, like the foreigners before them, the Americans would leave, and those who helped them would be left to face their enemies alone.

They drove on like this for miles, braking to avoid jagged stones that could shred their tires to ribbons. Now and then Hamid spoke of his young son, a gifted athlete, or the baby daughter for whom, unlike many Afghans, he desired a decent education. But that, too, depended on a fate America was unlikely to affect. The thought made Adam pensive. Not for the first time, he reflected that Hamid was his only friend in this place—or, at least, the only person outside his case officer who knew what Adam did. Through his aviator sunglasses, the film of dust on the windshield turned the undulating terrain a deeper brown. He could feel the Glock concealed beneath his Afghan shirt.

"I assume someone is watching us," Hamid remarked. "Friends, for a change."

"Several of them. They'll radio us when they spot our new friend's truck."

At last they saw the huge rock formation Adam had charted, and labored toward it up the side of a steep hill. Hamid pulled up behind it, concealing their SUV from anyone on the road. "Now we wait," Adam said.

Shaded by the rock, Adam and Hamid leaned their backs against it, sharing lukewarm water from a canteen. They did not bother to watch the road; other men, concealed in the hills above, did that for them. "This is the life," Adam said. "Manly work in the great outdoors."

Hamid did not smile. "Can we trust *this* man, I wonder?"

Adam shrugged. "Either way, it'll be a surprise."

The radio on his belt crackled. "Your man is coming," a voice said in Pashto. Leaving Hamid, Adam came out from behind the rock, backpack slung over his shoulder, and saw a white Toyota truck spewing dust on the tortuous road. Knees bent, he edged down the hillside, gun in hand, and stationed himself in the path of the truck. It stopped two feet in front of him.

As Adam had instructed, one of Hakeem's sons was driving. Walking to the driver's side, Adam told him, "Drive one kilometer down the road. Then stop and pull up the hood, like your truck is broken down. Wait there for your father."

Hakeem got out, his seamed face and narrowed eyes betraying no emotion. "Come with me," Adam directed, and led him away from the rock formation that concealed Hamid and their Jeep. They reached a ravine cut into the hillside, invisible from the road, but not to those who watched them from above. Scrambling to the bottom, the two men were alone.

Adam put away his gun. "Thank you for this meeting," he said courteously. "Have you brought me what I need?"

Briefly, the Afghan glanced up at the hills beyond, as though aware they were being watched. Instead of answering, he drew a parcel from inside his shirt and placed it in Adam's hand.

Opening it, Adam studied its contents. A precisely drawn map of a village, specifying the structure where al-Qaeda supposedly held the POW. A credible sketch of the house from various angles, showing the windows and describing its features—apparently, the only door swung inwards. The last document, a photograph that appeared to have been taken surreptitiously, showed two men who looked less like Pakistanis than Saudis, standing in front of the nondescript hut.

Unslinging his backpack, Adam put the parcel inside. "You've done well."

Still silent, the Afghan watched expectantly, waiting for payment. Instead, Adam took what appeared to be a rock from the backpack, and placed it in the Afghan's hand.

Hakeem eyed it suspiciously, then spoke at last. "What is this?"

"American magic," Adam responded. "This rock can hear voices. I want you to place it beside the house where they're holding the American."

The Afghan's gaze flickered. "How will I do that?"

"I leave that to you. But the deed is worth four times what I'm paying you today." He paused for effect. "This rock is also a secret of our government, and extremely valuable. If our enemies knew such a device existed, they'd want it very badly. You cannot lose it."

The Afghan simply stared at him, surveillance device in hand. Adam took a stack of American money from his backpack, bound by rubber bands. "Five thousand dollars," he said. "Count it if you like."

Hakeem inclined his head, as though to acknowledge the size of his reward. "I will do my best," he said in the same laconic manner. Adam tried imagining him as a dinnertime companion.

There was nothing left to do. Hakeem departed first, beginning the long walk to meet his son. Adam waited for a time. Then he climbed out of the ravine, followed by his own misgivings.

FIVE

With first light, Carla went to the deck with a cup of decaffeinated coffee.

At this hour, the world looked fresh and newly made, as awesome as Creation. Fall had long since come—the morning air was crisp and cool, and the light arrived at an angle. But the dewy grass glistened with green, and the ocean emerging from the dawn was a vast, shimmering aqua. Too long preoccupied with herself and the pressures of her career, Carla had become a noticer again, savoring the tranquil beauty that had been Adam's birthright on this island, whatever else he had inherited.

She thought again of his e-mail, a welcome distraction from her worries for the child she carried. Recalling his description of Ben, she imagined the boy he had been before time and circumstance had hardened him. Then her thoughts returned to the dangers facing her own son.

The waiting felt unbearable. She had never lived well with uncertainty—a residue, no doubt, of too many nights spent in her darkened bedroom, fearing the sound of her father's return. Since her visit to the doctor, she had not been to an AA meeting, and an ineradicable part of her craved the oblivion that alcohol could bring her, numbing her anxieties. At this moment, she felt that only her child, the source of these fears, stood between her and the reckless woman who had spiraled downward in a mindless, bottomless dark. It scared her to know how much she depended on a being who—should he live—was entitled to depend on her completely, the way she could never depend on her mother and father. Even now, she was everything to him. But without this child who would *she* be?

Instinctively, she fingered her mother's rosary beads, as cool as sand pebbles in the chill sea air.

Her mother had visited her at Betty Ford, mystified by what Carla had no heart to explain. All Mary Margaret Pacelli could do was press these beads into her daughter's hands—as though acknowledging, as she always had, her own limitations in the face of her husband's rages, Carla's self-destruction. Carla had found the gesture at once sad and pointless: a melancholy echo of a stunted past, a faith Carla had shed in her angry haste to leave it all behind. In her mind, women who prayed the rosary were gnarled old crones or, like her mother, had found their lives too overwhelming to cope. But now Carla was one of them. And this morning these beads, and the fragments of prayer they summoned, were all she seemed to have.

At once, Carla rebuked herself—she had yet to ask for help. Her sponsor was recording a new album in Los Angeles, and she barely knew the others at AA. Her food was running low, and someone should expect a call were she seized with new contractions. But she could always call 911, she had rationalized—the reflex of a loner, who believed that to speak her fears to a stranger would make them come true.

She closed her eyes, aware that her prayers for Adam and her son were an inversion of her childhood hopes that her father would perish. Her prayers felt better now. The beads in her hand were somehow reassuring, the words more comforting.

"Hail Mary, full of grace. Blessed are thou among women, and blessed is the fruit of thy womb . . ."

Before her downfall, repeating this would have aroused something she still felt deeply—anger at the male hierarchy of the church, the autocracy of men insulated from life, and the lives of women, by their own narrow holiness. Instead, she focused on the visit of the young, pregnant Mary to her older cousin Elizabeth, blessed with a surprising gift of her own pregnancy. These last weeks, Carla had experienced this same mystery, strange and secret and inexplicable to others, communing in silence with her invisible child, unknown to everyone else but so palpable to her. Which was why her mother had named her miraculous daughter Carla Elizabeth Pacelli.

Lost in the rosary, she imagined the stirring of the baby inside her, still alive. It took a moment to recognize the hollow but very real sound echoing through the guesthouse, a fist knocking on her door. For an irrational moment, she imagined that it was Adam Blaine, returned in answer to her prayers.

Rising gingerly, she walked through the house and opened the door. Framed in the morning light was a tall, pale man in his late thirties, slender yet sinewy, with black curly hair, a full mouth, and a thin, sensitive face. Though they were different in appearance, even had she not glimpsed him at the courthouse Carla would have known that he was Adam's brother. In her surprise, she thought Teddy a more handsome version of Adam's father, Jack. Then she reminded herself that Teddy still believed that Adam was Ben's son.

In momentary silence, they studied each other. Then she said, "You're Adam's brother. The artist."

The hint of a bleak smile touched one corner of Teddy's mouth. "The 'gay artist,' our father used to call me. The first word damned the second. Anyhow, Adam asked me to check in with you. To see if there's anything you need."

Even had Teddy not alluded to his bitter resentment of Benjamin Blaine, his tone captured the oddity of their circumstances. Carla hesitated, then said, "Why don't you come in."

Teddy's eyebrows shot up. "You sure? If you're like half the people on this island, which I expect you are, you still think I pushed him off the cliff. And unlike a lot of them, no doubt you're unhappy with me for it—enough to wish me a life in prison. When it comes to selecting good Samaritans, Adam has peculiar tastes."

Not for the first time, Carla suspected that Adam knew much more about Ben's death than he was willing to say—perhaps that the man in front of her was guilty of murder. Tartly, she answered, "I'm willing to assume you've bagged your quota for the year. In any event, I'm sure I'm not your favorite person."

"You weren't," he responded bluntly. "But Adam's my brother, and I promised him. In his estimate, you did us all a good turn when you didn't need to. So I'm willing to leave hating you to my mother."

Though his candor was unsettling, there was something about it Carla found bracing. "Come on in," she said, and waved him to the couch where, only weeks before, Adam had spent the night. The juxtaposition felt strange—as she settled back into a chair, Carla noticed him glancing at her stomach, swelling beneath her sweater.

He leaned forward a little, openly curious, his tone neutral. "It's all pretty strange, I have to say. I get it about you and our father—no surprises there. But you and Adam is where my imagination begins to flag."

Even his most acidic comments, Carla was noticing, had a trace of deflective humor—perhaps the weapon of a man who, though in different ways than Adam, had been hurt early in life. With a dryness of her own, she replied. "Don't let your imagination run wild— I'm pregnant, after all. I think your brother just likes babies. Never too late to discover your inner Mr. Rogers."

To Carla, her own remark sounded cheap and tinny. Before Teddy could respond, she amended, "Truthfully, I think he identifies with this baby. As though he wants things to turn out better for him than he thinks it did for the two of you."

"Wouldn't be hard," Teddy said more softly. "Even I can wish that much."

In her tenuous emotional state, Carla found that even this modest kindness caused her eyes to dampen before she looked away. "What is it?" Adam's brother asked.

Some impulse she could not name caused Carla to respond. "The doctor tells me I may miscarry. I'm sure that doesn't strike you as a tragedy. It certainly wouldn't disappoint your mother."

Teddy simply studied her. "Then why are you telling me this?"

"I really don't know. Maybe because you're Adam's brother and there's no one else to tell." She steadied her voice. "I'm not supposed to do very much, including shopping and errands."

Teddy settled his lanky frame back into the couch, regarding her with a quizzical look. "If you're asking me to shop for groceries, no worries. I shop for myself anyhow. Both you and I seem to have lost our partners."

Despite the arid allusion to Ben's death, Carla felt a rush of gratitude. "If you don't mind, I can give you money and a shopping list."

"We can sort out the money later," Teddy responded. "Thanks to you, I'll have money of my own—despite my father's best intentions." He paused for a moment. "Just out of curiosity, how did you put up with him? Was there someone inside there I didn't know?"

The sardonic question, Carla guessed, expressed the hurt of a child denied a father's love—which even adulthood, she knew well, could never quite erase. But she could not give him a truthful answer: that Clarice Blaine's infidelity had left Ben with grudges of his own, and Teddy with a brother who was also his cousin. "For me there was," she answered simply.

Teddy frowned, thwarted in any hope of understanding. "Anyhow, I'm happy enough to help you, for Adam's sake. God knows he's complicated, too, but I can't imagine a better brother. So I'll do whatever you need me to."

Beneath this offhand gesture, Carla sensed, lurked the decent man Adam had described. "Adam feels the same about you," she told him.

Teddy hesitated. "Do you hear from him?"

"Yes."

"Then maybe you know what he's doing over there."

Once again, Carla reflected that she had been drawn into the web of evasions among the Blaines. "Not really," she replied. "As you may have noticed, your brother can be remarkably uninformative. But he seems to think he's running a fool's errand. I find myself hoping that he'll find another line of work."

"We both hope. He doesn't need to keep retracing our father's reckless footsteps. No offense meant."

"None taken," Carla said at once. But his careless remark was another reminder, if she needed one, of all that stood between her and Adam Blaine. "About my pregnancy," she added, "Please don't tell Adam. He's got enough to worry about as it is."

Clearly uncomfortable, Teddy stood. "Fair enough. Make me a grocery list, and I'll give you my phone number. In case you ever need me."

In silence, Carla went to the kitchen and scribbled out a list, then took down Teddy's number. When she gave it to him, he turned and headed for the door.

Pausing there, he said, "I'll drop these off this afternoon. If no one answers, I'll leave them by the door." On his way out, he turned again. "I'm serious about calling me. And good luck with the kid. He's our brother, after all."

And then he was gone, leaving Carla torn between relief and all the questions she could never erase.

SIX

Ten days later, Hamid and Adam were summoned to Kabul.

Sitting in the back of a noisy transport plane, the translator had asked Adam for an explanation. Adam told him less than he knew, which was little enough. "Your man planted the device," Brett Hollis had reported to him. "The voice of one of the Arabs guarding the house matches that of a known al-Qaeda operative, and his maps coincide with the area in western Pakistan where we think the rest of them are hiding. If this is a plant, whoever dreamed it up is taking a lot of chances with his people—and hanging Colonel Rehman and his Afghan friends out to dry. So we have to consider the probability that your new agent and his information are good. Or at least, as you say, that he believes it."

Adam still felt edgy. "What should I do with the Afghan?"

"Pay him. Then you and Hamid are meeting me in Kabul."

Adam tried to imagine why, but did not ask. And so the last part of his account to Hamid had been truthful—he had no idea what Hollis wanted with either of them. Now they sat outside Hollis's office in the American Embassy, waiting to find out.

Trying to keep his mind blank, Adam found himself imagining Carla. It was still early morning on Martha's Vineyard—she would be sleeping now. Her e-mails had said little about her pregnancy, so perhaps her worries had come to nothing. Another month or two, he guessed, and the baby would be safe for delivery.

Interrupting his thoughts, Hollis emerged from his office. He shook hands with Hamid, at once warm and brisk, assuring him that he would be briefed shortly. And then he motioned Adam inside his office and closed the door behind them.

The room was as Adam remembered it, windowless and sterile, like a command post in the bowels of a bunker. Though in his early forties, Hollis looked older and wearier than when Adam last had seen him, and the first sign of a belly showed over his khaki pants. The way he ran his fingers through his thinning brown hair struck Adam as a sign of nervousness, not distraction; the somber speculative look he gave Adam was too focused for that. "Keeping fit, I can see. That's one of us."

Adam shrugged. "The compound has treadmills and stationary bikes, so I don't have to jog among the natives. What a joke of a death that would be."

To Adam's surprise, the casual remark induced a brief silence. Hollis regarded him with a studied lack of expression. Then he said, "You've been given an assignment from on high. 'A mission for your sins,' to quote *Apocalypse Now*."

Adam felt a tug of apprehension. As statement, not question, he said, "They've planned a rescue mission. Inside Pakistan."

"Yep. One the Pakistanis know nothing about. You know how much we trust their security services. There's something about harboring bin Laden which makes our overlords hold a grudge." Hollis paused for questions, then saw that Adam would ask none. "Among the other things the Pakistanis aren't supposed to know is that we have a forward operating base near where they're supposedly holding our POW. A targeting team, made up of specialists with spectrum scanners to transmit signals and voices back to NSA, plus special ops guys to call in a drone or go out and kill any Taliban or al-Qaeda we identify. Whatever works best. With the right preparation, they'll go in and snatch Bowe Bergdahl."

"Risky. And once you send them out, your forward operating post is blown."

Hollis grimaced. "You know the reasons. We place a high priority on POWs—no leaving our boys behind, and all of that. By bringing this guy back alive, we prove our loyalty; show the bad guys that we're better than they are; boost the morale of the American public; and, not coincidentally, bolster our own reputation. Killing bin Laden did a lot for us, and this would polish that particular apple." Studying Adam's expression, his case officer added, "We're all aware of the trade-offs, Adam. We risk losing a lot of brave and highly trained guys to free a single army grunt. We're not even sure how he got his ass captured. But once he did, he took on a value all his own."

Hollis, Adam realized, was talking more than usual. Bluntly, he said, "You didn't call me in to explain the moral peculiarities of this particular trade-off. Let alone to tell me secrets I don't need to know. So what's my job here?"

Briefly, Hollis puffed his cheeks. "They'll go in after him at night. Your job is to facilitate the assault."

Adam willed himself to feel nothing. "How, exactly?"

"Two nights from now, you and a guy from Seal Team 6 will cross the Pakistani border. Using a GPS, you'll drive up into the mountains through some pretty bad terrain and locate the forward operating base. They're holding a special piece of equipment— another 'rock,' this one about the size of a hockey puck. Concealed inside is an infrared beacon that transmits signals to the special ops people, pinpointing its precise location. Essential equipment to a night raid in hostile territory the Taliban and al-Qaeda know better than we do."

Here Hollis paused again, as though hoping for another question. Through an act of will, Adam asked none. He tried to feel as little emotion as he showed.

"Using night observation equipment," Hollis went on, "you'll move down into the village. You'll dress in local clothing to create a silhouette that appears innocuous to anyone who notices you, adopting the posture, gait, and mannerisms of local people—maybe carry a walking stick to suggest you're a shepherd or an old man. Concealed beneath your shirt will be the beacon, a multiband radio attached to an ear and mouthpiece and, of course, body armor and a weapon.

"Once you're there, you're to find the target house without being seen by the guards, and plant the infrared beacon beneath a window. The targeting team will provide overwatch, monitoring you through their own night observation devices, ready to respond with sniper fire if you report trouble through the radio. But they won't expose themselves unless you call them in." Hollis's tone became confident and reassuring. "If all goes well, you'll get in and out. The next night our team goes in, and gets our POW out of there— followed by kudos for all. Questions?"

"None worth asking."

His case officer's chest moved in what might have been an inaudible sigh. "No choice but to do this, and you're right for the job. We can't trust an Afghan or Pakistani—they might give up the equipment, or sell out the forward operating base. Fuck this up, and we lose the beacon; our base; an entire Delta Force assault team; and, more's the pity, the humble soldier we're trying to bring home to mom and dad. You're fluent in the language, and you've got the combat and navigational skills to pull this off." Hollis leaned forward, his voice soft and flat. "Bottom line, people at the highest level—meaning the president—are watching. We can't screw this up by sending the wrong guy."

Better to get the right guy killed, Adam thought but did not say. Then he realized that the right guy—the man he had become before meeting Carla Pacelli—might not have thought this at all. "It's what I signed up for," he replied. "But why call in Hamid if you're worried about Afghans? He's got a wife and kids."

The latent fatalism of the inquiry caused Hollis to give an arid smile. "Odds are they'll be seeing him again. We're not telling him a lot, and he'll be dropping out before you get to Pakistan. And the guy who's crossing with you enjoys this kind of thing."

SEVEN

Sitting down at her computer, Carla felt awkward—her center of gravity had relocated to her belly and her body, swollen by water weight, seemed to have been taken over by some alien force. But that force was her son, and this morning she had felt him stir inside her. Once her profession had made her near obsessive in her pursuit of fitness and litheness of movement. Now she could smile at herself, this awkward creature, happy at any sign of her baby's health. To become a mother was by far the most important supporting role of her all too self-focused life.

But it was that life about which Adam Blaine was curious. "I know you were drawn to acting," he had written. "In some ways, all of us are actors. To my detriment, I've spent the last decade playing different parts, often within minutes of each other. But few of us become famous for it."

So he was willing to acknowledge this, Carla thought—at least in a letter. To the extent she could trust herself, every instinct she possessed told her that at heart Adam was a good and compassionate man. But she wondered whether his layers of self-protection, all the scar tissue she did not fully understand, were so deep that he could never peel them away.

Still, his last e-mail suggested depths of feeling that he wanted to express, at least at a safe distance. Safe for her, as well—with painful honesty, she acknowledged that she was writing a man she might never see again. "So tell me about your career," he had written. "The parts they left out of *People Magazine*." For both their sakes, she would try to do that.

"Let me start with the obvious," she typed. "I craved acting so deeply because it allowed me to escape. The roles I loved most were the furthest from my own reality. For a couple of hours I was in another place—there, not here—every part of me vibrating with this imaginary person who inhabited me completely. The Carla Pacelli people responded to was a vessel who allowed the real Carla to forget herself. Until the only self I knew was the woman hell-bent on gobbling up chances to become someone else.

"I got a scholarship to UCLA to study theater. No one in my class worked harder—as I think about it now, I was running for my life. Even my minor, psychology, was—or so I told myself—another way of understanding why imaginary people were the way they were. Another tool that allowed me to escape the fears of the child, the nights I woke up believing I still heard my mother's cries as my father's hand cracked against her face."

Carla stopped here, remembering Ben's description of his own father's brutality to his mother. With surprising gentleness, he had told her, "At least when I turned sixteen, I was able to beat him to a pulp. All you could do is get away, any way you could. And now you feel bad about it. In Vietnam, we called that survivor's guilt."

This was true, Carla had realized. The nights she described to Adam had left a residue of shame—the beatings were still real, she knew, and all Carla had accomplished was to leave her mother behind. But she could not explain to Adam that Ben, whom he hated, had allowed her, at least partially, to forgive herself.

Instead, she wrote, "I'm sure this sounds melodramatic. It probably is. But the isolation of an only child, taught to hide her family's shame, increased my sense of being alone. With other people, I was able to conceal that by becoming what I might've described as a 'vivacious social drinker.' An incipient drunk, in other words, who also dabbled in cocaine. But my driving need for theater kept me from going over the edge.

"When I graduated from college, I moved as far away from San Francisco as I could—to New York, a magnet for any would-be stage actor. I was a walking cliché: I lived in walk-ups with people I barely knew, did temp work or waited tables and, believe it or not, filled in as a singing waitress while a roommate with a better voice worked off-Broadway. So glad you weren't there." Carla smiled at this—in retrospect, she had been truly awful. "But my basic routine was get up at five a.m.; hang out in the Equity line at Times Square in whatever crummy weather, waiting to sign up for auditions; race off for a morning's worth of secretarial work; come back for a one or two-minute audition; then pray for a call back while I ran off to hustle tips as a cocktail waitress.

"I had no agent, of course. Still, I landed a few roles in new plays way, way, off-Broadway. All that did was feed my hunger and desperation. 'Why not me?' the inner Carla kept crying out. No one seemed to hear me. And another voice kept telling me that I lacked that resonance that would leave casting directors as slack-jawed as I needed them to be."

This account of her inner voice, Carla well knew, was less than fully honest. But recalling the real turning point still made her burn with shame.

Among her means of scraping together cash had been modeling. She refused to do lingerie ads, having heard from other young women stories of scarifying indignities. Instead, she showed up at a catalog company that also featured sportswear. The man in charge of selecting models—a slick, slender Italian with the face of a handsome ferret—told her to change into some swimsuits in a large, bare room with a black square she quickly realized was a one-way window. But the job paid a thousand dollars if the guy chose her, and her rent was due next week.

The man came out again—to her further shame, she no longer recalled his name—while a photographer took pictures. Then he praised her "energy of beauty," and asked her out to lunch.

Carla had a callback for a bit part in two hours, and part of her knew better than to accept. But she smiled and said yes—after all, she might charm this guy into giving her the job. And lunch turned out to be surprisingly pleasant. The man was easy, yet authoritative, possessed of a certain practiced charm, asking questions about her life with seeming interest, smiling or laughing at her clever and utterly inauthentic answers. They drank two bottles of wine.

After lunch, he invited her back to his office—to sign a contract, she tried imagining. Instead, he offered her cocaine. Both high and dazed, Carla bent over his desk to snort a second line of powder. As she did, she felt the man reaching beneath her dress. Stunned, she realized that his finger was inside her, then his avid hands were pulling down her panties. In a tight voice, he said, "You want this, don't you?"

In something like a fever dream, she remembered glimpsing her mother after a beating, tears staining her face as Carl Pacelli pushed her against the kitchen wall and entered her from behind. Neither parent knew what she had seen. But now, as a stranger pushed inside her, she realized he evoked her father, and heard herself whisper, "Yes."

He came swiftly, then watched in silence as she arranged herself, unable to meet his eyes. "I've hired someone else," he said. It was all she could do to raise her head and walk out the door, a pathetic pantomime of pride.

Afterward, filled with nausea and self-disgust, Carla had recoiled from the memory of her mother's face as her tormentor took her from behind, a shattered yet stoic mask, and wondered whether she had sought her own humiliation at the hands of this Italian stranger. But the next day, and for a time after, she stopped using alcohol or drugs. Within a month, she had applied to the master in fine arts program at NYU.

To Adam, she wrote simply, "So I applied to graduate school."

The rest was nothing for a letter. The story, if she ever told it, would require more love and trust than she had ever felt with anyone.

"To my surprise," she continued, "I was awarded a full scholarship at NYU. It was like an answer to the prayers I no longer said. I could live and breathe theater, part of a golden group of men and women whose talent uplifted and inspired me. For the first time, I felt close to other people, a group whose ambitions I hoped would be realized with my own. I started liking myself better. And I became good—really good."

Carla found herself typing faster, spurred by remembered energy. "NYU was a great school, with a buoyant and brilliant faculty that turned out serious actors. I did summer theater, got my best reviews anywhere, and won a good part in *Equus*. I found an agent—not a big name, but a hardworking woman who believed in me. She pushed me to stick out my three years of school—I was not only beautiful, she assured me, but I could have a real career, on stage as well as in film. 'I only make money if you do,' she told me. 'The day our business takes me seriously is the day you become a major star. We're each other's get out of jail card.' And pretty soon she'd found a first-rate casting director who started paying attention to me.

"The time I wasn't in school or learning roles I spent with my friends. We catered parties to make money; did a little cocaine; sweated through exercise classes to stay in shape. Sometimes at pool parties in the Hamptons, coke-addled guests invited the caterers to jump in with them—the ones with the sleekest bodies—leaving the most light-fingered of us to scrounge leftovers for the rest. I went out with guys, but nothing serious—I was too busy, I told myself, and that was true enough. For the last two years of school I lived with a girlfriend in a fifth floor brick walk-up in the West Village, and the man both of us saw most was the masturbator in the next building. Par for the course, my roommate assured me—there was a pervert for every block in Manhattan.

"Day after day, I dedicated myself to acting. I never wanted to be a tabloid personality or a red-carpet actress. I wanted to stretch myself in the most challenging parts, to play them with nuance and humanity. I learned my plays cold, then experimented with the best way to deliver each line. I was always on time for work, and supportive of the other actors, knowing we could make each other better. My career was going to be about the craft, not the money. I knew very well about the harsh equation for actresses—career dwindling as they age, scratching for bit parts as the mother of some guy barely younger than they were. I was obsessed with becoming that rare, exceptional woman who was good enough to last.

"And then, at twenty-seven, it started to happen."

Stretching to rest her back, Carla felt a sharp, sudden pain, the baby kicking her stomach. She touched the place where this happened, as if to answer him. It took a moment for her to recall the state of mind she described to Adam.

"It was just after graduation, and the part was in a small independent film. But I had the lead—a beautiful but destructive young woman who can't give or receive love, and ends up sabotaging her own happiness." Pensive, she felt her typing slow. "I was, perhaps, too good. I seemed to know the role from the inside out.

"When they opened the film at Sundance, I was praised for the 'frightening authenticity' of my portrayal. Truth to tell, I even scared *myself* at little. But I understood something else. As confident as I was on stage, my first and greatest love, my face registered in close-ups. What I felt wasn't vanity, but a cool, knowing appraisal of the woman other people saw."

Pausing, she considered this, a fateful pivot in her own life. "So I expected change," she went on. "But not something so profoundly different and, beneath the surface, so potentially corrosive.

"A television executive was in the audience at Sundance. A month later, he asked my agent if I'd audition for the pilot of a proposed series for NBC. Your all-time favorite television program," she added dryly, "the grittily authentic dramatic landmark, *Deep Cover*. A virtual documentary of the life of an undercover espionage agent, complete with constantly shifting identities, luxurious hotel suites in pseudo-European settings, and the ultimate weapon of any well-trained operative—cleavage. Acting, I was assured, was also desirable.

"It was so far from what I had in mind that I told Betsy—my agent—I didn't see the point. But there was no harm in doing it, she argued—it was good exposure, and I probably wouldn't get the part. She probably knew better all along. I was an actor, not a model— when I did the screen test, I absolutely nailed it. They wanted sex appeal: what they got, the producer told me, was an actress who popped through the screen. I was perfect for playing a tough girl, he told me, and that was certainly right. I *was* one. Or so I thought.

"Anyhow, I had to decide. The role would put me on the map, and Betsy with it. I could see how much she wanted this, though she spelled out the pros and cons as fairly as she could. To carry the show, they needed an actress with physical agility and sex appeal: the 'almost feral complexity' I brought to it (her words, not mine) would stamp the role as my own. They'd pay me a lot less than a bigger name—$10,000 a show to start, roughly a quarter million if the show was green-lit for an entire season—which still was way more money than I'd ever seen. If the series flopped, I wouldn't lose much—I was more of a stage actress, after all. And if the show took off, I'd be a household name, sought for the female lead in plays or movies whenever I was on hiatus.

"Still, the downside of success was plain enough. A TV series would be a big diversion of energy from serious acting. Worse, they wanted a seven-year commitment, albeit with ever-escalating money. I'd have to move to LA, leaving my friends behind, for a 24/7 immersion in a part that didn't speak to my soul and threatened to make me feel like a hamster on a wheel. And I'd be a celebrity, suddenly recognizable in ways I never wanted. For me, acting was about hiding out, the polar opposite of being famous. With an almost chilling premonition, I knew that signing on would be bad for me.

"But I was a blue-collar girl, really, and I felt guilty sneering at a chance other actresses would kill for. And for years, I'd just been scraping by. I told myself that the money would buy me the security later on, to do the parts I wanted to, not snatch at anything to pay the rent. And too many good actors, I knew too well, went broke and wound up selling real estate. So I took the role, hoping in the deepest part of me that the show would tank."

Her fingers stopped. "Your mother," she informed her stomach, "was delusional." Then she continued typing.

"You know the rest, Adam—you once admitted to watching me on Monday nights. The show was the big new hit of the season, especially among our target audience, guys your age. So thanks a bunch." She grimaced at the line, then added swiftly, "Truth to tell, mea culpa. I was too good an actress not to give it everything I had. The Emmy nomination that followed lulled me into thinking I'd done the right thing. Sure enough, offers started pouring in for me to do movies over the summer break.

"But in real life, I began playing the hamster. The schedule was a killer. Six days a week I'd get up at four, go to hair and makeup for an hour and a half—I was the girl, after all—and then act in virtually every scene. Fifteen or sixteen hours later, they drove me 'home' in a limousine to a rented place in Bel Air, filled with art and furniture someone else had chosen for me.

"During breaks I checked in with my 'people.' Suddenly I had a lot of them—Betsy; a business manager to look out for my money; the accountant he'd hired to help; a publicist; an assistant to keep my schedule and fend off calls; a personal trainer. Thanks to my manager, I suddenly had my own production company, with people to run it. Most of them were on commission; the rest on salary. It was like a parody of success from a Hollywood movie about Hollywood—later on, when I pieced it all together, I realized I was keeping about 25% of what I made. But I was too busy and too important to do the counting myself. Too busy, even to grasp how lonely I was.

"The only people I saw regularly were on the show—actors, writers, the directors and the crew—or the people I was paying to look after things. Guys were coming out of nowhere, wanting to date me, but I had no time. Every now and then I'd coke up to get myself through some late-night party." She closed her eyes, feeling again the vertiginous rush of change. "I became this little industry—posing for the cover of magazines, endorsing a line of makeup. All, my manager assured me, to enhance my income and career.

"The reality crept over me by increments. Two seasons later, I was getting $150,000 an episode, about $3 million a year. But the series had defined me. Other actresses were getting roles I wanted but had no time to pursue. The plots grew more out-landish, the role numbingly the same—to amuse myself, I started doing accents I'd learned at NYU, a mockery of the serious work I'd trained to do. I was under more pressure to stay beautiful and slender; the cleavage grew ever deeper. Now and then I'd imagine adopting a child."

Which omitted, Carla acknowledged to herself, the crucial sub-ject of men. But she was not ready to broach this to Adam; it was too personal, and who knew if he really cared. And if he did, that would lead inevitably to the incendiary subject of Benjamin Blaine.

"Somehow, I'd imagined success would help me to discover the 'real' Carla Pacelli. But there *was* no real me. The one truly authen-tic thing about me—my passion for the craft—was crumbling.

"Even if you didn't already know it, you could guess the rest—another cautionary tale from lotus land lacking even the virtue of originality. I was exhausted, mentally and, I suppose, spiritually. So I rationalized that alcohol would calm me down, and that a little coke in my trailer would keep me going. After a while, I threw in Valium to help me sleep.

"At first, the producers pretended not to notice; whatever kept me going was fine. But when I started getting shaky on the set, over-acting or blowing my lines, they wrote in a secondary role for a very pretty and aggressive younger actress, playing my protégé and rival. If anything, the fact that she couldn't act much deepened my insecurity and self-contempt. When I could stand myself no longer, I started going to more parties. I'd found a new role—Carla Pacelli, the television star, acting out a downward spiral. The woman you saw in that mug shot, headed for Betty Ford."

She stopped to read her own words. "Again, I worry that so much of this is self-indulgent, a woman with too little to say answering questions you never asked. But your question about my career inevitably raises why it ended. And what I faced when the dreamscape turned real.

"The money vanished, too. My business manager, it transpired, had told me just enough to keep me from questioning where my income was going—to line his pockets, and that of the eminent Ponzi scheme operator who'd conned him. A tsunami of dishonesty and greed that stung a number of his show business clients."

What seared her, Carla thought now, was her own carelessness—as though riches were her due, and would keep on coming endlessly. It took a real lack of character, she reckoned, for a girl who had no money to become a women who took it for granted. But that led Carla to the void within her.

"Coming to Martha's Vineyard was another escape, it's true. But what I really wanted was peace, more time to face hard truths with a certain merciless clarity. I'd been running all my life, and what I finally learned was that you take your demons, or your emptiness, everywhere you go.

"Dorothy Parker once wrote that 'hell is other people.' But I'd made my own hell, and the men and women I encountered at Betty Ford wound up enriching my life. As I get stronger, I'll reach out to friends I valued in the past and lost track of. Perhaps I can even help my mother, as much as she cares to be helped. But no other person, not even this child, can fill the empty spaces, or change someone who doesn't want to change.

"It seems simple, I know. But it took me thirty-three years to understand that there is no magic that can transform you. Only honesty and, I hope, a certain level of compassion. I'm not sure I'll ever forgive my father. He's responsible for all the damage he did, to my mother and to me. But I also know that none of us are Adam and Eve. Our parents start as children; the sins they practice aren't original."

Including Benjamin Blaine, she thought but did not write.

Motionless, she reflected for an indeterminate time—lost to her—before she went on. "This may seem presumptuous," she concluded. "Perhaps it's instinct; the sense of one being for another she doesn't truly know. But, however obviously different we may be, I think some common themes may permeate our lives. And you've shown me more grace and understanding than I had any reason to expect. So I guess what I'm trying to do is open up things between us. For whatever that means, and for whatever good it does.

"Please know that I'm thinking of you."

She stopped there, unwilling to erase the last paragraph, yet troubled by her own confusion. What she was raising was a possibility of a more intimate relationship, though it was hard to imagine how that could be—she was an alcoholic who had failed in her only career, pregnant with Ben's child, and but for his troubling death and poisonous will they would not have met at all. A real prize, no doubt, especially for Adam Blaine. But she had written these last words, and could not bring herself to retract them.

Before, she had chosen men who could never meet her needs—whatever they were—and so could always imagine, and even desire, the end of a relationship. And acting, and all the issues surrounding her father, had kept romance at bay. Her first relationship in recovery had been with Benjamin Blaine. Though she valued his strength, and his support, she had known it could not last—first, there was his marriage, flawed though it was; later, there was the inevitable fact that the cancer in his brain would kill him. However sad, an end. Just as Afghanistan might be the end of Adam Blaine. Yet she prayed this would not be so, and knew that these prayers were not entirely selfless.

Perhaps she could not disentangle this impulse from Ben himself. As a father, Ben had damaged Adam, as he himself was damaged. Did she have some mystical, perhaps neurotic belief that she could reach back in time, salvaging Adam as no one could salvage Ben? Or did their mutual entwinement with Benjamin Blaine preordain another ending and, yet again, eliminate the emotional risk to a woman who might never learn to trust?

Hand resting on her stomach, she spoke to her son.

"I hate to tell you, sweetheart, but your brain-addled mom still has a ways to go. So I hope you can bear with me. But if it's any incentive to get yourself born, even though we haven't met yet, you may be the only man I've ever really loved."

The telephone rang.

Strangely apprehensive, she answered it, "This is Dr. Stein," he told her in a somber tone. "I'd like you to come in."

EIGHT

The next morning, Adam and his new team collected a Toyota SUV and began the long drive from Kabul to Khost, a frontier town near the Pakistan border.

There were four of them: Hamid, who drove; Philip Rotner, a saturnine and burly special forces medic; and Steve Branch, the Navy Seal who would go with Adam into Pakistan. Less than twenty-four hours ago, Adam had not known that Rotner or Branch existed, or that the fate of the POW would implicate his own. Now he thought of Benjamin Blaine. "All of us," he had told Adam, "live five seconds, or five feet, from tragedy. But most people never learn that."

Ben had meant this to contrast the obliviousness with which normal men meandered through existence—dodging random chance while never perceiving that tragedy lies in ambush—with his own venturesome and often dangerous life: combat heroism in Vietnam; covering wars and savagery for his novels. He savored each day more, Ben had argued, because he never forgot its perils. Ten years ago, Adam, too, had assumed these risks and, with them, a certain fatalism. But now, thinking of Carla, he envied the "sheep"—as Ben had called them—the heedlessness they thought to be security.

He wondered if his companions entertained such thoughts. When they had met the afternoon before, his clearest impression had been of competence and resolve. Gathering their weapons, supplies and strike rations, they had reviewed their plans with a phlegmatic air that, in the case of Branch, did not quite conceal his adrenalized anticipation of a mission that was his reason for being. Now, Branch sat in the rear with Adam, a lean, sandy-haired man with sculpted features and narrow blue-gray eyes that were sharp at their edges, as if a youth spent hunting in rural Alabama—scanning bushes for deer, or the sky for birds—had changed their shape and function.

Adam, too, had grown up outdoors. But when he refused to join his father in, as Adam had put it, "murdering Bambi's mother," Ben had rejoined that Adam was too much like his *own* mother. Like his real father, Adam supposed Ben had meant. Jack had despised hunting—to Adam's knowledge, the only life Jack had ever taken was his brother's.

Enough, Adam rebuked himself. The past or future had no place here. He willed himself to feel the blank resolve he read on Branch's face.

Laconically, the two men talked about their recent past. Branch related his regrets about missing out on the bin Laden raid, remarking, "I hear Osama's porn collection redefined the term 'double-standard.'" In turn, Adam gave an account of his role as dispenser of Viagra to a tribal chief. "A true hearts and minds operation," Branch observed. Neither man ceased his careful survey of the rugged foothills outside. Under Adam's shirt was a Glock 19 with a threaded barrel and flash suppressor; on the belt that secured its holster was a straight blade knife. Beneath the seat was an AK-47.

The SUV was ordinary civilian gear—special features like black-out windows would only draw attention. In the glove compartment cards bearing the CBS logo—of which the network was wholly unaware—identified them as "logistics producers" for CBS News.

If they were stopped, Hamid would speak for them, concealing that the others were fluent in the two major regional dialects. Their first order of business, by no means assured, was to position themselves near the border.

Angling toward the southeast, they began the climb up and through the difficult mountain passes. In late fall, the lower areas still had temperate weather, but as the SUV labored ever higher there was snow on the ground. Soon they stopped to put on snow tires; as the road grew narrower the strain showed on Hamid's neck and shoulders. The closest comparison, Adam thought, was driving through Colorado at 12,000 feet on a single-lane road. But the greater threat was Pasha Khan, a casually vicious warlord whose minions ran drugs, guns, and whatever contraband they could smuggle through these passes. They did not like strangers, much less Americans.

On the left, the ravine became sheer. Grunting, Hamid strained to negotiate a vertiginous curve. With barely a foot between the tires and a hundred yard drop, he braked so abruptly that Adam tensed in anticipation of a free fall.

The car crunched to a stop inches from the cliff. Filling their windshield were three bearded Afghans with rifles at their hips. Adam saw no vehicle—it was as if they had dropped from the moon. As though he were at a toll booth, Hamid rolled down the window and greeted them in Pashto. The men did not explain themselves; they did not need to. Adam felt certain that they belonged to Pasha Khan.

Calmly, Hamid told them that he was the guide and translator for an American news crew, requesting passage through the mountains. Adopting an air of mystified concern, Adam kept his gun hand free. Branch did the same. If the men tried to search the SUV, Adam would kill the Afghan closest to the window. Jumping out with the car door for cover, Branch would take the man beside him. Rotner would shoot the third man through the windshield. Silent, Adam's target regarded Hamid with a deep displeasure.

"If these foreigners are newsmen," he said at length, "where are their cameras and transmitters?"

"They are not newsmen," Hamid responded irritably. "Their job is to find quarters and vehicles for a crew who is coming. Let me show you their credentials."

Left hand raised in a plea for trust, he opened the glove compartment. Gingerly, he pinched a phony CBS card between his thumb and forefinger, tendering it to his interrogator as though it were a missive from God. Pointing out the trademark eye on the card, Hamid explained that this was the symbol of American television. "They know nothing," the translator said of his passengers in a scornful tone. "So I am driving them to Khost and helping find what they need. Without me, they are children—only with beards, which they believe makes them more acceptable. But I have real children to feed."

Their antagonist cocked his head, looking past Hamid at Adam. Miming fear, Adam mustered a nervous, ingratiating smile. He could feel Branch's stillness. As the Afghan studied him, Adam allowed his smile to fade, exposing the naked terror of a civilian.

With a disdainful air, the Afghan gestured them forward.

Thanking him, Hamid inched their SUV around the cliff as the Afghans backed against the sheer rock on the right. No one else looked back.

"Nice performance," Branch murmured to Adam. "You were the scaredest looking guy I've ever seen."

Adam felt the tension seep from inside him. "Some days it's easier than others."

Shortly, they began their slow, laborious descent. Skirting Gardiz, they avoided Camp Chapman, the site of a CIA installation ringed by Afghan guards and American troops. Though the presence of the CIA was not a secret, these four men, and their mission, could not be associated with the agency. They were on their own.

In twilight, they reached the town of Khost. Its location near the Pakistan border was convenient to their mission;

its character was not. The city was marbled with Taliban and al-Qaeda; its roads, laid out on a grid, centered on an enormous mosque financed by Osama bin Laden. Near this was the bunker-like headquarters of the Afghan police; across from that a ruined building blown up by a suicide bomber who, intending to destroy the headquarters, had taken fire that caused his truck to veer off course. The few Afghans on the street no doubt included people who—a decade before—had supported the Taliban in harboring the attackers of 9/11.

By prearrangement, Hamid drove them in to the police compound, where a mustached Afghan colonel greeted them as honored American aid workers—their cover for this purpose—and offered them a dinner of stewed lamb. Hamid left to secure a room, insulating the Americans from inspection by a potentially hostile landlord. In Khost, the Taliban network had tentacles everywhere.

After dinner, the colonel took them to a quiet room with chairs and oversized Afghan pillows. Against his better judgment, Adam distracted himself by taking out his laptop—innocuous civilian equipment—and rereading Carla's e-mail, as though he were an aid worker away from home. Carla's description of her career told him a good deal he had not known. But he suspected that in its margins, unspoken, was more pain and dislocation than she felt safe in describing. Still, he appreciated her honesty, and the effort this no doubt required. He imagined her bent over the computer, her lovely face intent and serious, her body swollen with the child growing inside her.

What would become of him, he wondered, and of her? Who would nurture the boy, and share this woman's love? He had always told himself that his lack of attachments was a virtue. There was no one to distract him, and his death—should it happen—would not distort the life of a wife or child left only with their imaginings of a father. His return to Martha's Vineyard had ripped the scab off his past, exposing the gap between the archetype of a family and the reality of his own life. But some irreducible part of him, which he had thought dead, had stirred with the fleeting vision of a future different than his past.

Closing the computer, he focused on the danger outside their walls. "It's good we're moving out at night," he observed to Branch.

The Seal nodded. "I took that crater across the street as a negative indicator. Just like the demographic trends of the last two centuries. Makes you wonder why our British friends signed up for a second go."

"That's easy," Adam answered carelessly. "We promised them that this time would be different."

Deep in the night, Hamid led them to the room he had secured.

He had gotten a key to the building—they did not require the assistance of a landlord who would know them as Americans, or wonder what equipment they carried in their heavy suitcases. As Adam had requested, the room was on the second floor and had a balcony that overlooked the street below. Once inside, they drove wedges beneath the door. Duplicating a common practice of Afghans who were cleaning their rug, Rotner draped a carpet over the railing of the balcony, blocking the view from the street. Adam took out the satellite telephone receiver and placed it behind the rug, assuring optimal reception for text messages. In appearance, the phone was standard NGO equipment. The giveaway to any intruder would be the body armor, guns, and ammunition concealed within the room.

So as not to be associated with them further, Hamid left. Before the others slept, Branch placed a wooden chair against the door. They lay on top of the beds, keeping their hands free, trying to rest as best they could. Before commencing his own broken sleep, Adam e-mailed Carla. "I'm on a road trip," he tapped out swiftly, "and tied up for a while. As soon as I can, I'll send you something longer." The words underscored the chasm between Adam's life and what he could tell her. But in a day or two, this might not matter at all.

Shutting off his computer, he mentally rehearsed each move in the darkness as he approached the building where—his superiors hoped—al-Qaeda held the POW.

As dawn broke—a thin ribbon of light peering over the mountains to materialize the tan, low-slung city—Hamid returned to the room.

Overnight, he had switched out their SUV for a Mitsubishi to confuse anyone who had seen the Toyota. But his face was graver than normal. Handing Adam a piece of paper, he said, "Night letter. The Taliban left it on doorsteps around the city."

As Branch and Rotner sat on the edges of their beds, Adam read the letter aloud. There were Americans in the city, it said baldly—the Taliban would kill any Afghan who helped them. But a person whose information allowed a spy to be taken alive would receive $10,000; a man who killed one would receive a lesser bounty of $5,000. The difference, Adam did not need to add, was a measure of how merciful it was to be killed instead of captured.

"Think they know we're here?" Rotner inquired in the tone of a man seeking information about the weather.

"No way of telling," Adam responded. "Because there's a CIA station nearby, they do this pretty often. We came in at night, dressed like locals. So maybe it's coincidence."

This did not sound satisfactory to him or, from their expressions, the others. Hoping for more information, he crept onto the porch behind the cover of the rug.

There was a text message on the satellite receiver. But it contained nothing about the Taliban. Instead, cryptically, it said that their time line had been accelerated. Branch and Adam were needed at the forward operations base before nightfall.

Swiftly, Adam reflected. Unless his superiors had learned that it was too risky to stay here, the likely reason for this change was information that al-Qaeda would move the POW in the next twenty-four hours. But it was far more dangerous for Branch and

Adam to strike out for Pakistan in daylight. Everything about this order narrowed their chances of survival.

Telling Branch, Adam said none of this. He did not need to. Taking in their new orders, Branch was quiet for a moment. Then he shrugged, saying only, "Good thing we look so much like Afghans," as he fingered his blond, sandy hair.

NINE

When Carla emerged from the doctor's office, Teddy Blaine was waiting.

As he looked up at her, concerned, Carla saw a young, obviously pregnant woman glance from her to Teddy in obvious surprise. For an instant, the incongruity of any relationship between Carla and a man still suspected in Ben's death penetrated her shock. Then what she had just learned overcame her. All that she could manage was to give Teddy the briefest of nods, a signal to leave, then walk slowly out the door and down the long hallway toward the parking lot.

A few people were coming the other way—visitors or patients, a nurse pushing an older man in a wheelchair. Carla barely saw them. With Teddy at her side, she looked straight ahead at the swinging glass doors until he pushed them open. She walked a few more steps and then, noting the cheerlessness of a dark, lowering sky, stopped to draw chill air into her lungs.

"What happened?" Teddy asked with quiet urgency.

Staring at the pavement, Carla could only shake her head. Like an automaton, she followed Teddy to his vintage Mercedes sedan, once Ben's, and slipped through the door he opened into the passenger seat, her stomach heavy, her heart leaden.

Putting his key in the ignition, Teddy stopped to look at her. Oddly, it was the expression of concern on his sensitive face that shattered Carla's self-control.

She sat back, shivering once, and felt the tears running down her face. "I'm sorry," she said in a husky voice, though she was not sure to whom.

Teddy simply waited. At length, with no one else to lean on, Carla told him what she had learned.

When the exam was finished—the usual indignities somewhat leavened by Dr. Stein's crisp professionalism—he had asked Carla to dress and come to his office. Once she did, he closed the door behind them, gesturing her to a chair with unwonted gravity that suggested their conversation would not be perfunctory or pleasant.

"So these contractions keep coming," he began.

Nodding, Carla watched his face. "Every other day or so, usually with spotting. I try to keep myself calm, and eventually they stop. Does that tell you anything?"

"Nothing definitive. Perhaps it's simply hereditary, reflecting the problems your mother had carrying a child to term." Stein folded his hands in front of him, regarding her with studied calm. "It could also suggest problems with the baby. We have the test results back, and they're somewhat worrisome."

Carla felt a constriction in her throat. "In what way?"

A brief, involuntary grimace left a residue of concern in the doctor's eyes. "Your blood test indicates the probability—though not the certainty—of trisomy 18. Most babies who have this anomaly die in utero, and there's also a significant risk of stillbirth . . ."

"Why?"

"If—and I emphasize the 'if'—your baby has this genetic disorder, it raises the prospect of heart abnormalities, or kidney problems, or other internal organ diseases. Sometimes the esophagus doesn't connect to the stomach. The heart defects are particularly lethal. But any or all of these problems can lead to a very low survival rate." Stein paused to let her absorb this, then added quietly, "I'm sorry."

Stunned, Carla crossed her arms, as though hugging herself against cold air. "Is there any hope?"

"There is. Though there are subtle signs of trisomy 18 on the ultrasound, they're inconclusive. The statistical probability that your child has this disorder is just that—a probability, not a certainty. Mostly we're going off your blood test. The experts in Boston compared it to a group of pregnant mothers whose fetuses have similar indicators. It's a little like forecasting the weather: we say there's a twenty percent chance of rain because, when the meteorological conditions are the same, it rains twenty percent of the time.

"Based on that comparison, they place the possibility that your baby has trisomy 18 at a little over fifty percent. Which leaves a significant chance that you'll have a completely normal baby." He hesitated, this meager note of encouragement draining from his voice. "But there's an equal or greater chance of miscarriage, or that your child won't survive the birth itself. And, if he does, that he won't live past infancy."

Carla felt nausea overwhelming her first spasm of disbelief. "What can I do?"

Stein gave her a look of clear-eyed candor. "For the baby, nothing. But I have to tell you that termination is an option some women choose. That way, the mom avoids the probability of further suffering—for herself, and for the child . . ."

"No," Carla cut in angrily, and realized that she had sat bolt upright. "I'm Catholic enough to believe that this baby is a life. We still don't know that there's anything wrong with him. And even if we did, I'm going to give him every chance. That's my obligation as his mother—not to spare myself 'suffering' by ripping him out of the womb . . ."

Stein held up his hand. "I'm your doctor, Carla. I had to present the options."

Carla had the sudden, superstitious fear that to continue this conversation threatened her son's life. "You did," she snapped. "The subject's closed."

Stein's quiet look of regret tamped down Carla's rage. "Then we need to monitor this," he told her. "I recommend that you see me every other week. If I understand your wishes, you'll do everything possible to take this child to term."

"Yes."

"Then we should talk about delivery. I'd like to contact a high risk pregnancy specialist in Boston. At around the eighth month or so, should your pregnancy proceed, you should find a place there until the baby is born. It would be better if he were delivered by a specialist."

Her anger gone, Carla felt enervated. All she did was nod.

Leaving Stein's office, she felt as if her life had changed, and that the child inside her, perhaps already doomed, might become another death to mourn. To see Teddy Blaine felt shattering.

At the end of her narrative, Teddy fleetingly touched Carla's arm, a gentle brush of his fingertips. "How can I help?"

Carla touched her eyes. "Please just keep doing what you've done. And don't tell Adam. There's nothing he can do."

"Does he know you're afraid of losing the baby?"

"No," she answered softly. "After all, he's not the baby's father, is he?"

She felt, rather than saw, his quiet acknowledgment of the complexity of her position, and that of Benjamin Blaine's ostensible sons—only one of whom, though Teddy did not know this, would be her unborn child's brother. "I should take you home," he said at length. "Don't forget your seatbelt."

They drove to the guest house in relative silence. Arriving, Teddy noted the Ford parked in front. "Company?"

"I'm sure not. Sometimes Whitney has gardeners here, or handymen. But they don't come in when I'm not home."

Teddy faced her. "Count on me for the groceries. And if you have some emergency—day or night—call me." He paused, then added, "Actually, you don't need a reason. You're pretty alone here."

She gave him a faint, rueful smile. "Pretty much. My own doing, but that's what I needed."

"I know the feeling," Teddy said with a certain wry understanding. "When people take a certain kind of interest in you, it tends to make you antisocial. I've been like that for months now."

Carla gazed at him, reminded by this elliptical reference that, in the minds of many, Teddy remained implicated in Ben's death. "Thanks for taking me," she said, and got out as quickly as she could.

Alone again—except for the baby, Carla reminded herself—she paused in front of the guesthouse.

Its walls would close around her soon enough—since her forced inactivity, the hours and days had passed too slowly. Still, she had done her best, scrupulously maintaining her morning ritual of prayer. She researched healthy foods, and all the ways where she could help her body sustain this baby. Mercifully, Whitney Dane's lifetime accumulation of hardcovers had spilled over to the guest house, and so Carla's regimen of self-improvement included consuming novels she should have read long before—*The Brothers Karamazov, Tender Is the Night,* and more contemporary, David Foster Wallace's brilliant but occasionally head-scratching *Infinite Jest.* She scoured the *New York Times* online and, until she reached her daily saturation point of cleverness and bloviation, followed politics on cable news. But the baby, her only companion, was the source of constant worry. When was the last time, Carla asked herself, that she had laughed aloud, or been overcome by gratitude for the sheer wonder of being alive?

She could no longer remember. At times, she felt like a house that had never been furnished, or brightened with warm colors. For years, she had been a striver, desperate to outrun her stunted beginnings. Then she had become Carla Pacelli, more vivid in the minds of others than in her own. Then she was Carla the alcoholic, standing in the ruins of her barely examined past, stirring the embers for clues. Struggling to maintain a semblance of dignity, to construct a personal code of honor, the foundation for a new life— all the while pursued by a tabloid press that feasted on her affair with Benjamin Blaine, the meaning of which was too personal to her to make excuses to anyone else. Though Carla could be mer- ciless in self-appraisal—a necessity, she believed—she gave herself credit for trying. But this willful effort to wrest sobriety and grace from turmoil did not create much space for spontaneity, or joy. And now there would be more days spent killing her allotted time on earth, darkened by the shadow of heartbreak over the transcen- dence she longed for as the mother of this child.

Reflexively, she touched her stomach. Had she felt him stir last night, as she had assured Dan Stein with a mother's insistence, or had she merely felt the pulse of her deepest hopes? She truly did not know.

But it was time for her to sit again, the sole protection she could give her child. She walked slowly to the unlocked door and opened it.

Standing in the doorway, Carla felt herself start.

The antique rocking chair where she often sat, imagining that her child enjoyed this gentle motion, was occupied by a thin, dark-haired woman who scrutinized Carla with probing brown eyes. Carla knew very well who she was—the reporter from the *Inquirer* who gnawed at Ben's death like a vulture. Her proprietary air stoked Carla's fury.

"What are you doing here?" she snapped.

"Waiting for you," the reporter said with willful calm. "Whether you like me or not, we really do need to talk."

Carla fought for self-control. "If I'd known you were coming," she said coldly, "I would have invited you. But I didn't, so you're trespassing. Get out."

The woman stared pointedly at Carla's stomach. "You're preg- nant with Benjamin Blaine's child. Now you can help me find out which Blaine killed him."

For an instant, Carla was caught between anger and curiosity, the instinct that one of two men had murdered Ben, then lied about it. The report of the medical examiner's inquest was still pending, but the testimony, at least what Carla knew of it, felt hauntingly incomplete. Then she focused on her first priority—the health of her baby, and therefore her own peace of mind. "When you find out," Carla retorted, "I assume you'll tell the world. In the meanwhile, you're not welcome here."

Ferris ignored this. "I don't know who pushed him," she continued with an assurance that made Carla squeamish. "But Adam Blaine knows. He broke into the courthouse, stole the investigative files, and choreographed a cover-up. I met with him twice, feeding him information about the case before I knew what he was doing."

Carla fought back her surprise. "Then you can prove all that without bothering me."

"I can't. But you seem to have become strangely close to a very frightening man. Perhaps you know what I only suspect—that he's a skilled practitioner of the darker arts. Lethal ones, in fact."

The memory of Adam's fleeting confession briefly silenced Carla. With considerable effort, she said, "You're everything I despise about the media, wrapped up in a single person. If you're not gone one minute from now, I'm calling the police. And if you ever break in here again, I'm getting a court order and suing you and the *Inquirer*. The dog vomit you collect doesn't give you a license to invade my home."

"However humble," the reporter replied in an insinuating tone. "A bit of a comedown from your rented McMansion in Bel Air. That should remind you how much you owe to a dead man who remembered you in his will. Unless, like his grasping and toxic family, you view his death as a convenience." Her voice sharpened. "Quite probably, Adam Blaine is an accessory to murder. Now, you're in a position to learn things from him. I'll give you time to decide whether your debt to Benjamin Blaine means less than your interest in his son's attentions—whatever form they may have taken. If so, you'll be his partner in the murder of your unborn child's father."

Suddenly pale, Carla opened the door wider, forcing herself to stare at this woman until, it seemed, she had willed Amanda Ferris from her chair.

Pausing in the doorway, the reporter gave Carla a last, long look. "My card is on your kitchen table. If you decide this wasn't a mercy killing, call me."

Carla turned away. When she heard the woman's footsteps on the porch, she closed the door behind her. But the house no longer felt like a refuge.

For a moment, Carla stood there, shattered by all that had happened. When she sat at the kitchen table, she saw Ferris's card atop a place mat. She wished that she could purge this place of her presence. But throwing away the reporter's card felt like complicity in a crime she could not yet name.

Placing it in a desk drawer, Carla sat in the rocking chair vacated by her tormentor, hoping to soothe a child she might never meet in life.

TEN

Before the morning brightened, Adam and Steve Branch took off for the Pakistani border, leaving Rotner and Hamid behind.

The Mitsubishi was balky starting. The problem was electrical, Branch concluded—that was why the dashboard lighting went in and out. Putting up the hood, he did a hasty fix on the wiring, his demeanor focused but untroubled. Adam was beginning to like the laconic Seal—Branch struck him as a highly skilled version of a certain American type, the man who could fix things and was undaunted by a challenge. There was comfort in this. For the next few hours, their fates were intertwined.

Adam felt less certain about their vehicle. The electrical problems might recur, and the SUV had a right-hand drive with a gearshift operated by the driver's left hand, something neither man had experienced. Electing to find this amusing, Branch volunteered to drive. It became Adam's job to keep watch to the front, back and sides, ready to react at the first hint of trouble. Both men had AK-47s beneath their seats.

They passed through the outskirts of town, Adam noting the pedestrians or peddlers along the patchy dirt road, then a cluster of stooped laborers making bricks with mud, clay, and hay, laying them out to dry in the sun. Without turning, Adam said, "Wonder how many centuries they've been doing that."

"No way of telling," Branch responded. "But we could drive past here decades from now, and their grandkids will be doing the same damn thing. Here a century lasts a thousand years."

Adam nodded. "No joke. One guy I met in a remote village thought I was a Russian, even though they left here with their tails dragging twenty years ago. This place has a certain timeless indifference."

They were in the countryside now. The dips and heights of the terrain became steeper, the rocks and potholes more punishing, sending jolts up Adam's spine. They began fording shallow creek beds, the first few dry before they slowed to a crawl for another, this one swollen with water. Briefly, their tires spun, spattering rivulets of muddy water on the front and side windows. Branch jerked the gearshift, rocking the SUV back, then forward, straining for a purchase on the mud beneath. "Don't like this for the wiring," he observed. "Getting wet won't help a bit."

Looking out the window, Adam hoped that the SUV would not get stuck here in the open, leaving them exposed. The tires kept grinding until, mercifully, the four-wheel-drive skidded forward onto dry land, a last stretch of rolling terrain before they hit the mountains. "Got a football team?" Branch inquired.

"College or pro?"

"College, to start."

"Not much to say," Adam confessed wryly. "I went to Yale."

Shifting gears, Branch shot him a look. "I can see the problem. What about pros?"

"I used to follow the Patriots."

"I'm a Cowboys guy," Branch said with satisfaction. "'America's team'—a stadium that looks like Disney World, and cheerleaders with perfect teeth and artificial boobs. Only one who's had more plastic surgery is the owner. If that's not All-American, I don't know what is."

"Guess you'd have trouble with the Patriots, then. Their bus has the demeanor of a second-tier Kremlin bureaucrat. It doesn't exactly warm the heart."

Branch shrugged. "At least tell me you don't watch soccer. Never got it—a bunch of guys in shorts running around in circles, most of them from shitbag countries that don't like us. And now they've got actual teams all over our great land, like sleeper cells. I keep asking myself which of them are illegals. Makes me wonder what we're fighting for, I can tell you that."

The commentary, Adam realized, captured a surprising streak of irony, Branch riffing on his Alabama background. He was about to respond in kind when a goat cantered onto the road ahead of them, followed by two more.

The seemingly prosaic sight made Adam instantly alert. A string of goats blocking the road could be happenstance, or the precursor to an ambush. Swiftly, he glanced around them. They were stuck—to the right was a four foot wall fronting some mud houses; to the left, trees lined the bank of a deep creek bed. More goats filled the road.

Branch braked to a stop. "No choice," he said, and felt for the weapon beneath his car seat. "If there's a stupider animal alive, I haven't met them."

Amidst the goats, a human being appeared from behind the wall—a boy in his early teens, Adam judged, prodding the recalcitrant beasts with a shepherd's crook. He glanced at the SUV, then kept moving his charges along. As the last goat crossed the road, Adam felt himself relax a fraction, and then four other men appeared behind the herd.

They were of a different cast—bearded, hard-looking men who stopped in the road, openly staring at the Americans stalled five yards away. Adam felt Branch thinking along with him, trained to survive, knowing that at any moment they might have to kill these men. He could not tell whether the Afghanis had weapons concealed in baggy shirts. What was certain is that they had seen two men who, despite their dress and beards, were betrayed by Branch's coloring as foreigners.

"So?" Branch inquired.

Adam thought quickly. "Let them go, or we'll have to shoot the boy as well. Even if we do, we'd be leaving five corpses in an inhabited area. No point drawing that kind of attention before we've even started."

The men kept staring at them, as though marking their faces. "If they call the wrong guy on their cell phone," Branch observed, "we're fucked." But the fatalism in his voice conceded Adam's point.

At last, the four men resumed following the young shepherd and his flock. In solemn imitation of an imperial despot, Branch intoned, "Let the boy live."

He resumed driving as Adam glanced around them. One of the Afghans, turning, gave the SUV a final look.

They drove another eight miles or so, at some unknown point crossing the Pakistani border, unmarked by wire or sensors or guards. A no-man's land—the province of warlords, jihadists and Adam's sometime business partner, Colonel Rehman, whose Afghan agent had set their operation in motion. A hall of mirrors, Adam amended.

"That shepherd," Branch remarked after a long silence, "sort of reminded me of my oldest boy. Stringy like that, with the body of a pass catcher."

This scrap of information made the Seal seem complex. "You have a family?" Adam inquired.

"I have kids—two boys and a pretty girl in the middle. Looks like her mom, who had the ingratitude to divorce me." Hitting the brakes, Branch slowed to navigate the steep twisting road. "Called me uncommunicative, if you can imagine that."

"I can't. Think of how close we are already."

"Soul mates. Guess it helps to have killing people in common." The humor bled from Branch's voice. "You're with your family, and you remind yourself they're the reason we do stuff like this—that, and the thrill of it all. But they don't really want to hear about it, and you don't really want to tell them. So you just wall it off."

The observation struck a chord from Adam's sessions with Charlie Glazer. "What choice do we have?"

Branch glanced at him. "You married?"

"Nope. I've been hoping to miss the first divorce."

"Got a girlfriend, at least?"

Involuntarily, Adam found himself distracted by an image of Carla—her face close to his, the electric jolt that came from the feel of her lips, the press of her body. "Not really. Just someone I'd like to see again."

Only after he spoke the words did Adam appreciate their context. He looked around him, seeing nothing but the harsh, jagged terrain of the mountains that enveloped them as they climbed. His last phrase lingered there, unanswered.

At length they reached the snow-topped ridges that marked the beginning of their descent into the badlands. "Crappy place for an operating base," Branch observed, "but perfect for al-Qaeda. They could stash our POW anywhere."

"Guess that's what the rush is about. Right now, we may actually know where he is. But once they move him, he's a ghost again."

They crept with agonizing slowness down a narrow twisting road, Branch braking constantly, glancing at the GPS as Adam scanned the terrain—a sheer cliff hugging the driver's side, a deep ravine on their left. Branch slowed the SUV to a crawl; the drop was at least two football fields in length, and skidding would be fatal.

Suddenly, the motor died. The SUV was still, a metal shell.

"Fucking electricals," Branch said between gritted teeth. "Why now?"

Both men knew their roles. Grabbing his weapon as he jumped out of the driver's side, Branch slung it over his shoulder and raised the hood. Adam closed the passenger door behind him and leaned against it two feet from the ravine, cradling his weapon as he looked to the front and back for any sign of trouble.

Peering beneath the hood, Branch began tinkering with the wires. "Like the goddam Gordian knot," he said. "No wonder Japan got so screwed up." Then his concentration became too intense for speech.

"Hate to ask," he finally said. "But I need you to hold a wire."

Reluctantly, Adam abandoned his surveillance. Taking a string of green wire from the Seal's hand, he scanned the road behind them, his sight line partially blocked by the hood.

"Getting there," Branch muttered, and then Adam detected a faint new sound. Like the buzzing of a swarm of bees, he thought, but could not yet pick up its direction.

"Hear that?"

Branch glanced up, cocking his head. All at once, there was a crack of glass breaking, the percussive sound of bullets striking metal like the banging of a ballpeen. From the road, Adam thought, and cried out, "Down . . ."

A hammer blow struck the center of his back, a round pinging off his body armor. Adam jerked upright. A second bullet passed through his left shoulder with the force of a blow from a steel bat.

Blood spurted out as Adam dropped to the ground, stunned, instinctively using the truck as cover. Clamping his wound with his good hand, he peered out from behind the truck and saw two men on a motorcycle—a driver and a shooter. "Behind us," he shouted.

Kneeling, Branch began spraying bullets. The driver veered to evade fire, the shooter stymied from aiming. "Loading magazine," Branch spat.

Out of bullets, Adam knew. Pulling himself upright, he felt a searing pain course through his left arm, then saw the motorcycle steady itself, the shooter taking aim as they sped closer.

With one hand, Adam jerked his AK-47 and began firing at the driver, the percussive recoil jabbing his good shoulder. The motorcycle wobbled; in slow motion, the driver tipped to the side and toppled with his vehicle onto the hard dirt road. The haze of shock filled Adam's eyes, white flashes obscuring his vision. As though he were watching from a distance, he saw the shooter rise to his knees and begin returning fire.

A round popped by Adam's jaw. The shooter's head snapped back, a gaping hole where one eye had been. As Adam slumped against the windshield, he saw Branch fire again, the shooter's chest twitching as he fell backward.

Adam dropped his rifle, right palm pressed against the hole in his shoulder. It pulsed with pain; blood seeped from between his fingers. Without glancing at him, Branch ran forward, firing at their prone attackers. Their bodies skittered with each bullet in an eerie death rattle. Only then did Branch turn to see Adam sliding down the side of the car, his white shirt soaked in carmine.

ELEVEN

Adam was bleeding profusely. Hurriedly, Branch grabbed a medical kit from beneath the rear seat and wrapped a compress around his shoulder. "You saved my ass," he told Adam. "I'm getting you out of here."

Slumped by the SUV, Adam leaned his shoulder against a tire to help the compress stop the rush of blood. He could not argue. The mission was done; if the POW had ever been in the village, he would soon be gone. He felt the weight of their failure merge with shock and enervation. His wound was serious; unless he was tended to, the loss of blood and pressure would kill him. As to the men they had shot, he felt nothing except a vague relief that his training had not failed him.

Watching Branch throw the bodies and motorcycle into the ravine, he considered the logistics of their dilemma. "We can't turn around here," he told Branch when the Seal had finished. "You drive forward until we find a place to turn. Then I'll take over driving and you ride shotgun. Your aim will be better than mine."

Branch glanced around them. "It's a left hand shift," he objected. "Your wound's going to hurt like a son of a bitch."

Adam's shoulder felt as though it had been crushed by a sledge-hammer. "It does now. I'll go as far as I can."

He stood, wrenching the passenger door open with his good arm. Branch gave the wiring a last tweak before getting behind the wheel. When he pushed the gas pedal, the SUV started.

Branch expelled a breath. They inched forward for agonizing minutes, at last finding an indentation in the cliffside big enough for them to circle back toward Afghanistan. Both were silent—their failure confirmed, dangerous hours still ahead.

Branch stopped so they could trade seats, taking his AK-47. Throwing the car into drive, Adam felt a bolt of pain shoot from his shoulder to his fingertips.

"What blew it?" Branch wondered aloud.

Jaw clamped against the pain, Adam husbanded his speech. "Could be anything. But if our sources set us up, the Taliban would have watched to see where we went. The guys we killed were amateurs."

Branch considered this. "Fucking shepherd," he said under his breath. "Didn't help they sent us out in daylight."

Adam said nothing. Edging along the ravine, he peered down into its depths. He already felt weakened by the strain of keeping the SUV from plummeting over the side. Each jolt from the road caused a stabbing pain; the compress was soaked with blood. Adam wondered how long he could keep driving.

He stopped talking altogether. As the sheer, rugged terrain closed around them, he kept shifting with his damaged arm, steering with the other. A feverish sweat dampened his forehead.

The SUV reached the summit again, began creeping downward with Adam shifting and breaking. Still they saw no one. Perhaps an hour passed. Though his shoulder screamed in protest, Adam forced himself to keep driving. If they could make it to Camp Chapman, they would be safe. The idea of sanctuary began merging with an image of Carla Pacelli.

His shoulder started freezing up, drained of feeling—at once a mercy and a warning. He was still losing blood, and the harrowing descent through the stark mountains showed no sign of ending. "Shoulder's done," he told Branch. "I'll tell you when to shift."

Adam gave an instruction. Rifle cradled in his left arm, Branch shifted with his right. This worked for perhaps a mile. "Enough," the Seal said. "My turn."

Adam did not argue. He was too faint, and his arm felt dead, a limp appendage.

He braked again, stopping the car. Stepping out, he felt his legs buckle. Inhaling deeply, he sucked in the chill air of late afternoon, its bright blue sky slowly fading. He seemed to walk from muscle memory.

Branch began driving. Window cracked open for air, Adam kept looking to the front and back, AK-47 in his lap. Each turn of his head produced wrenching pain.

At last the road began flattening out. In what seemed like a mirage, Adam saw the village where the herd of goats had stopped them. Their fatal moment, most likely. He tensed, finger on the trigger of his rifle. But they passed the mud wall without seeing anyone.

Taking out his cell phone, Branch called the number they were given for emergencies. When someone answered, he said, "We've had to abort mission. My partner's hit. We need medical assistance at Chapman."

Branch listened intently. Adam knew what they were asking—"how bad?"

"Pretty bad," the Seal answered. "A through and through wound to the shoulder, and he's lost a lot of blood." He paused to listen and then said tersely, "Yeah, he's still conscious. Don't know about walking, but he could an hour ago."

Adam forced himself to detach, keep looking for potential danger. In a tone both angry and resigned, Branch told his listener, "I hear you," and got off.

"Hope you're up for a drive to Kabul," he told Adam, biting off the words. "In their infinite wisdom, you're not bad enough to

jeopardize the security at Chapman. They reminded me they don't
know us."

Adam felt hope yield to resignation—this was what he had
expected. "There's more medical supplies at the room in Khost,"
Branch went on. "We'll have to go there, alert the other guys."

Adam grimaced. "And anyone else who sees us."

Glancing around at the broad open plain, Branch stopped the car.
He got out swiftly, using the butt of his rifle to knock out the remaining glass in the shattered rear window. Getting back in, he said, "Now
we won't look so bad. Except for you."

Adam's shoulder was throbbing again, and he was afraid of passing out. He could think of nothing to say. All he felt was a primal
desire to survive.

Carla, he thought. A formless prayer for something he could not
define.

Pushing this away, he resumed his taut vigilance out the windows.

On the outskirts of Khost, they passed the same Afghan laborers
making bricks from mud and straw and clay. To Adam, it was as
though nothing had happened in the hours since he had first seen
these men stooped over their work. A reminder of how Afghanistan
swallowed foreigners without a trace.

As they drove into town, a haunting call to prayer issued from
bin Laden's mosque. Suddenly the streets were crowded with pedestrians and beat up cars rushing to heed the summons of Islam. The
SUV crawled to a stop amidst the traffic—its rear window missing,
its sides pocked with bullet holes, its passenger's shirt covered in
blood. Their rifles were beneath the seats again, harder to reach.
Now and then, an Afghan stopped to stare.

Hurriedly, Branch called Hamid, asking him to be at the guest
house. Under his breath, the Seal said, "We look like the last survivors of a massacre. Sure don't want to linger."

The clutter in the streets thinned at last, as though vacuumed up
by the mosque. The SUV began moving again. When they reached

the guest house, the Toyota they had driven to Khost was parked in front, and Hamid had left the main door open.

Adam followed Branch upstairs, the last steps appearing distant, as though he saw them through the wrong end of a telescope. When Branch knocked twice, Rotner opened the door, murmuring "shit" as Adam stumbled past him. Then he grabbed a first aid kit and tossed it on the bed. "Want me to do this?"

Adam shook his head. "I will."

Inside the kit was a hypodermic needle, lidocaine, and a vial of antibiotic powder. Adam poured the powder into the lidocaine, then sucked the murky fluid into the needle. Pulling down his pants, he stabbed himself in the thigh, hoping to ward off infection. His shoulder hurt so much he barely felt the needle.

Awkwardly, he stripped off his bloody shirt and put on the fresh one Rotner gave him. On the balcony, Branch was throwing their gear down to Hamid. "Let's go," he barked at Adam.

Quickly, Rotner changed Adam's compress. "There's morphine in that kit," he said. "But you can't take it, no matter how bad the pain. You need to be functional, and with the blood you've lost already, lowering the pressure means you'll die. So don't."

Mute, Adam nodded. Rotner and Hamid had risked their lives by being here. He would do his part.

They hurried down the stairs, Rotner grabbing Adam's good arm, each step jolting his shoulder. When Adam got in the Toyota, Branch gunned the engine and began speeding through the primitive streets, making Adam grit his teeth against the pain. "Those two are going separately," Branch said. "We're on our own."

Eight hours, Adam thought.

Leaving town, they crossed creeks swollen with rushing water and began their ascent into snowcapped mountains. Warlord country, the redoubt of Pasha Khan and others like him, who might kill or sell them to al-Qaeda or the Taliban. Adam's wound was leaking through the compress, dappling his new shirt with blood and rendering their cover story useless. With fresh anger, he absorbed the pointlessness of their mission.

As they climbed, Branch stopped the SUV at vantage points overlooking the terrain, allowing him to scan the road ahead for checkpoints. Then night fell, and they could see nothing, their headlights—a necessity—a telltale beacon of their presence. Rocks the size of baseballs shook the car, each fresh surge of agony sapping Adam's consciousness. Without morphine, his only relief would be blacking out, an abandonment of his duty to keep himself and Branch alive.

For minutes and then hours, he forced himself to focus on his pain, the only antidote to sleep. Their headlights illuminated a vast, daunting emptiness—ravines, snow, mountains, an endless black sky barely silvered by a quarter moon. Patches of ice ground beneath their tires.

Pushing Carla from his mind, Adam forced himself to keep staring out the windows through half closed eyes. An infinite night enveloped him.

"Fuck," Branch spat in the darkness.

His voice jerked Adam from some bottomless netherworld. Through the windshield, the twin beams of their headlights seemed to conjure three men whose outlines grew clearer. They moved to block the road, their motions almost ghostly in their loose pants and flowing shirts, the steel barrels of their rifles dark against white clothing.

"No choice this time," Branch said. His voice was even now, the years of training and discipline kicking in. It struck Adam that this might be the last minute of his life.

"None," he concurred. A signal that he was ready.

Branch eased the Toyota to a stop. As the Afghans stepped forward, both men lowered their windows. Drawing their enemies' attention, Branch opened his car door and raised his left hand in a placating gesture. Adam gripped the door handle.

In a single fluid motion, Branch's right hand came up and through the window to fire his AK-47. Adam jumped out of the car, rolling sideways. Sickening pain tore through his shoulder as he aimed and shot. The second Afghan fell to the ground, his mouth gaping open in surprise. In the headlights, the survivor fired at Branch. As his bullet pinged on metal, Adam shot him in the forehead.

The Afghan crumpled to his knees, pitching forward. Branch walked into the light, firing one bullet into each man's skull.

The shots echoed in the vastness. Adam used his right hand to push himself upright, watching Branch hastily throw corpses down a ravine for the second time in hours. Rushing back to the Toyota, Branch said tensely, "Least I can do is get you back alive. So hang on tight."

Branch began driving. Adam's last reserves of strength were gone. Already the firefight felt like something he remembered from being stoned, uncertain of what had happened. For miles, he struggled to stay upright as consciousness slipped away. With mild curiosity, he wondered if this was dying, then ceased to wonder at all.

Adam fought back through darkness, disoriented. For an instant, he imagined waking on Martha's Vineyard. Recognizing Kabul, he wondered why he was there. Then the pulsing in his shoulder helped reality kick in.

"Sorry," he told Branch.

"No worries. You used yourself up back there. All I needed was for you to keep on breathing, so there'd be some point to this."

They stopped in front of the guesthouse where they had met in Kabul. "They've set up a makeshift surgical ward," Branch informed him. "Don't want us anywhere near an army base."

Arm around his waist, Branch dragged Adam up the stairs. Inside the dimly lit room was a crew-cut medic with an operating table and IVs. The medic helped Branch lift Adam onto the operating table and then stripped off his body armor. "Judging from the dent in the back," the medic remarked, "that round would have pierced your spine, heart, and lungs. Comparatively speaking, you got off light."

The pounding in his shoulder made Adam want to vomit. "Give me the morphine, for Christ's sakes."

"Not yet. Lie on your right shoulder while I clean this wound."

Grinding his teeth, Adam turned on his side. Alert now, he watched the medic fill a turkey baster with salt water. Stepping behind Adam's back, he took off the compress and pushed the baster into the open wound. As Adam stifled a cry of pain, the medic shot the contents through him.

Blood and salt water trickled down Adam's chest. "Twice more," the medic said.

Grabbing a sheet, Adam bit down. To distract himself, he looked at the heart rate monitor on his watch. He winced at the second spurt of bloody saline, then bit down again for the third.

More salt water dribbled from the front of his wound, clearer now. His shoulder felt like ground meat. "My heartbeat is okay," Adam said tightly. "Give me the fucking morphine."

The medic hesitated, looking hard at Adam, then hooked up a morphine drip. "Now," Adam snapped, and the medic jabbed the needle in his arm.

As the medic swathed his wound in a compress and bandages, Adam felt warmth spreading through him. He had never felt so grateful to lose control.

A cosmic trembling all around him snapped Adam awake. Hearing the crack of incoming fire, he groped blindly for a gun, his mind foggy in the semidark.

At the foot of his bed, Branch popped up. Grinning, the Seal inquired, "Was that as good for you as it was for me? The earth sure did move."

Staring at him, Adam realized that he was feeling the last tremors of an earthquake. "Fucking Afghanistan," Branch complained "you'd think this shithole would cut us a break."

It was the funniest thing Adam had ever heard. He kept on laughing until tears welled in his eyes.

Branch watched him with a half-smile of comprehension only they could share. "Yeah," he said softly. "Good to be alive, isn't it."

TWELVE

Two days later, they flew Adam to Dubai for treatment and recuperation.

The agency put him up at the Dubai Hilton, with tall windows looking out on the phallic competition of empty high-rises thrusting toward the sky. The surroundings added to his sense of the surreal, and of himself as suspended between an escape he remembered in freeze frames and a future he could not envision. Branch had remarked on his nervelessness. Perhaps it was his training; perhaps it began when Benjamin Blaine had held out the example of Ted Williams, then drilled him in the virtues of coolness under pressure. This was another strand of his tangled legacy; in those few moments, Adam had felt nothing, and did not know how to feel now.

But his wound was clean, with no complications. A week after the shooting he could do the breaststroke in the hotel pool. This became his routine; now and then, he would leave a small trickle of blood, but no one saw it. He never spoke to anyone except to order room service.

He slept well enough. Sometimes he would wake up with a start, look around in the darkness before recalling where he was. But he began to accept that Dubai, however strange and artificial, was an island of safety. Afghanistan felt far away, fleeting glimpses in the slipstream of a car. To his surprise, he had no dreams of death.

Days passed. One morning he came back from the pool, and found an e-mail from Carla Pacelli, whose face was commingled in his mind with images of killing and flight. "It's been awhile since you've written," she said. "Are you okay?"

A good question. But at least he was alive to seek the answer.

Placing the groceries on Carla's kitchen table, Teddy Blaine saw her mother's rosary beads. Hesitant, he asked, "Does that really work for you?"

Carla gave him a thin smile. "We'll find out, won't we? As a child, I was taught that you're not supposed to ask for God's favors so concretely, like wanting a new dress for Christmas." Then she recalled praying for her father's death, and added, "But sometimes I did. Now I pray for other people—your brother, and my son."

Teddy raised his eyebrows. "Nothing for yourself? There must be a dress you want."

Carla shook her head. "What I want for myself can't be hung up in a closet. For me, prayer and reflection is an end in itself."

Teddy opened the refrigerator and began putting things away. Over his shoulder, he asked, "Did you ever discuss this with my father? A godless man if there ever was one. He insisted that any particular religion was a function of its followers' ignorance and superstition, quickly cured by one semester in a comparative religion class."

Carla took an apple from his hand, placing it in a bowl of pears and oranges. "It does sound familiar, actually. I did politely point out to Ben that, at its best, religion also teaches kindness, personal responsibility, and the grace not to judge people by the worst moments in their lives. And that the forgiveness of others might be something he could use."

Teddy glanced at her. "You've got that right."

Turning, Carla focused on a beam of sunlight that burnished the mahogany table. Again, she experienced the discomfort of wondering whether this man, so surprisingly considerate of her, had murdered his own father. Evenly, she said, "You still loathe him as much as Adam does, don't you? Perhaps more."

Teddy moved his shoulders. "Don't forget my mother and uncle. Among the four of us, it's a vigorous competition. Still, I suppose it's special for his sons. You end up caught in a web of confusion between what you need from him and what he forces you to recognize. Maybe you survive, as we did, but it's like a fish hook in your guts. Even worse, you feel infantile and guilty—never worse than at his funeral, relief warring with the childish wish that he'd really loved me. And then you realize you're stuck with this miserable ambivalence, too deeply embedded to ever quite go away."

His voice softened. "You weren't there, and I guess in the final months he gave you something different. I don't mean to stomp all over that by singing sad songs for myself—family is tough for a lot of people. But there's no understanding Adam unless you grasp what the father of your child was like as our father."

The ironic formulation reminded Carla of a painful truth—that Adam's tortured relationship with Ben, whatever its causes, could damn anything they might have. Quietly, she asked, "Do you and Adam ever talk about this?"

"More lately." Teddy's voice held resignation and regret. "But another gift from Dad is that he made Adam a cool one. When we were kids, Adam was fundamentally sweet-natured—even though he was my kid brother, when it came to our father he did his best to stand up for me. Even now, I can feel the kindness I remember—God knows he still looks out for me. But after he broke with Dad it was like seeing that person behind protective glass, impossible to touch."

But for fleeting moments, Carla thought, she almost had. "Do you know why he left the island? All I get from him is the sense it involved someone else than Ben."

Closing the refrigerator, Teddy sat across from her, regarding her with kindness and perplexity. "You really do care about him, don't you?"

Carla rested her folded hands on her stomach, a rueful reference to their circumstances. "Call me silly, if you like. My track record the last few years is pretty miserable."

"Join the party." Teddy gazed past her, as if pondering her question. "Adam refuses to talk about why he left—all he says is that he got fed up. That's bullshit, obviously. But all I can tell you was that the Blaines weren't the only people Adam left behind.

"He had a girlfriend then, Jenny Leigh. In the way of any small community, most people thought they'd get married—me included. He certainly gave a pretty good impression of a twenty-three-year-old in love. But he bailed on Jenny like he did the rest of us." Teddy refocused his troubled gaze on Carla. "The day after he left, she went to the beach below our house and tried to kill herself with pills. My father found her and rushed her to the hospital. After she recovered, she and my mother had this special bond—though she was never at the house much, they hung around a lot.

"And then, to everyone's shock, my father left her exactly a million dollars—exactly one million more than he left our mother or me. Next to you, Jenny was the big winner. Explain that one to me, if you can—except as another act of sadism. God knows the rest of us are stumped."

Carla felt a formless disquiet surface from her subconscious. "Is Adam?"

Teddy's eyes narrowed in thought. "Excellent question. Adam is the original cat who walks alone, every thought a secret. God knows what he knows."

At once, Carla thought of the reporter. "I don't know who pushed him," Ferris had told her. "But Adam Blaine knows." As though seeing her troubled expression, Teddy added quickly, "We can't blame him, Carla. He started young—when a kid can't rely on either parent, he becomes a loner, looking out for himself. That makes it challenging to become a trusting soul."

He could be talking about her, Carla knew too well. Perhaps this likeness was part of what she sensed in Adam, and wished that she could touch. But this very kinship meant that she, too, found it hard to wholly trust him.

Teddy, she realized, was watching her closely. In a tentative voice, he said, "On the subject of trust, there's something I'd like you to believe. I'm not supposed to talk about this, to anyone. But I didn't kill my father.

"I was there that night, it's true. It's also true that I lied to the police about that, which is part of why they were planning to indict me. But when I left him there on the promontory, he was still alive." Teddy seemed to wince. "In the midst of his usual scorn, he almost apologized for how he'd treated me. It was the closest thing to human he'd been in years. Which made his death more painful— unresolved feelings forced to the surface, too late. But maybe being with you had done him some good."

Carla met his eyes. He had lied then; he had every reason to lie now—especially to her. But her instinct, however foolish, was to believe him. "So how did he fall off the cliff?"

Teddy shook his head. "I don't know. But Jack says it was an accident, and I've got no reason to disbelieve him."

Once more Carla could hear Amanda Ferris—Adam Blaine, she insisted, had broken into the courthouse, stolen investigative files, and choreographed a cover-up. "I do," Carla said flatly. "So does the district attorney, and the judge who's rendering that report. Like you, Jack lied to the police about seeing Ben that night. He only came forward after Adam returned, and you became a suspect."

"So why did Jack stick his nick in the noose?"

"To save you," Carla rejoined. "Tell me this: did Adam know that Jack was there?"

Teddy hesitated, his face closing. "All I can tell you is that I didn't do it, and that I believe what my uncle says. Jack is a completely decent man."

And Adam's father, Carla thought again, with whatever debt that might create. More softly, she said, "I do want to believe you, Teddy. You're even gentle when you put away my vegetables."

Relief stole into Teddy's eyes. "It's the soul of an artist. I've always been solicitous of broccoli."

Carla's telephone rang. Startled, she turned to it.

"Want me to get it?" Teddy asked.

She shook her head instinctively, pushing up from her chair and walking carefully to the kitchen counter. Seized by instinctive worry, she hesitated before picking up.

"Hello?"

A moment's silence. "It's Adam." His voice was a long-distance echo. "Sorry I've been out of touch."

For an instant, Carla was speechless—he had never called her before. "That's okay," she managed to say. "I know your life is complicated."

As Teddy looked at her with an inquiring expression, she heard Adam briefly laugh. "A little complicated. I got shot. But don't worry—I'm fine now. I can tell you about it when I get there."

Carla felt a wave of surprise, relief, confusion. "You're coming back?"

"Only for a little while, on leave. My employers are benevolent that way. Is the baby okay?"

Carla hesitated. "Fine. We both are."

"Great. Has Teddy been watching out for you?"

"Yes. Believe it or not, he's here right now."

"Then say hello. I'd better go now—off for a final checkup. See you in a couple of days."

"That's wonderful," she answered softly, and then Adam said goodbye.

As she put down the phone, Teddy looked at her quizzically. "'Fine?'" he repeated. "You two really are a pair."

True enough, she thought. "The important thing," she told Adam's brother, "is that he's coming home alive. At least for now."

An answer to her prayers, and yet so confusing and so tangled.

PART FOUR

The Return

Martha's Vineyard
November 2011–December 2011

ONE

When the cab dropped him at his mother's home, Adam paused, gazing at the sprawling house that struck him as familiar yet strange. Then he crossed the lawn to the front door.

It was late November, the beginning of a season that could be so bleak and prolonged that Adam once called it "torture for depressives"—months spent on the harsh, bare island that the tourists never saw, chafing the raw nerve-ends of those who endured it. The grass in the frozen ground was brown and stunted, as slick beneath his feet as Astroturf. He tired more easily, he realized, and his shoulder felt stiff and painful in the cold.

He found his mother in the kitchen. Seeing him, her face brightened, evoking the beautiful younger woman she had been. Rushing forward, she hugged him tightly before leaning back to regard him with maternal concern. "You look drawn," she said. "Are you feeling all right?"

"Fine," he assured her with a smile. "Just a little low on stamina. All in all, getting shot is not something I'd recommend."

Taking his hand, Clarice led him to the living room, sitting on the couch as Adam took the oversized leather chair he still thought of as his father's. "At least," she said pointedly, "we can drop the pretense that you're an agricultural consultant."

"We can," Adam concurred. "One less evasion might be good for all of us. Anyhow, I'm done in Afghanistan."

Her face softened with relief. "What about this job of yours? I'm not asking what it is, but whether you'll keep doing it."

But the future was a blur to him. "I don't know yet. If I don't think about it too much, maybe the answer will come to me. I've got time now."

"I'm very grateful for that, Adam. It's so good to have you home."

Adam wanted to respond in kind, but the words could not seem to come. "Dare I ask what's new?"

Her gaze flickered. In a tentative voice, she said, "Among other things, Jack is living here much of the time—though we're quiet about that, of course. If it's awkward for you, he's prepared to leave for the duration of your visit."

"I'm thirty-four years old, Mom. Getting petulant about the two of you would be a little arrested—not to mention trivial, given all I've learned. Anyhow, a good son should want his parents to be happy."

His mother regarded him more coolly. "You may be Jack's son, but sometimes you have Ben's tongue. Another of my regrets."

"And mine," Adam acknowledged. "Does this mean you're getting married?"

"I don't know if that's required. And before your next observation—yes, I continue to care about appearances. You'll recall that George Hanley is still sniffing around us, and that the judge has yet to state his conclusions. To say the least, rushing to marry Ben's brother might raise questions." She gave him an arid smile. "Some might even call it poor taste."

Adam considered her. In the same dispassionate tone, he said, "Not to mention that my father is a woodworker. By your account, that kept you apart after I was born."

Clarice stared out the window at the gray, sunless day. "That was part of it," she said at length. "But perhaps not in the way you're thinking. My own father was kind but weak. In my late teens, I grasped that we were standing on financial quicksand, and that the life I'd grown up to expect might vanish overnight. So what I felt was less about status than about a man's ambition—how he defined himself.

"Call me shallow, if you will, or dependent. But the world for women then wasn't as it is now. Without knowing your grandfather as I did, you can't understand how compelling I found Ben's determination to wrest what he wanted from life. From the beginning, I saw someone determined to place a stamp on the world, who could give me what I was used to having." Meeting his eyes, she said, "And then provide you with what I wanted any son of mine to have. You may not respect that, but I can't change my answer any more than I can change what I did. Or the price we all paid.

"So now I have to live with my regrets. I wounded Jack terribly, and I let Ben hurt both you and Teddy. I even hurt Ben, however richly deserving he might've been. In the bargain, as you've so acutely noted, I helped initiate the perverse cycle that led to Carla Pacelli and her unborn child—a constant, public and humiliating reminder of how badly it all went wrong. The only thing that could make it worse is the one thing I could never have imagined—that my own son, who is at the heart of all this would be drawn to Ben's woman. So I have to ask, Adam, if you mean to continue seeing her."

This was the longest speech he could remember from his mother, at least about her own pain and vulnerability. More gently, he said, "At least while I'm here."

Briefly, Clarice closed her eyes. "Can you understand how hard that is for me? It's more than female jealousy, or hatred of a young and beautiful woman who, I firmly believe, schemed to take from all of us what I paid so dearly to keep. She holds up a fractured mirror to my own life."

"As do I, it seems. But if it's any consolation, Carla holds up a fractured mirror to mine." He gave her a curious look. "But there seem to be complications everywhere I turn. I chose not to mention this last fall, but Rachel Ravinsky popped up here before I left. I gather that you and Rachel's mother have some memories in common. Now and then I've wondered what they are."

Clarice studied him, discomfort and reproof warring in her eyes. "You are getting around these days. I suppose I should take some comfort in that. In any event, you're asking about something that happened over forty years ago."

"And in all that time you and Whitney Dane have barely spoken. Another secret involving Ben, I assume, who seems to inspire long memories. Though if you stole him from Whitney, I think she'd be more grateful."

"If that's what you think," his mother said stiffly, "I'll leave it there. Whitney was my closest friend once, and I count her as another loss. Beyond that, I won't account for myself in matters that don't concern you. Please, Adam—enough."

All at once, Adam felt weary of himself and oddly sad for his mother. With greater force than ever, he realized how lonely she was beneath the well-bred veneer—and, perhaps, had always been. He could live his own life, whatever that might be, without picking at her wounds any further.

"You're right," he said. "And I'm sorry. Please don't take this personally, but I'm renting a place to live while I'm here. It's just better for all of us—Jack, you and me."

Clarice's lips parted, as though she wanted to argue. Then her manner became resigned. "Do you think you can ever accept him as your father?"

Adam could find no answer. "It's complicated, Mother. That seems to be my mantra for everything, I know."

His mother studied him, her expression wistful. "I love you very much, Adam. As the past begins to recede, I hope all of us can find peace with each other, and become a family again. I trust you'll come to understand that Carla Pacelli is one person too many."

But what defines a family? Adam wondered.

Teddy opened the door of the guesthouse he used as both studio and home. Seeing Adam, he broke into a grin, hugging his brother so fiercely that despite the pain in his shoulder Adam had to laugh. "Easy, Ted. If I'd known coming back would create this kind of excitement, I'd have gotten myself shot sooner. A shame to have missed Thanksgiving."

Teddy shook his head. "You're such a fucking moron, and this latest proves the point. Please tell me you're not going back."

"Not to Afghanistan. And you're sounding like our mother. Do I have to stand here and explain myself? At least she let me sit down."

Teddy waved him inside. "By all means, sit. Do you need fresh bandages, or spare ammunition?"

Adam laughed again. "I could use a beer, and the pleasure of your company. Perverse as it seems, I've missed you."

"And I you, bro. Though sometimes I think you're as crazy as the rest of us."

"A sobering thought." Sitting in a somewhat uncomfortable armchair, Adam glanced at the painting on Teddy's easel, a bleak landscape of Martha's Vineyard in winter. "Still trying to please the masses, I see. Another Hallmark card."

"The masses don't live here in the winter, when the natives get cooped up. Less Eden in winter than Grimm's Fairy Tale. Nonetheless, I hope you'll linger awhile."

"A little while, in any event. They've given me some recuperation time."

"Nice of them. I certainly hope you're changing jobs."

"You do sound like Mom." Adam's tone became more serious. "Truth to tell, I don't know what I'm doing after this, or whether I'm much suited to anything else than the work I can't tell you about.

There's a part of me you no longer know, and I'm not sure I can change. Sorry if that's unsatisfying."

"'Unsatisfying' is not a synonym for insane."

"Other people in my business get hurt, Ted. Some even appreciate life a little more."

Teddy took a beer from his refrigerator, handing it to Adam, then pulled up a stool and sat across from him. Soberly, he asked, "Any chance you'll become one of them?"

"A good question," Adam answered with equal weight. "And impossible to answer."

"You might start by finding another line of work." Teddy paused a moment. "Have you ever considered writing?"

This time Adam's laugh held a trace of sourness. "Like our father, you mean? He always commended my wisdom in not trying to compete with him. At least in the endeavor where, by his own admission, every other living American fell short of him. Who am I to box with God?"

"Adam Blaine," Ted said firmly. "You could always write, and you come with an actual heart." His tone became quieter, but no less insistent. "He was afraid of you, Adam—always. He may have haunted you, but something about you haunted him. He didn't want to find out you were better."

That's not why I haunted him, Adam thought but did not say. "I've considered it," he admitted. "But in how many areas of life do I want to drag his corpse behind me? A sane man—if that's what I am—cuts his losses."

Teddy regarded him closely. At length, he said, "Which inspires me to wonder if you've seen Carla."

Though he followed Teddy's thoughts, Adam chose to smile again. "You are becoming our mother, Ted. You've perfectly nailed her first three questions. No, I haven't seen her yet."

"Then you should."

Adam maintained his pretense of amusement. "That's where you and Mom diverge. You need to check in with her for a refresher course on Carla Pacelli. Thief of husbands and, not so incidentally, our fortune."

"I remember, Adam. And I'm sure you'll recall that I felt the same way she does. Then you asked me to look in on her, and the experience is complicating my lack of faith in human nature. But never mind that. What has Carla told you about the baby?"

"That they're both doing fine."

Teddy gave him a disgusted look. "And a bullet in the shoulder's nothing. At some point, stoicism becomes lockjaw, to the detriment of both of you. She may well lose the baby, and that could be a mercy. Based on the tests she's had, the odds are better than even that our brother-to-be won't live past infancy. And shouldn't."

Adam felt the shock of this run through him. "Tell me about it."

In considerable detail, Teddy did. Listening, Adam felt a sadness so profound that it numbed him. "Jesus . . ."

"I know," his brother said glumly. "She's devastated and, in my own way, so am I. Despite my best intentions, I've become invested in things turning out right for her. I'm very afraid they won't." Teddy hunched forward, looking into Adam's face. "How do you really feel about her?"

"You asked me that before, Ted. I didn't know then, and I don't know now. I've been gone, remember?"

Teddy ignored this. "I'm asking for her sake, not yours. She's pretty guarded. But I think she has real feelings for you, however confusing it may be." His voice lowered. "One member of the walking wounded can tell another. I don't want to see her hurt anymore, that's all."

Adam stared at the floor. "I don't want either of us hurt. And God knows I want this baby to be okay."

"Not good enough," Teddy persisted. "If you can't care for her, don't let her believe you can. She's become pretty strong, I think. But I can sense there've been hard things in her past—more than just her fall from grace. She doesn't need another blow from life after all that's happened. And may happen with this baby."

"I get that."

"But do you really think the two of you could have something? Or is the ghost of our sainted father too big a distraction?"

Adam met his eyes. "Do you understand what she wanted with him, Ted?"

"I used to—money. Now I don't have a clue. But I think she had her reasons. I don't have to comprehend them, just accept that they existed. But if you can't come to terms with that, it's fatal."

"I appreciate your concern," Adam said softly. "But you're telling me things I already know."

Teddy grimaced. "Then let me tell you something you don't know. Not only has the coroner's inquest lingered for an ominously long time, but George Hanley has refused Avi Gold's request to tell the judge that he won't prosecute Jack—or any of the rest of us. Which means our problems remain very much alive."

Adam felt the past closing in again. "Does Avi know why?"

"No. Although he divines that the woman from the *Inquirer*, Amanda Ferris, has gotten Hanley's ear. I know she's still around here."

For a reflexive moment, Adam wondered how to get rid of her. Amidst the tangle of worries—for Jack, and for himself—it struck him that Ferris was yet another impediment to any relationship with Carla, even were he capable of one. Feigning unconcern, he told his brother, "Other than trailing slime, I don't know what she can do. Just stay away from her until this thing is over. And Hanley, of course."

Teddy nodded. "Of course. But you don't have that option, bro. According to Avi, Hanley wants to see you."

Two

By the time Adam parked in Edgartown, a driving sideways rain had started, and the few pedestrians braving the foulness of winter carried umbrellas or walked hunched against the storm. Adam's shoulder hurt; already tired, he did not treasure getting soaked. But it was better to surprise George Hanley, and he needed to know what Hanley thought and where Amanda Ferris fit. So he hurried across Main Street, its asphalt glistening with moisture and puddles, and entered the red brick courthouse, glancing briefly at the alarm system he had thwarted months before.

As Adam well knew, Hanley's office was on the second floor. Seeing his door ajar, Adam knocked, and heard the district attorney say gruffly, "Come on in, whoever you are."

Without responding, Adam entered, took the chair in front of Hanley's desk, and gave the older man his most amiable smile. "Heard you wanted to see me, George. So I came as soon as I could."

Hanley studied him, his own half-smile not affecting the cool curiosity in his eyes. "I thought you were in Afghanistan."

"I was. But my employer has a liberal vacation policy."

Hanley paused, a hint of his displeasure at being surprised by a man he so clearly mistrusted. Bluntly, he asked, "Do you know Amanda Ferris?"

Adam raised his eyebrows. "The *Inquirer's* gift to journalism? She's accosted me a couple of times."

Hanley rearranged his features, adopting an expressionless mask. "Only that?"

Adam let a puzzled look answer for him. Eyes narrowing, Hanley said, "She claims to have met with you in secret, and that you were trying to ferret out the evidence against your brother. She further suggests that you were pulling together a cover-up to exonerate Teddy, and that you broke into the courthouse to rifle my files. The ones I kept right here."

Adam smiled a little. "All that? What proof is she offering?"

Hanley stared at him. "She says you only met at night, on the beach. According to Ferris, you were very careful to leave no evidence you knew her."

"Because there is none." In a cooler tone, Adam continued, "I'm everywhere, it seems, but no one ever sees me. Yet you have a security system and a bunch of cameras. Only a ghost could break in here."

"Unless they were very accomplished," Hanley retorted. "Someone worked a bypass on the system."

"Come off it, George. To shut off your alarm system I'd have to sneak into the building, setting off the system. A bit of a chicken-egg problem, you'll agree. And if I somehow managed to do that, you'd have me on camera. But you don't, or I'd be languishing in your downstairs jail."

"Someone else did it," Hanley said in a cold, inexorable voice. "We think it was a breaking and entering specialist disguised as a service guy, come to look at our system."

"Then I guess he's the one who took your files."

Hanley shook his head, regarding Adam closely. "We have him on camera—a stocky older guy with thick glasses and mustache. But the man two of our cops saw running away from the courthouse that night was tall, obviously young and in great shape. Someone like you. So when Ferris came to us, it sort of resonated."

Adam shrugged. "Sorry I can't help you. But I don't know what night we're talking about, so I don't know where I was. I wouldn't remember anyhow—I had other things on my mind than keeping a calendar. Like my father's death, and that poisonous will he'd left behind . . ."

"But you do remember mailing copies of my investigative files to Teddy's lawyer. His secretary certainly remembers receiving them—however reluctant she was to say so." Hanley leaned forward, arms on his desk. "Interesting how the story Teddy told at the inquest put an innocent gloss on all the physical evidence suggesting he pushed your father off the cliff. Along with Jack's somewhat belated explanation exonerating everyone."

"Truthful explanation, I'd say. Anyhow, that's your department, George. I was halfway across the world when my father died, and I'm certainly no lawyer."

"You're also no fool. As I recall, you went to law school before breaking with Ben."

"So I did. Among the things I learned is that it's a crime to obstruct justice. Which you seem to be accusing me of."

"Who else, Adam?"

Adam adopted a tone of mild contempt. "Unlike your new reporter friend, I don't go around nominating people. But if you ever find out, George, please let me know. You're making me curious."

"Then I'm sure you wouldn't mind testifying," Hanley suggested pointedly. "I can reopen the inquest, so you can tell the judge what you just told me."

Adam shook his head. "Please don't do that on my account, George. I don't feel the need to testify yet again because some reporter pisses on my leg."

Hanley looked at him askance. "Are you saying you'd invoke the Fifth Amendment?"

"If that's your perspective. Mine is that I've already given at the office. Once was enough, thanks. Anything else?"

Hanley's obdurate frown deepened the lines at the edge of his eyes and mouth. "Not now, Adam. You've already gotten what you came for."

Adam stood. "I came because you wanted to see me, remember?"

With that, he left, reviewing his points of vulnerability, his avenues of escape.

The problem was Amanda Ferris.

Five months before, Adam had met Ferris on the beach beneath the promontory.

On the surface, little had happened since Ben's death. Whatever inquiry George Hanley and the police had launched—an exhaustive one, Adam was certain—they had suppressed any news of the incident itself. The previous day Teddy had flown to Boston to buy art supplies; only Adam knew enough to guess he had been summoned by his lawyer. No one had questioned Adam about anything: with the security cameras disabled, all Hanley had was a faceless man, swift and resourceful enough to vanish, eliminating a host of potential suspects while creating a dead end.

Knowing this, Adam had the familiar sense of having set events in motion without leaving any trace. But he continued to parse the varied narratives surrounding the will and his father's death, including from his family, sensing that none of them was truthful or complete. And now he had the problem of Amanda Ferris.

As at their prior meeting, he had followed her from Edgartown; he still wanted no evidence that they had met. But the woman was nothing if not clever. Now he would learn how fully she understood their chess game.

The air was balmier; the seas calm; the wind smelling faintly of sea salt. This time, she had not tried to conceal a tape recorder. By now she grasped that their conversations were damning to them both.

"Too bad I couldn't get the pathologist's report," she said with quiet acidity. "But you may not have to wait long. Only until Hanley indicts your brother."

Hearing this made Adam edgy. "Tell me about that."

Ferris shifted her weight, adding to the restlessness animating her wiry frame. "First, there's the evidence at the scene. A footprint matching your brother's boot. Plus skid marks suggesting someone dragged your father toward the cliff."

And mud on his father's heels, Adam thought, but Ferris did not know this. "What else?"

"There's a button missing from his shirt, suggesting a struggle—"

"Have they found it?"

Ferris hesitated. "No."

Because I found it, Adam thought. "Then it means nothing."

"There's also the neighbor who was walking along the trail. He thought he heard a man screaming, then saw a figure leaving the promontory—"

Nathan Wright, Adam knew. Feigning curiosity, he asked, "Man, or woman?"

"He couldn't say." Ferris's tone became more assertive. "But the crime lab found a hair on your father's shirt that matches Teddy's DNA."

This Adam had not known. "Anything more?"

"Your brother's cell phone records. About 8:15, well before sunset, he received a call from the landline in the main house—no doubt from your mother. At 9:51, after the neighbor saw this unknown figure, Teddy left a message with an ex-lover—"

"Concerning what?"

"It wasn't specific, though he sounded distraught. But the time between calls leaves an hour and a half for Teddy to go to the promontory, and push your dad off the cliff. Maybe in response to something your mother told him."

"Or," Adam interjected, "maybe she and Teddy gave him a shove together. He was pretty big, after all."

For an instant, Ferris was silent. "You see my point," Adam said with the same indifference. "You're still awash in 'maybes.' So are the police."

Ferris crossed her arms. "Then why did Teddy lie? Not only did he say he hadn't gone there that night, but he said he never went at all. Just like he claimed not to remember Clarice calling him at 8:15. How could that be?"

"Maybe because the phone call was so ordinary. And even assuming the footprint was Teddy's, we don't know whether he left it before 8:15, or after—or anytime near the time my father died. You haven't given me a murder, let alone a murderer."

Once more Ferris hesitated. But she did not know, as Adam did, about the bruises on Ben's wrists. "Let me ask you this," he pressed. "Did the crime lab find any DNA under Teddy's fingernails?"

"No."

"So let's catalog what you don't have. First, definitive proof of a murder. Second, a murderer. What you do have is this boot print, the drag marks, the shadowy figure, the phone records—all subject to multiple interpretations. A first year lawyer could defend Teddy in his sleep." Adam paused, then prodded, "So now that we've acquitted my brother, what do you have on Carla Pacelli?"

"Her DNA on the dead man's clothes and face. But is she strong enough to throw him off a cliff?"

Adam flashed on Pacelli at dinner. "She looks pretty fit to me." His voice became sharp. "On the question of strength, my dad was dying. He might even have had a stroke—in which case, an average woman could have tossed him overboard. That would explain the drag marks. So you can add Carla to the list of suspects."

Ferris shook her head. "She's a dead end. I can't find anyone she told about the will. Present company excepted, she's the most guarded person in America. You tell me what that means."

I've only lied to you once, Carla had told him, for reasons of my own, and not about Jenny or the will. "Maybe she's in mourning," Adam rejoined. "But every instinct I have says she's hiding something serious. According to my mother, a few nights before he died she saw my father on the promontory with a woman. Who else but Pacelli?"

"Quit trying to divert me," Ferris said in a relentless tone. "I've got more than enough for a story. We're going to print that Edward

Blaine is the prime suspect in his father's murder, and spell out the evidence against him."

In the half-light, Adam looked into her face. "Actually," he told her softly, "you're not."

Ferris gave a short laugh. "Can I ask why?"

"Several reasons. Unless Teddy's indicted, he'll sue you and the *Inquirer* for libel . . ."

"Don't try to threaten me," Ferris shot back. "We have lawyers for that."

"I'm counting on it. You're the one who gave my friend money for information. He and I never talked at all."

"You led me to him."

"So go ahead and confess to bribing a cop so he'd slip you documents and information critical to a murder investigation. Then ask how long it will take the police to indict you for obstruction of justice. Because if you print another word about my brother, I'll make damn sure they do."

"That's bullshit. You told me your cop friend needed money." Suddenly her voice was shrill, uncertain. "Go to the police, and you'd go down with me."

"Would I? You're the one who passed the money, not me. You have no evidence we've ever spoken. And if you try to trace your calls to me, you'll find out that you can't. That also goes for the anonymous call I'll place to the police." Deliberately, Adam muted his voice. "You lose, Amanda. All you can do is leave this island for good. But before you go, you're going to give me the piece you're still holding out. Something about an insurance policy."

She looked away, caught, then met his eyes again. "If you already knew, why ask?"

Ask Teddy about the insurance policy, his guileless friend Bobby Towle had said. "Because you're telling me what you know. So that you remain in my good graces."

Ferris's face twisted, a study in stifled anger. "Four months ago, according to your friend, your mother took out a one million dollar

insurance policy on your father's life, with her and Teddy as ben-
eficiaries. They collect unless Ben committed suicide, or one or the
other killed him. Or," she added spitefully, "if they knew he was
terminal, and bought it to cash in."

Jarred, Adam mustered an air of calm. "From which you
conclude—"

"That they knew about his will, and lied to the police. And that
one or both knew that he was dying, and lied about that, too." She
gave him a sour smile. "Any comment?"

Adam shrugged. "So many questions, so few answers. The only
person who knows what they knew is dead."

"Conveniently so." Ferris's tone became chill. "Your brother will
be indicted by summer's end. Then I'll print my story, and there's
not a damned thing you can do. Especially from Afghanistan."

That much was true, Adam realized. "We're through now," Ferris finished with palpable bitterness. "I don't need a lawyer to know
that you poison anything you touch." She laughed. "Poor Carla."

She turned from him, walking swiftly away as though fearing for
her life. A good thing, Adam supposed.

An hour later, he had found Jack and his mother on the darkened porch, sitting in Adirondack chairs beside a radio tuned to
the Red Sox game. "I thought they'd invented television," Adam
remarked.

This drew a wispy smile from Clarice. "Memories," she answered.
"When I was a little girl, I'd sit here with my father listening to the
games. We had Ted Williams then, and always finished behind
the Yankees. But it felt magical—just my dad, me, the crickets, the
announcer's voice in the darkness, and the sounds of a game far
away. This may be the last summer I can relive that."

Turning, Jack regarded her with avuncular concern. "It'll work
out, Clarice. This place is meant to be yours."

There was something old-fashioned about this scene, Adam had
thought—not just the radio, but that his mother and uncle seemed

like actors in a play from another era. Amanda Ferris had curdled his mood.

"I need to talk with you," he told his mother.

As she looked at him in surprise, Jack regarded him more closely. Then Clarice said, "You can help me make fresh coffee."

He followed her into the kitchen. Stopping by the sink, she poured out the scalded coffee, then carefully ladled more beans into a grinder. "What is it?" she asked.

"The insurance policy."

Glancing up, she asked in a thinner voice, "Where did you hear about that?"

"Not from you. Or Teddy, for that matter."

"Don't reprimand me, Adam." She paused. "The police know, of course. But it isn't that important. After all, it won't let me keep the house, and with Ben having cancer when we applied for it, I don't know that I'll collect. At least that's what my lawyer tells me."

She made not telling him sound innocent enough, Adam thought, but this was not the real problem. Evenly, he said, "The police must wonder why you took it out. So do I."

Clarice put down the bag of beans. "So now you're looking at us like you're George Hanley?"

"Please don't try guilt, Mom. I outgrew it. What concerns me is the answers I'm not getting. Did you expect that something would happen to him?"

"Not anything specific. But when you've lived with someone for forty years, you notice not-so-little things like drinking too much, or losing one's balance for no reason. Or Ben's indifference to being caught out with this actress." She paused, as though finding her own answer. "I didn't imagine him falling off that cliff, or changing his will. Nor did I know that he had brain cancer. Except for worrying he might drive his car into a tree some night, it was nothing that concrete. More a sense that the ground was shifting under us in ways I couldn't identify. When you're as afraid as I was, and as defenseless, you become good at reading tea leaves."

"Did you discuss this with Teddy?"

"In a general way, yes. But the initiative for the insurance was mine." Her voice became clipped. "Are we quite done with this now? We've left your uncle sitting there."

"One more thing," Adam said. "Why did you call Teddy the night he died?"

Clarice cocked her head. "Did I? When?"

"About 8:30."

"I really don't remember. So it can't have been significant." Clarice frowned. "I certainly didn't call him to predict your father's death. Which leaves me wondering why you seem to know more about me than I can remember."

"Because Teddy's in trouble," Adam said curtly. "Do you recall anything else about that night? Specifically anything that would make it harder for the police to suspect my brother?"

"I know this much," Clarice responded firmly, "as a mother. No doubt Teddy feels protective toward me. But he's the last person on earth capable of killing Ben. You're imagining Teddy as yourself."

Turning, Clarice had foreclosed any further discussion, leaving Adam with still more questions, the ones George Hanley must have had. But only Adam had learned the truth.

THREE

When Adam reached the guest house, the long Vineyard night, spitting rain, was a deep black relieved only by the light glowing in Carla's window. He felt a moment's disbelief; the last time he had been here, the landscape had been green and verdant, and he would soon be returning to a harsh terrain he might never leave. Now there was life ahead of him, a future he could not define.

Carrying French bread and a container of clam chowder, he knocked on the door. When Carla answered, she stood back, and for a moment they gazed at each other in silence. She was very pregnant, he saw at once; following his eyes, she lowered her gaze as though to conceal a smile, shaking her head with a kind of wonder—perhaps at herself, perhaps simply that he was here. In a gesture of mock surrender, she opened her arms and, when he reached for her, rested her face against his shoulder. Huskily, she said, "I'm so glad you're back."

Adam could smell the womanly freshness of her. "Was there a question?"

"I thought so. In most jobs people don't get shot."

Her soft voice carried a hint of another question, perhaps the hope that he would leave the agency. But he had no answer for this, or for anything else. Instead, he kissed her gently. "I brought dinner," he said. "I gather you've lost some mobility."

She leaned back, her eyes much graver. "Teddy told you."

"Yes. I wish I'd known."

Once more, Carla shook her head. "I didn't want to worry you. And what could you have done?"

Softly but firmly, he answered, "Not the point."

Her expression became questioning. Do you really want to be part of my life? he imagined her wondering. "I should probably sit down," she told him. "These days I'm only good at occupying space. But all I can do is give this baby every chance."

She did not need to say that he might already be doomed, or how devastating that would be for her. Sitting beside him on the couch, she reached out with curled fingers and touched his shoulder. "How is it?"

"A little tender still, but healing nicely. As wounds go I lucked out."

She looked at him intently. "Tell me what happened—all of it. Dinner can wait."

With some reluctance, he complied, dwelling on Steve Branch's courage rather than his own ordeal. He did not tell her that, in the moments of his desperation, he had imagined coming back to her. "There's one part you're leaving out," she prodded. "Weren't you the least bit scared?"

"Sure. When I felt the earthquake."

Carla gave a rueful laugh. "Great. I waited all this time to have dinner with John Wayne."

All at once, Adam needed to tell her the truth. "You heard my nightmares, Carla. The best I can do is try to put all that behind me. Trust that I appreciate being alive, never more than at this moment."

"Please keep that in mind," she said, then glanced down at her stomach with a look that told him everything. "I just felt the baby move," she added softly. "I never thought I'd be so grateful to be kicked by a man."

After dinner, Adam started a fire with logs and kindling from the covered porch outside. They sat on the couch watching the orange yellow flames spit and flicker in the darkness, Carla sitting between his legs with her back against his chest, her hair grazing his face. She should not like this too much, she told herself, or imagine other nights with him.

"I really enjoyed your letters," Adam told her, then added more softly, "Actually, they meant a lot."

Carla smiled to herself. "I'm relieved to hear it. I worried that there were Exhibit A in the annals of narcissism—first, last and always about me."

"Only because I asked. Anyhow, I've seen true narcissism first-hand. Along with the damage to other people, the casualties include honesty and self-reflection. You're more than capable of both."

Carla chose to avoid the clear reference to Benjamin Blaine. "If so, it's only because I learned the hard way. There were countless times when I wish I'd had known myself earlier and better."

She felt him pause again. "Including with men?"

He was asking about Ben, she was now quite certain. But that was a hard conversation, to be reserved for another time that might never arrive. "The subject of men," she finally answered, "begins with my father. You know the essence of it—he was physically and verbally abusive. Not to mention frighteningly unpredictable, especially on the all too frequent evenings when he was drunk. Just for fun, throw in harshly judgmental: if I got an A, I was great; if I got B's or C's, I was worthless.

"When there's no in-between, you don't know how to feel about yourself. Are you a bad person, or good one? And what to make of it when your strict Catholic father and mother marinate you in the evils of sex outside marriage—and then you find out he's cheating on the woman to whom marriage brings so much suffering that all she can do is cast her eyes to God."

"Makes for a confusing childhood, I imagine."

He was also speaking about himself, Carla sensed, though he could not admit this without mentioning Ben. "And a confused adult," she replied. "I was ambitious, driven, assertive, and able to fight through adversity and rejection. But I didn't know how to value myself as a woman. Nothing good comes from that kind of emotional whipsaw. Including my choice of men."

She would have been happy to stop there—though honesty had become her touchstone, she was still a woman, and she felt too keenly her own desire not to diminish herself in the eyes of Adam Blaine. Perhaps she should forgive herself for this—trust still did not come easily to her, and the man who held her remained an enigma. Then he said quietly, "I'd really like to understand that, Carla—for my own sake. Not the names or details, more the feeling of it."

Was he also wondering about himself? Carla mused in silence. After Jenny Leigh, she knew from Teddy, there had been no one important in Adam's life. But his reasons must be different than her own. At length, she answered, "I did what I thought any sensible woman would do—pick men who were different from my father. I certainly can't fault my success in that way. Not once did anyone hit me.

"Too bad, in a sense—the first time would've been the last. Instead, I picked men who were 'gentle.' I failed to notice that they were also weak or adolescent or passive aggressive or disengaged or narcissistic—more often than not, most of the above. But all of them had one overriding virtue: because they couldn't see inside me, I didn't have to deal with my own psychological baggage, the need to hide which fit so perfectly with my career. The attention I craved—to me as a person—also scared the hell out of me. So 'Carla Pacelli' became just another role, as unreal as the rest."

"The success you had was real enough."

For a time, Carla gazed at the fire, caught between her present and her past. "And never enough," she amended. "All the attention I got wasn't for me—assuming that I could've told you who I was. The most pathetic part was when I got the lead in *Deep Cover*. Maybe, I told myself, Dad will be proud of me at last. Instead, he felt threatened by my success; all he could do was tear down the show, and me for doing it. That I was devastated tells you how empty I was, how completely unable to reach out for what I truly needed."

"Which is?"

The answers, Carla knew, were much easier listed than found. Self-awareness counted. And empathy. Intelligence, of course. Fidelity, thank you very much. Sobriety. Openness. A companion who could love her as she was, with all her flaws and weaknesses and complications. Someone to support her in a recovery that would continue as long as she lived. A bond of mind and spirit where each made the other better. The ability to laugh at his own quirks—and hers. A man who could love her son, should he live, as much as he did her. Oh yes, God—don't forget never quite getting enough of him, the spontaneous, irrational desire to drag this man off to bed. Which reminded her that, more than likely, Adam possessed at least some of what she wanted most. But his capacity to be the other things she craved was obscure enough to worry her, and she did not know him well enough to hope. Above all, she doubted that he could ever forgive her relationship with Benjamin Blaine.

"The specifications are many," she said demurely. "And I like to keep them a surprise. Do you know Puccini's opera *Turandot*?"

Adam laughed. "I saw it once at the Met. As I recall, the story involves a Chinese princess who'll only marry the man who guesses the secret word that unlocks her heart. The losers got beheaded."

"You've caught the essence of it. But the music is beautiful, isn't it."

"Incomparable. Fortunately, all I had at risk was the cost of a seat in the rear balcony. So when did you develop these rigorous standards?"

For a moment, Carla watched the crackling flames cast shadows in the room "It began at Betty Ford. The first step was the obvious: to realize that I had no examples of a healthy relationship, and that my own confusion started with my mother and, especially, my father. Trying to escape him, I kept picking men who couldn't love me—just as he couldn't. No surprise that the result was an emotional life as empty as I was. To change that, I had to change how I understood that life."

"How did you go about that?"

"I'll spare you," Carla demurred. "Too long, too boring, too self-referential. But, if you like, I can tell you a story about dreams."

"Go ahead," Adam responded softly. "Somehow I think I can relate to that."

Though his embrace was gentle, Carla could feel the warmth of his chest, the strength of his arms. Settling back against him, she began, "I started having it after I'd been in therapy for a while. It was always the same. I was a small child again, running across a barren field—terrified, because a carnivorous bear with red eyes and bloody teeth and claws was chasing me.

"I'm trying to get to a chain-link fence, to escape to a meadow on the other side. But it's too high—when I get there, I can't climb it. I can hear the bear coming closer. I look around desperately, and suddenly see a house. But there's no one looking out the window, no one to hear my cries. As the bear reaches out for me, I wake up sweating."

"How often did you have it?"

"All the time." Recalling the dream, Carla found, still left her feeling exhausted and alone. "So tell me what you think it means."

"Some of it's plain enough, I guess. The bear is your father." He paused a moment. "In the dream, do you think the house is empty?"

"No."

"Then the person who doesn't hear you would most likely be your mother."

Slowly, Carla felt herself relax. "You win, Adam—there'll be no beheadings tonight. Foolish as this sounds, my therapist at Betty Ford handed me colored pencils and asked me to redraw the dream as I would have wanted it to be. In my picture, I'm feeding the bear, who's now benign, and my mother is riding on its back. It sounds silly, I know. But I stopped having the dream. The larger lesson, of course, was that I had to transform my inner life before I could change my life in the world."

She could sense him forming questions. After a time, he asked, "Did your parents ever come to visit you?"

"Only my mother. Dad was too disgusted with having such a weakling for a daughter. But Mom did her best to encourage me. My recovery came first, she said—alcohol was a curse to my father, and she didn't want that for me." Carla hesitated. "Toward the end, when I was due to get out, she said wistfully, 'I only wish you had a man in your life.'

"The answer was on the tip of my tongue: 'That depends on what kind of man.' But all I said was, 'I'll be okay, mom.' It's so pointless a blame her, or even him. As I said to you before, every parent was a child once." Including Benjamin Blaine, she did not feel safe in adding.

"Still," Adam ventured, "when you came home you must've felt pretty lonely. Especially because you were giving up your career."

Another probe about Ben, Carla thought—however elliptical. But she chose to answer the question as he asked it. "Backing off from celebrity wasn't so hard. That was always a burden, and the notoriety around crashing and burning became a nightmare. What was hard to let go was acting. Since I'd decided to become an actress, I never once considered quitting. Sometimes I used anger to keep me going—'why not me?' But I was so determined that I backed myself into a corner, deliberately acquiring no other skills I could fall back on. If I had no choice but to push forward until I succeeded, I told myself, then I would."

"Sounds familiar," Adam responded. "In the last few years, I've made myself do things I'd never imagined, by forcing myself into situations where I had no choice. A hard way to live, but hard to give up. It's like violating your deepest superstition."

For a moment, Carla allowed herself to hope that he could find another path. "It was like that for me," she acknowledged. "Every fiber of my being screamed 'don't quit.' Deep down I believed that I'd be no one if I did.

"But that's the challenge, isn't it? To change how you see yourself, and find other reasons for being that are healthier and more fulfilling." Saying this, she felt a tinge of fear. "For me, the baby has been the biggest one. It's frightening to think I may never know him, to lie awake wondering night after night. But if he lives, the point is not to lean on him, but to be good for him.

"So I need something else to do in the world. As a therapist I could reach out to other people—like acting, I suppose, but in a much more intimate way. Where I can see a person in front of me, and know whether I've been helpful."

Adam held her a little closer. "I think you'll be very good at it, Carla. Some things I simply know about you. That's one."

To her surprise, she felt a rush of gratitude. "Believe it or not, that means a lot to me. So thank you."

The other man to whom she felt grateful in this way, Carla knew, was Benjamin Blaine. Yet to say this might spoil the moment. No doubt she had good reason to fear that. But there was no doubt that, at least with Adam, she remained the former Carla Pacelli—slow to trust, afraid to place herself at risk.

It was way too soon to admit this, or to even know if she should. Nor had she admitted the deepest truth about her choice of men— knowing that they could never meet her needs, she had also known that each relationship would end. Even with Ben, her only man after becoming stronger, they both knew that he would die. As terrible as this had been, she could see her way out.

But Adam Blaine unsettled her. For months she had feared, yet anticipated, his death. Now he had survived. She wanted him to be free of the past, just as she was trying to be. But Adam's hatred for the father of the child she bore might tear them apart. Another man, another exit. She did not know whether it was right to want him, or to fear him.

"Cat got your tongue?" he asked.

"I'm just sleepy."

"There are other nights," he said easily "I forgot that you're sleeping for two."

Perhaps she only imagined that he was as troubled, and as questioning, as she. Because of her, or Ben, or himself. And perhaps because of things he did not want her to know.

"I missed you," he said at last.

"And I you."

He kissed her gently, and was gone.

FOUR

Driving home, Adam reflected on what he could not tell anyone—Carla least of all. Including that he had believed Teddy guilty of murder and had tried to offer Carla in his place. A piercing memory came to him then, another turning point in the maze he could not seem to escape.

It was just after his final meeting with Amanda Ferris. Walking to the guesthouse that night, Adam had seen Teddy through the window, seated at his easel with a glass of red wine beside him. The stillness of his posture suggested a trance.

When Adam entered, pulling up a stool at Teddy's shoulder, his brother's only movement was to pick up a brush. This canvass was abstract, with garish colors to which Teddy began adding slashes of bright red. He worked with what seemed a terrible intensity, the sheen of sweat on his forehead; but for the obstinacy of his brother's concentration Adam might have believed that Teddy did not notice him. For an instant he had recalled watching Teddy as he painted—Adam at twelve, Teddy at fourteen or fifteen—and how magical it was to see his brother fill a blank canvass with such startling images. Calmly, he said, "Any time you're ready, Ted."

After a moment, Teddy turned to him, his smile guarded. "What is it, bro?"

"I know you were on the cliff that night. I don't mind that you lied. But George Hanley and the cops mind quite a lot."

A shadow crossed Teddy's face. "How do you know all that?"

"That's irrelevant. All that matters is that they're preparing to indict you."

In the harsh illumination from above, Adam saw the first etching of age at the corners of Teddy's eyes, and, more unsettling, the deep vulnerability of a man who felt entrapped. Teddy lowered his voice, as though afraid of being heard. "My lawyer says not to talk about this."

"Good advice for anyone but me." Adam's tone became cool. "The first thing I ask is that you listen, then tell your lawyer what I've said without disclosing who said it. That conversation is covered by the attorney-client privilege. Understood?"

Silent, Teddy nodded.

With willed dispassion, Adam recited all that he had learned from Amanda Ferris and the files he had stolen: the unknown person Nate Wright had seen at the promontory on the night Ben died; Teddy's boot print; the drag marks; the bruises on Ben's wrists; the mud on his boot heels; Teddy's hair on his shirt; Clarice's call to him; his call to the ex-lover; his fantasies about killing their father; the insurance policy on Ben's life—all rendered more damning by Teddy's lie. "I'm sure your lawyer knows most of this," Adam concluded. "But not all—unless you've told him more than I think you have. If there's anything you've left out, tell him now. Then start perfecting a story that covers all this and still makes you out to be innocent."

Teddy flushed. "So you think I killed him?"

"I don't give a damn. You've paid too big a price for him already."

A brief, reflexive tremor ran through Teddy's frame. "And if I tell you what happened?"

"It never leaves this room."

"It can't," Teddy said with sudden force. "This involves more than me. You'll have to be every bit the actor I've come to think you are."

Adam felt a stab of dread, a sense of coming closer to a reckoning with truth. "Go ahead."

Teddy bent forward on the stool, hands folded in his lap, then said in a husky voice, "We didn't tell the truth—not all of it. Mom called me that night, close to frantic. Dad was drunk and rambling, she said, not really making sense. But the essence was that he was leaving her for Carla Pacelli."

Adam felt this revelation lead to others: that his mother and brother had lied to him and to the police; that—at least on this point—Carla Pacelli had told the truth. "Why didn't you tell that to the police?"

"Because I knew that Mother hadn't. She told me she was afraid that could make his death look different than what it was—an accident."

Adam tried to envision Clarice suggesting this, further complicating his sense of who she was. Quietly, he asked, "Because she believed that? Or because that's what she needed other people to believe?"

Teddy rubbed his temples. "I can't be sure. See, I concealed the truth from her, as well. She still doesn't know that I went to the promontory."

"This family certainly has a gift for candor, doesn't it? Tell me when you went there."

"After she called me." Teddy's voice became harder. "That sonofabitch had tormented me for years, and now he was humiliating our mother. So I decided to confront him." His words came in a rush now. "He was standing there like he had a thousand nights before, staring at the fucking sunset like it was the last one in human history, and he was there to bear witness."

Just imagine not looking at this, Ben had said to their neighbor Nathan Wright. *Can you?* "Maybe he was," Adam said. "After all, the man was dying."

"I didn't know that. All I knew was that he treated her like dirt." Teddy shook his head, voice thickening with emotion. "God help me, I wanted to push him off that cliff, just like I'd imagined ever since I was a kid. Instead, I just stood there waiting for him to notice me.

"When he finally did, he gave me this look—not disdainful like normal, but more puzzled. 'What are you doing here?' he asked. 'You hate this place.' It threw me off guard—suddenly he had the tone and manner of an old man, and his face looked ravaged. My idea of him was so strong I hadn't noticed he'd become his own ghost.

"'I'm here for my mother,' I told him. 'For years, I've watched you degrade her in private, humiliate her in public, and exploit her fear of being abandoned. She's the only parent I ever had. You were just a sperm donor, and even that makes me want to vomit.' He tried to muster that supercilious smile, but even that was a ghost. 'Then go ahead,' he told me. 'Just keep it off my boots. They're new.'"

Adam tried to imagine the ferocity of will that made his father, dying, still prefer hatred to pity. But Teddy seemed transported back in time. "Maybe I'll push you off this cliff,' I told him. He just kept looking at me, almost like he was curious what I'd do. Then he spoke in a strange new voice, tired but completely calm, 'If you hate me that much, do it for your mother. Or better yet, yourself.'

"He sounded like he didn't care, that he'd be willing to die if that would make me feel whole. All at once, I saw him as he was, this aging husk of a man. I couldn't move, or fight back the tears." Briefly, Teddy closed his eyes. "Looking back at me, he seemed to slump. 'Jesus,' he said in this heavy way I'd never heard before. 'What have I done to you, Teddy? Did I make you like this?'

"I don't know whether he meant gay, or too weak to act in my own behalf. Then he finished: 'To come to the end, and face this. It's not your fault you could never be like Adam. It was foolish of me to want that.'"

For a moment, Adam could say nothing. Then he said softly, "He certainly had a gift, didn't he? Only he could issue an apology meant to cut you to the quick."

Teddy continued as if he had not heard. "I started toward him. He just watched me, not moving, when suddenly his eyes rolled back in his head. Then he kind of collapsed like he was too tired to stand, and sat there in the mud near the side of the cliff, his eyes as blank as marbles." Pausing, Teddy looked into Adam's face, as though recalling he was there. "He was utterly defenseless. But killing a helpless man is what he would expect from me. So I grabbed him by the wrists and dragged him to the rocky area, where at least it wasn't muddy. Then I sat there, studying his face as though he'd gone to sleep, trying to remember when I'd loved him.

"Suddenly his eyes snapped open. He looked at me, surprised, then said, 'I passed out, didn't I? It's happening more often.' Then he asked in this quiet voice, 'Why didn't you kill me, Teddy?' I gave him the only answer I could think of: 'Too easy.'"

Someday people won't read you anymore, Adam remembered telling his father. *You'll be left with whoever is left to love you. It's not too late for Teddy to be one of them.* Finally, he asked, "How did he react?"

Teddy swallowed. "His eyes seemed to focus, like he'd never seen me before. Then he sort of croaked, 'I'll change things, Teddy. At least those things I still can help.'"

"The will?"

"Maybe," Teddy answered. "But I didn't know about that, and I'm sure Mom didn't either. So what I imagined him saying was that maybe he wouldn't leave her.

"Suddenly I felt exhausted—not only by what happened between us, but by being in that place. Without saying another word, I left him there. I never saw my father again." Teddy looked at Adam intently, finishing with lacerating bitterness, "For all I know he jumped or fell. Whatever happened, the sonofabitch fucked me one more time. Instead of fixing the will, he made me the prime suspect in a murder I could only fantasize about."

Silent, Adam struggled to distance himself from Teddy's story and his desire to believe it. Finally, he asked, "Why did you call your ex-boyfriend?"

"Jesus, Adam—wouldn't you call someone after an experience like that? Or would you just pour yourself a drink and switch on the Red Sox game?"

"I really don't know. But I might have told Sean Mallory what you just told me, instead of framing myself for murder. Assuming, of course, that anything you've told me is true."

A moment's anger flickered through Teddy's eyes, and then he looked away. "You've met Mallory," he said in a dispirited tone. "I took one look at him, and knew he wouldn't believe me. I don't think George Hanley would, either. All I'd do is get myself and Mom in trouble."

"Instead of just yourself," Adam rejoined. "But now you're right to protect her, I suppose, given what you say she doesn't know. A sudden recollection of her phone call might not help either one of you."

Looking up, Teddy met his brother's gaze. "Do you believe me, Adam?"

Adam weighed his answer. Too much of Teddy's story was implausible. But it had the virtue, at least, of accounting for the evidence Adam had siphoned to his lawyer—suggesting its essential truth, or more likely, his brother's considerable ingenuity. A jury might not— probably would not—believe him. But Adam could not bring himself to reject the story outright. Then it struck him that if Teddy's account was true, and Ben had resolved to revise his will yet again, Carla Pacelli might have had reason to kill him. But this assumed that Carla had come to the promontory, and that Ben had told her. An assumption that, as of now, was as unprovable as the other indispensable assumption: that Carla had known about her inheritance.

"It doesn't matter what I believe," Adam said at length. "Your story covers the evidence as I know it—except for the button. Tell me how that came off his shirt."

"I have no idea," Teddy insisted. "I never touched his shirt. For all I know the button was already missing."

Adam considered this. The button had not been missing; Adam had found it at the scene, and the hair on Ben's shirt suggested closer contact than Teddy admitted. But if his brother were telling the truth, then someone else—perhaps Nathan Wright's elusive figure—had ripped the button off. And only Adam knew that.

Watching his face, Teddy said, "You don't believe me, do you? I'm pretty sure my lawyer doesn't, either. I guess that's what happens when he gives you a lie detector test, and it comes out inconclusive. All I could tell him is that my fantasy was so strong that sometimes I feel like I killed him. Doesn't inspire much confidence, does it?"

Adam did not answer. "Just keep our mother out of this," he instructed. "Including what I know about her not-so-small lapse of memory. At least until I figure out what else to do."

Teddy stared at him. "You sent my lawyer those documents, didn't you?"

Adam stood. Then he had smiled a little, placing a hand on Teddy's shoulder. "What documents?" he replied, then returned to their mother's house, his expression as he said good night to her seemingly placid and untroubled.

Arriving at the house, Adam sat in the driveway.

In hindsight, he had been as innocent as Teddy. He had not known who his father was, or that Jack had killed the man, Carla's lover, whom Adam had hated as a son. Now he was part of that, as guilty as his father.

FIVE

The next morning was chill and leaden, with sheets of wind sweeping off the gray roiling waters of the Vineyard Sound. Thoughts in turmoil, Adam knocked on Charlie Glazer's front door.

Answering, the psychiatrist gave him a cheerful grin. "Glad you made it back."

"Me, too."

Charlie beckoned him inside. As they went to his living room, his expression became inquiring. "So this part of your life is done?"

"Only in Afghanistan. I haven't decided about the job."

"It seems we'll have enough to talk about. You like your coffee black, I remember."

Adam took a chair near a window that framed the white-capped sea. Returning with two mugs, Charlie sat across from him. "How is it to be back?"

Adam sorted through his thoughts. "Confusing. For whatever reason, I was expecting to die. But when the moment came, I did my damnedest to survive, and killed some Afghans in the bargain. I'm not sure I've processed it all yet. But here I am, and this place is every bit as complicated as when I left." He shook his head in dismay. "As you said, I'm living in compartments. Too many."

"Such as?"

"Carla, for one. I saw her last night."

Charlie's blue eyes betrayed interest and concern. "How was that?"

Wondering how to express this, Adam described what he learned from her letters, and from the evening before. "She's like a kaleidoscope," he concluded. "Moment to moment I see something different. Ben's lover; a mother desperately fighting to save a baby who may be doomed; a scarred and complicated, but deeply honest person; this woman I seem to want, and who wonders if she wants me; a fantasy of the future whose image kept coming back to me when I was fighting to survive. And I don't even know what all that means—or should mean."

"Still worried about your capacity to love?" Charlie inquired gently.

Adam accorded the therapist a somewhat sour smile. "I really missed you, Charlie. We could have worked that one out by now." He took a sip of coffee. "As it is, too often I still experience the same detachment, this wanting to withdraw when I sense someone getting close to me. Even with Carla—no, especially with Carla. Every time I imagine her with Ben, anger and revulsion bubble up. And when I try to get her to talk about it, she won't."

Charlie raised his eyebrows. "Are you surprised? No doubt she's smart enough to imagine all the feelings that might open up. Maybe she's wondering whether it's safe to trust you—for good reason, as you admit. But neither of you seems emotionally prepared to make the first move." Charlie's voice softened. "Not even physically, I gather, given the precariousness of her pregnancy."

"She's pretty pregnant," Adam said dryly. "In the best of worlds, the logistics would be tricky." When Charlie merely looked at him, he confessed, "You're right enough about our dynamics. But there's something else that I can't shake."

"Concerning?"

"The medical examiner's inquest."

Charlie's eyes narrowed. "I know you've worried about your clandestine operations, as it were. But I thought Jack put all that to rest."

"Not so. When I left here, I hoped that the hearing had buried all that—and Ben with it. But George Hanley's still poking around. Along with a tabloid reporter who thinks all of our testimony—my mother's, Teddy's, Jack's, and my own—was shot through with lies."

Charlie pondered this. "I won't ask what really happened," he said at length. "But I suspect this may be not only a problem for you, but potentially destructive to any relationship with Carla."

Hearing this spoken aloud depressed Adam further. "This is nothing you can help me with, Charlie. Trust me about that."

"Still," the therapist persisted, "what you're implying suggests something pretty loaded. You didn't kill Ben—that much everyone knows. But it's clear you're still carrying your family on your back, at whatever cost." Leaning forward, Charlie continued, "Seems you're in a quandary, Adam. You're dealing with a near-death experience most men would find traumatic. That raises basic questions about the purpose of your life—by itself, more than enough reason for reflection. Instead, you're coping with the web of secrets arising from Ben's death. And whether Carla Pacelli is Ben's last taunt from the grave."

Fighting back despair, Adam said, "Not a pretty picture. But we have to start somewhere, don't we?"

"True enough," Charlie agreed crisply. "Where should we begin?"

"Maybe with my work," Adam responded in a pensive tone. "Conceptually, I don't regret anything I've done. We've prevented another 9/11 by decimating the leadership of al-Qaeda and the Taliban. That was my job, and I'm more than okay with it." Adam took another swallow of lukewarm coffee. "But challenge and danger become addictive. I'm not sure what else I'd do, or whether I'm suited to the life most people want—that I used to want. Now that seems like a long time ago."

"It was, Adam. And a lot has happened to you since then. Mind telling me how you got wounded?"

For the next few moments, Adam complied, trying to drain the emotion from his account. When he finished, Charlie gazed out at the sound, his tone and manner reflective. "When I look at dangerous waters, I often think of Ben. He'd sail in damned near any weather. What he was most afraid of, I came to think, was acknowledging his own fear." Pausing, he faced Adam, "I always thought you needed to live up to that—to find out if you're as brave and resourceful as he was. Few men would've taken on the work you did, and fewer would've survived it. In the process, you saved the man who rescued you. That's a lot to know about yourself."

Once again, Adam wrestled with his sense of failure. "I understand that. But we didn't bring back the man we were sent to find."

"Not your fault. The point is that you passed the test, and you're still alive. The question is what you do now."

"Any suggestions?"

"Not my call. But you've begun to seem more inquisitive and open—maybe even a little softer. You may not believe it, but I don't think you're lost to yourself or to others." The therapist looked at him intently. "You know the issues. Whether you stay with the agency. Whether you can deal with the effects of the last ten years. Whether—especially given the apparent risks still looming from Ben's death—you can reach some peace with your mother and Jack. And, of course, with a dead man." Charlie's tone softened. "Which brings us back to your relationship with women—specifically, with Carla Pacelli. At least for now, she's bound up with everything else. So let me pose a few thoughts. Not as definitive truths, but as questions you might consider."

"All right."

"Start with Carla's life before you met her. As I understand you, she had a destructive and abusive father—much like Ben's father, ironically enough, and there's even a resemblance between her childhood and how Ben sometimes treated you. She may associate love with pain; certainly, her relationship with men seems to have had a self-destructive quality. So did her use of drugs and alcohol, which destroyed the one identity she had . . ."

"I think she's stronger now," Adam objected.

Charlie gave him a measured look. "True, she went through recovery. From the sound of things, she's more in touch with herself. But, at least on the surface, Ben was another questionable choice. Which suggests that she may still have the capacity to self-destruct.

"I worry about what happens to her if there's some tragedy with this child. Like you, I think Carla is seeking redemption; as you do—though it's neither of our fault—I would guess she has a dark side. So the next man she chooses may help determine what happens to her."

The last remark hit Adam hard. "Is that a warning?"

"It's an observation. You've spent the last decade trying to outrun Benjamin Blaine. Maybe you should want your own woman, not Ben's lover. If that's not what you want, perhaps it's because you're still competing with him." Charlie held up a placating hand. "Ben will never be the love of Carla's life—he's dead. Maybe you can be. You might even become a better father to his son. But unless you're very clear about your reasons, you and Carla could fall back into Ben's vortex when you both need to escape."

"Oh, it's not as bad as all that," Adam replied softly. "At least he wasn't really my father."

Charlie chose to ignore the irony. "And a good thing," he responded. "Even before Jenny, you sensed that aspects of your relationship were abnormal for a father and a son. It must have been a relief to discover why."

"In some ways. Though it doesn't help with Jenny."

"A crucial point." The therapist leaned forward. "I'm somewhat reluctant to say this. But I wonder if, by taking Jenny, Ben was doing to you what your real father—his brother—had done with your mother."

Adam expelled a breath, "Jesus . . ."

"Pretty dark," Charlie conceded. "But it makes a certain twisted sense. So you have to ask yourself whether—however subconsciously—you risk continuing this particularly vicious cycle. It's a question I've raised before, and now it's more germane than ever."

Adam stiffened with anger. "Do you really think I'm that screwed up?"

"I'm not saying that I'm right," Charlie answered calmly. "But you need to understand what Carla means to you. And to know whether you can accept her relationship to Ben—whatever her reasons—with enough compassion to overcome the revulsion you acknowledge feeling. If so, both of you could help each other find transcendence. But only you can figure out if you're capable of that."

Weighing this, Adam felt suddenly, woefully inadequate. "I don't know," he confessed. "I just don't know."

Charlie nodded gravely. "That's a start, Adam. Let's leave it there for now."

Six

After leaving Charlie's house, Adam drove to the dock of Menemsha Harbor. Ignoring the raw weather, he sat hunched on the pier, staring sightlessly at the battered fishing boats as he pondered Charlie's questions. He needed to be alone; he did not want his thoughts broken by the emotional static that pervaded his mother's home.

He wanted Carla—this much he knew. He could imagine making love to her, the intense desire to reach her essence, break down the walls between them. But his feelings were too complicated, and he feared the harm he might cause them both. Nothing he could do felt right or certain. In his life, Benjamin Blaine had done great harm; now Adam feared being too much like him. He felt angry at Charlie Glazer, and untrusting of himself. The inquest hovered over him like an albatross.

After a fruitless, dismal hour in this mental cul-de-sac, the piercing cold forced Adam home. When he arrived, the kitchen phone was ringing.

Clarice Blaine answered it. Her face was expressionless, her tone cool; for a moment he imagined that, against reason but out of some deep need, Carla had called him. Then his mother handed him the phone, saying in her most arid voice, "It's Rachel Ravinsky."

Surprised, Adam took the phone. "Enjoying the day?" he asked.

Rachel laughed. "Not really. I was feeling cold even before announcing myself to your mother. She has a lovely way of reminding me I'm Whitney's daughter."

Adam glanced at Clarice, who had resumed putting away dishes with an inscrutable expression intended to speak volumes. "You wanted to experience winter," he reminded her. "I suffered it for years. Hope it doesn't spoil your writing."

"Actually, this weather is part of why I'm stir crazy. But the real problem is writing a first novel. I've typed in lots of words, most of which form sentences. But it still feels like trying to catch lightning in a bottle—while blindfolded."

"Sounds dire."

"Desperate, actually," she agreed with mock dismay, which, Adam sensed, was deployed to mask her genuine doubts. "And against all odds, I'm becoming tired of myself. But then I saw that you were home, and hoped you might divert me."

"Saw," Adam wondered to himself, then realized that her mother's guesthouse, where Carla lived, was no doubt visible to Rachel. Warily, he asked, "What did you have in mind?"

Catching his reserve, she answered, "Nothing which would complicate your life—unless you have some qualms about allowing a sad and lonely woman to take you out to dinner. I'm hoping you can cure me of seasonal affective disorder."

Adam could find no graceful reason to refuse. "Where should I meet you?"

The lilt of relief entered Rachel's voice. "I'll pick you up about 6:30." She laughed again, more softly. "If it's awkward, you can wait for me on the porch. Even without me, your social life must be a sore point."

She was a provocateur, Adam thought again, and this banter was a form of playfulness, meant to keep him off balance while satisfying her deeper curiosity. But part of him was grateful for this distraction. Blandly, he said, "I try to bring happiness everywhere I go. See you at 6:30."

Hanging up, Adam caught his mother smiling to herself.

Rachel drove him to the Harborview in Edgartown. It had been dark since 4:30; by 7 o'clock, the darkness was so profound that it felt like midnight. The great houses they passed along the waterfront were vague shadows, abandoned for the winter, and the lighthouse across from the hotel was black against the starless sky. Parking, Rachel observed, "It feels like we're the last two people on earth."

This was strangely true. Entering the restaurant, they saw only a few couples, most of them looking stunted by the relentless embrace of winter, the certainty of three more months like this to come. "These are our fellow survivors," Adam informed Rachel. "By morning they'll all be dead from nuclear poisoning, leaving us to represent mankind by ourselves."

Rachel shot him a grin. "Mankind could do worse. Actually, I think I saw that movie—Nicolas Cage's finest performance, adduced by the great auteur Michael Bay. All that kept it from greatness was the screenplay."

They sat by a window, its panes squares of black. There was no one near them, and the small candle on the table lent an air of intimacy. "So why are you home?" she asked. "Not that I mind, but I had the impression you'd be gone much longer."

Adam was tired of reciting his story, and felt no need to do so. "My tour was up. This hasn't been the easiest stretch for my family, so I decided to take some leave while the company works out the next contract with USAID." To change the subject, he requested, "Tell me about the novel. Has retreating to the Vineyard helped or hurt?"

Rachel frowned in thought. "Hard to say," she confessed. "I'm not sure how much of the bleakness I'm feeling is external versus internal. For better or worse, we take ourselves everywhere we go. Though I don't like myself for it, I'm a person of highs and lows, and right this moment I'm slogging through the slough of despond. A lot of it's the writing. I'm a gifted miniaturist, I realize—a natural at short stories. But the scale of a novel feels a little daunting."

"Is your mom any help?"

"Yes, and no. Frankly, and no doubt to my discredit, I've always considered her the stereotypical WASP, as a woman and in her novels. Steady and craftsman-like, but lacking that touch of genius and spontaneity that would elevate her from a very observant and thoughtful white lady, the author of well-structured novels dissecting the haute bourgeois." She smiled wonderingly at herself. "Now I realize I've underrated her character, both in life and in her art. The architecture of those novels is near-flawless. Clearly, that comes from knowing the arc of her story before she writes it. A lesson to me, who began my novel without a clue how it would end."

"Isn't that often the way?"

"So I hear. But not for my mother or, as I read his novels, your father. Did the two of you ever talk about that?"

"Never," Adam said bluntly. "It was enough for him to suggest I was incapable of duplicating the genius that made him who he was. The one thing I'm sure of is how dogged he was—drunk or sick or sober, he always showed up for work. Which makes me think he was also pretty methodical."

Rachel nodded glumly, her dark, expressive eyes sober and reflective. "I expect so. Maybe Melville got up one morning suddenly envisioning a big fish, and decided to see where he was fifty pages out. But somehow I doubt it. Perhaps I should have wondered about that before I set my minnows into motion."

She sounded a little bereft, Adam thought. "I've read a couple of your stories," he told her. "On my e-reader, just this afternoon. They were too vivid and arresting for this book you're writing not to end up being good."

"God, I hope so." She paused, looking at him gratefully. "It was thoughtful of you to read me, Adam. Really, I'm flattered."

She was touched with insecurity, he saw, despite her intelligence and exotic looks, the somewhat kinetic air that might be taken for self-confidence. "De nada," he said easily. "I wouldn't have reached the second page if you hadn't engaged me so completely on the first. There were quite a few real insights, I thought."

Rachel smiled at this. "Years of therapy," she responded in a mock confessional tone. "I try not to be a danger to others or myself. Whatever my shortcomings in real life, it's been useful on the page. The only place where I can delete all my mistakes."

The touch of humor did not quite conceal her underlying ruefulness. As if regretting this, she added quickly, "But enough about me, as they say. Tell me more about your work."

Over dinner, Adam pretended to do this, spinning a fiction of his own so practiced that it felt like pushing a button. Rachel listened carefully, asking the occasional question, her thoughts obscure. At length, she asked, "Is this what you really want, going forward? I'm sure you've seen more interesting things and places than almost anyone I know, following the erratic path of the American Imperium. But what's it all mean? The life sounds itinerant, and more than a little lonely."

Suddenly they were closer to Adam's truth, whatever the lies that had led here. Shrugging, he answered, "Maybe I'm just restless. But I'm giving it some thought."

This seemed to please her. When the check arrived, she took it with a decisive air. "My treat, remember?" She hesitated, then looked into his eyes. "Why don't we have a snifter of my parents' very good Armagnac. Perhaps we can even identify something else for you to do."

At once he thought of Carla. "Aren't you writing in the morning?"

"Of course. But I'm a trouper, like your father. I'll write no matter what I've been up to the night before, and tonight I'm tired of my solitary thoughts." Smiling, she added teasingly, "Besides, we can hardly hang out at your mom's house, can we?"

When, Adam thought, had he ever turned down a woman this smart and attractive? The reality of the last ten years of his life, which he had reviewed so mercilessly on the dock, did not present a reason to be different. With misgivings and an inner trace of melancholy, he said, "We can't. So I guess it's your place, or nothing."

"Nothing," she answered quietly, "is unacceptable."

The Dane's summer home was commodious and well appointed, decorated in the antiques of New England. "It allows us to commune with our ancestors," Rachel remarked. "Or at least my mom's, given that dad's forbearers washed up here after fleeing a pogrom."

They took two snifters of Armagnac to the porch, its windows shut against winter. Rachel seemed edgier, the rhythm of her speech quicker and a bit disjointed. When she stopped herself in mid-sentence, abruptly gazing into his face, Adam knew what would happen.

With an air of resolve, she put down her brandy and put one hand behind his neck, guiding his mouth to hers. Her lips were warm and insistent. Breaking off, she murmured, "I've been waiting for this since I was seventeen, remember?"

Thinking of Carla, Adam felt a stab of regret. "So you told me."

Rachel gave him a questioning look, as though suddenly shy. Seeming to will this away, she offered another kiss that was long and deep enough to leave no doubts. Then she pressed herself against his chest, sighing a little. Though she was tall, her body felt light in his arms.

The rest was up to him, Adam realized. When his hands slid beneath her sweater, touching the slender planes of her back and shoulders, she made no protest.

Still kissing her, Adam unsnapped her bra. He leaned back slightly, touching her flat stomach with his palms, then reaching under her loosened bra to cup her small, firm breasts, the tip of his thumbs grazing her nipples.

He felt her shiver. Mute, she raised her arms so he could pull the sweater over her head. He did that, obscuring her face for a moment. Then the sweater was a clump on the floor, and her eyes held his with an intensity Adam felt to his core. Shrugging the bra off her shoulders, she exposed perfect breasts, brown nipples raised with desire. "Now you," she whispered.

He took off his sweater. Bending slightly, she kissed the thin line of black hair running down his chest and stomach. Then she looked at him, and gently touched the scar that marked his exit wound. "What happened?"

"I was mowing the lawn. The blades threw a rock."

Even as her lips opened to form a question, Adam saw her eyes reserve it for later. They had more urgent business now.

Still looking at him, she stepped out of her shoes. As he kissed her again Adam unbuckled her belt, then knelt in front of her, sliding down her jeans, then her sheer silk thong. His lips grazed the black fur between her slender hips and then, briefly, a more intimate place.

He heard the murmur of satisfaction in her throat. Then she reached beneath his arms, pulling him up to her. "My turn, Adam."

Avidly, she repeated what he had done, helping him step out of his jeans. Then she went to her knees, taking him into her mouth. Her lips were moist and soft, her hand stroking so gently but rhythmically that he stiffened to the point of bursting before she withdrew, standing before him again. Then she took his hand and led him down the hallway to the master bedroom.

It was dark and shadowy, the blinds drawn save for a single window. Firmly, Rachel closed the door, switching on one dim lamp, and Adam saw them captured in a mirror. Following his gaze, Rachel pulled him to her, their bodies touching, watching their reflection in the silvery glass. Then she broke away from him, lying back on the down bed cover. Gazing up at him, she slowly opened her legs, exposing the pinkness between.

"Do you really want me, Adam?"

His voice, thick with desire, concealed his confusion. "Yes."

He slid onto the bed, kissing the place she had shown him until it was moist, and her torso began to writhe. "I so want you," she told him, a fervent exhalation of breath.

How long had it been? Adam wondered. Since before Ben's death, he realized, though it troubled him that he could not recall which woman. Arms raised, he pulled himself on top of her, her hand guiding his shaft inside her, snug and warm and wet. "Deeper," she demanded.

He gave her all of him, then began moving, slowly at first, then harder, faster, still controlling himself, staying distant from his own desires so that he could please her. "Yes," she urged him.

He moved faster still. Suddenly she gave a small cry, her hips thrusting against him with primal urgency. He felt her tightening, and then the tightness broke, and with a fierce spasm she cried out, "Oh, Adam . . . ," his name breaking off in a cry of pleasure, and then she was shuddering more gently until, with a final twitch, she became utterly still, gazing up at the ceiling as though stunned by some revelation.

"My God, Adam Blaine," she whispered in a tone of wonder, and then looked searchingly into his face.

He smiled a little. "You're not disappointed?"

"Why on earth would I be?"

"You never found me a job."

She kissed him gently. "That's for later. What I want now is to make you lose control."

Not so easy, Adam knew. He had been too practiced, and too detached, for too long. But she was lovely like this, and she could not read his mind.

She began to move with him, head darting to take his nipple between her teeth, nipping at him to inflict both pain and ecstasy. He willed himself to think about nothing but her, nothing but this. At last he felt his shaft tighten beyond help. With the final excruciating rictus he burst inside her, and then this slowed, his pulse still racing as the warm tingling of release spread through his limbs.

When he opened his eyes, she was looking intently up at him, as though drawing his soul inside her. "That was certainly worth waiting for. I only hope . . ."

He cut this off by kissing her. "It was," he assured her. "I'm grateful for your patience, all ten years' worth."

She smiled with relief. "I thought so, too. Whatever happened with your father and my mother, it couldn't have been nearly as good as this."

Close to one o'clock, as happened often now, Carla stirred awake, her sleep broken by the awkward position in which she laid and the discomfort of her swollen limbs and belly. But then she felt the baby kicking and was overcome by gratitude.

Please, she implored him, live.

She had not been to church since the first threat of miscarriage. Now she rose, putting on her robe, and went to sit at her kitchen table.

Her mother's rosary beads were there. Fingering them, she bent her head, praying that her child be born safe and strong. She felt a deep vulnerability, a consuming love like nothing she had experienced before this—fighting with all her soul and body to bring this child into the world.

A beam of light struck her front window. Apprehensive, she struggled upright, and went to peer through the glass.

A familiar SUV was idling in the driveway of the main house, motor warming in the cold. It was Rachel, she thought, relief mingled with curiosity. Then she saw the man captured by headlights as he climbed into the passenger side.

It was only a few seconds. But she knew him at once. His frame and movements were so like Ben's.

With a sudden sickness of spirit, she forced herself away from the window and sat back down at the table, shaken. There was only one reason for him to be there at this hour, with this woman. An alluring, talented woman, she amended.

Carla felt her eyes close. She had no reason to feel betrayed, as though Adam had deserted her. They had no commitment to each other, had never made love as he surely had tonight with Rachel. And that must be the least of it for Adam—Carla was known to be self-destructive, and she was pregnant with Ben's child. She had no right to feel as though her heart had been ripped open.

Perhaps he was truly his supposed father's son, as other people had experienced Ben—a predator, and Adam's only model through the years as growing up. But despite her fears, she had sensed a goodness in Adam and imagined an affinity he might feel as well. Perhaps he was a good man, needing only the fresh start she could not give him. Perhaps with Rachel Ravinsky.

But Carla was no judge of men, her life had made all too clear. She felt jealous, confused, craving a certainty she could not find. And, most of all, afraid of Adam and herself. She had made mistakes too many times. All she knew for sure was that she wanted a life different than the one she had had, a man different than all the unstable and selfish men she had known as an actress.

Perhaps this was unfair to Adam Blaine. Perhaps that was why she found herself crying.

"We'll be all right," she promised her son. "Just get here, please, and I'll be all right for you."

Rachel dropped Adam at the head of the driveway. With feigned concern, she whispered, "Think she's waiting up for you?"

"Probably. It's past my curfew."

Adam still felt strange to himself, as though he had betrayed Carla. He could not shake this; the guesthouse was too close. In this way, he was not Ben's son.

Interrupting his thoughts, Rachel swiftly kissed him before leaning back to study his face. "I hope this isn't the last time," she said softly. "I like being with you, Adam. It feels like there's more to do, and to say."

Perhaps there was, he thought. There was no reason, really, not to find out. "I'm getting my own place," he responded. "The next time we'll go there."

Rachel looked at him, her expression briefly vulnerable, as though she had divined his thoughts. But all she said was, "I'll look forward to it."

SEVEN

Leaving to look at rental properties, Adam encountered Jack repairing a rotted corner of the front porch.

"Termites," Jack muttered, then drove another nail into a new plank.

With nothing to say, Adam headed for the car before hearing Jack softly call his name.

He turned to face his father. Still kneeling, Jack looked up at him, squinting slightly in a thin winter sun. "I hear you're moving out."

Adam nodded. "Better that way."

Jack's deep brown eyes were questioning and somber. "Is it? Your mother doesn't think so."

Afraid of being overheard, Adam moved closer, speaking under his breath. "She might if she knew what happened between you and Ben that night. But I would think she knows enough. You and mom should have whatever you both need—God knows you waited long enough. But the three of us can't go back and rewrite history, playing mom and dad and son." He glanced toward the guest house. "Besides, there's Teddy to consider. For everyone's good, the less

Ted knows about our family history the better, including that he's only my half brother. Which also makes us cousins, I suppose—sometimes I lose track."

Jack winced, deepening the lines of age in his weathered face. "I wonder if you can ever accept me. Or who I am to you."

Caught between sadness and fatigue, Adam sat beside his father. "What can you be? I make no judgment about what happened between my mother and you. And I'll never forget what a good uncle you were to us both. But you weren't a father to me when it mattered."

"So it doesn't matter now."

"I wish it did, Jack. But nothing can change the past, or what we're dealing with in the present. I contrived this cover-up so that neither you nor Teddy spends a life in prison for my quasi-father's death—sealing my mother's sadness in the bargain. But as long as I stay in this house, I'm living that every moment. It's suffocating."

Jack ran a hand through his dark silvering hair. In a low voice he said, "God knows I'd like to go back to when you were a boy, tell you 'I'm your father, and I love you.' I always felt I was watching you through a window—completely miserable, unable to make myself known. But I had to live by your mother's rules."

"And Ben's. So here we all are, living out the choices I had no part in making." Feeling compassion war with candor, Adam placed a hand on Jack's shoulder. "I don't hate you, Jack—far from it. I don't want Mom or you or Teddy to keep paying the price for who Ben was. But I can't pretend to feel things I don't, or to forget what can never be forgotten."

Jack looked down. "At least that's honest. Far more than we could ever be with you."

There was nothing more to say, Adam knew. He let his hand rest on his father's shoulder for another moment, then went to find a place to live, still suspended between his past and future.

* * *

Driving to meet the rental agent, Adam reviewed yet again what George Hanley knew or believed—that Adam had broken into the courthouse, stolen files, and sent them to Teddy's lawyer. The one piece Hanley did not have was Adam's manipulation of Bobby Towle, once his teammate and friend. Adam's deepest shame.

Shortly after Ben's funeral, Adam had met Bobby at the bar of the Kelly House.

In ten years, it was little changed—dim lights, wooden tables, and a bar jammed with tourists and islanders, the din of laughter and conversation bouncing off walls covered with old photographs or Vineyard memorabilia. His friend sat at a small table in the corner, looking bulky and awkward in blue jeans and a polo shirt big enough to double as a beach towel. In the instant before Bobby saw him, Adam had the affectionate thought that he looked like Baby Huey all grown up—a little bulkier, a lot sadder.

With a smile, Adam sat down. "So pal, how've you been the last decade or so?"

Bobby mustered a smile of his own. "You know how this island is. Days pass, then years, nothing changes much. Pretty soon that's your life."

But something had changed, Adam sensed. For a guy like Bobby, being a cop, and married to the prettiest girl in their high school class, should have felt better than it appeared. Bobby ordered two beers, then asked, "And you? Seems like you just disappeared."

Adam nodded. "One day I woke up, and decided to see the world. For me everything changes, every day. I don't know which is better."

The puzzlement lingered in Bobby's eyes. "Everyone thought you'd be a lawyer. Maybe marry Jenny Leigh."

Adam felt the familiar ache, the memory of a life torn asunder. "So did I," he answered. "I found out that wasn't me."

A young waitress brought two beer mugs full to the brim. Hoisting his, Adam said, "To victory over Nantucket."

Clicking mugs, Bobby replied nostalgically, "That was a game, wasn't it?"

"Yup. I'll remember the last play on my death bed. They're two yards from the goal line, five seconds to go, a quarterback sweep away from beating us. He almost gets to the goal line. Then you knock the sonofabitch into tomorrow, and the ball loose from his hands—"

"And you fall on it," Bobby finished. "Happiest moment of my life."

"Happier than marrying Barbara?" Adam asked lightly. "Football games are sixty minutes; marriage is supposed to last a lifetime. Or so they tell me."

Bobby's face changed, his bewildered expression followed by a slow shake of the head. "That's what I always believed." He stopped himself. "I don't much like to talk about it, Adam. With what happened to your dad, we maybe shouldn't even be having this beer."

It was another sign, if Adam had needed one, that George Hanley and the state police thought someone had killed Benjamin Blaine, and had focused on a member of his family. Shrugging, he said casually, "This is the Vineyard, not Manhattan, and we're old friends. That doesn't entitle me to anything you don't want to tell me. But if it helps, I'd like to hear more about you and Barbara."

For a long moment, Bobby looked down, then shook his head again, less in resistance than sorrow. "It's all just so fucked up."

Adam gave his friend a look of quiet commiseration. After a time he said, "I guess we're talking about your marriage."

Bobby puffed his cheeks. Expelling a breath, he murmured, "Barb got mixed up with a guy where she worked. At the bank."

This required no elaboration. "Sorry," Adam proffered. "That's tough to take, I know."

Bobby looked past him, seemingly at nothing. "You start to imagine them together, you know? Still, the unfaithful part I could have gotten past. But this douchebag was into crystal meth." His voice became almost hopeful. "I think that was what Barb was into, more than him."

Keep telling yourself that, Adam thought, *if it helps.* Signaling for a second beer, he asked, "Did you guys break up?"

Bobby stared at the table, as though examining the wreckage of his own life. "She begged me to take her back. But by that time, it had gone on way too long, and she was way too deep into meth. I had to put her in a treatment center."

It was the kind of thing Bobby would do, Adam thought—even in high school, he had been a responsible kid, stepping up when a lesser person would not. "When did all this happen?"

"She went away six months ago, to a treatment center on the Cape. She's still there." He frowned. "It sort of reminds me of the actress your dad got mixed up with. Except she had the money to get straight."

"Oh, it worked out fine for Carla," Adam said. "For her, this island became a profit center. But I guess helping Barbara gets expensive."

"Like lighting hundred dollar bills on fire," Bobby answered resignedly.

When the waitress brought their second beers, he barely noticed her. Adam thanked her, then asked his friend, "How are you affording that?"

"I'm not. Had to take a second mortgage on the place we fixed up together. Only reason I could buy it is my granddad left me a little." A look of bleakness seeped through Bobby's stoic mask. "You haven't been here for a while. I love this place, for sure. But us ordinary folks are getting squeezed out of the real estate market by summer people with money. Not to mention we're losing work to these Brazilians and day laborers from the mainland, and property taxes keep going up. Families who've been here since time began are barely hanging on." He looked at Adam, as though recalling the difference in their circumstances. "Your dad always had plenty of money. Still, you're well out of all this. Except for what happened to him, I guess."

"More to my mother. I guess you heard about the will."

"Oh, yeah." The words were weighted with significance. "We've heard."

"I guess everyone has," Adam said resignedly. "How has it been working with the state police?"

"About what you'd expect. They send over this sergeant named Mallory—thinks he's a hotshot, and that cops on this island are all buffoons. Not that he says that. It's more the way he's so patient and polite. Like when I was talking to Grandma after she got Alzheimer's."

Adam had to laugh. "From now on, Bobby, I'll speak very slowly and distinctly."

Bobby's grin was rueful. "It really is like that, you know."

"So how long do you have to put up with these guys?"

"As long as they keep digging."

Adam shook his head. "I can't believe that anyone killed him. I don't know why they'd think so."

"Well, they do." Bobby looked away, then into Adam's face. "Is anyone in your family getting legal advice?"

Adam feigned surprise. "They've got no reason to lawyer up. What with the will, they can't afford to anyhow."

Bobby stared at his beer. "Maybe they should try," he said in a flatter tone. "I know where they can get a second mortgage."

"Not on a house that belongs to Carla Pacelli. I'm the only one with money, and not much at that." Adam paused, then asked quietly, "How much should I worry about them, Bob?"

Bobby considered his answer. "All I can tell you," he said in a lower voice, "is there's a problem with the autopsy report."

"What kind of problem?"

For what seemed to Adam a painfully long time, Bobby concealed his thoughts behind half-closed eyelids. "How close are you to your brother, Adam?"

With difficulty, Adam summoned a look of composure, maintaining the same puzzled tone. "Teddy? We used to be very close."

Bobby seemed to inhale. "If you still are, you might ask him the last time he was at the promontory. Depending on how you like the answer, tell him to get a lawyer—"

"Bobby," Adam interrupted. "I know my brother. He hated that place."

"So he says. Problem is, he also hated your father."

"No more than I did."

Bobby shook his head. "Maybe so. But Teddy stuck around." Pausing, he glanced at the nearest table, then continued speaking under the din. "Might as well tell you what Teddy already knows. Your brother used to have a boyfriend on the island, and Mallory and George Hanley went to see him. Seems like Teddy used to fantasize about giving your dad a shove, then watching him hit the rocks head first. Pillow talk, I guess."

Adam's skin went cold, and then a memory pierced his consciousness. The brothers had set up an old army tent to camp in the back yard. Teddy was twelve, Adam ten—the evening before, Teddy had refused to join the family picnic at the promontory, and Ben had mocked his fear of heights. "I guess you're made for sea level," their father had concluded. "A metaphor of sorts." Lying in the tent, Teddy repeated this, then said, "Loves those sunsets, doesn't he?"

"Yeah."

"Ever think about giving him a shove?"

Teddy's tone of inquiry had unsettled Adam badly. All at once, he had felt the difference between them, the line of demarcation that was their father. "Not really, no."

"Because I do, all the time. Sometimes it feels like the bastard is choking me to death—"

Facing Bobby, Adam shook his head, as if to clear it. "That sounds like something a kid would say. Even at that, it doesn't sound like Teddy."

"People grow up," Bobby rejoined, "get serious about life. Maybe there's a lot he hasn't told you. Like that he called his ex-boyfriend the night your father died, leaving a message that he needed to talk."

"About what?"

"The message didn't say. But your brother sounded desperate, almost out of his mind. Not like I remember him from high school, this kind of gentle guy." Bobby stopped to stare at him. "You don't know anything about this, do you?"

"No," Adam conceded. "Nothing."

"That's pretty interesting, don't you think? Anyhow, I've made my point, and said way too much to do it. But ask yourself which neighbor of yours likes to walk that trail after dinner."

Adam searched his memory. "Nathan Wright used to."

"Tell Teddy to see a lawyer," Bobby repeated. "That's all I have to say. If you want to talk about old times, I'm happy to stick around. Or you can tell me about what you've been up to."

Bobby's misgivings were palpable, and in his last words, Adam heard a plea—*help me make this a night with an old friend.* "Then let's switch to whisky, Bob, and do it right."

For the next few moments, waiting for two glasses of Maker's Mark on ice, Adam spun stories about Afghanistan—in his telling a strange and exotic place in which Adam was a seriocomic bit player. Over one whisky, then another, they began reprising the Nantucket game, recalling key moments in a night that made them champions of their league. "You know," Bobby said in a thicker voice, "my dad always said that, next to Ben Blaine, you were the best quarterback we ever had."

Adam laughed briefly. "Funny, Bob. My dad said that, too."

At length they got up, leaving crumpled bills on the table. Outside it had rained; the night air had cooled, and shallow pockets of water glistened on the asphalt. The two men embraced, and then drew back, looking into each other's faces.

"Good luck with Barbara," Adam said. "I hope it all works out."

Bobby's shoulders slumped. "Me, too," he murmured. "I always wanted kids, you know."

"So did I," Adam replied, and realized that this was true. "A family of my own, where I made things turn out better."

Bobby looked up again. "Ask Teddy about the insurance policy," he said, and had walked unsteadily toward his car.

* * *

You might ask Teddy, Bobby Towle had told him, *the last time he was at the promontory.*

It had only taken a week for Adam to betray his friend.

In the dead of night, Adam had taken the ladder down the promontory.

Reaching the bottom, had had turned from the site of his father's death, walking toward the water. Here the tide was a continual low rumble, punctuated by the deep echoing surge of six foot waves striking land. Thick clouds blocked the moon. His surroundings were monochrome—starless sky, dark water, darkened beach.

Walking toward him along the shoreline was the lone figure of a woman. He waited, shivering in the chill wind.

Spotting him, she briefly stopped, then closed the remaining distance. Only when she stood before him could Adam see her features.

Amanda Ferris looked into his face. "Why are we meeting like this?" she said. "At midnight, in the loneliest place on earth. I keep wondering if you're a serial killer."

The reporter's voice was slightly louder than required to carry over the pounding surf. Perhaps it was nerves, Adam thought; this was their first meeting. But perhaps it was something more. Calmly he said, "First take out your tape recorder. I'd guess it's in the pocket of your blouse."

Her face and eyes became immobile. "What do you mean?"

Now Adam was quite certain. "Do it," he snapped. "Or go back to the swamp you came from."

Ferris's shoulders turned in, as though she were hunched against the cold. Then she reached into her pocket and held out a digital tape recorder in the palm of her hand. "Erase my voice," Adam ordered. "Then throw it at the water."

Ferris stiffened. "Take it, if you like. Then give it back when we're though."

"With my fingerprints on it?" Adam said coldly. "Quit playing with me. You're not qualified."

Ferris stared at him. Then she erased the tape and flung it into the surf with an angry underhand motion. "Who are you?" she demanded.

"You've already researched me on the internet," Adam replied. "Not to mention calling the consulting firm I work for. As to why I'm doing this, you'll understand by the time we're through. But 'off the record' doesn't cover this encounter. Except for the benefit to your career, the next half hour never happened."

Watching her eyes, Adam took stock of her once again—bright, determined and aggressive, with a good measure of cupidity and amoral curiosity. Her job was not about anything save the public desire to pick the bones of celebrities like Carla Pacelli and his father—or, perhaps, become one. At times Adam was glad that he no longer lived in America.

"All right," Ferris said sharply. "Let's talk about what both of us want."

"I already know what you want," Adam replied. "You think someone killed my father—that's why you're still here. But you're getting nowhere with the state police." Adam glanced up at the promontory. "Like you, I'm curious about how my father fell from there to here. Unlike you, I can't pay people to find out. But I do know who might take your money."

Shifting her weight, Ferris studied him with narrowed eyes. "Explain to me what you get from this."

"First let's talk about what you need. To start, you want the complete autopsy report, focusing on the marks on my father's body or evidence on his clothes—rips, mud, hairs or saliva that weren't his. The report is under wraps, so that's a bit of a trick—"

"In other words," she interjected, "someone will have to sell it—"

"Next you'll want the evidence they found on the promontory, including footprints and any signs of a struggle. Beyond that, you'll need the witness statements—especially from my family, Carla Pacelli, and Jenny Leigh."

"That's a lot to get."

"You're a clever woman, and money will make you smarter. As for me, I want copies of everything—starting with the autopsy report. And I expect to hear what you know before you print it." Pausing, Adam spoke slowly and deliberately. "Don't even dream of holding out on me, Amanda. If you do, I've already figured out how to get you indicted for obstruction of justice—"

"You're joking."

"Hardly. You've got three choices—failure, a career making story, or a potential stretch in prison. The risks you should be taking aren't with me. From what I've learned, your career is on the bubble. So how badly do you need this story?"

Almost imperceptibly, Ferris seemed to recoil. In an undertone, she said, "You're a very strange and scary person. It's pretty much common knowledge that you couldn't stand your father."

"I'm rethinking our relationship. So how much nerve do you have? I can always go to TMZ."

Ferris clamped her lips, then nodded.

"Good," Adam said. "While you're at it, check out Carla Pacelli. From the rumors I've picked up, she claims to have known nothing about the will before he died. Prove that false, and her entire story unravels. That would interest me."

"And the *Inquirer*," Ferris agreed. "So tell me where I start."

Feeling the tug of conscience, Adam hesitated. His deepest loyalty, he told himself, must be to his mother and brother. When he spoke, his mouth felt dry. "There's a policeman in Chilmark," he answered in a monotone. "As best you can, I want you to protect him. But he's in desperate need of money."

After she had gone, Adam had remained on the beach, his soul leaden. His mind framed useless apologies to Bobby Towle.

How did I get here? he had thought. *How did all of us get here?* Now the link that bound the three of them—Ferris, Bobby and Adam— was all Hanley needed to convict him. And all that protected him was that this connection was equally damning to the others.

EIGHT

After securing his own place—a secluded house across the road from Quitsa Pond—Adam decided to drop in on Carla.

As he passed the main dwelling, he saw Rachel's car in front, increasing his ambivalence at this sudden impulse. He was not cheating on anyone, he reminded himself: this was not a triangle, and his chief concern was Carla and her baby. But as he knocked on her door, he felt restive and uneasy.

Opening it, she appraised him in silence before asking, "What is it, Adam?"

For an instant, he wondered if she knew about Rachel. "I'm just checking to see if Teddy's doing his job."

"Very nicely, thanks—I'm flush with vegetables, yogurt, and all the nutrients an expectant mom could have. Your brother is extremely reliable."

Something in her tone suggested that her answer was as pro forma as she believed his inquiry to be. Hands thrust in his pockets, he asked, "So when do you go to Boston to have the baby?"

Adam thought he saw impatience flicker in her eyes, though perhaps it was worry. "I thought I told you. Two weeks from now, when I reach seven and a half months."

"Will you need a ride?"

"Teddy's already volunteered. Anyhow, I might fly—quicker may be safer."

There was a distinct coolness in her voice and manner. After a moment, he asked, "Is something wrong?"

"Should there be?" Watching his face, she said more evenly, "Is there something you want to talk about?"

Adam hesitated. "I wouldn't mind spending a few moments. If you've got time."

Carla considered this, then stood aside to let him in. She took a place on the couch, an open book face down beside her. Sitting across from her, he said, "You seem to be in a mood."

"Not for passive-aggressive fencing. If you've got anything in particular to say, then say it."

Though the impulse came to Adam suddenly, the subject was always close to the surface, and speaking it aloud made him feel less defensive. "There's something going on with us, Carla—enough that we've trusted each other with a fair amount. But there's a very dead elephant in the room, and we keep pretending it isn't there. So let me ask a direct question. How you could have learned so much about yourself, and still chose Ben?"

Her look of surprise was followed by a smile with little humor. "Men continue to amaze me. I could've sworn there was something else on your mind. But why should there be, after all?" She paused, then seemed to reach a decision followed by a shrug. "No harm in discussing something with so little emotional baggage. I've certainly given it enough thought."

"So have I. But I knew him too well to understand it."

"Try to let go of how much you hate him," Carla retorted, "assuming that's even possible. Then maybe it won't be so hard for you to grasp. Like me, Ben knew what it was like to be famous, so we could see past that in each other. We both had abusive fathers and passive mothers; both of us were driven to break out. He learned to write, and I found out that I could act. To succeed, both of us became as tough as we needed to be. People like Ben and me don't stumble across each other every day."

To Adam, this had a rote quality, pasteurized from a few rounds of psychotherapy. "That's biography, Carla. You see other people; he never could. Selfishness and cruelty are not your most obvious characteristics."

Her frown conveyed both understanding and irritation. "I've heard the stories, all right? Even Ben had deep regrets about his performance as a father—though neither of you would ever tell me the reason for your break. But you assume he was such an irredeemable bastard that there was nothing he could give me other than a roll in bed.

"Let's leave that one alone, for both our sakes. But just as l could only face myself after I hit rock bottom, he saw himself more clearly once he saw death coming for him." Her tone became ironic. "In that sense, cancer was good for Ben's character. At least he had the grace to choose reflection over self-pity. And given my own limitations, the exit sign hanging over his head was also good for me. There's no one safer than a dying man."

For a moment, her candor startled him. "That's a novel way of looking at it."

"Why? I saw him plainly enough to know that he could never completely change—all that charm, all that self-involvement and, yes, all the hurt and insecurity he tried so hard to conceal. But he came to me knowing that he'd destroyed his relationship with both you and Teddy, and filled with regrets about staying with Clarice and all the damage it caused. He wanted to be good for someone—me, as it happened—and he understood better than most people why I'd self-destructed.

"Still, he was married—no matter how tattered the marriage was, he wasn't a healthy choice for me, and I knew that I had to end it." Her voice softened. "Two things changed that—my pregnancy, and his illness. By some miracle, he'd given me the child I'd always wanted. And I was strong enough—at last—to take care of a man who truly needed that from me." To Adam's surprise, her eyes briefly moistened. "Watching him try to accept death without flinching was unspeakably sad. I didn't have to worry about his flaws or whether this made any sense in the long-term. By dying, Ben became safe.

"That allowed me to help him face the end, knowing that someone cared. When the tabloids began feasting on our relationship, I refused to run away." She paused, and then her tone became strong and level. "If you can't accept that about me, it really doesn't matter. Because I've accepted it, and I wouldn't change it if I could."

Once more, her honesty silenced him. "I'm sorry," he offered. "But it's hard to put myself in your place."

"I can feel that." She looked off in the distance, quiet for a moment. "You know what's strange to me? You both had nightmares. Like you, Ben woke up screaming from his. I'm not making excuses for him, and I'm certainly no expert in PTSD. But after growing up in an abusive home and going through combat in Vietnam, he seemed to fit the profile." She faced him again, her voice even and dispassionate. "I'm not making excuses for him, but that's what caused his nightmares. Maybe also the drinking, and his legendary absence of impulse control—including around women. Though Ben always claimed he was turning the tables on Jack and Clarice for their affair—of which you, regrettably, were a constant reminder. Tragic for both of you, really."

For an unnerving moment, Adam recalled Charlie Glazer asking if wanting Carla was Adam's psychic revenge for Jenny Leigh. Feeling his discomfort become sarcasm, he said, "I guess I should feel more sympathy."

"That's hardly my point," Carla retorted with renewed impatience. "Doesn't what I'm telling you make any sense at all?"

Abruptly, Adam recalled the only time that Ben had confessed to weakness. "At least in one way," he acknowledged.

*　*　*

Adam had been twenty-one then; Ben still in his prime. They were fishing off Dogfish Bar on a pitch—dark night, so chill that the stiff wind from the waters cut through their flannel shirts and down vests. But it was a point of pride between father and son that they fished under conditions that drove others home. Now and then, they passed a bottle of whiskey back and forth, it's warmth inside them thawing the ice in their bones.

Suddenly, Ben started and looked swiftly around. Seeing and hearing nothing, Adam asked, "Expecting anyone?"

Ben gave him a long look, and then laughed, a sound soft yet curiously harsh. "Only the Viet Cong."

Surprised, Adam inquired, "Bad memories?"

"More like reflexes. We spent a lot of time in the dark or in the bushes, not knowing where they were. Sometimes, when it's night and a bit too quiet, I go back there." He faced the water. "I know it sounds crazy. But for a moment in this nothingness, you and I were waiting for something bad to happen. Except that only I knew that."

Adam tried to find words to console a man who had never needed this. "You were a hero, Dad. I've seen the medals."

Ben shook his head. "I got them for surviving a war as meaningless as it was murderous. My platoon lived in its own world—there were no rules, nothing made sense, death was random and pointless, and too many damned officers were set on climbing the ladder by getting our heads blown off. We spent our time taking and giving up the same hill, hoping to survive, with blacks and whites not trusting each other." His voice grew quieter. "I was sure I'd die there, for nothing. Instead I got a best-selling memoir out of it, and wound up famous instead of dead."

Adam stood closer to him. "You also know that you're not a coward. In a strange way, I envy you that."

"Maybe so," his father answered with muted bitterness. "You might ask your uncle, who managed to wriggle out of serving. But my 'manhood' came at a price. I'm jumpier, more impulsive and prone to anger, and I drink too goddamned much. Sometimes it feels like I'm going to explode.

"I'm not a complete mystery to myself. There's a reason I still go to war zones. I hate it, and I need it—to prove myself, again and again." Turning, he gazed closely at Adam, then put a hand on his son's shoulder. "If there's another war, it'll be in the Middle East, and a fucking nightmare. Don't be in any hurry to chase after it. There are other ways to prove that you're a man."

Recounting this to Carla, Adam found that his mood had subtly altered.

"I'd almost forgotten that," he finished. "It was that rare time he forced himself to be introspective, which he absolutely hated—except, it seems, with you. It was the clearest sign that he actually gave a damn."

"He loved you," she insisted. "At least as much as he could. Maybe he found it easier to care about people who weren't embedded in his own torment." She gazed down, reflective. "Whatever the reason, he did care. When I was on top, I paid the usual Hollywood lip service to the usual causes. But Ben campaigned against the death penalty, wrote about famine in places no one knew about, funded scholarships to Yale and the writing program at UMass. By the time he wrote that will, he'd given a lot of his money away."

Adam had heard this speech, so often that he could almost quote it. "I like money as much as anyone," he recalled Ben saying at the dinner table. "But no one in this country got rich by themselves. No one. I became wealthy because a publisher believed in me; reviewers praised me; and the economy was good enough that people could afford to buy my books in hardcover.

"They shipped those books on highways built with other people's tax money; sold them in stores other people started, to customers who'd learn to read in public schools. Half the old people who read me—and too damn many of my readers are old—pay with precious dollars from Social Security, or go to libraries built and maintained with public money." His father took another swallow of wine, then added fiercely, "Those greedy sons of bitches who make millions and then whine about their taxes make me puke. Class warfare isn't making the rich pay taxes; it's letting these bastards pull the ladder up behind them. I went to Yale on someone else's dime, supplemented by other people's tax money. As far as I'm concerned, I'm worth every goddamn penny, and so is anyone this country helps to realize their potential. The point is that I'm not just my own creation—I'm the sum of what a person with talent and ambition can do when society gives them a chance. So now I'm going to be one of those people who gives a damn, simple as that . . ."

"What I could never figure out," Adam said now, "was whether he remembered being poor, or remembered hating rich people like Whitney Dane's father."

"No doubt both," Carla answered. "But what does it matter? He gave away his own money, and his politics cost him readers. As for Whitney's father, from what Ben told me he loved Whitney before he married your mother. But Charles Dane did everything in his power to drive them apart—including getting Ben drafted into the army. That would certainly explain Ben's dislike, and cast a different light on his history with women. Particularly after Whitney slipped away from him." Carla paused, then added mildly, "Whitney says she's not a beauty like her daughter. But I've gotten to know her well enough to see she's that smart and strong and grounded. So maybe Ben lost what he most needed, long ago."

Studying Carla, Adam wondered about her passing reference to Rachel. "'Til there was you," he said.

"I certainly don't compare myself to Whitney," Carla responded coolly. "I'm merely suggesting that marrying your mother damaged Ben as much as her." She gave him a long, pensive look. "No doubt you suffered the consequences. Perhaps someday, if it matters, you can tell me why you ended up bolting the island. But it probably won't matter at all."

Adam found himself without words. "Back to the baby," he finally said. "When he's born, I'd like to be there."

Carla raised her eyebrows. "To do what, exactly?"

"I just don't want you to be alone."

A shadow crossed her face. "I'd prefer not to share the delivery," she said tartly. "You skipped all the birthing classes, where they teach men to say 'push' while the women lie spread-eagled in unspeakable agony. A little too intimate for us, don't you think?" Her voice became smokier, yet softer. "What are we to each other, I have to wonder. And I don't know what will happen to my son, or how I will be when it does. Best for me to do this by myself."

Awkwardly, Adam stood. "Until then, mind if I keep looking in on you?"

Carla smiled faintly. "You don't have to make a special trip. Just whenever you find yourself nearby."

Something had changed, Adam knew, but she was leaving him to guess. "I'll do that," he told her. "What goes on with you and your son matters to me. It also matters that you know that."

After a moment, she nodded, almost imperceptibly, and he imagined a trace of doubt and sadness in her eyes. Touching her shoulder, he said, "I appreciate the conversation," and left.

NINE

"I'm curious about Jack," Charlie said. "Since you came back, you've barely mentioned him."

The inquiry threw Adam off-balance; he had just sat down in Charlie's living room, and his thoughts were focused on Carla and Rachel. "Funny you should ask. We had a talk yesterday, of a kind. He seems to hope I'll feel things I can't."

"Such as?"

"A paternal connection, for one."

Charlie shot him a curious look. "Since discovering he's your father, do you feel less warmth for him?"

Adam pondered this. "It's hard to sort out," he said at length. "Growing up I loved Jack as an uncle—he didn't have any parental archetype to fill, and he always took what I saw as a kindly interest. But no doubt part of me internalized Ben's contempt. Jack seemed passive; Ben was my father, voracious for life. Instinctively I wanted to be like him."

"And now that you know who Jack really was?"

Adam felt the same involuntary coolness. "His benevolence looks worse. The last thing I'd do is to give my son to Ben."

Charlie took a contemplative sip of coffee, then looked up at Adam again. "In your mind, who is your father?"

The question surprised Adam; the answer he found depressed him. "It's still Ben," he said in a flat tone. "When I was a kid, needing a father, all of them let me think that. For better or worse, when I hear the word 'father' Ben's face appears."

"So it's still not helpful that preying on Jenny wasn't a father's betrayal?"

Once more, Adam fought back the same vivid, shocking image. "No," he answered softly. "It doesn't change how it felt to see them."

Charlie cocked his head. "Memories are powerful—traumatic ones in particular. But you also have a future. So perhaps you can find a way to reinterpret the past."

For an instant, Adam thought of Carla, redrawing her dream of the voracious bear. "In what sense?"

"You feel that Jack abandoned you. But he was always there to talk with. Or to show up at your high school games whenever Ben was gone . . ."

"True," Adam cut in harshly. "He also encouraged me to compete against Ben for the sailing championship that summer, knowing how psychologically loaded that was. By winning, I triggered Ben's desire to sodomize a psychologically fragile young woman I happened to love. But, of course, no one's to blame for any of this but Ben. No wonder he felt such contempt for Jack."

"Not just contempt—anger. Isn't that what you feel for them both?"

Adam felt himself close down. "This is arrested, Charlie—a complete waste of time. I'm getting too old to feel anything but sadness and a sense of responsibility for people with less coping skills than I have. No point in sniveling about Jack."

Charlie held up a hand. "Obviously, this subject isn't welcome. But I wonder if you're better off resenting Jack—which you clearly do—or asking him to help sort through your confusion. It can't have been easy for him to sit by, trying to do the best he could for you. Which was the only choice your mother gave him."

Despite his best efforts, Adam felt the unfairness of this. But Charlie did not know, and Adam could not tell him, that he was protecting Jack from a charge of murder. "I'll consider it, Charlie. Let's move on."

"Fine with me," Charlie said equably. "What would you like to talk about?"

Adam hesitated. "Do you know Rachel Ravinsky?"

Charlie raised his eyebrows. "Whitney Dane's exotic, dark-haired daughter? I've certainly met her, and I've read her stories—impressive. Dare I ask why she deserves more attention than Jack?"

Adam considered his choice of words. "We may be involved."

To Adam's surprise, Charlie gave him a quizzical smile. "You remind me of today's teenagers—they fuck for months, and still can't describe their relationship. So take pity on a dinosaur, and help me out."

"No need. I think you've caught the spirit of it."

Charlie sat back, steepled fingers touching his lips. "My first instinct was to say that I'm surprised. On reflection, I suppose I'm not. Are you?"

"I'm neither surprised nor unsurprised. Tell me why you're not."

"Let's start with the easy part—the reasons Rachel would appeal to any man. She's smart; talented; and extremely attractive. As I recall her from cocktail parties, she's charming and a bit quirky, with a certain kinetic sexiness. She's a good age for you, with none of Carla's baggage—Ben, this baby. All those toxins from the past." Charlie stopped himself abruptly. "Before we go further, how are you dealing with Rachel in relation to Carla?"

Adam folded his arms. "Not well. When I went to see Carla yesterday, she seemed much more remote. Maybe she knows or senses something; maybe I just felt guilty. Though God knows why I should—we've never slept together, and she has no claim on me."

Charlie looked at him intently. "But you want her, don't you."

"Yes."

"Yet you're also afraid of those feelings?"

Adam found himself staring at a square of sunlight on Charlie's Persian carpet. "For good reason. But you already know that."

"Do you think being with Rachel may be a way of destroying your relationship to Carla? Or, for that matter, that she's a surrogate for Carla?" When Adam did not answer, Charlie inquired, "May I ask how the experience we dare not name felt to you?"

Adam expelled a breath. "Through no fault of Rachel's, I still felt the same detachment. Like I have ever since Jenny."

Charlie nodded, his eyes grave. "Psychologically speaking, who did you think you were really with—Rachel or Carla?"

"Rachel. She has a way of compelling your attention."

A corner of Charlie's mouth flickered. "I can imagine. But later you felt guilty about Carla?"

"True. I also felt stupid for it."

"When you saw Carla after sleeping with Rachel, did you still want her?"

Adam stared out the window. "Yes. But even if her pregnancy didn't make sex impossible, her manner wasn't exactly an aphrodisiac. Neither was our conversation."

"Which concerned?"

"Ben and the reasons she was drawn to him—common backgrounds, mutual understandings. Her notion that terminal illness seemed to have improved his character—including a deep regret about his family. Oh, and the fact that she was pregnant with his child."

"That must've been interesting," the therapist remarked dryly. "Who initiated this conversation?"

"I did."

"That's new," Charlie observed. "What moved you to pursue that?"

"I don't know."

Charlie looked at him keenly, then chose to let this go. "It's also interesting that she responded, given that she could've told you to go pound sand. Did any of what she said resonate with you?"

"Intellectually, I think so. But Ben's not like some ex-husband I say hello to when he's dropping off the kids. Of all the men on earth, Carla chose him."

"As opposed to Rachel," the psychiatrist observed, "who represents all the women on earth who've never slept with Ben. Despite his best efforts, a considerable number—a good many of whom are potentially available to you. But let's stick with Rachel for the moment. What do you make of her?"

Adam tried to synthesize his impressions. "I hardly know her. But I'd say she's venturesome, maybe a little impulsive and high strung. One interesting thing, though she won't quite acknowledge it, is that she both admires her mother and is jealous of her—as a novelist, and as a woman. And now she's torturing herself to produce a novel."

"Unlike you," the therapist observed, "who Ben discouraged from writing. Is that why you chose law school?"

Adam gave him an ironic smile. "No doubt Whitney was a better parent. I'm not sure if Rachel knows who she really is. But she's certainly not inhibited from going after what she thinks she wants . . ."

"Like you?"

"Like her idea of me. This is all about a crush she had when I was still with Jenny. She knows nothing about me, obviously, which covers some pretty important ground."

"Think you'll ever be inclined to tell her?"

"Impossible to know, and that's contrary to my instincts. But it's pretty clear she means to give me the chance."

"Believe it or not," the psychiatrist suggested gently, "Rachel's attraction to you may be perfectly normal. And why not? As you point out, she knows so little about you."

Uncomfortable, Adam laughed. "You're quite a help, Charlie."

Charlie smiled at this, and then grew serious again. "For someone who spent one night with her, you seem to have gotten some clear impressions—a woman with hopes and needs, desires and insecurities. Who, I surmise, also exposes what you perceive as your own coldness." He paused a moment. "You've acknowledged feeling guilty about Carla. Are you afraid of hurting her?"

Adam felt a renewed melancholy. "She's been through too much already."

"Do you also worry about hurting Rachel?"

"I sense that I could. So it bothers me, yes."

"Over the last ten years, how often did you dwell on the feelings of the women you were with?"

Adam stared out the window. "Not as much as I should have," he acknowledged. "I was too busy keeping my own secrets, or getting away."

"In short, protecting yourself by avoiding intimacy. But now you're also concerned with protecting a woman from yourself. Carla, certainly, and perhaps Rachel."

Turning, Adam gave the psychiatrist a bleak smile. "Nice to know I'm making progress."

"You may be joking. I'm not. For the first time, I hear you saying 'I want to love, and live life more fully. I want to be a better partner and father than Benjamin Blaine.' But you're still afraid you can't be, true?"

"Yes."

"I see that as a good thing, Adam." Charlie's voice softened. "You're changing, and don't want to live with hurting either woman. But hurting them both could be even worse—especially for you. A good thing to consider."

Adam bent forward, briefly closing his eyes. "I know that," he answered. "Let's call it a day, all right?"

Sitting by a window that filtered the faint winter sunlight, Carla studied her photograph of Benjamin Blaine.

Ben had asked her to take this picture, before the ravages of brain cancer did their worst. But his face was already gaunt, as though he were collapsing from the inside out. "I could give you a book jacket photo," he had told her, "from when I was younger and better looking. But I didn't know you then, and you've stayed with me as I am.

I want our son to know what I looked like, and that I didn't want to leave him."

He had said this not in his usual baritone rasp, but gently, a world of regret in his voice—that he had failed so utterly with Teddy and Adam, his own doing. But gratitude, also, that Carla would be with him until the end. She had no heart to tell him that only his end had made this possible.

What had she wanted from Adam, she asked herself now, when she could not even trust him? Why, knowing about Rachel, had she willed herself to explain her relationship to Ben? Did she still imagine breaking through to him, for her own sake as well as his? Or was she simply tired of all that remained unspoken, and so decided to tell the truth?

At least as far as it went.

But she did not owe Adam even that. Though she had given him the chance, he had said nothing about Rachel. Which made him no worse than many men she had known, but perhaps no better. Adam Blaine had told her more, she guessed, than he told most women in his life. But he still held his secrets close. Perhaps if she knew them, she would wish that she did not.

The telephone rang.

For a moment, she was hopeful, though she did not know why. But she stood slowly, afraid of causing a premature labor that might keep her from delivering in Boston. But there was another reason for her caution, she acknowledged as she reached for the phone— until she delivered, she could imagine holding her baby, pink and healthy and alive.

"This is Amanda Ferris," her caller said

Carla felt her stomach clench. "How did you get this number?"

The reporter ignored this. "I'm wondering if you're ready to talk about Adam Blaine."

Carla considered hanging up, then hesitated. "I don't know anything about Adam Blaine," she snapped.

"But don't you wonder?" Ferris asked. "I've told you about his activities on this island. You must suspect that he knows who killed his father—your baby's father—and is covering it up. Which means that the murderer, a member of his family, is walking around this island loose with Adam's blessing.

"You're the one he talks to. I'd like your help, and so would the district attorney." The reporter paused, then added in a softly insinuating tone, "Unless you've transferred your affections from father to son. If so, it's too bad that Adam tried to pin Ben's murder on you. Just ask George Hanley . . ."

This time Carla hung up, more slowly than she should have. Certain that this last was true—or, at least, once was.

What had Adam learned? she wondered. The truth about his paternity struck her yet again. She no longer thought Teddy capable of murder. But the years of hatred spawned by Adams birth might cause one brother to kill another.

Outside the Blaine family, only Carla knew this. A closed circle, except for her, which might conceal a murderer.

Inexorably, she felt herself drawn back to the photograph of Ben. For a long time she gazed at it, sickened and confused, then placed it on the kitchen table where she could see him.

Why could you never tell me, she asked him, what happened between you and Adam?

TEN

On the first Saturday morning in his new home, Adam awakened to a heavy snowfall blanketing the meadow outside his window. Shortly thereafter, Rachel called.

"What do the natives do with this?" she inquired. "You seem to be missing a ski slope."

Adam smiled at this. "We're missing a lot of things in winter, except for alcoholism and spousal abuse. But you can always ski cross-country."

"Such drudgery, so boring. I miss the sensation of speed."

This triggered a memory from Adam's youth. "Too bad you're not a kid. On days like this, my father would pack up sleds and take us to the third hole at Farm Neck. The tee is at the top of a hill—not a big one, but when you're five or six the trip down feels exhilarating."

"Who says I'm not a kid?"

"I do. Didn't we establish that the other evening?"

Rachel laughed softly. "Depends on what kind of mood I'm in. So are you taking me sledding, or do I have to find some other guy?"

Quickly, Adam considered his choices. "This is winter, Rachel—there are no other guys. But I'm willing to meet your inner child."

"Good," Rachel answered in a cheerful tone. "In some ways, you'll find her quite advanced."

The golf course was empty, its terrain obscured by a blanket of snow that powdered the bare branches of oaks lining the fairways. Trudging through the snow with their sleds on ropes, they saw a trail of footprints heading in the same direction, some larger than others. "A dad and his kids," Adam observed. "Not much changes here in winter."

Rachel surveyed white rolling landscape. "Still, on a day like this it almost seems idyllic."

Once more, Adam recalled Ben waiting at the bottom of the hill, laughing as his four-year-old son sped down the hill for the first time, gripped by ecstasy and terror. "I thought it was, then."

At length they reached the third tee, overlooking a snow-covered fairway that culminated in a sweeping pond, its waters gray beneath a matching sky. As Adam had anticipated, at the bottom of the hill a father watched his small son and daughter as they spun toward him in metal saucers. Seeing Adam smile, Rachel asked, "Can you ever see yourself with kids?"

Briefly, Adam thought of Carla and the unborn son she prayed for. "I can imagine lots of things. But I'm not sure they'll happen. And you?"

Lightly, Rachel answered, "I always fancied being the only child of my marriage, and I've never met a guy who changed my mind. Maybe that's because the ones I've been with started seeming like children themselves." Her voice became reflective and a touch self-questioning. "I see pictures of my mom before she was married, and she just looks like a woman who is meant to be a mother. Maybe I'm too selfish, but when I look in the mirror all I see is a writer."

Adam watched the little girl swirl down the hill toward her father, her blond ringlets sticking out from the knit cap pulled tightly over her ears. "You never know, Rachel. Life is long."

"But not endless. I'll be thirty before I know it—after that, there's only so much time to develop a maternal instinct. And once I'm past thirty-five, there's a real chance of something going wrong."

She had thought about it, Adam realized, and then his own thoughts returned to Carla. For a moment, wanting the best for her and her son, he forgot where he was.

Rachel eyed him quizzically. "You look pensive."

"Just vacant." Adam turned to her. "So who's going down first?"

"You are, so you can catch me at the bottom. I'm the child, remember?"

Feeling vaguely foolish, Adam waited until the boy and girl below were out of his path. Then he lay flat on the sled he had last used twenty-five years ago, and pushed himself down the hill. Feeling his oversized limbs skidding at the edge, Adam marveled that this gentle ride, so quickly over, had once seemed like an adventure. He wondered if Ben, watching him, had seen the world through the eyes of a son.

He stood, brushing the snow off his jeans, then called back up to Rachel. "Traverse Mount Everest, if you dare."

Grinning, she threw herself on the sled with mock abandon, pushing herself off the edge. At the end of a creditable glide, swifter than his own, she wound up at Adam's feet. Quickly rising, she brushed the snow off her flushed cheeks, and kissed him. "Was I good?" she asked.

"Exceptional."

"Then that's two things we can do together. Why don't we combine them and go skiing in New Hampshire? If we can get a cabin there, I know the perfect place."

For a moment, Adam hesitated. "You're changing," Charlie Glazer had said, "enough that you don't want to live with hurting either woman. But hurting both of them would be worse." Then he caught the look in Rachel's eyes, hopeful and imploring.

"Let's check the weather," he suggested.

"I already have," she answered with a smile. "Lousy here, white powder there. Seems like a perfect time to get away."

Just before dawn on Monday, Carla awakened to nauseating contractions that made her curl, shuddering with pain. Outside, a howling wind propelled sheets of rain against the windows with a harsh percussive sound.

Shaken, she hobbled bent over to the telephone and called her doctor. "There's no time to get you to Boston," Stein said quickly. "Especially in this weather. I'll meet you at the hospital."

Putting down the phone, she parsed her jumbled thoughts, then instinctively called Adam Blaine.

No one answered. With the next contraction, Carla shut her eyes. There was no time, and Adam was somewhere else.

From memory, she dialed Teddy's number. When he answered, voice thick with sleep, Carla said, "I'm sorry, but I think the baby's coming early. I tried to call Adam, but he's not in."

"Don't worry," Teddy assured her. "I'm on my way."

Wrenched by another contraction, she thanked him and got off.

As swiftly as she could, Carla dressed and packed for the hospital. Please, she implored whoever listened, let him be all right. As though her fervor might induce a bargain.

When Teddy's truck appeared in driveway, another contraction ran through her. Shaken, she opened the door. He ran toward her, head bent against the rain that struck his hood and slicker. Conjuring a smile, he said, "Nice day you chose."

Grateful, she hugged him. "We'll be all right," he promised. "I'll wait for you at the hospital however long it takes."

The cabin was at the foot of the mountain, set off by itself. Fresh snow had fallen overnight, perfect for skiing, dusting the pines with fresh powder. Turning from the window, Adam saw Rachel emerging from the shower, a towel wrapped around her slender body, her eyes still bright with making love at first awakening.

Naked, Adam stretched out beneath the sheets. "Is there room in there for me?"

She gave him a teasing smile. "There was room before, actually." She paused, as though reluctant to say too much. "This is nice, Adam. I'm glad you decided to come."

On the nightstand, Adam's cell phone rang. Looking surprised and apprehensive, Rachel asked, "Who could that be?"

"Someone who'll have to leave a message," Adam said, then glanced at caller ID and amended, "I'd better take this."

Pushing the answer button, he asked, "What's up, Ted?"

"Carla's started having contractions, bad ones. I'm at the hospital now, and thought you'd want to know."

Adam tensed. "How is she?" he asked quickly, and saw Rachel freeze at the corner of his vision.

"Scared to death about the baby, though she's trying to stay calm. No way for her to get to Boston—her day of reckoning has come early." His brother's voice quickened. "She called you first at home, and no one answered. Where are you, exactly?"

Adam imagined Carla, listening as his telephone rang unanswered. "Jesus . . ."

Sitting beside him, Rachel touched his arm, whispering, "Is it about your mom?"

Briefly, Adam turned to her and shook his head. "I'm in New Hampshire," he told his brother. "Skiing."

A brief silence. "Not alone, I take it."

"No."

"Never mind, then," Teddy responded in a tired voice. "I've got this covered."

For a moment, Adam was silent. "There'll be other snowfalls," he said at last. "I'll get there as soon as I can."

Pushing the off button, he turned to Rachel.

She studied him, her eyes probing. "That was about Carla Pacelli," he said reluctantly. "She's gone into labor early, and there may be a problem with the baby. A fatal one."

Quiet, Rachel absorbed this. "You're leaving?" she asked with muted incredulity.

"I have to," Adam responded, then realized how absurd this must sound to her. "I promised Carla I'd be there. As bizarre as this may seem, we've become friends, and if he lives this kid will be my brother."

Never, Adam thought, had he seen a frown express such skepticism and wonder. "Please," she responded with surprising evenness. "This is about Carla Pacelli, not the unborn. If it weren't, your brother could represent you nicely."

Adam looked into her face. "There's something in that," he acknowledged. "But I can't tell you what. All I know is that, however much I want to stay, I'd feel lousy if I did."

"Then go to her." Her voice was flat, as though she were suppressing her own anger and disappointment. "I can hardly keep you, can I?"

"Are you coming with me, or should I call a cab?"

Rachel shook her head in astonishment. "Leave here to drive back into a howling rainstorm, all so you can be with your father's lover when she delivers his child? Under the circumstances, we might find it hard to make light conversation."

Adam grimaced. "I can't imagine it, either. All I can do is apologize."

"Just figure this out," Rachel requested in a gentler tone. "I'll try not to think of you while I'm skiing." She hesitated, then gave him a quick kiss that somehow felt defensive. "Please, Adam, just go."

Arriving at Boston Logan, Adam rushed to the counter of the small commuter airline that serviced Martha's Vineyard. There were no passengers in line, only a middle-aged reservationist who looked bored. "Are you still flying?" he asked her.

"For now. But the weather's getting worse. Right now, the next flight's due to leave at noon."

"Got room for me?"

She gave him a wry look. "Nothing but. Funny, but we're short of eager travelers."

Hurriedly, Adam bought a ticket and fretted his way through the security line, glancing repeatedly at his watch, wondering about Carla and then Rachel. When he arrived at the gate and presented his ticket, it was 11:45. "Have you boarded yet?"

The attendant shook his head. "Still waiting for clearance. Don't know if we're going."

Noon passed, then 12:30, with no word. One other passenger, an older woman, waited in the gate area.

Abruptly, the attendant called out, "You're boarding."

Adam followed the woman onto the tarmac and into a driving sleet, then up the metal stairs to the nine seat propeller plane. Its size did not faze him; he had flown on third-world airlines with hair-raising safety records. But the weather did—it hardly suited this aircraft. The pilot looked to be sixty-five, at least, and there was no copilot. For the sake of balance, the older man explained, Adam and the woman should sit across from each other in the last aisle. Noting the pack of cigarettes in his pocket, Adam hoped that his cardiac health was unimpaired.

Settling into the front of the plane, the pilot pushed the throttle. As they taxied down the slick glistening tarmac, fresh gusts of wind caused the plane to vibrate. Outside, the weather was so gray and close that Adam could not make out the Boston skyline. Glancing at his fellow passenger, he saw her jaw tighten.

The plane gained speed, then abruptly lifted off at a severe upward angle, buffeted by wind and rain. A series of jolts rocked Adam back then forward as the plane strained toward thick black clouds. Suddenly they were amidst them, with no visibility that Adam could discern.

For minutes, they bounced up and down and sideways, then began a series of abrupt, sickening dips, the motor grinding as it fought against the weather. The plane felt like Nature's plaything, divorced from the normal rules of flight. They were somewhere over the water now, Adam knew, though they could see nothing. Even in Afghanistan, he had never allowed himself to fear. But he could not help it now. Perhaps this time was different because he had no control, or escape.

The plane dipped again, shaking abruptly. Across the aisle, the woman gasped. Without speaking, Adam reached for her hand. After all he had survived, he suddenly thought, to crash while flying to see Ben's pregnant lover would be a truly cosmic joke.

Minutes passed, the woman squeezing Adam's fingers, her own frozen white. There was another loss of elevation, the motor snarling like a buzz saw. "Ten minutes now," the pilot promised.

Adam felt the plane begin its descent, falling then rising with fresh gales of wind. Suddenly they were below the clouds, rain pelting the windshield like gunshots, startlingly close to the slick asphalt of Martha's Vineyard Airport, a haven in the stunted winter landscape. There was a last dip of the wings to one side, and then the plane landed with a bump, safe.

As the woman released his hand, Adam felt his tension seep away. "Nice flying with you," he told the pilot.

The man grinned at him. "Your lucky day. I'm retiring the day after tomorrow."

At once, Carla consumed Adam's thoughts. He got off the plane and hurried to a taxi.

Eleven

.

Wrenched by spasms of pain, Carla fought to focus on the baby, barely conscious of the delivery room around her.

Teddy had helped her through the emergency entrance, where a nurse put her in a wheelchair and whisked her to the triage room for an evaluation. When she arrived her forehead was damp, and each contraction caused her to exhale sharply. As Teddy sat outside, a stout blond-haired nurse with a thick New England accent and a pleasant but no-nonsense manner helped her change into a hospital gown and awkwardly climb onto the bed. Then the nurse inserted an IV in her arm and strapped a fetal monitor on her stomach. "Helps us check the baby's heart rate," she said matter-of-factly. Though she surely knew the dangers facing Carla's son, she gave no sign that this delivery was anything but normal. "The head is down," she added, "and the heartbeat sounds fine."

Another contraction, then another, timed by the nurse. Breathing deeply, Carla tried to will away the pain, staring at the white ceiling through slitted eyes. The door flew open, and Dr. Dan Stein was there.

"How are you feeling, Carla?"

Were it not for her fears, the genial absurdity of the question would have made her smile. "That nature could've designed a better process."

"Another sign that God is a male. If you want, later on we can give you morphine for the pain."

This time Carla did smile, though with effort. "Thanks, but I exhausted my quota of drugs a couple of years ago. I'll settle for an epidural when he's closer."

Stein nodded. "He's coming, no doubt of that. But you're a first-time mom, so that may be some hours yet." He paused, then spoke more quietly. "There'll be a pediatrician here for the delivery. If there's a problem, we'll get you and the baby to Boston as soon as possible."

If he's still alive, the doctor did not need to add. Caught between hope and dread, Carla simply thanked him.

Quickly, they took her to the room for labor and delivery. It was as large as a hotel suite, the walls a soothing beige, with a couch and two chairs near the head of the bed. As they helped her lie down, Carla noticed the clock on the wall.

Once again, the nurse placed a fetal monitor on her stomach. "Your baby still sounds strong," she assured Carla. "Just hang on."

When Adam arrived, Teddy was slumped in an uncomfortable looking chair outside the delivery room. Standing over him, Adam said, "I bet this is one experience you thought you'd never have."

Beneath the harsh fluorescent lights, Teddy eyed him with weary tolerance. "Why should predators like you have all the fun."

Adam glanced at the door. "How is she?"

"Gritty, as usual—I've been looking in whenever they're not doing weird stuff to her anatomy. But she's got a long hard stretch ahead of her, and that may not be the worst part."

Against his will, Adam imagined Carla presented with a still-born child. "Anyhow," he told Teddy, "it's my turn. Did you tell her I was coming?"

His brother frowned. "Given the complexity of your circumstances, I didn't know if you could make it. So where do things sit with you two, exactly?"

"I have no idea, and right now it hardly matters. I just needed to be here when he comes—whatever happens."

Teddy gazed up at him. "Fine. But I'm waiting this out right here. You gave me this assignment, after all, and now we're in it together." Glancing around, he added in a lower voice, "I like her too. Even though she may still wonder if I killed this baby's father."

Despite his tangled knot of worries, Adam felt a deep wave of affection for his brother, the only member of his family he loved without ambiguity. Placing a hand on Teddy's shoulder, he said, "If they'd given me a choice of brothers, Ted, you'd be the one I picked."

When Adam appeared by her bed, Carla was squinting with pain, her face pinched and wan. It took a moment for her to realize he was there. Her eyes froze, surprised yet serious, before she managed to say, "I wasn't expecting you."

"I'm sorry I wasn't home. Teddy tracked me down in New Hampshire, and I came as soon as I could."

She studied him, absorbing what he had not said. "That can't have gone over well."

Adam shrugged. "No better than I deserved."

A trace of a smile appeared at the corner of her mouth. "A nicer woman would feel more sympathy."

"No doubt. Nonetheless, I'm here."

She nodded solemnly, as though trying to absorb this. "I wish I could be more effusive, but there's a lot going on with me." She hesitated, looking into his face. "I've never been this afraid."

Given what Adam knew about her life, the admission pierced him. He moved closer to her bedside. "Maybe it won't help, Carla. But I'm staying here as long as you want me."

Something in her eyes changed. Her gaze, though tentative, lingered on his face. "You truly are an enigma, you know."

Adam smiled a little. "You should try being me."

The doctor came in, glancing from Carla to her visitor with apparent surprise. "Adam Blaine? I haven't seen you since that football game where you and Bobby Towle beat Nantucket. Looks like the entire family is here."

Though well intended, the circumstances made Stein's remark slightly tactless. Don't expect my mother, Adam imagined saying— though if I told you my father were still walking around, it really would be a surprise. Instead, he responded evenly, "We'll try to keep out of the way."

Turning his attention to Carla, Stein studied the fetal monitor. "He's still got a strong, steady heartbeat," he informed her. "A very good sign."

A smile of hope crossed Carla's lips. To Adam, she seemed to enter a realm of her own, containing only a mother and the baby she already loved. He considered saying something, or simply touching her, then realized he was outside the mystery of their connection. So he found a chair in the corner of the room, absorbing in silence how deeply he wanted her child to live.

As the hours wore on, and day became evening, Adam waited. He sat at the head of Carla's bed, not speaking much, leaving when he should without being asked. Sometimes she would turn to him, speaking a few words or just affirming his presence with her eyes. But in the deepest sense, he knew, Carla was alone.

They gave her ice cubes to suck on for hydration and, to vary this, a popsicle. By midnight, her contractions were coming quicker and stronger. Her breaths became gasps; her forehead shone with sweat, and her gown was soaked. "Go ahead and scream," the nurse said. "Everyone does."

But Carla seemed to fight this, as though she believed yielding to her own pain would jeopardize her son's life. Stein constantly checked the fetal monitor, nodding at the steady heartbeat. When he examined her again, Carla did not object to Adam's presence—no doubt because he was positioned to spare her any embarrassment. Over the long night, Stein and his nurse had seemed to accept that he was there as long as Carla wished. At some point, Adam realized he had not eaten. But he did not wish to leave.

Briefly, Carla fell asleep from sheer exhaustion. When the next contraction jolted her awake, she emitted a small cry.

Stein examined her again. "You're dilated to five centimeters, Carla. Time for your epidural."

A youthful anesthesiologist appeared. Introducing himself, he inserted the tube, explaining that this would numb her from the waist down. "He's getting closer now," Stein told her. "I want you to push with each contraction."

The next one came quickly. Carla thrust her hips beneath the sheet, eyes shut, lips clamped to suppress a cry. "Good," the doctor encouraged her. "Just keep it up."

"Easy for you to say," Carla complained between gritted teeth. But when her eyes opened again, fixed on the ceiling, Adam could read her fear—not of the pain, but for the son she was struggling to bear.

The nurse wheeled in a baby warmer with blankets. Instinctively, Adam took Carla's hand, and felt the brief answering pressure of curled fingers.

An hour passed, then another, with almost no sound save the doctor's instructions, Carla's thin animal cries of pain. Adam kept holding her hand. After another fierce contraction forced a louder cry from between open lips, she protested, "The epidural's wearing off."

The doctor checked her yet again. "He's very close now, Carla. You've dilated to ten centimeters. I'm going to give you a local, and make a small incision."

The nurse stood next to him at the foot of the bed. Her face intent, she gave Carla a shot; moments later, the doctor positioned himself on a stool and produced a scalpel. To Adam's eye, the instrument disappeared; when it appeared again, its edges red, he felt himself wince, his fingers tightening around Carla's. She did not ask him to leave.

Stein reached beneath the blanket. "He's coming now, Carla," he said encouragingly. "Just keep pushing."

Another middle-aged woman appeared in the room—the pediatrician, Adam guessed. He felt a fresh surge of dread: even were the baby born alive, so many other things could doom him. Though he had not told Carla, he had scoured the Internet to learn about Trisomy 18. Leaning close to her, he murmured, "Do you want me to stay?"

Silent, she squeezed his hand, her face ashen with pain. Another spasm twisted her body.

"I can see his head," Stein said encouragingly. "You're doing great."

Taut, Adam could not see the baby; he could do nothing but clasp Carla's hand. He felt her grip tighten as she struggled to raise her head, straining to glimpse the son she might be losing. At her feet, the nurse used a syringe to clear the unseen child's nose and mouth.

"There's a shoulder," Stein said quickly. "One more push."

Releasing Adam's hand, Carla thrust her torso upward with both palms, the strain and anxiety showing in her eyes, wide open now, body tremoring with the final push. Adam saw the doctor's gloved hands reach beneath her gown. "Please God . . ." she implored in a soft, clear voice.

Stein was holding the child now, Adam realized, as the nurse hurriedly swabbed him with a towel. Agonizing seconds passed, and then the doctor held the baby aloft for his mother to see, still connected to the cord inside her.

The newborn was still, Adam saw, a tiny, waxen figure with dark, matted hair. Carla sat bolt upright, rigid with apprehension. Hurriedly, Stein gave the infant a quick slap on the rear.

The baby seemed to shudder, then emitted a brief cry, extending an outstretched arm in protest. Grinning, Stein said, "Pretty stoic, this guy."

He passed the baby to the pediatrician. Placing him on a baby warmer, she told Carla apologetically, "I just need to look at him."

She examined the child closely, then put a stethoscope to his chest. At length the pediatrician smiled. "Seems pretty healthy to me," she informed the boy's mother. "Good muscle tone, fine skin color, a strong heartbeat, and a first-rate pair of lungs. Seems like this boy is going to be with you for a very long time."

Carla gazed at her son in wonderment. Suddenly her face broke into an incandescent smile that Adam had never seen before, even as tears began streaming down her face. "Lie back down," Stein requested gently. "I think he wants to meet you."

Carla complied, her expression serious now. As she held out her arms, Stein placed the baby on her chest. Tentative, she kissed the swirl of dark hair before looking into her son's brown eyes. "Hello, Liam," she said softly. "I'm your mom."

Adam felt the dampness on his face, a bond with this woman and her child that left him speechless As though she sensed this, Carla turned, looking gravely into his face. Then she turned to her newborn son again, and all else seemed forgotten.

Suffused with joy, Carla saw the child's hand reaching instinctively toward her face. In that moment, it seemed to her, they were utterly sufficient to each other, and to themselves.

Feeling her son's touch, she thanked God for the gift of his life, and promised Liam that she would earn it for the rest of her own.

PART FIVE

THE RECKONING

Martha's Vineyard
January–March 2012

ONE

An hour before Adam would arrive for dinner, Carla Pacelli nursed her son, watching Liam's dark head bob as he attacked this project with his customary enthusiasm.

Their ritual both warmed and amused her. She was now the host in a symbiotic relationship with a boy who was, at least based on anecdotal evidence, unusually voracious. Of course, he had ground to make up; after all, he had insisted on arriving seven weeks early, and she was glad to see him becoming plumper. But the irregularity of his appetite at odd hours was matched only by the noisiness with which he announced it. It was though he understood that the pitch dark of early morning required the lung power to break through his exhausted mother's narcolepsy.

"It's not like I didn't ask for this," she told him. "But do you always have to prove that you're a guy?" In answer, his mouth clamped down harder. "I get the message," she reproved him fondly. "Everything really *is* all about you."

But Liam would not be rushed; she was in their rocking chair for the duration. Over time, she reflected, this stage would pass, and then the next, and the one after that. Though she would miss what was lost, her purpose as a mother was to raise an adult, confident and self-sufficient, without the damage which had wounded Ben or Adam—or her. Liam was a separate being, and she would school herself to let go.

But for many years, he would depend on her, and she would be making choices for them both. Which brought her to the puzzle that was Adam Blaine: so compelling yet so troubling.

I'll do the best I can, she promised the infant tugging at her breast. Of the men in my life, you come first.

While Adam got the lobster pot boiling, Carla set the table and lit candles.

Over his shoulder, he remarked, "I've got to say you're looking remarkably like your former self."

Carla smiled. "Lots of yoga and floor exercises—I didn't enjoy my stomach looking like an accordion. Despite my deepening spirituality, my vanity is still intact."

"I'm sure Liam doesn't mind." Finishing, he went to the bassinet set near the fireplace to gaze at the infant who, replete, was resting up for the next encounter with his food source. "He doesn't have to do much to be fascinating, does he? He just is."

"And a good thing," Carla responded wryly. "His routine is pretty much limited to intake and evacuation, with moments of staring I choose to interpret as love. The burden of glittering conversation falls on you." She lit the last candle. "Still, the helpless stage drives home how much Liam depends on me. Including for a childhood that doesn't give him nightmares."

Adam glanced at her. "No lousy marriage, in other words."

"Better no marriage at all. As you and I both know."

Adam fell silent. Perhaps her remark was gratuitous, Carla thought—she was far from knowing what they wanted from each other. But she felt the need for honesty in a situation so obviously fraught, and Adam might serve best as a caring man for Liam than as something more for her. Contemplating Liam, Adam told the boy, "Your mommy says no losers."

"Let's hope that 'Mommy,'" Carla rejoined, "develops some talent in that area."

Returning to the stove, Adam dropped two lobsters in the pot. "By the way," he remarked, "does Liam know that he has an ethnically incongruous name?"

"Liam Edward Pacelli? If I'd known you cared so much, I'd have asked you to submit a list."

Adam smiled at this. "You might have done worse, I suppose—his middle name could be Milton. But where did Liam come from?"

"My maternal grandfather. I remember him as gentle, though maybe it was merely because he was so old."

Adam shot her a look. "You really are a cynic, aren't you?"

"Just warier these days."

Slicing pads of butter into a cup, Adam placed it in the microwave, then glanced at her sideways. "Are we talking about us, by any chance?"

"Perhaps as a case study," Carla quipped, and then turned to him. "Should we be?"

He paused to consider his answer. "Ever since Liam showed up, things seem different. Maybe it's just me."

Carla served the salad. "That you showed up meant the world to me. It also gave me a lot to think about."

"Such as?"

She waited for him to bring two lobsters to the table. "I know you're capable of feeling," she said gently. "But I think your feelings about me are complicated, and you're not sure what they are."

Adam sat across from her. "And you?"

She gave him a long, level look. "It's not easy for me to trust any man. But you're often very hard to read. I wonder if the life you

chose has made you addicted to danger. And if you've ever committed to a relationship, I don't know about it." She paused a moment.
"So maybe we should talk about Rachel Ravinsky."

This was the first time she had mentioned Rachel directly. To his
credit, Adam did not feign puzzlement. Instead, he made a surgical job of liberating her lobster from its shell. "All right," he said at
length. "What would you like to know?"

She tried to compose her thoughts. Among the unspoken things
between them was a palpable sexual tension—they had never made
love, and Carla could not yet. Finally, she answered, "Not whether
the two of you shared an experience that we've never had—clever
girl that I am, I've already puzzled that one out. I don't even blame
you that much. But I can't help wondering where things stand."

He looked at her seriously, face shadowed in candlelight. "You
could say we're in a state of limbo."

"So what are we doing, exactly?" Carla's voice softened. "I don't
expect anything, Adam. I don't even know what I want. If all you
want is to be a caring presence in Liam's life, I'd be content with
that."

Reaching across the table, he touched her hand. "It feels like
something more. It's also clear that we need more time."

Carla nodded, steeling herself to say the rest. "I certainly agree.
But if you're interested in me as a woman, you should figure
out what's happening with Rachel. It's your privilege to be with
her, of course. But I can't let myself and Liam become part of a
competition."

His eyes held a trace of annoyance. "You really didn't have to tell
me that, all right? Because of me, and also because of her."

"So she's waiting?"

"Perhaps. But I've made no claim on her patience."

Carla gave him a thin smile. "If it's any comfort, I'm guessing you
don't need to."

"I wouldn't know. She's gone back to Manhattan for a while. It
seems she found this housing arrangement a little awkward." There

was another change in his expression, tentative yet impatient. "If we've exhausted the fascination of this particular subject, there's something else I need to tell you."

"Such as?"

"I resigned from the agency this morning. That part of my life is over."

Astonished, all Carla could do was ask, "Why?"

"Because if I don't change that, nothing else I do will matter."

Carla felt emotion thicken her voice. "Does this have to do with us?"

Adam looked into her eyes. "Not all of it. But without this, anything more would be impossible, wouldn't it?"

She drew a breath, then reached across the table for his hand. "I never could've asked that of you."

Adams fingers tightened. "I know that. I also know it's what you need."

For a moment, she averted her gaze. "What will you do now?"

"Strange as this may sound, try writing. I've started working on an article about Afghanistan. Not what I did, or for whom, but what I saw. Most of it is about my translator and his daughter and what will happen to women once we're gone. If my 'father's' name helps me place it, then so be it . . ."

Carla felt herself fighting back tears. "What's wrong?" he asked softly.

She shook her head in wonder and confusion. "I don't know that anything is. But you've just told me you're changing your whole life. Suddenly, nothing else can decide this for us, but us. And there's so much we have to deal with."

Adam gave her a humorless smile. "Like Ben, you mean? You'll be happy to know I'm seeing a competent psychiatrist. No doubt I'll keep him busy for a while."

Carla felt hope warring with misery. "There's something else. Something I can't put off telling you anymore. It's about that reporter from the *Inquirer*."

Adam's face went blank. The only hint of emotion was a fugitive change in his eyes, quickly gone and impossible to decipher. "Amanda Ferris," he said flatly.

Carla nodded. "Before Liam was born, she came to see me."

At once Adam's voice turned cool. "You let her in?"

"I found her sitting in that rocking chair. It was a bad day—I'd just found out that my baby might have Trisomy 18. Before I could throw her out, she made accusations I can't just brush aside."

"Involving what?"

Carla held his gaze. "She claims that Ben was murdered, and that you may know who killed him."

It was eerie, she thought, how little his face showed. "Clever of me, Carla. Given that when he died I was twenty thousand miles away . . ."

"Ferris also claims that you broke into the courthouse last summer, stealing documents to help you protect Teddy. She surmises you've got the skills to pull that off. I know you do."

"Then damn me for telling you anything," Adam said sharply. "Do you really think that Ted's a murderer?"

She could not let herself back down, Carla knew. "It's hard to conceive of Teddy killing anyone—even a man he hated. But you and I both know how much hatred there was between Jack and Ben. And why."

All at once, she could feel Adam slipping away from her. In a weary monotone, he said, "Jack already explained how Ben died. I'd like to keep this poison away from us."

"So would I. That's why I had to tell you."

"But you can't forget about it, can you?"

She gripped his hand. "Not without some help from you. I know what scum this woman is. But Ben would never have killed himself, not with me here, and he knew that promontory too well to risk falling. Deep in my soul, I believe that someone killed him." Her voice lowered. "I've always known there are things you haven't told me. I just don't know what they are. Can't you see how hard that makes it to live with your family secrets?"

Adam looked away, a reaction so uncharacteristic that it unsettled her still more. "I'd never ask you to. All I can do is hope that someday all this will stop mattering. However pointless the wish."

Carla could not answer. She almost welcomed Liam's cries of hunger.

Two

With Liam sated, Carla resumed reading the first draft of Adam's article.

He had given it to her reluctantly, concerned that his prose would not meet her expectations. But as the pages turned, she read more swiftly, at first surprised, then relieved, then impressed. He wrote with a clarity and humanity, evoking his translator's daughter so well that it hurt Carla to perceive how the web of ignorance and custom would ensnare her once the Taliban resumed control. It was the best kind of journalism, she thought, capturing a social landscape through the people caught in it. It was something Ben might have done, yet so clearly Adam's own—more particular, somehow, and more poignant. Then she heard the sharp rap on her door, and went to answer.

Though she would know this woman anywhere, Carla was astonished to find her on the porch—still striking in her midsixties, her gray-blond hair perfectly coiffed, her blue eyes clear and cool, her patrician features barely conveying the disdain she was too well mannered to express. Without preface, Clarice Blaine said, "May I come in?"

It was not phrased as a request. Silent, Carla stood aside. Clarice entered, barely casting a glance toward Liam's bassinet before taking a chair. Carla sat across from her, resolved to say nothing until Adam's mother spoke again.

An arid smile briefly crossed Clarice's lips. "It's obvious you've been spending time with my son. You seem to have mastered his talent for Delphic silence."

This was meant to unnerve her, Carla knew. But while she did not have this woman's breeding, Carla had not been an actress, or a celebrity, for nothing. "You came here for a reason," she responded evenly. "I'm sure you'll tell me when you're ready."

With an ironic lift of her eyebrows, Clarice took note of Carla's self-containment. "I thought it was time we spoke."

"Why now?" Carla inquired. "We were doing so well as it was."

A chill amusement surfaced briefly in Clarice's eyes. "You've certainly been doing well. First my husband—and now, it seems, my son. Not to mention a considerable chunk of Ben's estate."

Carla forced herself not to react. "I can understand your point of view. Is there anything else you want to say?"

Clarice's face set, her anger still repressed. "You tried to steal my husband and my security, using your pregnancy as a crowbar. Now you're moving on to Adam. There are words for women like that." She paused, speaking more deliberately. "There's been enough, Carla. I don't want you in my life, or with my son."

Still Carla held her temper. "I don't intend to be in your life. But Adam's life is his own. You can't choose for him—especially when it concerns my son, who's no more at fault for being here than Adam was. I'm sorry for your pain and humiliation and to have been any part of that. But perhaps we have too much in common."

Clarice stiffened. "You really do flatter yourself."

"Flatter myself? Let me see if I understand you. You had an affair, as I did, the difference being that you were also committing adultery. You became pregnant, as I did—and, like me, decided to have the child. Then you protected that child—and your own reputation—by signing over your marital assets to Ben. Too bad my reputation took the beating you were so eager to avoid. But I can live with that." Carla's tone became quieter. "When I learned about Ben's will, I gave you most of what he left me. Not just out of sympathy for you—Adam had been through enough without feeling guilty about being born. I'm sure that part was particularly humiliating. Given that you were so determined to leave my son and me with nothing."

Clarice stiffened. "So you really think this is about my pride? You may fancy playing your new role as a mother for an audience of one. But from the day he was born, I've loved Adam more than you can ever understand. Far too much to see him settle for an alcoholic has-been whose greatest talent involves lying on her back."

Carla gave herself a moment to regain her calm. "I don't expect you to thank me, Clarice. After all, being taken care of by others has always been your due. But you can take your hypocrisy elsewhere. As for having me in Adam's life, I suppose you could end up with Rachel. Then you can deal with Whitney Dane, who seems entitled to some grudges of her own."

Clarice's eyes froze, betraying how startled she must be, her sudden fear of what Carla might know. But Clarice could not ask. Nor did Carla choose to say the rest: that before settling on Ben, Clarice Barkley, Whitney's closest friend through college, had betrayed her by sleeping with Whitney's father. Instead, she finished coolly, "You're wondering what I know, of course. A good deal, actually. But you've disenchanted Adam quite enough already. Besides, the Blaines have so many secrets I'll enjoy sharing this one with you. As with Ben's will, you can thank me later."

Standing, Carla went to the door and opened it. There was nothing Clarice Blaine could do but leave, her posture erect and her head held high, though she could no longer look Carla in the face.

When Rachel appeared at his door, Adam was not surprised—to show up unannounced matched his sense of her, and he had not expected her to vanish. "I'm glad to see you," he said, and found that this was true. "When did you get back from Manhattan?"

"This morning, and I only plan on being here a day." Stepping inside, she looked around her—for traces of Carla, he imagined. "I came to see you, actually."

He hoped his smile was not as uneasy as he felt. "A house call is way more than I deserve. I'm still sorry about what happened."

She sat with him beside a window framing the meadow, lit by slanting winter sun. "So am I," she answered quietly. "Especially because it wasn't my choice."

Adam touched the bridge of his nose, a nervous gesture—he seemed to be losing his gift for emotionless calm. "Carla's baby could've been stillborn. You and I were only skiing . . ."

Rachel shook her head. "We were doing more than skiing, I thought. I had the delusion we were starting something."

"Perhaps we were," Adam acknowledged. "I hated having to leave."

After a moment, Rachel nodded slowly. "Is the baby all right?"

Despite his best efforts, the thought of Liam made Adam smile—a few days before the tiny boy had wrapped a death grip around his finger, looking into his face, and Adam had imagined a glimmer of recognition. "Oh, he's fine. Just hungry all the time."

Rachel looked at him with new directness. "Then I guess you don't need to worry anymore."

"Not about his lungs, certainly." He was skirting the truth, Adam realized, and Rachel deserved much better. "As for the relationship between Carla and me, I'm not sure yet."

She smiled at this, a reflex. "But there is a 'Carla and me.'"

Adam nodded. "At least for now. But neither of us know where this is going. So I'm not counting on a happy ending."

Across the table, Rachel seemed to steel herself, her striking features assuming a determined cast. "A reasonable person wouldn't. A truly reasonable person might even call this a Freudian nightmare."

Adam chose not to defend himself. "Only if it feels that way."

"How can it not?" Rachel persisted. "Your father's girlfriend? Your father's son? Why not start wearing his old jackets, and writing sequels to his books?"

This struck close enough to home that her words stung him. With an edge in his voice, he said, "I'm sorry that I hurt you, Rachel. And so quickly at that."

At once, her gaze broke. "I guess it's my turn to apologize. Maybe I imagined something that wasn't there. I make things up for a living, after all."

"You've got too much going to believe that. In bed or out, I wasn't just killing time."

Rachel looked up at him. "I hope so," she said in a firmer tone. "I do care about you, Adam. But you actually seem to be contemplating a future with your father's mistress and your infant half brother, rubbing salt in your mother's gaping wounds—not to mention your own. Are you still so tied to Benjamin Blaine that his leftovers are sacred relics?"

The question both angered and unsettled him. Quietly, he answered, "Whatever else, I don't see Carla and Liam as leftovers. Another sign of my deep emotional problems."

Rachel bit her lip in obvious dismay. "I've really lost my gift for words, haven't I? No doubt tact is not my greatest strength. But do you honestly think you can untangle all this?"

It was a good question, Adam thought, even from a woman who knew only what was apparent on the surface. "I don't know," he admitted. "Even if I can 'untangle all this,' what happens isn't just about me."

"Oh, she'll want you, Adam. Why wouldn't she?" Rachel touched his arm, speaking in a lower voice. "Please don't hold what I've said against me, all right? No matter what, I'll want to know what happens to you."

"And to you, Rachel."

She stood at once. Walking her to the door, Adam ventured, "Are you still working on the novel?"

She smiled for a moment. "Religiously. I've discovered that mixing self-doubt with unhappiness is the writer's friend. Anyhow, thanks for asking."

She turned in the doorway, and kissed him, long enough for Adam to wish he could respond. Then she pulled back, looking into his face. "Damn you, Adam Blaine," she said, and walked swiftly to her car.

THREE

Driving to the doctor's office from an AA meeting in Vineyard Haven, Carla hoped that Liam was not scarred for life by having such an anxious mother.

It was her first time away from him in his six weeks on the planet, and Carla had to restrain herself from taking out her cell phone to call the babysitter. It was time to let go a little, she told herself. Her son had been the focus of her hopes and fears for so many months that she had not allowed either of them to breathe—not to mention that it might be a mercy to everyone if he settled for a bottle now and then. So she tried to reflect on the renewal she had felt at the meeting, the man she had never seen before—his face ravaged, but his blue eyes clear and gentle, as though he had come back wiser from some terrible place. She, too, felt stronger now; she had a life to live, and was determined to live it fully.

Waiting for the doctor, she thought about Adam Blaine. He no longer had nightmares; surviving Afghanistan seemed to have freed him from the sense that his own life was foreshortened. They saw each other frequently now: more often than not, he was smart and wry and perceptive and curious about her and Liam's progress and her applications to graduate school. For all the good it did them, every day she found him more attractive. But Adam never spoke of the inquest or Amanda Ferris, and he still retained an elusive quality, creating the sense that something still pursued him, that part of him could never quite be with her. The dark and light of the Irish, she remembered from her own youth, but his moments of opacity felt like much more than that. Yet there were times when Carla felt she could almost reach inside him, touch what she could not see. Perhaps an illusion, however tantalizing, conjured by her own desire.

But when it came to Adam, Mary Margaret Pacelli's only daughter had many desires, and one of them was very simple.

When the examination was over, Dr. Stein assured her, "Everything looks good. As far as I can tell, young Liam did no further damage to the plant. Seems only fair, with all the trouble you went to for him." He sat down in his chair. "No guarantees, Carla—even if you wanted to, it will never be easy for you to get pregnant and take the kid to term. But it happened once, when you least expected it. So you need to start thinking about birth control."

Carla felt a rush of gratitude—irrational, perhaps. But it felt oddly hopeful to think she might be able to have another child. "Does that mean I'm no longer off-limits?"

Stein smiled. "If the mood strikes, you can have sex in the parking lot. But the pill and IUD have already caused you problems. So I suggest we fix you up with a diaphragm before you face the outside world."

Carla felt herself flush—there were far more immediate possibilities than childbirth, and the thought of her dinner date set off a wave of nervousness and anticipation. After a moment, she said, "I don't know about the parking lot. But I probably shouldn't leave here without something. I'd just hate calling 911 in the middle of the night."

* * *

That night, having placated Liam for at least an hour or two, Carla went with Adam for dinner at State Road.

It was February, and bitter outside—the other diners, year-rounders all, showed less interest in the two of them than would the summer crowd, avid for gossip. In the candlelit seclusion of a quiet corner, Carla felt as much at ease as her new circumstances permitted. "When I got home today," she informed Adam, "Liam actually smiled at me. I was so pathetically grateful I nearly wept."

"Sure it wasn't gas?"

"It was rapture," she insisted. "He was simply ecstatic to see me."

Adam gave her breasts a satiric glance. "That much I believe. But the boy needs to broaden his interests a little." He thought a moment. "The next good day, why don't we stuff Liam in a snuggly and take a walk in Menemsha Hills. You've been housebound too long, and it's time he started appreciating the natural environment."

"Our world has been a little small," Carla allowed wryly. "Even going to an AA meeting felt like a jailbreak." She paused, wary of prodding him, then let curiosity overcome her. "Did you send off that article, by the way?"

Adam nodded. "To *Vanity Fair*, which used to publish Ben's travel pieces. Maybe it was the connection, but I heard from them today. They say their readers will be interested in what I saw of Afghan women, and so they're publishing it. Not that anything will change."

Carla was surprised, then deeply pleased. "It's already changed for you—you've become a published author in record time. How does it feel?"

Adam frowned in thought. "Pretty good, I guess. Though I can't help but wonder where he leaves off and I begin."

Nettled, Carla replied, "So why don't you just become an astronaut? Or did Ben orbit the earth when I wasn't looking?"

To Carla's surprise, her tartness induced a short laugh. "Spit it out, Carla. When you're obscure like that, I can't tell what you're driving at."

Carla could no longer stifle her impatience. "All right. If you want to make everything you do about him, you can—including this success. For that matter, you can simply run away from it. Whatever you choose, please don't let me interfere."

From Adam's expression, he understood too well that her change of mood was not only about his article. "Point taken," he responded. "All the way around."

Now it was Carla's turn to feel rueful. "In my experience," she said more gently, "there are too few nice surprises in the world. I'm just happy for this one."

Raising her iced tea, she toasted his first publication, and their conversation elided easily into dinner, covering a novel of Vietnam they had both read and admired, *Matterhorn*; whether Robert Mitchum was, as she insisted, a great American film actor; and Adam's seriocomic assertion that the latest Republican presidential debate had rendered *Saturday Night Live* redundant. Over dessert, he proposed, "I rented a movie we could watch. Interested?"

"What is it?"

"A classic screwball comedy—*Bringing Up Baby*, with Cary Grant and Katharine Hepburn. I thought about *Hamlet*," he added dryly, "but it feels like we've lived that one already. I figured we could use some lighter entertainment."

Carla felt a moment's reticence. "On that general subject," she said, "there's something else I ought to mention. I went in for my checkup this morning."

"And?"

"I passed. No damage done except to my sleep cycle." She hesitated, glancing at him with a barely perceptible smile. "Dan Stein was so excited that he recommended birth control."

Adam gave her a sideways look. "A good man, Dr. Stein."

Their eyes met for a longer time. "I'm glad you think so," Carla told him.

Together, they gazed fondly at Liam in his bassinet.

He had accepted his bottle readily, the babysitter had reported, drifting into somnolence after a sequence of deep burps. "How like a male," Carla remarked to Adam. "Take without discrimination, then nod off. But I suppose we should be grateful."

"As should he. It's so easy to love them when they're sleeping."

Still they lingered there, fingers touching, watching Liam's chest rise up and down beneath his absurdly small pajamas, enjoying the profound sleep nature bestows on infants. Save when he was hungry, Adam thought, Liam seemed to have a peaceful and contented nature—as was true of Adam himself as a child, his mother had told him long ago. It was a sobering thing to be charged with a life so unmarked.

After a time, Carla turned to him. "Why don't we let him rest," she proposed. "He was doing so well without us."

He gave her a querying look. In answer, she touched his face, looking into his eyes, and then kissed him. The kiss deepened, the desire for her overcoming Adam so swiftly that he could no longer escape how long, and how much, he had wanted her. When his lips brushed her neck, Carla shivered, and he heard her whisper, "Yes."

Breaking away, she took his hand, drawing him into the darkened bedroom. She left the door ajar, thin light coming from the living room, enough for them.

She stood apart, moving to the foot of the bed. Without speaking, she reached behind her to unzip her dress, letting it fall to the floor. As she did the rest, Adam felt a kind of awe.

She was stunningly beautiful—full breasts, slender hips, her stomach flat again, her body lithe and sculpted. Adam could scarcely believe that she was real; or that this moment was theirs. At first, he could not read the question in her gaze.

Quietly, he said, "Sorry. But I can't take my eyes off you."

The slightest of smiles. "That's good, then. But, in itself, your admiration isn't helping me."

As quickly as he could, Adam undressed. She came to him then; the first touch of her breasts against his chest sent a current through him, and he began kissing her mouth, her throat, her neck, trying not to hurry, feeling a sense of consequence that was new to him. Their bodies pressed together as if this alone could save them.

"I've been waiting for so long now," she murmured.

He wanted to answer this. But she was leading him to the bed, barring his need, or his ability, to speak. They found the covers together, his lips grazing her nipples, her stomach, her thighs, his tongue probing between them.

"I want you," she insisted.

But he kept moving his tongue until she cried out softly, shuddering, a plea for what she needed from him. Then he slid on top of her, feeling the warmth of her body, the desire to look into her face, whatever followed. "Now," she urged.

As he slipped inside her, Adam felt her moistness, her strong thighs drawing him deeper, saw a question appearing in her eyes, the intensity of her need to see inside him. His torso began moving without conscious thought, as though their skin could not touch enough, that he could never reach the deepest part of her. She grasped his hips to pull him farther inside, eyes still meeting his. He thrust harder now, reason gone, thought vanishing, overcome by desire for this woman—Carla Pacelli. Desperate, he felt the blood rushing to his hardness, the pressure of their bodies seeking release, her fingernails digging into his back. She pressed against him fiercely, craving more, the inside of her tightening as he fought to resist the tide of her for one last, transcendent moment.

Suddenly she cried out, his name on her lips, and he lost himself entirely and they were shuddering together, warmth coursing through his limbs—their eyes still locked, Adam needing to confirm for Carla her uniqueness, to have her see him, no one else. At last the rhythm of their bodies ceased, their stare so intense that neither one could break it. He could feel their heat and moisture, the beating of his heart. He was lost to himself, yet home.

"My God . . . ," he murmured, an offering.

Her eyes remained searching, though she at last smiled a little. "So you think we achieved adequacy?"

Adam shook his head, so astonished that he came close to tears. "You don't understand, Carla. It's like you've taken a piece of me." He hesitated, speech failing him. "It's too hard to explain . . ."

"You don't have to."

Touching her face, he replayed the ambiguity of the words. "Tell me how you feel."

Her gaze became more serious yet. "I'd like to," she answered softly. "More than you know. But I just want us to be as we are, right now. At least for a while."

Perhaps she knew what he must wonder, and wanted to avoid it. "I understand," he told her. "But for me, being with you was about so much more."

Softly, Carla kissed him. "For me, too. If that's what you wanted to know."

Some of it, he thought. But not all.

As Adam slept, dreamless, Carla's fingers grazed the wound on his back, the skin puckered by the bullet that had nearly killed him. Gently, she kissed it, achingly grateful that he had lived. Like the child in the next room, the man did not stir.

Better this way, she thought. He had wanted to know about Ben, but could not ask. Nor did she know how to answer.

Still, Carla understood in the depths of her soul how much she was at risk. This night had told them some things, but not others. There were questions no lovemaking can answer, fears it could not quell.

From the living room a thin squall came, the first announcement of Liam's hunger. A reminder, should she need one, of who was now at the center of her life, Carla's to protect from her own mistakes.

FOUR

Next morning the sun lingered, filtered through a thinning fog which signaled a warmer day. Weary of winter, Adam and Charlie decided to walk along the rocky beach near the mouth of Menemsha Harbor. As the therapist surveyed the choppy waters with a sailor's anticipation of spring, Adam thought of Benjamin Blaine, his father then, eager to get his sailboat back on the waters, his enthusiasm sparking Adam's own. Hands thrust in the pockets of his down vest, Charlie turned to Adam. "So what's new? I can always count on something."

Adam scanned the ground in front of them, picking his way through boulders and jagged rocks. "Carla."

Charlie glanced at him sideways, and then comprehension stole through his eyes. "Oh, I see."

"I'm not sure you do. This was different."

"How so?"

The words felt hard to come by. "In every way. Afterward I felt close to her, and wanted to be closer. Ever since Jenny, with other women I'd just go somewhere else—even though we'd just made love, I felt empty." Acknowledging this, Adam was struck by a solitude so profound that he could barely speak. "But not last night . . ."

The muffled phrase made Charlie stop, facing Adam with a look of compassion. Head bowed, Adam murmured, "I've just felt so fucking alone."

This was all he could manage to say, but it captured the last decade of his life. Charlie waited in companionable silence until Adam got his bearings. "Little wonder," the therapist told him. "Long ago you learned to protect yourself, and take care of everyone else. If you can finally resolve that, you may be free to care for a woman who also cares for you. But somewhere you've lost the ability to ask for what you need. You don't know how, and it scares you." He paused, then asked simply, "Do you still feel like running away?"

Unable to look at Charlie, Adam felt the sadness of his answer. "Not this time. But I don't know if I can make this work. Or even if it can."

"How does Carla feel?"

"I'm not sure. But I think she's as scared as I am." Adam shook his head, a gesture of confusion. "In many ways, she's the most startlingly honest woman I've ever known. There are times it feels like I can trust her absolutely. But I don't think she can trust me, and she needs that as much as I do." Restless, he began to walk again. "And then there's Ben," he finished softly. "Always Ben."

Charlie scrutinized him closely. "Last night, did you think about Carla with Ben?"

"Only later. When we were together, all I could think of was her. Funny to become so lost."

"Funny for you, maybe. And maybe wonderful. But then Ben crawls into bed with you." Charlie's tone grew pointed. "Are you still competing with him, or is the thought of him with Carla just too repugnant to live with?"

The question stopped Adam where he was. "You certainly get to the heart of things, Charlie." Fighting his discomfort, he finished harshly, "Competing with Benjamin Blaine is a hard habit to break, and so is hating him. You don't forget seeing your father sodomize your girlfriend."

"Have you mentioned that to Carla?"

"No. I still have this odd reluctance to nauseate her. And even though the son of a bitch is dead, he's still the father of her child. For whatever strange reason, she loved him—however much that sticks in my throat."

"I think it's worse than that," Charlie said bluntly. "It sounds like you have contempt for those feelings and, to that extent, for her."

Adam flinched inside. "That's an ugly way of putting it."

"Is it? By your own account, you despise him. Yet you're deathly afraid you're like him: the restlessness, the risk taking, the emotional unavailability—especially with women. How can you respect Carla for loving a man like that?" Charlie's speech slowed. "Although I'm left to wonder which man—Ben, or you?"

Mute, Adam stared at him.

Unfazed, the therapist continued, "Time for a refresher course, all right? Ben was a narcissist; you're not. You're so different in fundamental ways that I can't list them all. But the biggest difference is that Benjamin Blaine would never be standing here—willing to look at himself, trying to find a different life. He could never escape his own past. I think you still can. The question is whether you can do that with Carla Pacelli."

Adam exhaled. "Not so easy, I'm finding. Perhaps for both of us."

Charlie picked up a sand dollar, and flung it into the lapping aqua waves, producing three skips before the tan disk vanished. "Maybe you can start by accepting the good things Ben helped to give you—at one time or another, you've acknowledged them all. A love of sailing and the outdoors. A venturesome nature and great personal courage. The resolve and resilience to master challenges, and make things turn out the way you want. Not to mention the strength it took to protect your family after his death—despite learning some very hard truths, and at considerable risk to yourself."

The risk was still there, Adam thought—a prosecution that could land him in prison, erasing any chance for a life with Carla.

"Those are incredible attributes," the psychiatrist went on. "Exemplified by a man who—as brutally as he betrayed you—loved his brother's son as much as his own nature and the circumstances allowed. Surely you must remember feeling that."

Gazing out at a lone fishing boat that plied the waters between the Vineyard and the Elizabeth Islands, Adam recalled Ben's stories of lobstering with his father, their curious mix of bitterness and nostalgia. "When I was away, Carla asked me about memories. So I wrote her about the better ones—too painful to remember, after Jenny. But I knew she wanted to hear them, and now they keep on surfacing."

"For instance?"

"The other day Liam reached out to grab my finger, and I imagined for a moment that he knew me. Then I remembered being very small—touching the whiskers on Ben's face before he shaved, and thinking someday I'd be a man like him. Ironic."

"Perhaps not. When you hoped that Liam would know you, what were you to him?"

Adam studied the rocks in their path. "A father, I guess. Someone like that."

Charlie gave him a faint smile. "That's worth discussing further. But let's consider how Liam managed to get here. Whatever Carla's obvious appeal for a man like Ben—and given his history, you can choose to be as cynical as you like—by fighting for recovery she presented him with one last chance to be a decent human being, at least for as long as he was able. When she became pregnant, maybe he imagined leaving behind a son less scarred than you or Teddy. And so, for that time, he may have become more like the man you'd wanted him to be."

Adam shoved his hands in his pockets. "That's a hard place for me to get."

"Perhaps. But there's no interpretation of this triangle too deep for me." Pausing, Charlie cocked his head. "This may sound strange, but perhaps Carla presents you with a chance to absorb the good things about Ben—at least with respect to her—and to accept that you once loved him as she did. A complicated task, but a necessary one, certainly for your own sake, and perhaps for Carla's. At least if there's to be any hope of a relationship."

Feeling the wind in his face, Adam put on aviator sunglasses, caught in the jumble of his thoughts. "As you say, it's complicated."

"And germane to many things. How goes the writing?"

"Hard to know, in the long run. But I just placed an article in *Vanity Fair*. Where Ben used to publish."

Charlie considered him. "A real breakthrough, don't you think? But I take it you're wondering who that's about."

"Of course. When I expressed my doubts to Carla, she suggested I become an astronaut instead."

To Adam's surprise, Charlie laughed aloud. "I'm beginning to like her. So why did you choose writing instead of space travel?"

"It just feels natural to me. I've seen a lot in Iraq and Lebanon and Afghanistan—around the world, really. There's nothing more compelling than human beings faced with challenges and hardships—war, famine, repression from dictators or kleptocrats or religious fanatics. In too many places it's that much worse for women." Adam's voice quickened. "Americans need to know about this, instead of worrying about their iPhones and paying less in taxes. I look at this country after ten years away, and see the decline of Rome with that special touch of Paraguay—conspicuous consumption; financial predators who don't make anything; people divided into gated communities of the mind; political campaigns financed by legalized bribery; armchair warriors piously mouthing patriotic slogans while they send other people's kids to fight their wars. Maybe nothing I say will matter at all, but you have to live like it does. Or what's the point of any of this?"

Though smiling a little, Charlie gave him a penetrant look. "Not a speech you'd have given six months ago, when we were pondering whether you had a death wish. I'd count that as progress. It's also interesting that I heard nothing about Ben."

"Oh, he's in there," Adam retorted. "Growing up, I never wanted to compete with him at writing—he was all too ready to assure me that I could never be as good. But he helped make me curious about the world, and he never lacked for enterprise or ambition. Which he realized by forcing himself to be the most disciplined son of a bitch I've ever seen. Now I am, too—writing by seven, revising each day's work until it's as good as I can make it. That much is thanks to him."

"No doubt the man was a professional," Charlie observed in his driest tone. "How is your writing, by the way? Or is *Vanity Fair* just indulging a mediocrity because of your last name? Though perhaps it's hard to tell."

Despite himself, Adam was forced to smile. "I grew up reading his novels, so I know what's good. Push me to the wall, and I'd say I'm good enough."

"Then it all adds up for me. Like Ben, you need to be active and engaged in the world. Without that, I think you're adrift and depressed. But what does Carla say?"

Adam parsed the implications of the question. "So far she's been encouraging—I need to do something that has meaning to me, and after the life I've led I can't change myself into an office worker. But longer term? She's a single mother who needs stability in her own life, and she's wary of commitments that might be bad for her or Liam. I'm not sure she appreciates how much I'd be traveling if this works out, or the occasional risk involved in going to the places I'd be writing about. If I understand her at all, she wouldn't love that. She's dealt with too much loss."

"You'll never know unless you ask."

"It's way too soon, Charlie. There are other things that may keep us from ever getting there."

Charlie sat on a large boulder, inviting Adam to do the same. "So maybe we should talk about the boy. It must be a relief to know for sure that he's okay."

"It is. For both of us."

"You don't hold his father against him?"

"How could I?" Adam responded softly. "Ben did, and look where it got us both."

"So it's different with Liam than Carla."

Adam nodded. "Like my mother, she chose Ben. Liam had no choice to make."

"But you may," Charlie answered. "So perhaps you should consider if you're capable of fathering this boy. What do you want for him?"

"Some of what I had, and all of what I didn't have. A father who loves him flat out—no competition or ambivalence or secret resentments. A father who's able to see him as a separate person—not like Ben was with Teddy, curdled with disappointment that his 'real' son wasn't more like him. A father Liam can do things with, but also learn from, and who's determined to bring out his son's best self." Adam hesitated, then finished softly, "A father who Liam knows loves and respects his mother."

Charlie raised his eyebrows. "A fairly comprehensive list. I see you've thought about it."

"I've had a lifetime to think about it, Charlie."

"So can you do all that? Not just to be superior to Ben, but because that's what Liam deserves."

Pensive, Adam faced the water. "Ben was the only father I've had, and that's where you learn—for good or ill. But I have the will to be different, and Carla would insist on it."

The wind stirred Charlie's gray-white hair. Distractedly, he brushed it from his forehead, still intent on Adam. "You've got some real work ahead. But it seems you're getting started, and maybe Carla can help." He paused, speaking quietly and reflectively. "I think you know that when this first came up, the mere suggestion of a relationship between you and Ben's pregnant girlfriend gave me whiplash. But despite her messy life—from childhood, it seems—she's clearly a survivor with impressively sturdy protoplasm.

"Like you, she's come back from some pretty dark places. The question is what risks she's willing to take with you, and you with her. But she may turn out to be different than Clarice, Jenny or even, perhaps, Rachel—more stable and consistent, able to be present for you and honest about herself. Still alluring, to be sure, but not a mystery." Briefly, Charlie laughed in wonder. "Imagine all this actually making sense."

"Yes," Adam said softly. "Imagine that." But there were other things he could imagine, and all of them would put Carla and her son beyond his reach.

FIVE

In late afternoon, with Liam asleep and sunlight grazing her bedroom window, Adam and Carla made love.

It was sweet and intense, surer now. With their bodies joined, their eyes searching each other's, Adam could not imagine wanting another woman. This thought was shadowed by melancholy; with this woman, there was so much he could not say.

Afterward, they lay facing each other, a questioning look replacing the softness in Carla's eyes. The undertow of his imaginings flooded Adam's consciousness; the thought of Carla lying with Benjamin Blaine in this same bed was too vivid to escape. As though reading his thoughts, she said softly, "Will he ever stop sleeping with us, I wonder."

In his surprise, Adam could say nothing. "How long were we going to avoid this?" she asked. "Silence doesn't make anything go away. Our own families taught us that much."

Adam felt their closeness slipping away. "So now we're bringing him back to life," he said stiffly. "What would you like to talk about?"

"Everything," Carla's voice turned cool and level. "Are you really that scared of him? Because what scares me most is avoiding the truth. So let's start with what neither of you could face telling me—how Ben caused so much hatred that only his death allowed you to return."

Against his will, the images of that day, vivid as photographs, filled Adam with a visceral anger that turned on Carla. "It's a very pretty story," he said curtly. "How much detail would you like?"

His tone and expression caused Carla to cover herself. "This is about Jenny, isn't it."

"Yes."

"I'd already guessed that." Snatching at her robe, Carla pulled it on and sat at the edge of the bed. "Please don't spare my feelings, if that's what you're doing. The truth can't be any worse than being punished without knowing why."

Adam steeled himself. With merciless precision, he told her what Ben had done to Jenny, omitting nothing.

Carla listened in silence, impassive, though her face became paler. Only when he had finished did her eyes shut. "My God, Adam . . ."

The anguish in her voice incited him, a decade of hatred spilling out. "Maybe that's why the sonofabitch despised Teddy so much. One drunken night with my mother, he shared some special memories of a fellow soldier. But he was too 'manly' to face up to it, or to treat Teddy with the compassion he damned well owed him. Instead he turned his sexual enthusiasms on my girlfriend—and, of course, my mother."

Carla's eyes snapped open. "That must have been a lovely mother–son conversation," she said in a harsher tone. "Obviously, I haven't given your family enough credit for selective candor. So if you're asking me if we had anal sex, the answer is no. There are only so many mental images I want you to suffer." She turned from him, her voice muted and despairing. "I finally understand the depth of Ben's shame—and your hatred. I don't see how we can ever get past that."

Carla's misery was so palpable that Adam felt his anger soften. "Do you even want to try?"

She shook her head. "I'm not sure it's safe—not after this. It might be better for us both if you turned to Rachel, or anyone who isn't me. But I wanted us to tell the truth, so I might as well give you mine." Composing herself, she faced him. "I don't know whether you'd ever betray me. But given what I've been through, you can stake your life on the fact that I'd never betray you."

Reaching across the bed, Adam touched her arm. "You don't need . . ."

"I'm not done. The only hope for us is honesty—in or out of bed. I've never known a man who didn't want to be better at sex than the guy before, and with you it's outright toxic. So let me tell you what that was like with Ben . . ."

"You don't have to do this."

"Come off it," Carla snapped. "You and your father—the one you had when it mattered—competed over everything: sailing, writing, and even women. If we don't confront that, your competition with a dead man will blow up in our face." As though to compel his attention, Carla gripped Adam's wrist. "When we became lovers, Ben was sixty-five years old. It wasn't hard to grasp why he wanted me, or what that meant to a man who felt time tapping him on the shoulder. I was an elixir that staved off his own mortality.

"For me it was different. Ben was terrified of death; I was afraid of committing to any man. My sponsor in AA put it pretty well: 'Maybe you don't believe you deserve a partner who will really be there.' If so, Benjamin Blaine is the walking definition of a self-fulfilling prophecy."

Carla's tone softened with self-recognition. "I knew she'd nailed the truth. But I needed to work through my own confusions about men, and I started with him. Ben was so intent on helping me stay sober so he was right for that moment. Maybe for the first time, I mattered to someone for more than my celebrity or my looks."

Adam tried to imagine her as she was, fighting against addiction and the damage of her own beginnings, strangely like Ben's own.

"Still," she continued in a rush, "I knew that I should break it off. But no sooner had I decided to than I found out I was pregnant. When I told Ben, tears ran down his face, and I felt how much this meant to him—and to me, the woman who could never have children. Then Ben found out he was dying, and would never know his son."

Adam spoke without inflection or intonation. "So you stayed with him out of pity, and concern for your unborn child."

"No," Carla said firmly. "There was some of that, it's true. But I'd come to love him, as much as I was capable then. It felt good to be strong enough to care for a man who was dying and afraid, no matter how it looked to the tabloids or the vicious gossips on this island. And if Ben still wanted to make love with me, I wanted him to." A new tone entered her voice, steely and determined to finish. "Don't misunderstand me—I'm not an angel of mercy, dispensing sex to the needy. Even at sixty-five and with brain cancer, Benjamin Blaine had more going for him than the handful of Hollywood guys I'd slept with. So it's hard for me to think he was as sexually equivocal as your mother suggests."

Though he fought against this, Adam found her rawness painful. "You're right," he said tonelessly. "I needed to hear the truth . . ."

"Then you might as well hear all of it. For so many reasons, you are so much more to me than Ben in a younger body. When you're not tangled up in the past, I can talk to you in ways I could never talk to him—or wanted to. No doubt it's completely twisted, but Ben got me to a place where I could be with you. That's what breaks my heart—knowing that you can be strong and sensitive and kind, a partner I might actually believe in. But because of him, you may never get there—at least with me.

"And yet here we are in bed. And there's just no way that Ben or anyone else has filled me with the craving I feel for you, at once completely satisfied and yet wanting the next time so much that it's a part of me." Her voice turned husky, and sudden tears welled in her eyes. "I can imagine going through life needing you, in every way. There's been no one like that before you, and I'm scared to death there never will be. But God knows what else you're hiding, or whether you're capable of getting over Ben. I don't know if you should even try."

From the front room came a brief cry, Liam stunned to find himself awake. "A timely reminder," Carla said. "At least for me. I won't let old resentments poison my son's childhood. All too often, a child sees his parents' misery and blames himself. With you, I'm not sure that Ben's son could ever escape it. Any more than Jack's son did."

Adam felt his chest constrict. "That's a lot to absorb, Carla."

Carla's eyes welled again. "Then go now. And if you honestly find you can't live with the past, please don't come back. I'd never blame you for it. But I'm through with this subject, and I can't go on living with you and Ben. It's hard enough right now."

Turning away, she went to Liam. When Adam left, Carla was in the rocking chair, the baby at her breast as she spoke in the quiet voice of a mother.

Six

That night Adam could not sleep, grappling with the questions Carla had posed with such lacerating clarity. When at last morning came, sunny and temperate, he went to his front stoop and found a Manila envelope beside his newspaper.

Inside was the latest issue of the *National Inquirer*. Apprehensive, he riffled it, stopping on page three. Atop the fold was a photograph of Carla gazing at him across the table at State Road, and another of Adam leaving her guesthouse the next morning. Beneath this was an article by Amanda Ferris.

Swiftly, Adam read a distorted mirror of the truth. He and Carla were "entangled in a shocking affair," even while the district attorney investigated him for impeding the inquiry into the death of his father, Benjamin Blaine—himself the father of Carla's infant son. "In exchange for his father's place in her bed," Ferris wrote, "Carla Pacelli seduced him to settle the will contest brought by Ben's aggrieved widow, Clarice. In this Greek tragedy of familial perversity, Adam betrayed his mother to satisfy Carla's greed, while striving to conceal the terrible possibility that his brother Teddy killed their father." Sickened, Adam reached the last lethal sentences. "For Adam Blaine, sex and money are truly thicker than blood. Especially when the prize is his father's mistress and his father's fortune."

Staring at the words, Adam heard his telephone ringing. Even before answering, he guessed who was calling.

"Read the article?" Ferris asked.

"Yes."

His terse, emotionless response caused her to hesitate. "I'm working on the next revelation," she told him. "That the DA believes you broke into the courthouse; stole evidence; fed it to Teddy's lawyer; then used it to enlist your uncle in a cover up."

Adam knew better than to react. Evenly, he said, "I wonder if you want to do that."

Ferris laughed at this. "I know what you're thinking—that I helped you by bribing Bobby Towle. But you'll never turn that around on me, will you? You'd be nailing your high school buddy and yourself." She paused for effect. "Suppose I write that Bobby leaked police evidence. The police can't trace the cash I gave him, and under Massachusetts law, they can't force me to reveal my sources. But they'll find the money running from his bank account to pay for his wife's stretch in rehab. And the unraveling of your clever scheme will have ruined two more lives."

This was the one thing that Adam had not considered. With studied calm, he said, "In this fever dream of yours, Amanda, you and I are Siamese twins. A smarter woman would have a care."

But she was smart enough, Adam knew, to understand that he could take her down for destroying Bobby Towle—once he and Bobby had nothing to lose, they could both become witnesses against her. "Only if you and Bobby confess guilt," she countered. "In the meanwhile, I wonder if Carla Pacelli would enjoy reading you tried to set her up as a suspect in Ben's death. She might hesitate to let you back in bed.

"No doubt people will wonder how any man can be so twisted. But word has it you were wounded in Afghanistan—not the kind of thing that happens to guys who work for USAID. Which explains the talents you brought to covering up for your brother, and the cold-blooded way you use everyone around you. That's the glue for my story—the truth about who you really are." Voice swollen with portent, she finished, "Your life is catching up with you. If you really care about Teddy, you'll make a deal with the district attorney—your confession in return for leaving your brother and uncle alone. Hanley might even take it, and I can move on to other things. After one last article, of course."

That was what she wanted, Adam understood—his cooperation in his own ruin, providing her with the career breakthrough he had thwarted the summer before. Though she was not quite there yet, she had already done great harm. He could not, after all, outrun the past.

Without responding, he hung up the phone and called Carla.

Eyes smudged with sleeplessness, Carla answered the door, clutching a copy of the *Inquirer*. "Ferris already called," she told him in a brittle voice. "She invited me to 'clarify' our relationship."

Mute, Adam nodded. "You should come in," she added wearily. "Before someone takes our picture."

Entering, Adam was struck by the thought that, hours before, they had spent the afternoon as lovers. Now all that was in ruins, with Ferris hounding them still. For a moment, he watched Liam struggle to turn in his bassinet, then sat with Carla at the kitchen table.

"What will you do?" he asked.

"I won't talk to her, no matter what she does to me. But she's already done more than enough to us." Glancing over at Liam, she finished, "We know what she wrote about us isn't true. But what happens when Liam's old enough to discover all this? What do I tell him then? That it doesn't matter to me how or why his father died, or who might have killed him? Or, as bad, who might have concealed the truth?"

The devastating litany left Adam without words. "All I can ask," he said at length, "is that you trust me, and believe that any choice I've made was for a reason."

Miserably, Carla shook her head. "How can I? I don't even understand what the choices are, or why you've made them. However hard, I was honest with you last night. It's way past time I get that much from you."

But she could not have it, Adam knew. Whatever the cost to him, the price of honesty would be to betray his father—and, by doing so, to ruin his mother. "If you know who I am," he said quietly, "that should be enough. Anyhow, it has to be."

But the truth, and his secrets, would follow them. Searching his face, Carla said nothing more. Then she turned to the window, a dismissal.

Adam stood. "My family is waiting," he told her, though it no longer made any difference.

He sat at the dining room table with his mother, Jack and Teddy, the article spread across it. Eyes clouded with doubt, Clarice asked her youngest son, "What is this woman implying about you?"

Unlike with Carla, Adam had no compunction about lying, and every need to do so. "That I know more than I do, I suppose. Which is no more than you do."

He did not look at his brother, who must suspect that he was dissembling—or at Jack, the reason for it. "Then why," his mother persisted, "is this reporter still poking around us? These vermin are too afraid of being sued to simply make things up."

"I don't read the minds of vermin, Mother. All I know is not to feed them. We've all said our piece, and it's time to let this story die."

"But it won't die, will it? Not when your affair with Carla Pacelli is keeping the story alive in the most distasteful of ways."

Wherever he turned, Adam thought, Ferris had secreted her poison. "Sorry," he said tonelessly. "Selfish of me to think I could live my own life."

"Ben's life," his mother snapped. "Ms. Pacelli has a gift for seducing the nearest Blaine . . ."

"Even me," Teddy cut in, facing his mother. "I visit her now and then, and as the only gay Blaine, I'm uniquely positioned to be objective. And she's a far better woman than you imagine." Unfazed by his mother's annoyance, Teddy went on. "What part of the article don't you believe, by the way? That Adam saved your inheritance so he could sleep with Carla? Or that he's covering up my murder of dear old dad. Because you don't get to pick and choose between one accusation and another."

At the corner of his vision, Adam saw Jack glance at him in uncomfortable complicity. Tartly, Clarice asked the others, "Is there really a question that this woman slept with my husband and son? Or have I gone insane?"

"You haven't," Adam said. "And neither have I. Best to leave it there. Amanda Ferris and George Hanley are the enemies, not me. So if we're done here, I'm going for a sail."

It was a lesson from Ben—at the worst moments of his life, he sought out solace on the water, alone. But when Adam stood to leave, Teddy followed him out the door.

"Thanks for the intervention," Adam said over his shoulder. "For a brief, unfilial moment, I considered strangling her instead of Ferris. One dead parent is enough."

"At least it was the right one." Teddy placed a hand on Adam's arm, to stop him. "I don't understand what's happening, bro. But something is closing in on you."

"Don't sweat it, Ted. I know what I'm doing, pretty much all the time."

"Not when you're watching out for all the rest of us." Teddy's face furrowed with concern. "How is Carla handling this?"

"Let's just say it isn't helpful."

"How can it be," Teddy responded. "The portrait this viper paints of Carla is pretty wounding—the kind of thing people remember and she'd never want Liam to read. And she can't help but wonder if you're covering for your homicidal brother. All she's got left is to protect her boy."

Hands in his pockets, Adam gazed out at the water, voice filled with sorrow and regret. "Last summer I thought it would end there, with the four of us making peace as best we could. But now I can see the damage I've done by reaching out for Carla and Liam. That's my legacy, it seems."

When Adam arrived home, George Hanley and two state troopers were waiting on the porch. Coolly, Adam said, "Afternoon, George. Can I get you guys a beer?"

The bulky district attorney regarded him with the bleak appraisal of a recording angel pondering a dead man's fate. "I don't suppose you'd mind if we search the place."

"I don't suppose," Adam responded mildly, "that you have a search warrant."

"Nope."

"I didn't think so—no sane court would find probable cause for one. So you're counting on my good nature."

"That," Hanley said in an astringent tone. "And your pristine conscience."

Adam made a swift calculation. "Search away, George—as long as you tell me what you're looking for. I always like to know what I've been up to."

Hanley shrugged. "Might want to confiscate your cell phone and computer."

This was what Adam expected—he had used a cell phone to photograph documents in the courthouse, a computer to print them out. Both had been issued by the agency, and were therefore untraceable; both now resided at the bottom of the Vineyard Sound. "I do mind that. What on earth do you need them for?"

Regarding Adam with amiable suspicion, Hanley rejoined, "I'm sure you know. Activity on a cell phone will pretty much tell you where the owner was—it's linked with the nearest cell tower. But there's a particular twelve hour time span last summer where your cell phone records show no activity at all."

Adam smiled. "Don't keep me in suspense. Those twelve hours must coincide with the break in, so you're wondering if I have a second phone. Fortunately, I've figured out my whereabouts that night. Would it spoil things to tell you I was fishing off of Dogfish Bar? Striped bass don't respond to phone calls."

"Nope. It wouldn't spoil things at all."

Adam gave a sigh of resignation. "Go ahead—take any cell phone or laptop you can find. Just let me visit them in a couple days, so I can transfer my files to a new computer. Unless you decide to give them back."

Adam saw the defeat surface in Hanley's eyes—and, with it, the understanding of what Adam had surely done. That much was foreordained. What unsettled Adam much more was that Hanley still persisted, spurred by Amanda Ferris. The medical examiner's inquest showed no sign of ending, and it had already damned any future with Carla.

"I'll do that," Hanley responded, and went inside to direct the search.

SEVEN

By the first of March, the Vineyard winter had proven itself unseasonably mild. Adam and Charlie Glazer sat on Charlie's porch, the sunlight warm enough that both men wore light sweaters. As Adam described Carla's account of her relationship with Ben, Charlie listened so intently that he became completely still. "She really put it on the table," the therapist observed. "Sex with Ben, her feelings about you. How did all that make you feel?"

Adam fell quiet, sorting through his emotions. "After a while, I was relieved. It made what happened with Ben seem less important than what was happening with us. It felt better to have everything in the open . . ."

Hearing himself, Adam felt his own entrapment. "And you?" Charlie asked.

"She's who I want, Charlie. More than I've wanted anything in my life."

"I wasn't sure I'd ever hear that from you," Charlie replied gently. "Somehow it makes my own life feel a little more worthwhile." He sat back, reflective. "Freud said that there are certain places where analysis is of limited value. Sometimes you meet a woman, and just know that she's your species—different from all the others. Mine was Rose. For you, that woman is Carla, and maybe you've always known it. It seems like she's faced the worst about herself, and come out stronger. Now she's trying to take you by the hand."

Adam stood and walked to the edge of Charlie's porch, both hands on the railing as he gazed at the Vineyard Sound. "She was. But it's too late, Charlie."

There was a long silence. In a quieter tone, Charlie asked, "Is this about Ben's death?"

"Yes." As completely as he could, Adam described his interactions with George Hanley and Amanda Ferris—the prosecutor's suspicions; his refusal to answer Hanley's questions; the search of his home; Ferris's article distorting his relationship with Carla.

"Hanley's measuring me for prisonwear," he concluded, "and all I can do is ask Carla to trust me. After this last article, I don't see how she can. Or should."

Charlie regarded him gravely. "Have you considered taking a chance, and telling her what you did?"

"I can't. This isn't just about what I did, but what I know."

Squinting at the floorboards, Charlie considered this before looking back at Adam, his gaze fixed, his voice soft. "I've always wondered if Ben was murdered."

Adam met the therapist's eyes, silence his only answer.

"I see."

Adam's stomach felt empty. "I can't put someone else's life in Carla's hands—for their sake, or for hers. Even if I could, how can I start a relationship by making her complicit in the death of her child's father? We'd be living with this albatross, and she'd always worry that Liam would find out. The truth would ruin us, and so does lying." He paused, mired in his own helplessness. "Yesterday, facing Carla, all I wanted was to get off the earth somehow. I never should have let myself care for her. But like a fool, I did."

"Like a human being," Charlie countered. "At last."

"But it doesn't matter, does it? I'm still living in compartments, each with its own lies and deceptions—all tied to how Ben died, and what I know but can never say. Especially to Carla. There's no way out for me."

Charlie frowned in thought. "Isn't there?" he inquired slowly. "Have you considered telling George Hanley what you know, and let whomever you're protecting take the punishment they deserve? Why should you take it for them?"

Because Jack's my father, Adam wanted to say, and I can't live with putting him in prison for the rest of his life. Crossing the porch, he put a hand on Charlie's shoulder. "You've done all you can," Adam said softly. "I only wish I could have helped you."

Jack found him at the mooring on Quitsa Pond, gazing out at the trim sailboat in which, ten years before, Ben had striven to defeat Adam for the prize he had won so many times. But, in the end, all three men had lost. The story of their family.

Silent, Adam looked up at Jack. For so many years, he had loved this man as an uncle. Now he was a burden and a curse. His only wish was that Jack would disappear.

Instead, Jack sat beside him, his face appearing worn and tired. "I thought I might find you here."

Adam still said nothing. Awkwardly, Jack placed a hand on his arm. "I was watching you the other day, after that article came out. Instead of gratitude, all I felt was shame."

And now here you are, Adam thought, *awash in self-pity*. In a monotone, he said, "I don't need the second emotion any more than I needed the first. It's done."

Jack withdrew his hand, sharing Adam's silence. After some time, he said, "You're in love with Carla Pacelli, aren't you?"

Adam felt his temper fraying. "It hardly matters."

"It does to me," his father persisted. "Your mother and I went through life apart. She thought she was protecting you. But it distorted everyone's lives. Now you're protecting me, and it's distorting your life—and Carla's." His quiet tone held bitterness and regret. "What did my life add up to? And who is better off for my existence?"

At last, Adam turned to face him. "Don't come to me for answers, Jack. Or for absolution. I'm not qualified."

The implicit rebuke caused Jack to wince. "I'm your father, Adam. There must be something I can do."

But there was nothing that could repair the damage stemming from his birth, seeping endlessly into the future. The last line of *The Great Gatsby*, once his favorite, came back to Adam again: "So we beat on, boats against the current, borne back ceaselessly into the past."

Perhaps Jack read this in his face. Without saying more, he stood and walked slowly back down the catwalk.

EIGHT

Carla sat on the deck with Liam, enjoying the sunny, mild morning. Face down on a blanket, the baby was making crawling motions, floundering on his stomach like a man trying to swim in quicksand. Watching this, she remarked, "No point in being an overachiever, Liam. I refuse to be a pushy mother. You'll get the hang of crawling soon enough."

At once, she became aware of a man approaching—Jack Blaine, she realized with discomfort and surprise. Faintly smiling at her son, he observed, "I used to see Adam like that, and wish that I could stay with him for hours. But I couldn't."

Carla felt a jarring intimacy—though they had never spoken, Jack knew that she shared the secret of Adam's paternity. "And I never thought I'd have one," she responded. "Like any baby, Liam takes his existence for granted. He'll never know what joy he brought me just by showing up."

Jack nodded his understanding, and then his long face became grave. "Do you mind if I sit? There's something I need to talk with you about."

Carla inclined her head toward the empty Adirondack chair. Sitting, Jack gazed out at the water, less to admire the view, she sensed, than to marshal his resolve. "There's no easy place to begin this," he said at length. "But Adam is carrying something he can't tell you, and I don't think he can ever escape it."

Feeling a terrible premonition, Carla forced herself to say, "This is about Ben's death, isn't it?"

"It is," Jack answered, his tone reflective, almost wondering. "How many times have I passed that promontory since the night he died? I passed it again today. The memory is always the same, always shattering. Yet I keep on living as I have, doing all the things any man would do." He faced her, seeming to force the words out. "I lied at the medical examiner's inquest. Adam is paying the price."

A chill ran through her. "What happened that night?"

Jack hunched in his chair. "Ben threatened Clarice with a change in the will, giving pretty much everything to you. I went to confront him. He was at the promontory, admiring the sunset, no doubt on his way to see you. When I found him, years of hatred consumed us both." His voice thickened. "He ridiculed me, as he had countless times before. He'd already changed the will, he said. When I grabbed the front of his shirt, filled with rage, Ben told me that Clarice would be looking for a rich man by Thanksgiving.

"'I lost control, forcing him to the edge of the cliff. I could kill you,' I told him. 'I've wanted to for years.' But Ben was utterly calm. 'You're a loser,' he answered. 'And you're about to lose again.'"

Stricken, Carla imagined the scene. "And so you pushed him."

Looking away, Jack said, "I held his face an inch from mine. 'Do you think that I can't do this?' I demanded. Then he gave me that smile of complete disdain, and spat in my face." In profile, Jack seemed to flinch. "I stared into his eyes, and suddenly felt my hands let go. For a split second, I was so blinded by hate that it didn't feel like murder. But as soon as he vanished into the darkness, I knew exactly what I'd done."

Carla swallowed. "And Adam knows all this."

"He forced it out of me," Jack answered wearily, "less than an hour after learning I was his father. I still can't imagine how that felt. But he couldn't let the DA prosecute Teddy, and he couldn't bring himself to turn me in for the murder of a dying man. Instead he tried to salvage all three of us, and hide what happened from Teddy and Clarice." Jack sat straighter, looking her in the face. "Lying to you is tearing him apart. But the truth would have endangered me and entangled you. Instead he forced Clarice to compromise the will contest, making sure that you and the baby were secure." Jack's chest moved in and out, as though revealing the truth had winded him. "So now you know our secret."

Sickened and confused, Carla struggled to accept that Adam's father had caused the death of Liam's father, and that Adam had always known this. "Why are you telling me?"

"To free Adam from the curse of the Blaines. My life is much closer to its end than its beginning. Adam's my son, and he deserves a better life." Jack's voice softened. "If you go to George Hanley, I'm prepared for that. I think I could make a deal with him—my confession to Ben's murder in return for dropping any charges against Adam. You've got no reason to protect me."

Carla touched her eyes. "Except for Adam. He was willing to risk everything to keep you from dying in prison. So now I'm part of this, no matter what I do." She felt her stomach clench. "I always suspected someone in your family had killed him. But it's so much worse to know that, and to know who did it."

Jack looked away. "Would you rather I'd never told you? If so, all this is for nothing."

Carla regarded her son, this small and innocent life. "How do you expect me to answer? Though at least you helped me see Adam whole."

Slowly, Jack nodded. "I won't tell him I came. You should have time with this alone."

"Thank you," she said in a dispirited voice, and felt the oddness of this courtesy.

He stood to go, then looked back at her. "Whatever else, please forgive him."

Carla could say nothing. Instinctively scooping up her son, she watched Jack Blaine walk away—the death of Liam's father on his conscience, and on hers.

Carla tried to go about her life, tending to Liam, scanning the graduate school applications on her desk. But the truth of Ben's death consumed her. Only at night was she able to sit quietly, her mind distilling all she knew.

At last, she was ready to call Adam.

He appeared at her door in minutes. Seeing her face, he said quickly, "What is it? On the phone you sounded drained."

"I am." She walked with him to the living room, sitting across from him. "Jack came to see me."

Adams face froze. "About what?"

"Ben's death." Carla struggled to compose herself. "He told me everything—what he did, and what you know. Somehow he imagined that would help us."

Adam bent his head, touching the bridge of his nose in an agonized gesture that somehow resembled prayer. "My God . . ."

"I understand that you were trapped, Adam. Jack explained that much."

"Not even Jack knows all of it," he said bluntly, then began speaking in a rush. "I didn't give a damn who killed Ben—in my mind, he was richly deserving, because of what he'd done to every one of us. At first, I thought it was Teddy. So I broke into the courthouse, stole investigative files, and used Amanda Ferris to bribe an innocent cop with a wife in drug rehab who was eating up his savings. Then I anonymously mailed everything I had to Teddy's lawyer and, in the bargain, tried to float you as a suspect.

"When I found out the truth, I concocted a story that absolved Teddy, and left the police without a solid case against Jack. So now you know what I've done, and who I am—an accessory to the murder of Liam's father." Adam looked at her with new directness. "There's more. I lied to you not just to protect Jack, but because I wanted to be with you. But all I accomplished was bringing our familial nightmare closer to your door. There's no apology big enough to cover that . . ."

"That's a pretty comprehensive list," Carla cut in. "But please stop being such a martyr. Any more self-sacrifice, and you'd have to climb up on the cross." Her voice filled with emotion. "Maybe who killed Ben was news to me, but I always sensed it wasn't news to you—I'm not completely stupid, after all. But did I kick you out? No. Because we're two of a kind, and I wanted you here. Despite everything."

Adam stared at her, hope and doubt warring in his eyes. "And now?"

"At least I don't have to guess anymore. Including about you." Carla found the next words difficult to say. "Ben was dying, and Jack's your father. So I'm not going to turn him in. He can live with what he did and, if he can manage it, with Clarice. I don't envy him either one. I just hope you can slip by the district attorney."

"And if I do?"

Carla shook her head in dismay. "How can you even ask me? I'll only know how that feels if it happens." She paused, speaking more calmly. "At least there's one thing that has nothing to do with us. By coming here, Jack risked everything for you. Whatever else, you'll always know that."

To her surprise, tears formed in Adam's eyes. Then he stood, kissing her softly on the forehead, and left.

Nine

For the next two days, Adam kept himself in motion—sailing for hours, making notes for a piece on sectarian strife in Lebanon. Anything to keep away from Carla. Constantly, he wondered if the price of truth was losing her for good. Better for her and Liam if it was, he thought. In his confusion, he avoided Jack.

On the third day, a call from Hanley broke his thoughts. "It's time for us to talk," the district attorney said phlegmatically. "I'll be in all day."

Apprehensive, Adam arrived at Hanley's office. The district attorney was in shirt sleeves, tie loosened, and greeted Adam with an impassivity that was impossible to read. On his desk were Adam's laptop and cell phone.

"You can have these back," Hanley said, giving Adam a shrewd look. "Not so easy to get your life back. Seeing how breaking and entering and obstruction of justice don't sit so well with me."

Adam wondered how to respond. Evenly, he said, "Suspicion isn't evidence. You've still got no case."

"You're not impressing me," Hanley retorted bluntly. "Forty years into this job, you learn to take chances if you think you're right. There are worse things than losing, after all. I'm retiring in six months, and the death of Benjamin Blaine is the last big thing on my plate. Do I want to end my career, I keep asking myself, by walking out of here with a potential homicide unresolved? Hard for a man like me to just throw up his hands."

"Wish I could help you, George. But I've got worries of my own."

"True enough, and not just about me. Amanda Ferris really doesn't like you. Use her like I'm sure you did, and she's malevolent enough to hold a grudge." Hanley shrugged this away. "Not that I mind when Ferris torments you. Though accusing Carla Pacelli of seducing you to get Ben's money is pretty close to repulsive. Compared to you Blaines, Carla's impressively straightforward, and she's sure as hell not a gold digger."

What was the reason, Adam wondered, for this discussion. "When it comes to women, you're an excellent judge of character."

"Actually, I am. So I can certainly grasp why you're drawn to Ms. Pacelli. But the small matter of this inquiry surely complicates your relationship. Even before you throw in the *National Inquirer*."

Adam chose to respond with care. "I've had better weeks, it's true."

"No more than you deserve," Hanley responded flatly. "You've had your fingerprints on this case ever since you got here. I also believe that Jack or Teddy murdered a dying man—and that you know which one it was." His phlegmatic words were etched with accusation. "Not hard to follow your calculations. If we go after Teddy, Jack's testimony creates reasonable doubt. If we go after Jack, the physical evidence suggests that Teddy is a better suspect. But you've understood that all along, haven't you. That's why you told Jack what to say."

It was so accurate that it took all of Adam's training not to react. As his silence stretched out, Hanley nodded. "A less disciplined man would protest. But you're too smart to bother, and it would only piss me off." The prosecutor leaned forward. "In one sense, you're a real altruist—sticking your neck out to cover up someone else's crime. Guess you thought you could blow the whole thing by us."

Still Adam said nothing. "Tell me who killed him," Hanley demanded bluntly. "Then you can walk."

Adam allowed himself a moment before sealing his fate. As calmly as he could, he said, "Sorry, George. No disrespect intended."

"That's what I expected." Frowning, Hanley stared at him. "I've thought about you long and hard. I don't like being gamed like this. But I've had a long and, I hope, honorable career, and I don't want to end it by turning my personal pride into a vendetta. Ben did enough damage when he was still alive.

"The judge has been waiting until he heard from me. Guess I'll have to tell him that I've failed." Hanley sat back, finishing coolly, "I'm not pursuing you, Adam. I'm not pursuing your family. It's done."

Fighting back emotion, Adam stood. "Thank you, George."

After the briefest hesitation, the two men shook hands. "Don't forget your laptop," the district attorney reminded him.

He found her on the deck, putting Liam in the bassinet. Seeing him, she became still, gazing at him so intently that it was a moment before he could speak.

"It's over, Carla. No prosecution."

Her lips parted, and then she looked down in confusion. "What are you thinking?" he asked.

"That I didn't want you in prison. I'm grateful for that much."

He felt his hope ebbing. "But what about the rest?"

She shook her head in amazement. "What on earth do you imagine I've been thinking about, over and over. Whether I can live with you—with this."

Adam tried to read her, but could not. "Can you?"

"I keep trying to imagine it. But at least I know who you really are, and how hard you tried to make things right—including for Liam. Ben was already dying, and I can't expect you to turn in your own father."

Was it still possible? he wondered. Searching for words, he heard himself saying, "I'm free to do what I want now. If writing works out, I'd be traveling to hard places, not working in an office. No Blaine has ever done that—not our grandfather or Jack or Teddy, and certainly not Ben. For better or worse, in that way I'm like he was."

Though she did not move, Carla met his eyes. "Do you think that one eluded me? You're curious and restless—a risk taker. But I want my own life, so it's fair that you have yours." She paused, her voice becoming husky. "I'd love to ponder the implications of your new career. But don't you suppose there's something else I might actually want to hear?"

All at once, he understood, like sudden knowledge in a man not smart. "My emotional equipment is rusted out," he confessed. "So this is hard for me."

"Just do your best, Adam. Try to remember you're asking me to live in the middle of a Shakespearean drama. Maybe I'm a single mother, but I'm reasonably intelligent and not bad looking. So a little effort from you might help."

Stunned, Adam tried to summon his resources. "All right, Carla. I look at you and see so many things. Both of us have been damaged; both survived. Both of us knew Benjamin Blaine. But we understand each other better than you and he ever could.

"You're smart, self-aware, honest, and empathic. You got to this point the hard way, and I respect you more than any woman I've ever known." He moved a step closer. "I can see so much in your face now. I thought you were beautiful when I met you, and now it's just insane. I can't imagine not making love with you. I can't imagine not being with you."

Carla watched and listened so intently that it seemed her life depended on it. "I could live without you if I had to," he hurried on. "But there would always be something missing. I'd wake up in the middle of the night, and want to tell you something. I'd look at a woman across the table, and wish that she were you. I'd wonder what you were doing, and how you are. You've taken up residence inside me, and the only way to live with that is to live with you."

As he took another step forward, her eyes welled up again. "I want you to have a life outside us," he told her, "one that you own and can take pride in. I want to help raise Liam. If we have our own kid, that's great. If not, we already have a family, and I mean for it to be the one we never had and always wanted." His voice steadied. "I'm in love with you, Carla Pacelli. Whether or not we're together, I'll love you all my life. So I'd really appreciate it if . . ."

Suddenly she came to him, letting Adam hold her, as though needing to feel that again. "If you can try," he heard her murmur, "I can. That's all I can tell you now."

Tilting his head back, Adam saw her expression of deep resolve. The stunning gift of his good fortune struck him all at once, so completely that he could not speak, caught in the rush of possibilities he had thought were lost to him. Then he remembered that someone else was there.

"Don't let go the thought," he managed to say, and went over to the bassinet. Picking up her infant son, he asked, "What about it, Liam. Think you can get used to me?"

In response, Liam stared at him for a moment, then gave a cavernous yawn. Behind them, Carla laughed with a lightness that gave him hope. "Don't worry," she assured him. "As Liam's mother, I can feel his enthusiasm."

Adam sat with his family in the living room of their house, its heavy furniture and third-world art still redolent of Benjamin Blaine. "There's something all of you need to know," he said. "Carla and I are leaving here, together."

His mother sat straighter in her chair. Seeing this, he told her, "I'm sorry about how you feel. But we mean to have a family of our own."

Sitting beside her on the couch, Adam's father looked relieved. Quietly, he responded, "That's something you should want, Adam."

And you never had, Adam thought. "Go for it, bro," Teddy was saying. "I wouldn't ask any of us to pick a partner for you."

Adam faced Clarice again. "Do the best you can with this, all right? It's my life now, and this is what I want. More than want—need."

Seemingly bereft, she averted her eyes. "How do you expect me to live with this?"

"However you decide to. I can't make that my problem—or Carla's."

For a time his mother was silent. At last she murmured, "I really don't have a choice, do I?"

"Not since you chose to have me," Adam told her. "For which I've been more grateful lately." Turning to Jack, he said simply, "Thanks for everything, Jack. It means a lot to me."

He could not say more; the others did not know. But his father's expression made Adam glad that he had spoken. Standing, he said, "Well, I'm off. I'll let you know when we get settled."

He embraced each of them in turn, his mother a bit stiffly. Then Adam walked away from the home of his past, into his own life.

EPILOGUE

The Family

Spring 2014

On a bright spring day in Boston, Carla Pacelli-Blaine and her husband Adam strolled down the shaded parkway dividing Commonwealth Avenue, heading for the Public Gardens.

The two-year-old Liam scrambled ahead, his resolute if somewhat teetering steps propelling him forward until, a little farther each time, he glanced back to verify that his mother and father were still there. "There's a metaphor in there," Adam observed to Carla. "Someday he'll stop looking back."

Carla smiled. "Not too soon, I hope. From the light in his eyes, you're supposed to chase him."

Adam glanced at the baby his wife pushed in the carriage. "Good thing Lily is a girl. All this competition is wearing me out."

With that, he took out after Liam.

Seeing this, the dark-haired boy emitted a throaty chuckle of pleasure and excitement, commencing a wobbly zigzag through the grass and trees, an evasive action designed to thwart his lumbering and less gifted father. Feigning frustration, Adam snatched at the air with each new change in Liam's direction, calling out in a voice of a cartoon giant, "I'm going to get you, Liam Blaine." This produced more triumphant laughter—from experience, Liam knew how hard it was for his father to keep up.

Watching this, Carla grinned—in the small but elastic world of children, anything was possible, including that a two-year-old could thwart a man as fit and athletic as Adam Blaine. At last, the boy stumbled to the ground, out of breath, eyes dancing as the man came forward with a final roar before swooping to toss Liam above his head, catching him at the last moment before he hit the grass. "You're my prisoner," Adam informed his son. "I'm never letting you go."

With this, Liam buried his face against Adam's neck. For a moment, Adam smiled to himself, caught in his pleasure at being a father entrusted with this boy's love. Returning to Carla and their daughter, he remarked, "It's a tough world here on Commonwealth Avenue. Sort of like Afghanistan."

"Enough of that," Carla responded, "really was enough." But she was grateful for Adam's skills and watchfulness—though she would never like his forays to dangerous places, she was glad his career had taken hold and knew that, for him, caution now came first. He had too much to lose.

As if sharing her thoughts, Adam glanced down at their sleeping daughter, Liam still nuzzled against him. Unlike many infants, Lily had skipped the Winston Churchill stage—at four months, her face was well formed and serene, with fair skin, a delicate mouth, and blond ringlets. "She really is a beauty," Adam observed.

"She is," Carla agreed wryly. "Remarkably like your mother."

It was true. To Carla's eyes, the Irish and Italian in their daughter had been laundered through so many generations of Boston WASP's that she mentally referred to Lily as "Clarice's revenge." Not that this mattered—Carla adored her, all the more so because of Adam's delight in having a girl. "One of each," he had observed matter-of-factly a few moments after Lily's birth. "Now we can quit. I'm ready for pointless sex."

"A more sensitive man," Carla had responded, "Might have waited for a day or two to raise that. And I object to the word 'pointless.'" But Adam was a very sensitive man—this had been his way of telling her, finally and forever, that Liam was his son. Over the years, they would explain to Liam, as best they could at a given age, the complications of his birth. The consequences worried her—despite their best efforts, Liam might feel deceived or even angry. But though they were keenly aware of the irony, Adam and Carla had resolved to keep only those secrets that must be kept, until Jack and Clarice were gone. At least, this time, the son would be secure in a father's love.

Watching them together, she thought of Ben. She often did, especially in the quiet hours of early morning, overcome once more by astonishment at her own destiny. So did Adam, she knew, still sorting through the past and what it had brought them both. Both would do this all their lives, for their own sake, and for each other and their children. But they felt no need to talk about this. Between them, it had all been said.

Beside her, Adam smiled at Liam. "Want to take us for a boat ride?" he asked his son. "Lily always likes that."

Carla sat back in the swan boat, holding Lily while Adam tucked his son between his legs, peddling as Liam helped him steer. The banks were filled with couples and families. As they cruised the pond beneath the overhanging branches of willow trees, Carla thought of an illustration from a sentimental children's book, a vision cleansed of the frightening and unpredictable. But there was time enough for those.

Her work reminded her of that. Despite a short break for Lily, she was close to finishing her master's degree at Boston University. Part of that involved seeing patients at the school—a refresher course, if she had needed one, in the varieties of human pain and need. So much came back to childhood and family: why couldn't they love me, why did I have to be like them, why did we never face what made us all so unhappy, how can I learn to be whole when I've been so damaged? For Carla, the familiarity of the questions did not diminish their individuality, or the hurt they caused. Perhaps because of Adam's life, and her own, she could find for each man or woman some well of empathy and patience. They seemed to trust her—even those who recalled her as an actress knew she had picked herself up from the bottom. There was a value for others, she had leaned, in her own mistakes.

"When are you visiting your mother?" she asked Adam.

He glanced over his shoulder. "Middle of the week, I think. She wants to meet Lily. I told her that the three of us are a package deal—I take both munchkins to the house, or neither, and that she doesn't get to pick and choose. I assume you don't mind being left out."

"Hardly—I don't want to replicate the 'meet the parents scene' from *Annie Hall*. But Clarice should know her granddaughter, and I won't use Lily as leverage to extort some grotesque semblance of togetherness. Whatever happens with her, I'll try to live with it. All I expect is that no child of ours will be treated as a second class citizen."

"Never," Adam said emphatically. "The curse really does stop here."

And for the most part, it had, or so it seemed to Carla. The relationship between Adam and his mother was unresolved, and pieces of it might always be. But now and then Jack would come over from Martha's Vineyard, visiting their apartment on Commonwealth Avenue or going with Adam to a Red Sox game, a ritual they had started with the expectation that it would soon involve Liam and, eventually, Lily. Sometimes it was better if Carla went out: she could never forget what she knew, or feel at ease with Jack. Yet she was also aware that Jack had made this new life possible, and grasped, perhaps before Adam did, that it was not too late for her husband to have a father. And so, however difficult, Adam and Carla were creating a family of their own.

The least ambiguous part was Teddy. Not long after the judge's report absolved the Blaines, over his mother's objections Adam had revealed to Teddy the true circumstances of his birth. Despite his shock, Teddy had resorted to edgy humor. "You're not his son?"

he had repeated. "Why do you have all the luck? So what are you now—my brother, or my cousin?"

"Actually, Ted, it's like the movie *Chinatown*. I'm both. So you can take your pick."

"Brother," Ted decided. "That's what you've always been, and I'm too lazy to change. Though it's no wonder I didn't grow up to paint like Norman Rockwell."

"That's the great thing about us," Adam observed. "No new surprise is worse than any other."

Ted gave him a sardonic smile. "Actually, it's kind of liberating when everyone chooses what they get to be. If you're now Liam's father, I can declare myself his uncle. The true definition of weird is for a thirty-six-year-old man to have a brother in diapers."

Together, they had laughed at the sheer absurdity of their circumstances. "Now that I'm an uncle," Teddy promised, "I'll knock myself out to be a normal one."

And so he had, Carla knew. On his trips to Boston, he never seemed to tire of being with Liam, and he had given the infant Lily more presents than a largely insensate being could comprehend. Beneath this, Carla understood that he shared their resolve to see both children grow up whole.

He also changed diapers.

Now, Carla watched Adam turn the paddles of a swan boat, helping their son to steer. Smiling to herself, she kissed the top of Lily's head, her heart overflowing with love. "A dad and a brother," she murmured to her sleeping daughter. "Seems like enough for any woman, don't you think?"

Afterword and Acknowledgments

Eden in Winter completes the trilogy that began with *Fall from Grace*, and continued with its prequel, *Loss of Innocence*, all concerning the Blaines of Martha's Vineyard, and those men and women affected—for good or ill—by this complex and turbulent family. Needless to say, I am grateful to all those who made this project possible.

As before, my friend Dr. Charles Silberstein was instrumental in helping me imagine the complex psychological makeup of my characters, particularly Adam Blaine and Carla Pacelli. Bob Baer, Howard Hart, and, especially, James Smith, gave me the benefit of their experience as CIA field officers in depicting Adam's ordeals in Afghanistan. And Tony- and Oscar-winning actress Marcia Gay Harden was incredibly generous and insightful in helping me imagine Carla as an actress and a woman.

For their assistance in understanding the ground rules for a medical examiner's inquest in Massachusetts, I'm grateful to Judge Lance Garth and Assistant District Attorney Laura Marshard. My friend Dr. Jason Lew, Dr. Stephen Ralston, and nurse Lily Brown helped me depict the complexities of Carla's pregnancy. My friends Al Giannini, and Dr. Maureen Strafford joined me in imagining Carla's relationship to Catholicism. Father Michael Nagle enabled me to explore the lovely Catholic Church in Oak Bluffs. And Betsy

Farver of the Betty Ford Center enabled me to better grasp Carla's addiction and recovery.

As always, I benefited from the perceptive support of my agents, Mort Janklow, Anne Sibbald, and Cullen Stanley; my wonderful assistant and critic, Alison Thomas; my wife and most faithful reader, Nancy Clair; and my closest friend, Philip Rotner.

Special thanks to my friend and longtime publisher in the UK, David North of Quercus, and to my editor, Jo Dickinson. I'm particularly excited to be part of Quercus's launch as an American publisher.

Finally, there is Dr. Bill Glazer, without whom this trilogy would not be remotely the same. With the keen understanding of a superb psychotherapist, Bill was tireless and insightful in helping me design the inner landscape of the Blaine family, and those they touched. As a keen sailor, he provided the sailing advice I needed in all three books, as well as suggesting the summer races that became the central metaphor of *Fall from Grace*. And as a dear friend, Bill has been wonderful company, and a continuing source of fun, counsel, and general wisdom about life. This book is hardly thanks enough.

Postscript

On June 23, 2013, well after I completed *Eden in Winter*, my dear friend Dr. Bill Glazer died after a long illness. I do not care to change the wording of my dedication—Bill remains alive in the hearts of his family and friends. But I do want to record Bill's remarkable grace in the face of an ending that came far too soon: his positive spirit, his embrace of life, his cheerful engagement with those who loved him, and, perhaps most remarkable, his unstinting dedication to his patients to the very last. For those eighteen months, he continued to add to our store of memories—of his humor, his boyish enthusiasm, his affectionate nature, and his deep wisdom and clarity of thought. Bill was, and always will be, one of the best men I have ever known.